# A
# CONVENIENT
# CATASTROPHE

Tracy Bayle

A Convenient Catastrophe

The characters and events in this book are fictitious. Any similarity to real persons, living or dead, is coincidental and not intended by the author.

Cover Design by: Yashodhan Jaltare
Editing by:
Formatting by: SkimStone Publishing

ISBN-10 : 1675915709
ISBN-13 : 978-1675915707

Published by: SkimStone Publishing
Winter Springs, FL, USA 32708

# THE SEA ISLAND SERIES

*HERE* IS A special place in the world called the Atlantic Ocean. Along this ocean's coast, on the eastern part of the United States, from South Carolina down to Florida, is a chain of tidal and barrier islands called the Sea Islands. The Sea Islands gift the inhabitants of these coastal towns with a glorious watercolor rendition of nature's most dynamic array of colors, as well as a continual symphony. Each island has a different flavor, but they all have been given a special sprinkling of enchantment.

It is that enchantment that brings visitors from around the globe seeking beauty and tranquility. But within every village there are the locals. The locals have families, jobs, homes. And the locals have secrets.

# Contents

The Sea Island Series......................................FM3

ONE.......................................................................1

TWO..................................................................15

THREE...............................................................33

FOUR .................................................................44

FIVE....................................................................54

SIX......................................................................62

SEVEN ..............................................................68

EIGHT ...............................................................77

NINE..................................................................84

TEN.....................................................................90

ELEVEN .............................................................99

TWELVE............................................................105

THIRTEEN ......................................................120

FOURTEEN.....................................................127

FIFTEEN ..........................................................140

SIXTEEN ..........................................................152

SEVENTEEN ...................................................172

EIGHTEEN.......................................................180

NINETEEN ......................................................191

TWENTY...........................................................200

TWENTY-ONE ...............................................210

TWENTY-TWO................................................221

TWENTY-THREE............................................240

TWENTY-FOUR .............................................260

TWENTY-FIVE................................................274

TWENTY-SIX ..................................................292

TWENTY-SEVEN ...........................................298

TWENTY-EIGHT ............................................305

TWENTY-NINE................................................308

THIRTY.............................................................313

Book two in the Sea Island series .................316

# *One*

I 'M THINKING ABOUT killing Eleanor."

There. I've finally said it.

Becky frowns across the booth at me, her face a mixture of confusion and inquiry at my proclamation. Words form on her lips, then realization floods her features and she traps her words back inside unspoken. It's apparent by this gesture alone that Eleanor isn't that important.

I get that, I suppose. Eleanor is fictional. Eleanor was created in my imagination years ago and has been shelved and re-shelved off and on for the better part of my adult life. She's been meticulously created and re-created so many times and, to Becky's credit, she hasn't been on my mind or in my discussions in a while. She's been shelved once again.

Here we are though, with our visit drawing to a close and the important, soul-searching discussions being kept at bay. I catch her eye and dare her to drop the subject of Eleanor and her impending fate. We could pick up this thread, re-invent a new ending for Eleanor and her love, Samuel, and avoid the reality of actual life. That would be the ideal thing to do.

Two women at the booth behind us are talking about a recent trip to a hypnotist. "I swear," one says to the other, "she said twelve pounds in three weeks." Dance Moms, both of them. The bane of my existence, aside from Madame Bienve herself. Fortunately, it's late afternoon and by this time Madame has locked her upstairs dance studio and gone home for the day. No more tapping of her stick on the floor above my head. No more scowling, looking down her long, thin nose at me, or correcting my speech. Until tomorrow, anyway.

"Well, maybe not brutally killing her exactly. It'd be pretty hard to combine horror with historical romance." I frown and gnaw at the skin surrounding my nail on my index finger, considering. "Maybe having Samuel *accidentally* kill her. Or maybe she and Samuel should die tragically together, instead of all this happily ever after nonsense no one cares about reading. Give the people what they apparently want."

"Still no bites?"

"Nope." I pop the *P* sound for emphasis. "Unless you consider twenty-three rejections a bite."

"Ooh." Becky swirls her latte with a stir stick, playing with her food, treading carefully. "Maybe it *is* time to let them die." She shrugs while she licks the stick like a child with a milkshake straw.

Surely she knows she's crossed a line. She knows how much *A Maiden's Voyage* means to me. She's been hearing about Eleanor and Samuel since the day I first put pen to paper, knows their story as well as she knows my own — or thinks she knows my own.

Truth be told, no one knows my real story — not even sure I do. I've constructed one that serves me well, but my life has more holes than a slice of Swiss cheese, and I'm uncertain how to fill them. Dwelling on them brings too much to the surface that needs to stay buried. That's why Eleanor keeps coming off the shelf, I suppose. I can fill in Eleanor's plot holes and, in doing so, avoid my own.

I place my elbows on the table in front of me and hold my head with fists under my chin. The new poster I had framed and hung over the lunch counter was a good choice. That pastry on the little china plate — the light captures the milkiness of the icing that drips off of it beautifully. Even the bit of tarnish in the hollow of the silver spoon that's been propped on the plate — nice touch. The tarnish spot blurs and takes on the shape of Texas as my mind meanders in directions I can't afford to let it, not now. I run my tongue over the soft flesh inside my cheek, tasting the chocolate chip cookie I ate hours earlier until I'm calm enough to change the subject myself.

"So. Hailey's last year." I sigh and rest the side of my face in the palm of my hand, scrunching it. "Me, the mother of an eighteen-year-old. She's graduating! We're officially old!" My voice rises with each proclamation and I lean in to show how good-natured I am, not angered in the least on Eleanor's behalf, not anxious about my meandering thoughts.

"Oh, jeez. Remember us at that age?" Becky watches my waiter, Cory, wipe down the counters with a washcloth and toss dirty dishes into a gray plastic bin. There are still crumbs under the barstool, sprinkled across the wood floor like a trail. Huge chunks of Pumpkin Maple Muffin left behind by that little boy that came in earlier with his mom.

"I try not to." I fold my hands in my lap, the mannerisms of a wayward girl turned proper, or attempting to appear so. "I was trying to graduate from high school and plan a shot-gun wedding."

"I was there. I remember it well." She flattens her lips. "So what's Baby Daddy Greg up to these days?"

"Same as always, I guess." I shrug and glance across the street at the bookstore and watch the owner, Deaton, maneuver his clearance rack through his doorway while thinking about my ex-husband's new life. "Still lying and sneaking around, I would imagine."

Becky follows my gaze. "Well, *he's* a looker." She raises her brows to see if I'll offer up any details on the man across the street who's now picking up a stack of books he's dropped.

"Deaton?" I make a face like she might be hallucinating. I squint and try to see what she might be seeing, but I can't. All I see is goofy Deaton, in his wire-rimmed glasses that he constantly adjusts up and down his nose like the doctor gave him the wrong prescription. Deaton's not a looker. He's just... Deaton. A friend, a brother of sorts, a big blob of geekiness.

Becky and I grow silent, both lost in our thoughts about every-thing that's happened, both of us continuing to avoid the real questions, the real truths as we know them.

*I should go back and try to find another poster to hang beside the new one—maybe a steaming mug of something to fill that space. The mug would need to match the dessert plate somewhat and...*

"How is she?" Becky asks with no change in tone, like we've been sitting here talking about *her* this whole time instead of made-up people I can control. Her voice is almost a whisper though, as if she's afraid to intrude on my thoughts. I know how hard this is. You're damned if you ask and damned if you don't.

*How is she?*

The answer to this question changes from day to day, depending on Ian. Depending on the weather. Depending on which foot hits the floor first in the morning and how hard. Depending on if she's found a doctor to keep writing the prescriptions.

"She's all right. She's plodding along." My response is unsure, noncommittal. "You know how it goes. Strong one day, broken the next."

She nods, nothing much else to say about it. It's been this way forever. But then, "Ames, don't you ever think it might be time-"

"No! I don't."

She tips back her head and finishes the last drop of her latte, glances at her watch, and settles things in her mind. "Welp, okay. I better get going. It's starting to look bad out there."

I glance out the window and unwad my napkin to wipe at the moisture that clouds my view, revealing the impending storm I hadn't even noticed. Deaton has managed to get his wheeled racks inside and close shop. By the clock, we should have another hour before nightfall, but the sky is already darkening, casting ominous shadows. A woman walking across the street is holding her hair back with her hand, and a lost dog flyer is sauntering down the street on its merry way. The bell on the café door chimes as my last customers, two Dance Moms holding their ballerinas' hands, leave. A strong gust blows the door out of their grip and it bangs against the nearby wall before slamming shut.

Cory runs from the kitchen to see what happened and disappears again, returning minutes later to wipe down the counters and top off all the filters for the next morning's rush. The rich scent of chicory and hazelnut fill the air, like spraying a can of calm. Talk of *her* gets swept up in the vapor and dissipates.

"When will you be back this way?"

Becky stands, securing her coat sash tightly around her thin frame. She looks like some old New York socialite, like one of those Olson twins, all five feet four inches of her, enveloped in furry warmth that swallows her whole. Her long blonde hair is held back off her face by the oversized sunglasses she had on when she arrived and she clutches a disposable coffee cup. "Not sure. Most likely Thanksgiving," she answers, tossing her cup into the nearby trash. "Depends on schedules — mine, Bryan's, the kids."

I nod knowingly, looking like a disappointed but pacified child. I hate this part of her infrequent visits, hate how far Montgomery, Alabama is from Flannery Cove, Georgia — how far her peaceful suburban comfort is from my chaotic tangle of lies.

The rain begins to pound. "Drive safe," I yell as she dashes for the white SUV parked at the curb. My words are beaten down by the sudden flood and washed down the nearby gutter.

After Becky leaves, I send Cory home thirty minutes early. "Not expecting any more today." I cut him off before he has a chance to tell me yet again how much he needs the hours for the new rims or whatever he's saving up to buy. "I'll lock up." I smile affably like I'm doing him a great favor, then stare out the window while he collects his things.

*The rain came down in sheets, soaking her skin and causing her blouse to cling to her...*

Not now! This is ridiculous. Eleanor can live for now, but I have got to stop writing these narratives in my head all the time and face facts. Stringing sentences together does not make one an author.

"But it does, Amy. It most certainly does," Mr. Scottsboro, my high school Literature teacher, would have said, while stroking his scruffy beard. Meaning that art is subjective. If you put color to canvas, you are an artist — words on a page, and you are a writer.

*Well, Mr. Scottsboro, publishers apparently don't see it that way.*

I open the door for Cory so he can manage his backpack, cell phone, and keys, then step out under my front awning to glance up and down deserted Sandpiper Street. I start to turn back when I see Deaton again, standing directly across from me, inside his bookstore doorway. He holds up a hand, then flips his open sign to the closed side. In a split decision, I run back inside and grab two Styrofoam cups, filling one with the last dregs of decaf, the other with half dark roast, half vanilla cappuccino, and two pumps of skim milk. After flipping my sign over, I sprint across the street in the pouring rain, tapping on the bookstore's glass door.

Deaton looks up from his register, where he's counting his day's take with a cordless phone propped between his cheek and shoulder, and he smiles. He grabs his keys and kicks a box out of the way as he strides purposefully back to the front door.

"Well, tell Patty I'm on her side," he says into the phone. "Bout time she threw that con-man to the curb." He holds up an index finger. I glance down at my sopping wet shirt and pull it out away from my skin as much as I can. "Gotta run, Mom. Call you tomorrow." He clicks the phone off and sets it on a nearby table.

I hold up the cup in my right hand. "I remembered how you like it."

"Thanks. What did you call it? The Socialite Special?"

I shrug, handing it to him. "Can't help it if you're a lightweight."

Atticus jumps from the window seat and weaves himself between my ankles, then moseys off toward the back of the store, his tail held straight and high, dignified. The smell of newly installed carpet and fresh paint almost seems toxic. It's too industrial for a bookstore. Things need to be scratched up a bit, spilled on a few times, made homey.

"That sounded interesting."

"Oh, yeah." Deaton wipes a hand across his lips and returns to his stool behind the register. "My mom. Her cousin Patty's been married twenty-some-odd-years to Larry the Loser." He grabs a handful of fifties and counts while still talking. "So yesterday at Wanda Wiggin's wedding..."

*Hmmm... there's a title: Wanda's Wedding... Wedding... beheading... Dreading the Wedding... That could be about a woman that...*

I miss a few words before I realize Deaton's tone has changed. "Anyway, Patty overheard some women talking about her husband Larry and Shirley Conway, who works down at Brennan's Department Store. Turns out Larry and Shirley have a thing going on and Patty is the last one in town to know."

"Hmph." I take a sip of my coffee and look for a place to throw my empty cup.

"So anyway," Deaton continues, laying aside the fifties and picking up the stack of twenties, "Mom says Patty has made up her mind, once and for all. She's leaving Larry," he proclaims and nods his head with finality, proud of this Patty, as if he's been trying to convince me for years that one day she would have had enough and I never believed it. The nod knocks his glasses, so he wrinkles his nose and works them back into place. "Her mother died last year, leaving her a dilapidated old house on the edge of town, and Mom says she's moving into it, determined to fix up the house and 'fix up her life.'" He puts air quotes around the phrase.

I nod, agreeing that Cousin Patty has had enough. Sounds like she needs to leave Larry to make his own chicken pot pies and wash his own overalls, or whatever people do in rural Iowa.

"Only problem is that Patty's son, L.J. — that's Larry Jr. — is foolishly blaming his *mom* for splitting the family up." He lays aside the stack of twenties and reaching for the fives. "Three hundred fifty."

I yawn, bored with talk of people I don't even know. Deaton's not the most interesting conversationalist, but he has a pretty good listening ear, for a man anyway. "Looks like a good day." I raise my brows and try not to compare it to my empty cash register.

"New Kathleen Barber book came out yesterday."

My mouth forms the word, "Oh", but no sound comes forth. Kathleen Barber's debut novel, *Are You Sleeping,* is being made into a ten-episode series and her second novel has just hit the bestseller list. For the second time in the span of an hour, Eleanor's future obituary floats through my mind as a possibility.

"Speaking of love lives." He glances up, wanting details of the blind date I told him I was going on last Friday.

*Why did I even tell him that in the first place?*

I bite at my lip, trying to remember the two of us a few weeks earlier, unpacking boxes of books in his back storeroom late into the evening. We'd been talking about the lack of people to date in this small town… in this big world. Deaton told me he hadn't dated anyone since he came out a few months ago and I hadn't known what to say to that, so I stupidly spouted off the story about how my waiter over at the café, Cory, had fixed me up with his uncle and we were going out the following night.

I roll my eyes. "Don't ask."

He picks up Atticus as the cat strides back into the room.

"Hey, your *T*." I nod toward the back wall where the name of his store is spelled out in tall black letters, without its full cast of characters. *Stories by he Sea.* A blank space is apparent between the *y* and the *h*.

"Yeah," Deaton frowns as he zips the day's cash close-out into a bank bag and closes the register with a loud ding. "It's supposed to arrive by next Thursday."

7

"Aah." My phone chimes and I pull it from my back pocket as a flash of lightning strikes close by and the lights flicker. I try pulling up my inbox, but the agonizing circle that shows no Internet connection keeps spinning.

"Wi-Fi's out." I hold up the phone to show him the maddening swirl and hand him my empty cup to toss into the trash behind the counter. "I better go," I announce, eager to get back to the café and see if I can pull up this message. If my phone dings with an email notification, it can only be from one source: A message to Unveiled Investigations. My side gig. My covert operation. One of my milder little secrets.

I wait in Deaton's doorway for about ten seconds and then make a run for my own, sloshing through the stream that's formed down the middle of the blacktop.

It's eerily quiet inside, aside from the splash of rain hitting the glass windows. I grab a leash and call for Otis, but he ignores me. "Otis, *come on!*" I yell out again after I wash out the carafes and check to make sure everything's set to brew early in the morning. I peek into my cluttered office and find him curled up in his bed, snoring loudly. Stumbling over boxes and bags of inventory and dog toys strewn about on my way, I snap the leash on him and pull him to his squat legs. "One day," I vow. "One day, I'm going to claim that storage closet away from Madame Bienve and clean all this crap out."

THE STORM CONTINUES, following me from the east side of town, across the railroad tracks, to the historic section, where the oak trees grow together and canopy the roads with low-hanging moss that dangles in the field of vision. My part of town! My refuge! All the way there my wipers work overtime, throwing water to the sides and echoing out their repetitive chant: Chea-ter. Chea-ter. Chea-ter. I cannot wait to check that email message and see who's been caught now, can't wait to change the course of my thoughts and shed the heaviness that's been weighing me down ever since my visit with Becky and her attempt to foray into the past and tell me what I should and shouldn't do about it.

"Home!" I nudge the heap curled on the seat beside me: fifty-two pounds of solid muscle, quivering at the rumbling skies and the thought of getting wet. My shoe skids a bit as I scramble out of the driver's seat, run around the front of the car, and open the passenger door, all the time struggling to open the umbrella with the two broken spokes that stick out dangerously. Mrs. Grimaldi, the neighbor who once joked I needed a real baby and a man to help me when she saw me carrying my dog in a blanket to the car on a cold morning, is watching the storm out her living room window. I once saw Mrs. Grimaldi honking her car horn very obnoxiously outside the convenience store on the corner while waiting impatiently on her crippled husband, whom she'd sent in to get a loaf of bread, so I take her opinions of my life with as much importance as a frayed thread. Once Otis sees the umbrella, he's willing to give it a go. I walk in the rain, juggling bags in my left hand and a leash and umbrella in my right. I crouch and waddle simultaneously, the umbrella held low, providing cover for a stubborn bulldog every slow step of the way to the door.

I'm gonna miss this house when they come knocking and tell me to leave it, as will surely happen soon. It has its oddities, I know. How could I not know? I've only had them pointed out by every real estate agent in town. But *I* love the dining room walls washed in Benjamin Moore Marigold Daydreams. *I* adore the white shag carpeting in the sunken living room. If anyone knew how hard it had been to find real shag carpet, especially snow-white, they would surely appreciate it too. I'd had to special order that from a mill in Virginia and I paid a hefty price for it. The dark eggplant-colored velvet sectional situated on the shag carpet is the ultimate indulgence, and I'm proud to say my original black-and-white checkerboard kitchen counters and backsplash have survived over fifty years without a nick.

Every time I enter this room it's hard not to picture my Nana, God bless her soul, standing over the stove sautéing a pot of something or at the counter stirring and sifting. The realtors call it out of date, over the top. I prefer retro and eclectic. But I'll be leaving it all behind soon if I don't figure out a way to pay the last six months of payments. I can't even bear to think about that right now. Nana would be so disappointed.

"Smells good in here." I inhale the garlic and let my bags drop on the Mexican tiled entryway. Authentic Saltillo tile. If you look closely, a few pieces even have markings where chickens walked across them before the clay was dry. So much more character than all that cold marble and granite everyone's after these days.

Hailey is setting bowls of chili on the little bistro table in the corner of the kitchen.

"Hey," she greets me. "I managed to get everything done before the electricity went out."

I glance at the overhead Tiffany-style dome, shining brightly down on the table.

"Just came back on. It went out for about thirty minutes," she says.

I scurry back to the entryway and find my phone dropped deep in the recesses of my purse before I settle myself across from her at the table, spooning chili with one hand and punching buttons with the other. Still that exhausting circle, swirling and trying to find a wave of Internet beams floating nearby it can grab.

I make a deep-throated growl of aggravation. "I have a message on Unveiled's email, but I haven't been able to see it yet."

Hailey's the only person who I can growl to. She's my daughter, but she's also my person — that best friend that gets me, cheers me on, feels my pain, and revels in my joy. She's one of the very few people who knows I'm the face behind the town's infamous investigation agency. No one would ever even suspect it's me, and so far Unveiled has been the only name anyone needed to know. I'm just the owner of a struggling little café down by the beach whose own husband was a serial adulterer. To the world, I'm wholesome, honest, an apparent open-book. Fresh-faced and starry-eyed, the picture of innocence.

The Final Straw started fiscally strong. All the beachside shops were flourishing before the expansion of the west side of town. No one saw that coming. "A mall in Flannery Cove? Never gonna happen." The old-timers used to sit in my very booths and declare prophecy, and we all banked on it. Now The Final Straw barely brings in enough money to pay the employees and the power bill, so I need Unveiled to grow beyond its small clientele into a serious, well-respected enterprise, and I desperately need to maintain its facade. Reputation and word of mouth are slowly getting me there, but not fast enough — not nearly fast enough! Flannery Cove is such a small town, I think my clients like the fact that my proprietorship is unknown. It allows me to stalk and eavesdrop to get the information they pay for. In a big city it might be different, but here the business growth depends on anonymity, and I intend to keep it that way.

"Oh!" Hailey says, between bites. She slurps tomato sauce back between her lips before continuing. We're a pretty casual pair, but I should probably encourage some better table manners in case she ends up dating someone classier than Jarod when she goes away to college. I mean, Jarod's great, but he's no descendant of Emily Post or anything like that. He wouldn't even notice my daughter's slurping sauce, or her long legs folded crisscross style in the seat of the chair, or her brand new jeans that look like someone tossed them on the expressway and let cars run over them for a week. She could meet a law student, someone from an aristocratic old mon-eyed family that wants to take her home to meet the parents and...

"So I guess you need to call him back." She looks at me and snaps her fingers in front of my face.

"Huh?"

"The answering machine?" She questions how much I've com-prehended what she's been telling me. Otis saunters in from the utility room, his nails clipping on the tiles. He grunts as if put out to find us doing the same old thing we do every night and plops himself down in the middle of the room.

"Okay," Hailey begins again from the top, making sure I'm listening this time. "The answering machine got erased when the power went out, but there was a message on there from Chappy asking you to call him."

I glance at the answering machine, even though she's just told me it lost power. The red light is still, unblinking. Crazy that I still have an answering machine, I suppose. Along with a house phone that plugs into the wall, although I guess I should look into dropping home phone service to save a little money. But then the vintage, princess-style phone I got off of eBay would be wasted.

*Dear God, the choices I'm being forced to make.*

"I wonder what Dad wants," I answer. My dad and I talk once or twice a week, but I just talked to him the day before, and he's usually only one for meaningless chit-chat, nothing heavy. There's only so much of that you can do in a week. Although he has been a bit better since he started dating Helena a year or so ago. I suspect she keeps after him about his obligations, trying to soften his edges. One thing I have to give her credit for. But then again, it's probably for the best that my dad questions little and remains somewhat emotionally elusive. It's served me well. Helena thinks she can change my father, mold him into some philosophical, mushy, marshmallow fellow, and maybe she can. Maybe she will eventually have herself a boyfriend that delves deep, unearths feelings and not just facts. Wouldn't be the first time I'd seen a flawed husband learn all his lessons from a first marriage and morph into the perfect man for his second.

I wonder if that'll be the case with Greg. Hailey tells me everything she witnesses between him and his girlfriend, Sherri. So far the man who used to leave all the dirty dishes towering in the sink, throw mud-caked work boots on the bathroom floor, and leave cracked eggshells on the countertops every morning has miraculously turned into a man who keeps an immaculate house. A "germaphobe" Hailey calls him. Ironic given the fact that I had medical tests run on me after we separated to make sure I hadn't contracted hazardous diseases from him. The verdict is still out on his monogamy. I expect Sherri to contact the anonymous me one day, questioning her boyfriend's fidelity, and it'll be a quick buck I don't even need to bother setting up a stake-out for. I have plenty of old photos of Greg coming out of hotels and lounges, his arm wrapped around some buxom blonde — sometimes two or three of them — that I can recycle. Cheaters don't change. All the post-divorce self-help books said so.

"Speaking of dads." Hailey takes a sip of her drink, then crunches her ice and swallows. "Mine wants to take me to dinner for my birthday. With Sherri, of course."

"Of course." I give a big, plastic grin.

*Gotta be happy for Daddy. Gotta love Sherri. Gotta love dad's cool, clean new digs, dad's hip lifestyle.*

Who am I fooling? Hailey knows what I think before I even think it. Well, mostly.

I'm not quite finished gnawing on my breadstick. It's grown cold and tough. I pull my legs up crisscross style onto my chair and pick my phone back up, logging on to my company email. It goes through, allowing me to give up on the breadstick and concentrate.

**To whom it may concern: I find myself with quite the dilemma.**

This is obviously written by a very well-dressed woman, not a frayed thread in sight. High collar, and sensible, low-heeled shoes.

Hair slicked back into a tight knot, and mouth puckered into a permanent sour grimace.

**My partner proposed to me this past Christmas. I have not accepted yet.**

*Umm. It's February now. Might want to check and see if the offer is still on the table.*

**He lost his first wife in a terrible accident many years ago; however, the authorities have never recovered her body. Understandably, I have my doubts about what really happened to her.**

*Understandably? Huh? Who doubts something like that? Well, I would, but that's different. No one else would.*

**There are questions, and I find myself unable to venture into this next phase of life until I know for certain. That is where you come in.**

*Wait, this isn't a cheating spouse case? I'm expanding into other investigative arenas?*
I take my eyes off the screen and stare off into space for a second. Hailey's filling the kitchen sink with hot, soapy water, and I'm off in a graveyard with a shovel and a lantern.

**I would like to hire you to prove that his first wife is indeed deceased. I realize this is not your usual area, but your services come highly recommended. I have connections at the Flannery Cove Courier, and if you can solve this case successfully before next February, (I have given my word that I will have an answer regarding the proposal by then) I will have the paper run a feature article on your business.**

*Oh!* My heart's fluttering. Something is poking at the periphery of my brain, but I ignore it and focus on this nice flutter. An article in the Flannery Cove Courier could expose me to a whole new clientele. Already I'm thinking: two pages long, but no accompanying photos. Can I be simultaneously famous yet remain anonymous?

Is it possible? *I'll make it be.* I'm ignoring all the roadblocks and concerns trying to squeeze their way into my mind.

**I also have connections at the Flannery Cove Country Club, and I can assure you...**

*Wait! What?*

A sensation overtakes me, but I can't identify it. A buzzing in my head, ghost ants crawling all over my nerves. I scroll back up to the beginning of the email and drop my phone on the table. It lands with a loud thud.

"What the..." Hailey turns off the faucet and walks toward me, drying her wet hands on the thighs of her new jeans.

I recoil, pointing to the phone that has landed in the middle of the table, and she picks it up, skims the message, and looks back at me with shock on her face.

"Oh! My God!" She says, a hand covering her mouth. She's stunned, and she doesn't even comprehend half of what this means — truly has no idea.

There at the top of the screen, in the sender's information portion of the email, is the address: **Helena1098@myFCcourier. com.** My dad's girlfriend and apparently, my future step-mother. And she wants me to prove my mother is dead.

My eyes meet Hailey's, and we speak volumes with one glance. *Of course she's dead. She's been gone for years. I've been motherless since I was a child.*

I'm the first to break away from the glance before my eyes can reveal, *but I had lunch with her just last week.*

# TWO

I
T SHOULD HAVE been an ordinary night. The kind we'd talk
about later and say, "Remember last Tuesday night? What'd
we do?" And the other one would say, "I dunno. Ate chili?
Watched Law and Order? There was that storm."

But everything changed with that email.

"Yo, Ames," Cory greets me early the next morning.

"Yo, Core."

I turn my key in the door and spend the next few hours focusing on espressos, mochas, and lattes. I've not slept a wink, but this
is what I do best — mixing and blending, melding flavors. It's
rote, so between greeting customers I *try* to think about Helena
and my dad and my mom. Mary, I'm supposed to refer to her. By
ten, the café is humming. Flannery Cove City Council members
have gathered at a round table for an early morning meeting. Five
Dance Moms arrived shortly after nine to drop off their prodigies
to Madame Bien.ve and have sat for an hour in their bra tops and
nylon leggings, talking about pilates. Madame Bienve herself is
tapping all over the place above me like a telegraph machine. My
attempt to concentrate gets me nothing more than a huge migraine
and some tingling nerves up and down the limbs I keep finding
myself nervously rubbing.

"What are you going to do?" Hailey had asked, and the obvious answer was that I would turn it down somehow. It would be easy to write back and say I did not do these kinds of cases, but no, that wasn't a good idea because if word got around I might not ever be offered another one like it. I was dying to expand beyond common old infidelity, which had grown tiresome and unprofitable.

"But the Courier." Hailey held her hands out as if that was my last hope at keeping my enterprise going.

"I know. But it's unethical. It's what they call a conflict of interest. Business 101: Never mix business and family."

"She's not family."

"Apparently she's going to be."

That's another thing I can't get over. It's not like I expect Dad to ask my permission. He's his own man. To think he might have asked me to lunch, taken my hand, and sought my approval before a life-altering event might be a bit reaching, but a simple heads-up? A conversation of some sort? I bet Buffy Barrington and the country club crowd had all been privy to this information weeks before it happened. She'd probably thrown a celebration and had never thought to include Hailey and me.

Well, I guess they wouldn't celebrate if Helena hasn't accepted the proposal yet. Poor Dad. I wonder if it crushed him. How in the world does my father's future end up depending on me? How has it come to be that I hold the answer to the biggest obstacle in Raulerson Chadwick's and Helena Delgado's path to marital bliss?

Standing behind the counter with a barely touched grilled eggplant on brioche, between the morning mob and the afternoon trickle, I make up my mind for good, not that there'd ever been any question. There is no way that I can do this job. I'm way too close to the situation, and I already know the answer to the puzzle. And I already know it's not the answer Helena wants, and it's certainly not one I can risk my dad or Hailey ever knowing. The lies I've raised my daughter on must always be her truth.

Cory sweeps past me with his wet washcloth, picking up my plate, cleaning underneath it, and depositing it back down where it was.

Madame Bienve appears on the landing. I know her next class isn't until two o'clock. Every weekday from nine to noon and two to four a steady stream of little girls dressed in cotton candy pink tutu's and ponytails pulled back tightly parade through the café and wave to their moms as they ascend the stairs up to The Madame Bienve School of Ballet. Every day during this time their moms hang around the café drinking green tea smoothies and discussing cellulite like it's leukemia. Cory and my other waitress Jenna have their little jokes, but these are the women who think nothing of a six-dollar cup of floating herbs or a ten-dollar salad that consists of nothing but romaine and almond slivers.

"Ahem." Madame clears her throat, and I glance her way. She's standing on the landing at the supply closet. There are about eight empty shelves and enough floor space in the closet to accommodate a twin bed. I covet that space, but Madame Bienve had her dance school upstairs before I had my café downstairs and had already claimed it for herself. And she's not budging, not that I have much to bargain with. Free pastries hardly tempt her, and I can't afford to pay her. She grabs a hand towel off the shelf and wraps it around the back of her neck. Her long, lean frame stands straight, disciplined. Seeing the scowl, the silent reprimand aimed at my curved vertebrae, I immediately bring myself to full height. Madame and I have some sort of unacknowledged competition. Who is more disciplined? More precise and structured? I unequivocally say it's me, but that large closet would help my cause.

"Good morning, Madame."

"It is one o'clock in the afternoon," she corrects me before pirouetting on her heel.

Retreating to my office and kicking boxes to the side, I clear a path to the little walnut desk I snagged from Dad's old house before it got sent to Goodwill. The drawers stick — one is even locked shut and I've yet to get a locksmith to make a key for it — and years of writing determinedly on thin papers have left behind dozens of nicks and marks. But it has character and has been around so long I imagine that some of those grooves belong to pencils my mother held. Plus it only takes up a small corner of the ping pong-table-sized room, and that's all the space I can afford with the entire wall of filing cabinets and storage bins I had built. Sitting down, I gather the papers strewn across the top and bundle them together, tapping their edges for a nice, clean stack. For a moment I breathe good, clean, deep breaths with my hands folded together. Tap, tap, inhale, tap. I want to work. I want to log onto my computer and start a new PDF. *Using Inventory to Maximize Profits.* Ideas are rolling around in my head that I need to see in list format to think through, then I need to call a repairman to look at the ice machine, and then order new pastry molds. So many things! Regardless, I pick up the phone.

Helena has a cell phone, but Dad does not. He retired last October, and if I want to reach my dad at any time without Helena's interference, I have to just hope he's home. Unless it's lunchtime, dinnertime, eleven o'clock A.M. on Tuesday, or nine o'clock A.M. on Saturday (his weekly tee times) he is most likely home. The trick is catching him there without Helena. She still has her condo over at Williamsburg West, but she spends a lot of time at Dad's place.

It rings four times. "Hello, Sparkle." He greets me heartily, his thin, feeble voice booming as much as possible.

"Dad. How'd you know it was me?"

He chuckles as if he's pulled off an amazing trick. "Helena talked me into getting something called Caller I.D." He enunciates the last few words as if introducing them to me for the first time. "Supposed to help eliminate those pesky telemarketing calls."

"You mean help prevent you from picking up the telemarketer calls," I say. "You're still gonna get them."

"Guess you're right." He chuckles again. "Can't teach an old dog new tricks."

I've no idea what that's even supposed to mean.

"Hailey said you left a message on the machine yesterday." I brace myself for the announcement. My dad has dated a bit in the years since Mom's disappearance, but not much and never with anyone for over six months or so. If I'd given it much thought, I'd have said we were safe, but then he met Helena at the country club through Hal and Buffy Barrington. The country club is full of Buffys and Biffys and Trixies and Dickies. Buffy and Hal have been around since my parents were married, Buffy's bifocals often aimed right at my family. I've despised her ever since the memorial service we had at the club where I overheard her telling another woman that my mother had been a "nonsensical sort of woman with her head in the clouds and not a care in the world besides herself."

"I was calling to see if you had any ideas about what I could get Hailey for her birthday."

*Strange.* Hailey and I always depend on Dad for a generic card and a ten-dollar check. He's a creature of habit, my dad, but not an imaginative or extravagant one. I suggest CDs, hair products, or Converse tennis shoes, and Dad hangs up without a single word about any engagement or proposal.

The upstairs tapping starts again, like plumbing pipes in a New York City apartment building. I also hear the continuous chime of the front doorbell, the ting of metal utensils against ceramic plates, the scrape of chairs on the wood floor in the dining area. Lovely money-making sounds! Coaxing Otis from his bed, I force him out the back door of my office that leads to the small grassy area where he can relieve himself.

The Shops of Sandpiper Street are two blocks from the ocean. I'd been ecstatic to find this space available after the divorce when I decided to open The Final Straw. By that time, I'd been ecstatic to stop taking additional classes at the college three nights a week working toward a degree I'd grown bored and burdened by, ecstatic to stop working days at the Starbucks near the college, and ecstatic to stop sweeping dried up mud from Greg's work boots off my bathroom floor. I was ready for a new life, cliché as a divorced café owner may be. Everyone thought I was better suited for a restaurant. "A real one that only opens in the evenings and has a long reservation list and a dark, boozy atmosphere," Johan, my regional manager at Starbucks had suggested. "That Lemon Souffle' you made for the Christmas party last year would draw crowds," he'd predicted. "And, Omigod that jalapeno cheese dip thing you invented."

But I'd opted for this instead. It sounded more normal, uncomplicated. I can honestly say I tried for normal. God knows I tried.

I lead Otis around on his leash until he finally agrees to stop smelling every blade of grass and get his business over with. Mr. Kent, who owns a bicycle shop next to the café, is outside his shop smoking a pipe and gazing out on the little slice of ocean we can see from our back doors. The day is clear but windy. The small slice of water I can glimpse is infused with whitecaps. Gulls holler in the distance, a lonely cry for my desolate mood. Mr. Kent is a dear. He once stayed with me when I accidentally locked myself out of the café after dark and insisted on follow-ing me home.

"Spring's a-comin'," Mr. Kent says. He always inhales the salty air and says "Spring's a-comin'," even when outside it's twenty degrees.

"Indeed it is," I reply, while I too take a big whiff of air like I'm some farmer with years of experience predicting the weather and the outcome of my crop.

*Her nostrils filled with the permeating scent of sea spray and sandalwood, signaling the end of a wicked winter.*

I shake my head, literally shaking off this annoying prose-forming habit. I've got real fiascos going down. I do not have time for this right now. Otis grows bored with his meandering and heads back inside to his bed.

"Stop in for a cup of coffee on the house sometime, Mr. Kent," I holler over my shoulder before shutting the metal door that will close me back inside for the rest of the afternoon. Back to my PDF file, my ledgers, my calculator.

When I return to the front, the afternooners are being well taken care of by Cory, Jenna is in the kitchen, and the same mother and son I've been seeing for the last few days are at the bar. The little boy is eating one of my famous Pumpkin Maple Muffins and his mother is dabbing at the corners of his mouth with a napkin she's twisted into a long corkscrew. Between dabs, she dips the napkin in her glass of water.

"So sorry about the mess," she says, looking down at the scratched wood floor that's now littered with crumbs. It looks like a dry-rotted sponge has disintegrated.

I wave a hand. "Glad to see him enjoying it."

The boy keeps going at the muffin, ignoring us. He is about eight years old with adorable sandy blonde curls and freckles sprinkled across his cheeks like constellations. Most little boys that age have ears that trumpet out the sides of their heads like fresh blooms, but he has the most adorable little buds. The most astonishing thing about his appearance, though, is his wardrobe. He's dressed like a World War II fighter pilot complete with khaki green pants, a leather bomber jacket, and aviation goggles affixed to his face making his little eyes appear bugged. I recall that the day before he had been wearing a superhero cape over red pants.

"I'm Margo," his mom says to me. She could be his aunt or babysitter, but I don't think so. Not the delicate way she wipes at his mouth and rubs a finger down the bridge of his nose, flicking it playfully when she reaches the tip.

I start to introduce myself, but the little boy turns his stool around and extends his hand. "Paulus," he says, his face set in a serious expression as if we're meeting in a board room to discuss company mergers.

"Paulus. What a neat name!" I speak like I'm on a children's morning show.

"His name is Paul, after my ex-husband's father," says Margo. "He likes to go by Paulus." She shrugs, indicating she's been trying to make sense of it for years.

Paulus stares straight ahead and begins his explanation. "Paulus is derived from the Latin adjective meaning small. During the Classical Age, Paulus was used to identify the younger of two people from the same family that bore the same name. Since my paternal grandfather was named Paul, I am called Paulus."

"Well," I declare once he takes a breath. "It's a great name, and I totally see your point." There's that kindergarten substitute teacher voice again. "I do the opposite with my name."

Margo looks at me and blinks. She clearly wasn't expecting a reply, much less a conversation. There's a wariness in her eyes. I know the look because I wear it often myself. Margo has something she's shielding. There's something... a guardedness, perhaps?

"My name is Amethyst. But, I hate hauling that silly name around everywhere, so I just go by Amy."

"The name Amethyst comes from the word intoxicated. At one time it was believed that the stone could offer protection from drunkenness," Paulus says, looking straight ahead as if he's reading the words from a teleprompter.

I follow his gaze, but there's nothing in his view aside from a window. Deaton is outside on the sidewalk arranging discounted books on his racks. "Before the 18th century, amethyst was thought to be one of the most valuable gems."

"Well," I say with an air of authority, smiling at Margo. I hold my head up high as if I've just realized my importance.

Behind me, I can hear a group of Dance Moms chatting away. "There's a Groupon for half off Botox at Serendipity Spa in Savannah," one of them — *Donna?* — says. Their conversation seems even sillier than usual after the knowledge and information that have just spewed out of the mouth of Paulus.

I glance up at the clock. "I need to do some more work in my office. It was so nice to meet you, Margo. Paulus."

"After the unearthing of extensive deposits in locations such as Brazil, amethyst lost most of its value," Paulus says.

Three o'clock. A good time to call Mom. She should be home from work by now counting down the hours until Ian gets home. If he's coming home. Ian's unpredictable. Ian's got a roving eye. Ian likes things that don't belong to him. Hence, my mother.

Mom sounds happy and relaxed. She speaks breezily of the weekend and how they enjoyed a walk in the park together and Ian bought a little watercolor from a street vendor. "We went for seafood at a little shack on the docks and watched a movie on television," she says. She sounds strong. I'm reluctant to burst her bubble of contentment, but I'd rather do it now than when Ian's on one of his overnight "business trips" or the wind isn't blowing in the right direction to ease Mom's multitude of anxieties.

Hailey bursts through the door of my office. I realize I should have called Mom earlier before Hailey got out of school. I point toward the kitchen, asking with my hands if she can go help Jenna and Cory. She drops her backpack on the floor. "Mary," I mouth, pointing to the phone before she walks out. Otis lifts his head from his pillow and eyes me, calling out my deception.

"Mom, I have to tell you about something that is going on," I begin once the door closes behind Hailey.

"Mary!" She quickly corrects me.

"Mary."

I replay the entire scenario from the night before, setting the scene. It's something I do when talking to my mom. She's an English teacher and appreciates a good story. I begin with Becky's visit and the storm. I take her through how the door slammed when the little ballerinas headed home after a day of practice, how Deaton's mom called him and told him about her cousin's troubles, how his *T* was missing from his store name decal, how Otis refused to get wet, and how Hailey made chili. The story ends in a panic with the email message I was finally able to retrieve after hours of my phone's taunting me with its spinning circle.

"Amy," she says after a moment of silence. I imagine her hand at her neck, twisting the gold locket Ian gave her on their tenth anniversary. Not an actual anniversary, just a day that commemorates the day they made their decision — the day she went from being my mother Caroline Chadwick to Mary in a matter of hours. "Honey, you don't have to do this," she assures me.

"Oh for God's sake, Mom. *Mary!* I'm *not* going to do this. But Helena's opened the box. She's determined." I run my fingers along the top of my desk, fitting my nails in the grooves pencils and pens have left in the soft wood.

"There are over five hundred thousand people in Atlanta, sweetheart. I'm well hidden."

She says this, but I can hear the rise in her voice. Even though I missed many years with my mom, I know her as well as I know myself. I know her moods, her gestures, her desires, and her fears. Being found is her second greatest fear. Losing Ian is her first. Being a bigamist and jeopardizing everything in other people's lives doesn't even register.

*She was a nonsensical woman with her head in the clouds…*

"It's illegal to marry someone while you're still married," I hiss through clenched teeth.

"Your father isn't married," she answers breezily, as if we're discussing whether he's a Ford or a Chevy man.

Hailey comes back into my office and plops down on a box of paper goods. Conversation over.

"I need to hang up, Mary. I need to unpack boxes and spend a little time talking to Hailey before she heads out."

My daughter blows a kiss toward the phone. "And she sends her love."

Hailey loves Mary — the Mary that supposedly taught English Literature to me in school and took a shine to me. She calls her *Aunt Mary.* "Felt sorry for me because my mother died," I had told her. This version of Mary moved to Atlanta many years ago and kept in touch with me, and now we're as close as mother and daughter. My father believes this same story. He has never met Aunt Mary, obviously, but he sure appreciates how she has taken me under her wing all these years and still, to this day, keeps in such close contact with me and my Hailey. And even though my dad means the world to me and to Hailey too, as far as female influence and solidarity are concerned, it's just Hailey, "Aunt Mary", and me against the world. Always has been.

From where I was standing, I saw no other way.

"I wanted to tell you I'm going to dinner with Jarod and his parents," Hailey mumbles while rifling through her backpack, intent on finding something. She produces a paper outlining how much a graduation cap and gown will cost and where to order them. Ninety-five dollars!

I walk her to the door and catch a glimpse of the backside of Madame Bienve as she's leaving. Her backside is one long, straight stick topped with a small, round, tightly wrapped bun that looks like a doorknob.

"Everything all right out here?" I look around at the almost empty room. Napkins are wadded up and discarded on plates along with the remnants of bread crusts and cheese. Only two diners remain, and I doubt any last-minute stragglers are coming in this late. Sandpiper Street goes fairly silent and closes down around six. I give the nod to Cory to wrap things up before I retreat to my office again.

My laptop lid is open. I check my Unveiled email and read the audacious message again.

*How dare she!* What right does Helena Delgado have digging up long-buried bodies? Okay, so there wasn't actually a body, but long-buried pain. Doesn't she realize how much suffering she's going to put us all through again, having to relive this tragedy? Is she even planning to tell us about it?

I get to the end, the part about the newspaper. Helena is the food critic for the Courier. "Food Journalist" she calls herself, though that might be a stretch. She always says rice instead of risotto, like they're interchangeable. Sorely, I note that she has never offered to do a review of The Final Straw's twelve different flavors of coffee or our Apple Butter Cinnamon Rolls, but she's offered to ask a colleague to promote the advancement of an investigation agency owned by a supposed stranger. Her future daughter-in-law is a chef, for God's sake, and she's oblivious — and I'd thought Helena and I were friends. Friendly, anyway.

Otis is cleaning his front paws, seemingly intent on something in particular on the left one. "I don't care," I say to him. "She and all her friends at the Courier can drink the ink." He keeps gnawing and moves over to the right paw, ignoring me. I remember the ninety-five dollar cap and gown, the six months of overdue bank payments, my car that has been acting up — trying to give me fair warning that it's gonna rebel soon. No matter. I am not taking this job.

**From: Unveiled@officeweb.com**
**To: Helena1098@myFCcourier.com**
**Subject: Investigation**

**Thank you so much for your consideration. We** — *I always refer to my one-woman operation as a "we" like there's a team of us busily scurrying around* — **are always happy to hear we come so highly recommended. Unfortunately, we have far too many commitments right now and will have to pass, but we wish you the best of luck.**

Deaton texts me just before I'm ready to head out.

"Got any Socialite Special left?"

"Plenty. No one else orders it but you and the Dance Moms."

"Pulling on my yoga pants as we speak!"

I make him a cup, lock up the café, and walk to the other side of the street with a smile on my face. I've put this mess to rest. I cannot help what a grown woman does, no matter how wrong it might be. My house of cards is not going to fall. Surely Helena won't get far with this.

Stray limbs and leaves still litter the sidewalk from the storm the evening before, but the air this evening is filled with a sense of solace as if the beast that had escaped and gone on a rampage has been captured and pacified.

Atticus jumps from his perch in the window seat when I enter his presence.

"I get the feeling he's not crazy about me."

"Don't take it personally. He's a loner."

"Ah," I mouth, tilting my head back in realization.

We settle into the club chairs Deaton has positioned in the back corner of the store, and I kick off my shoes, pull my feet cozily up underneath me, and try simply to be a normal person with her friend, not someone struggling to carry the weight of an elephant. Talk comes easily. Our conversation flows from businesses on Sandpiper Street to the struggling economy to the latest best-sellers and, finally, to Cousin Patty in Iowa.

"Well, she's moved into the old homestead," says Deaton. "Ran into L.J. in the mercantile and he turned the other way, and Larry

Sr. wants her to come on home and forget this nonsense, as he calls it."

I frown and tuck my foot further under me.

"Good news is, Tommy Mobley, the grandson of Earl Mobley who built the house in 1929, says she's still structurally sound and should be gleamin' and sportin' a whole new attitude before squirrel season."

"The house or Patty?"

It boggles my mind to think this is where Deaton came from, who his kinfolk are, especially when he's so urban and techy. I think of my own heritage and picture holidays at a table with Deaton's mom and Aunt Patty and various other cousins and aunts and uncles. Deaton's family sounds so much more fun and much less complicated than my own. Then again, so does John Gotti's.

"Hey, you want some pot roast? I have some in the Crock-Pot upstairs," Deaton says.

"As long as it's not made with squirrel."

I follow him to the back storage room and up the stairs to his apartment, behind Atticus, glad I'd had the foresight to feed Otis before I came over. If only I could have brought him with me, but Atticus would have never allowed it, and I'm not sure if Deaton would have been too thrilled about it either. The first time he came to the café and saw Otis he patted his head as if that were an unspoken requirement, and I could tell he hoped those few little pats would be enough to make Otis go away and stop staring him down.

"Wow. This is impressive." Deaton has transformed the upstairs space amazingly well. His apartment is a bit smaller than Madame Bienve's studio, but his play on texture and color, his ability to maximize the square footage, the way he's worked with the natural light — the result is breathtaking. There's just enough coarseness to the room to keep it from being sterile. Well, of course, he would have a way with fabrics and furnishings.

I try to think of things to keep the conversation going. "Did I tell you about one of the Dance Moms who recently got remarried? Nikki. They met on an online dating website. I'm kind of an eavesdropper," I admit between chews.

Out of curiosity, we pull up the Potion #9 website. "Let's do it," I suggest, and Deaton nods in agreement.

"We could just see what happens," he shrugs, good-naturedly. It's like a social experiment, not anything we're that invested in. It's the middle of the week in Flannery Cove. What else is there to do?

We start with my profile. Deaton reads the questions out to me, as I carefully consider each one. The screen reflects soft bluish light onto his face. I've moved from the table to the sofa, and I pull my legs under me and sit up straight like I'm about to clap my hands with glee. I try to relax against the pillows a bit, but I'm still a little eager looking — can't help it, this is fun.

"What's on your playlist?" He begins, cocking his head, interested in my response.

I haven't updated my playlist in years. It's still full of break-up songs: *I'm a Survivor, You Give Love a Bad Name, Before He Cheats.* I'm not sure I want to reveal this, so when I stare off into space like I'm trying to remember, I'm actually trying to think of what songs will make me look good, hot, confident.

"Quirks?" Deaton says, moving down the line while I'm still thinking.

"Quirks?"

"Yeah, you know. Like odd little things that are unique to you that no one knows. Name three."

I frown, trying to think of cute, dateable characteristics. *I think like I'm narrating a story.* No way! Not admitting that one. *I pretty much conjure up images for every thought that floats through my mind?* Nope again.

*I communicate daily with my mother who's supposed to be dead.* Is that a quirk? *I'm a liar and a fraud, but I'm a pillar of the community, a responsible business owner, and a beloved daughter, and mother, and faithful friend — so it's okay* — but is it a quirk?

I hold up a finger. "I feel bad for other people too easily," I say. "I mean, like people I shouldn't feel bad for. Like people I should despise, actually." *Like my mother.*

He looks up from the keyboard.

"Like if someone has been mean to me before, and I'm sticking pins in a voodoo doll of them, but then they say or do something nice or something happens that makes them appear vulnerable, I'm like a glob of putty. I make a million excuses in my head for their previous behavior."

*Probably because I hope someone does the same for me if ever… This Helena thing: If the truth came out could I be arrested? Could they say I covered up a crime, muddled an investigation? Conspired?*

"That's not a quirk," says Deaton. "That's compassion."

Heat builds in my cheeks. "Well, I hate it." I didn't mean to make myself sound better than I am, even though that is my specialty. "I'm not that compassionate," I assure him like I'm disclosing I'm not that smart after beating everyone at Jeopardy. "Honestly, I mean if Greg had fallen asleep in a running car with the garage door down I would've run to the bathroom for a good ten minutes or so."

"I don't think so." He raises his eyebrows, fairly certain of this.

*I do think so! I've been perfecting this facade since I was fifteen years old! I'm quite skilled by now.*

"No, really. I don't even know if Lyme disease is fatal, because it's something that's never concerned me."

"You *are* heartless."

"I like Pilgrims," I blurt out.

"Wh… what?" Deaton tosses his head back and laughs out loud.

"Well, I mean. Not that I *like* Pilgrims. I wrote a book about two Pilgrims that fall in love on their journey to America, and I learned a lot about them during my research. Really fascinating. Did you know the Pilgrims didn't steal the land from the Indians? No, it's true," I say as if he's doubting me — *as if he cares!* "The Wampanoags never challenged the Pilgrims' right to live on the land, and the Pilgrims paid for and purchased their land." Now I know what it feels like to be Paulus, and I purposely look Deaton directly in the eye in case I've been staring straight ahead in a trance with encyclopedic knowledge nervously pouring out of me.

"You wrote a book? You never told me this."

"A manuscript." I shrug my shoulders as if this is insignificant information. "It was years ago when I was still married, before I had the café and all the things I have on my plate now. I shelved it, but it doesn't seem to want to stay shelved — always poking around in my head."

"Has anyone read it?"

"It's been rejected a few times," I say.

"Okay, but has anyone *read* it?"

I try to think. No agents have read it beyond the first chapter, and no one ever asked for more. Becky doesn't like to read, so she wasn't a good one to ask. My dad would have said it was good, offering nothing beyond that, and I wouldn't have been sure he had even bothered. He might have even patted me on the head the way Deaton did Otis, hoping I would go away and stop begging. My mom had read it and said she loved it, but I wasn't sure that counted. Asking for my mom's literary opinion of my work was like asking her if I was pretty. "Of course," she would say. "You are the most beautiful girl in the world. And your written words are more eloquent than Emily Dickinson's."

"Not really."

"Can I?" He asks.

My heart skips a beat. I've been wanting an honest critique for a long time, but I'm not sure I can face it. It's like being asked to strip down and let someone examine all my moles for skin cancer.

"Um, gosh. I'd have to dig the thing out."

He studies me, trying to see if I'm evading the subject or if I really might have the manuscript buried somewhere under the rubble of brick and debris. "Show it to me and I'll show you..." he puts a hand to his mouth, thinking.

"Yes? What?"

"I don't know. My high school poems about my sexy math tutor? They're basically the lyrics to REO Speedwagon songs, but I'll dig them out too."

"I have knees like baseballs," I say, changing the subject back to quirks. Not that that one's any better than my slush-pile manuscript.

He looks down toward the middle of my legs, but I'm wearing long pants. I flex my muscles anyway, pulling those lumps tight.

It's true, the knee thing. The first time I noticed it was when I was fourteen or fifteen years old. I used to exercise like crazy, but they would never tone. Looking at the J.C. Penny catalog, I used to notice that all the models had knees that blended in with the rest of their legs, but I'd look down at mine and it was like God forgot my knees and stuck these little, round things on at the last minute, before shipping me out. To this day I still have them. Hailey says I'm imagining things, and my mom says my legs look like they were carved by a master sculptor, but I see them every time I look down. I've tried to get a close-up inspection, but if I crouch then they bend, and if I lean from the waist, the blood rushes to my head. But I know how my knees look. They can be seen in full-length mirrors.

"I'll keep thinking. Let's move on to you," I say, and again we go through the same lists.

"Your playlist?"

"Springsteen, Mellencamp." Deaton names people I never expected. I look at him with renewed respect.

What had I been expecting? Duran-Duran? Barry Manilow? *Well... yeah.*

"Quirks?" I ask. "We already know about your coffee."

He answers quickly having had time to think about his.

"I hang all my shirts facing the same way, color-coordinated, every button buttoned."

"O.C.D." I purse my lips to deliver the diagnosis.

"Okay, hmm." He starts to say something then waves a hand. "No. No, don't put that. Let's move on to the next section and come back to this."

"Okay." I turn the laptop back toward me and peer at the screen, running my finger down the profile form. "I don't even see this quirks thing on here. Where is it?"

"Oh, it's not. I was just being nosy."

I stare at him for a few seconds and mutter something about how annoying he is, then find my place back on the screen. "Describe your ideal mate."

"Easy." "My ideal woman," he begins.

*Wait. Woman?*

Hadn't Deaton told me he pitched for the other team? I search my memory. I can't recall those exact words. Was it the stereotypical love of books? The cat? The fabulously decorated apartment, or that pink oxford he'd been wearing the first day I met him? Probably it was that oxford, it'd even been starched. Or maybe it was the ability and forethought to put a pot roast in the Crock-Pot.

*Oh! He said he hasn't dated since coming out.*

I plunge straight in because my foot never strays far from my mouth. I should have mentioned that as one of my quirks.

"Now, you told me you hadn't dated since you, um, ya know, came out, er, if I remember correctly." I tap my index finger to my chin, business-like.

"That's right," he confirms. "I'd been dating the same woman for a few months, but things fizzled. We broke up before I came out here."

It takes me a second then, *Oh! Coming out. Moving out here!* No wonder I didn't get it. No one says they moved *out* to the coast of Georgia! My fourth-grade geography teacher, Mrs. Lampler, appears in my mind and clutches a hand to her heart.

Deaton continues describing his ideal woman while I try to focus on filling in the blanks on the screen as if I'm helping him fill out boring social security forms or something. He's thrown me for a bit of a loop, but whatever...

"Long hair," he says. "Prefer brunettes over blondes."

I run a hand down my long ponytail, catching a glimpse of Loreal's Natural Light Brown.

"Compassion is a must," he says. "The ability to forgive is a virtue."

I nod and begin tapping keys efficiently, trying not to read anything into something that's not there. He's not referring to my earlier comment. Everyone looks for kindness. No one says they are hoping to meet a tall, dark-haired vixen to take home to their mom.

"Big knees," he says. "I've always had a thing for big knees."

*No! No. No. No.* All wrong. Detour! Road-block! Five minutes ago I thought the man was gay. Deaton is like a brother.

*What have I done now?*

Otis and I get home right after Hailey. I'm so exhausted I wave a hand at her, and she goes upstairs to her room, and I go to mine. I collapse in bed and turn on my sound machine. Sleeping is a hobby of mine, but not one I get to enjoy that often. Most people invest in paints and canvases, diving gear, and gardening supplies while I stock up on cushy pillows, downy blankets, and anything that promises peaceful slumber. The atmosphere is changed to sleep conducive by pulling down the thermostat and covering up any lights on the electronics. I'd tried to get used to wearing a sleep mask, but I kept imagining someone standing over me and I had to keep pulling it down to peek, so it was counterproductive. That should have been listed as one of my quirks. I have a feeling those are going to be jumping out at me from every direction now.

I flip my pillow to the cool side and plump it. *Mmm, laundry detergent, Springtime Meadow.* What a day! My car barely made it home, I turned down a plum assignment, free advertising, and a much-needed paycheck, and threw another load of dirt on my mother's coffin while I solidified my good standing with my dad, and totally rocked being a single mother to my beloved daughter. And I made my best friend fall for me. It was probably that comment about sympathy, which made me sound like something I'm not.

Now I really need to find a man on that stupid website, if for no other reason than to be unavailable.

# THREE

I
N 2007 I started hearing about this phenomenon called
social media. Hailey was too young to use it, and I was too
busy. I was working, raising a kid, going to school, and trying to keep my husband satisfied. I was cleaning up his messes
— both literally and figuratively — and keeping my feet firmly
planted in two opposing lives. I wasn't the least bit interested in
any platform designed to shed light on myself — transparency
not being my thing.

When Greg's infidelities were no longer deniable, I became
more active online, searching for the women he was being linked
to. Old acquaintances found me, and I got sucked into the online
community. Suddenly I was privy to everyone's thoughts, their
family dynamics, even their constant whereabouts. It was oddly
fascinating that other people in the world lived out in the open
like that, truly who they said they were, who their friends and
family knew them to be. Turns out some people sharing their
real selves are constantly on the prowl for the next avenue of
their life, even if it takes them on a major detour from the one
they're on.

I had followed my husband. I'd done stake-outs. One morning
I'd even crawled through the window of his buddy Frank's bach-
elor pad, where he was staying after I had kicked him out. There

I found a little wooden box next to the bed he'd been sleeping in with letters from some woman named Felicity and receipts from the Comfort Inn.

I knew people who stayed with philanderers. I knew people who knew about it and turned a blind eye, people who suspected but had no proof, and people whose minds it had never entered but should have. And that's when I deviated from my own avenue and formed a company.

I was due to graduate from my business degree program in two months, which I did. But I'd minored in psychology, and I wanted to do something with it as well. It was a crazy, fleeting thought, but I grabbed on to it. *Why not?* I thought. *I know this by heart.* I enrolled in an online course, took a test, and got licensed by the state of Georgia as a private investigator. I'd been practicing the craft since I was a mere adolescent, after all. Becky helped me set up a website and an online presence, and after donating my wedding dress to Goodwill, I came up with the name: Unveiled Investigations. People assume it means uncovered, exposed. It does not. For me, it means freedom.

"Never tell anyone it's me." That was all I asked.

We shook on it and toasted the whole thing with ice cream sundaes and, to this day, no one except me, Mom — *Mary!* — Becky and Hailey knows anything about my sleuthing. And I can spot a liar from a mile away. Like a serial-killing cop, I bring 'em to justice and re-join the game with one less opponent in the world. It's not like I have a booming business. It's just a semi-profitable hobby, but it would be great if it could be more than semi-profitable. It's fun, it's adventurous, but it's not necessarily real. I don't dedicate near the time and effort to it I do to the growing list of gourmet recipes, the diligent book-keeping, and the marketing and public relations that my café requires. I'm the anonymous best friend to every woman in town who's been where I've been. So far, that's all it is.

I've had a few memorable cases, though. Once I sat outside the Methodist church until two o'clock in the morning to snap a picture of Pastor Grimm and the pianist, Mrs. Thibadeux, leaving together, and another time I pretended to be a homeless person on a park bench in the freezing rain to snap a photo of a widower who had remarried and still made daily visits to his first wife's grave. I tried to assure that client it only showed what a sensitive, loving man he was, but after that, I had to let it go. The Pastor Grimm case resulted in a small-town scandal that rivaled Watergate.

"I decided not to take it," I tell Hailey over bagels late Saturday morning. My eyes flit to the clock on the café wall, hoping it's past noon or getting close. Sandpiper Street shops are only open until two o'clock on Saturdays and closed Sundays. It's always been that way. It's in our lease agreements to keep the charm of the beachside separate from the commercialism of downtown and now the new west corridor. A few customers linger over cold coffee, wrinkled newspapers, and stale conversations. Apparently, weekends are made for malls.

"Of course you did," Hailey says. She doesn't even look up from her chemistry book. I can't tell if the tone is *Duh! I don't blame you,* "Duh! you never do anything exciting," or "Duh! I know you well enough to know that without you telling me."

I get up and sweep the broom under her table and she lifts her feet, still running her finger across the text of her book and mumbling as she does, committing it to memory. In the booth behind her, a mother and daughter are getting ready to go wedding dress shopping and already arguing about the color peony.

"It's peach." The daughter determinedly taps the table with the tip of a long fingernail.

"Pink" Her mother emphatically shakes her head and folds her arms across her chest — subject closed to further discussion.

After Hailey helps wash the dishes and leaves, I retreat to my office and log back onto Unveiled's email account. There's the message, back in bold, which means Helena has replied.

My phone dings with a text from Deaton. I've stayed on my side of the street since that evening we did our profiles, but I've missed having someone to unwind and banter with.

"Have u looked @ ur profile?"

I open up another window on my laptop and look. I already have an admirer.

Marvin F. is kind of cute. He's a swimming pool installer and likes camping, hunting, country music, and football.

"Hmmm. Sounds like he might be from your neck of the woods."

"Ha! Come over when u can!"

"K. In a sec."

After letting Otis out and finishing up a few things, I head over to the bookstore. Deaton is on a ladder putting his *T* decal in place.

"Look straight?" he asks.

Yes, he does look straight to me now. But I still see nothing sexy or handsome. I just see Deaton. And besides, someone out in cyberspace thinks I'm worth a second look.

"Tiny bit up on the left corner," I answer.

We eat the Mediterranean Turkey sandwiches on fresh, warm ciabatta I brought with me for lunch and try to find out everything we can about Marvin F., which proves to be not much without the help of a full last name. We end up on the subject of food, probably because of the ciabatta, and I tell Deaton about Helena being a food critic for the Courier.

"So your dad's been dating her for over a year?" Deaton pulls the cushion from the chair opposite the one I'm sitting in and props it against the wall. He stretches his long legs out on the carpet and reclines against the cushion.

"Yes. More than a year now," I say. "They're actually..." *Oops. I'm not supposed to know about the proposal.*

"Oh! Atticus, you scared me." I reach for the cat, but he strides away.

"Do you like her? Does Hailey?"

I don't know how to answer this, especially now. It's not as though I like or dislike Helena. She's done nothing mean to me, nor has she done anything especially nice. We're perfectly civil to each other. A few times we've shared a laugh, but it's always followed by awkward silence while we both try to think of something to keep the laughter going. Despite her country club lifestyle, she doesn't strike me as pretentious or snooty. Unless she's writing to a private investigator or writing her column and putting on an uppity, highly educated act, she uses words like flabbergasted and skedaddle. It's hard not to like that in a person. Until two days, ago I would have said, "I don't like her choice of friends, but she's fine." *Really!* I would have thought, *Better than fine.* But now I'm not so sure. Before, I would have thought if she made my dad happy that made me happy. Now I can't wrap my head around how she could possibly think what she is doing could, by any stretch of the imagination, make any of us happy.

*She's pure evil!*

"We like her fine," I say.

Deaton raises one brow, but he doesn't prod.


I leave Deaton's around three o'clock, stuffed and ready for an afternoon of mindless television. He watches from the sidewalk as I load Otis into the passenger seat and wave from the driver's side. I'm still waving and smiling from ear to ear when I turn my key in the ignition and nothing happens.

It's not long before I have my car towed to my house and load Otis and myself into Deaton's car to be driven home. This will be Deaton's first trip to my house. Sitting beside him, I'm trying to remember when I last vacuumed, if I've flushed my toilet, if I left the bra I had reached into my shirt and pulled out the sleeve the night before draped over the dining room chair. I haven't exactly been on my A-game lately. But maybe that's good. He'll see me as a sloth, a slob, a woman no man in his right mind would want.

It's a beautiful, clear night. Mr. Kent is right, spring's a-comin'. Jarod must've mowed the grass earlier in the day. Everything looks well kept, as if I'm not falling apart.

Great! Sympathetic *and* orderly.

*The afternoon shadows screened through the leaves of the majestic oaks like weak tea, not quite transparent, not quite...* "Hmmm?" I turn my face toward Deaton. "What'd you say?"

"Nice place."

Otis sits up like a school kid bringing a friend home for the first time, proud of his digs.

The tow truck pulls in right beside us and deposits my betraying heap of smoldering metal in the driveway. I throw up my hands. "Nothing I can do about this now. Let's go in."

I love to watch people's reactions when they enter my home. *It's good, isn't it? You like?*

Otis saunters off to the laundry room, so blasé. An entitled kid unaware that some dogs live in backyards.

"It's... wow." Deaton is speechless. The one reaction that always throws me. *Speechless good or speechless bad?* "How do you keep that white carpet so clean?"

"Well, it's just me and Hailey," I say. "Had it installed after my divorce." I'd vacuumed every last speck of dried mud and installed stark white carpeting in the living room. In a final declaration of independence, I'd stocked my closet with high–heeled stilettos that looked beautiful but killed my feet (Greg is only 5'10" and I could never wear heels with him.) Well, I'd also rented space a block from the ocean and opened up a café, but I will not think about that right now, even though I can see Hailey brought in the mail before leaving and there's something from the bank lying in the stack.

"How did you ever come to acquire such a plum piece of real estate?" Deaton asks. I feel like I'm bringing someone from another world into my home life, someone who only knows me one way. He may see a glimpse of the other me: the suburban, good neighbor, conscientious homeowner, eclectic decorator me. But he may also glimpse my threadbare towels, my lack of green thumb, and my stack of lies in the corner, so it's a risk.

"It was my Nana's — my dad's mom. She passed away when I was fifteen and left it to me. I've lived here since I was eighteen years old."

I run my hand down the dark, mahogany wood of the banister, remembering Susan and myself — Susan somewhere around ten, me six years old or so — flying down the stairs. Susan has that old Astro's cap on her head; I have a knit cap on mine. For the hundredth time, I wonder whatever happened to Susan, where she'd ended up going. She'd stayed on with Nana long after Gramps died but had gone to live with a different family an hour or so away when she started high school. I'd lost track when she turned eighteen and left the foster system and Flannery Cove behind.

I've looked for her online, but it's a needle in a haystack. Susan's gone, and I don't know where she lives now or if her last name is even Blakely anymore. She is another reason I never want to leave this house. One day I'm certain Susan is going to turn up looking for Nana, wanting to reconnect. Susan was the closest thing I ever had to a sister, but now she's another family member I can't claim. They drop like flies.

"Where's your restroom?" Deaton asks and proceeds down the hall where I point, carrying the bag he walked in with. When he emerges he's dressed in an old, stained shirt, and cargo shorts.

"Gonna take a look under the hood," he says, responding to my stare, and out the door he goes, taking charge. He gets in the driver's seat and tries once more to start the car. He lifts the hood and pulls things out, inspecting wires. I follow behind him kicking the tires, peering over his shoulder.

Deaton retrieves something from the bag he'd carried his work clothes in. "Circuit tester." He holds it up for me to see, as if I know what I'm looking at. It looks like a nice one, I guess. "Turn the key in the on position," he hollers, ducking beneath the hood again. I oblige

"Fuel pump," he determines, coming around to the driver's window and wiping his hands on his shirt. "That's what I suspected."

I nod my head meagerly, as if apologizing for being so hard on my fuel pump.

"Tell ya what," Deaton says. "I'll go down to the auto parts store and get what we need to fix this up if you'll cook me a steak dinner."

"Deal."

It's as if Deaton had read my earlier thoughts and is now doing everything he can to prove his manhood with auto mechanics and slabs of meat. *Me Jane, you not Tarzan!*

While Deaton's gone, I call my mom. "Mom… Mary. What in the world am I going to do about this whole Helena thing? I'm stressed beyond the limit over this, and I'm getting that terrible itch back," I say, rubbing my nails on my right hand up and down my left arm. My arms tend to break out when my mother gets under my skin.

She listens while I rail. "And Dad still hasn't even told me anything about proposing to her."

"That's your dad for you," she says. "Listen, you asked me why Helena was dredging all this up after all these years, and I told you I wasn't sure."

I stop railing and listen.

"That's not entirely true. I think I might know why. I'm not saying I know this for certain," she continues. "I'm just saying it's a theory. A plausible one."

"Okaaayyy."

"Your dad and I had life insurance. There was a two hundred fifty thousand dollar policy on me. Not a windfall, but still," she says. "Do you know if your dad ever cashed it? I'm fairly certain Helena might like to start their new life together with that added to their bank account. It would certainly benefit her for me to be dead."

"Would benefit her for you to be dead?" I laugh out loud. "You mean, aside from the obvious reason?"

"Just a theory," she snaps crisply.

I have to call Deaton and ask him to stop at the grocery store and pick up the steaks and potatoes and the makings for a chocolate cake. "My car is dead," I point out. "Write this down: half-inch thick New York strips. Fresh Rosemary. Two large baking potatoes. Fresh Asparagus. Feta crumbles. A container of cocoa and heavy cream for the ganache."

I spend the afternoon inside marinating beef and whipping up a chocolate macadamia cake while Deaton replaces the fuel pump in my car. Cooking calms me, but I hope Deaton doesn't think we look like an old married couple, he in oil-stained cargo shorts and a ripped T-shirt and me in an apron. As I measure oil and crack eggs, I try to imagine telling our kids one day how his manliness was the thing that got me.

"Every man should know his fuel pumps." Deaton will lower the newspaper and put his two cents in with a wink.

The image horrifies me.

While we eat, I study him. He has a strange way of lifting his fork up and out of his mouth rather than straight out. I've figured out another reason for my initial assessment of him. It's his hair. It seems blow-dried and styled like it's 1978 and he's headed to the disco. And his face, there's no stubble.

"So you said when you moved to Georgia you had been offered a position in the home office of... where did you work again?" I scoop another spoonful of potato over on the left side of my plate, far away from the pumpernickel roll.

Deaton lifts his fork up and out of his mouth like a toddler announcing his pureed carrots are all gone. "Braxton International. We distributed textbooks. Universities, schools, libraries, print on demand, e-book. Everything."

I stifle a yawn and pretend to be intrigued. "And why didn't you take it? Wanted a change?"

"I never said no, but I didn't jump on it as fast as I should have. I knew James Mandwell was more qualified, and I was trying to be a 'company man.' You know, think about what's best for growth, blah, blah, blah." He waves a hand in the air. "James ended up going to work for a different corporation, and I got passed over altogether. That's where that got me."

I frown and straighten my silverware. "Hmmm. Well, their loss."

"Moral of the story," says Deaton, "pick up the phone when it's ringing or you might not get a call back."

From: Helena1098@myFCcourier.com
To: Unveiled@officeweb.com
Subject: reconsider

**Dear Investigator,**

**I urge you to reconsider before turning down this case. I am giving your company the opportunity first because, as I stated before, you come highly recommended. Your reviews are glowing, and your research is known for being precisely accurate and impeccably documented. However, if you turn this down one of your competitors will be offered the chance to find out what happened to Caroline Chadwick.**

*Oh Gosh, seeing my mother's real name in print — it's been so long. I don't like Helena using my mother's name. It's sacred, that name.*

**That investigator will be the one to get an article in the Courier. That investigator will be the one to solve a decades-old case that the Flannery Cove Police Dept. detectives didn't — not that they really tried. Again, please reconsider. I am prepared to double your standard rates. Thank you, Helena Delgado.**

There's also an email from franandbob@commonlink.com. I had wrapped up a case for Fran two months earlier and unfortunately, it hadn't ended well. I had to present her with evidence of a husband who had rekindled a relationship with a former college flame.

**Dear Investigator,**

I would like to fill you in on what has taken place since I paid my final check to you and thanked you for your services. I hired an attorney and filed for a divorce from my husband. He was completely bewildered until I presented him with the pictures of him and Loretta together. Loretta is now a nurse for Dr. Marshall Lyons. Dr. Lyons is a Pediatric Orthopedist with a practice in Savannah. He has patients coming from all over the world to see him, and his waiting list is long. My husband and I have a two-year-old son with Skeletal Dysplasia, and he was using whatever loose connection he could find to get my son in to see this doctor without getting my hopes up in the process. Fortunately, he was successful in securing an appointment and Dr. Lyons has agreed to take Jeremy on as a patient. Also, fortunately, my husband and I are united in our marriage and the needs of our family. Unfortunately, we are out quite a large sum of money (to us anyway) for your services (not to mention the deposit I paid an attorney and the filing charges I incurred.)

I write to you today to ask you to please reimburse my fees to me, as I am very dissatisfied with the lack of actual investigation. I felt it only fair to ask you this before I take to the internet and post a very negative review of your business.

I've been holding my breath. I exhale and run a hand through my hair. I don't feel in the least responsible for this, and I didn't say what Fran's husband had been doing with Loretta. Fran contacted me when she already suspected something between them and had asked me for proof. She had signed up for the least expensive option on my website, so I had taken the pictures, uploaded them, and sent them to her. I had left the conclusion up to her.

I've already given her money to the grocery store in exchange for fresh produce and a few pounds of chicken breasts, and to the doctor when Hailey had strep throat and needed an antibiotic.

I reply asking her for an account number I can deposit to, and then I glance back at Helena's email.

*Pick up the phone when it's ringing, or you might not get a call back.*

I'm reminded of something. I go over to the kitchen counter and flip through the stack of mail. Buried beneath the Victoria's Secret catalog and the outrageously high power bill is another delinquent notice from my bank.

**From: Unveiled@officeweb.com**
**To: Helena1098@myFCcourier.com**
**Subject: reconsidered**

**Dear Ms. Delgado,**

**Please send us the specifics of the case to review and pay a deposit to our payment tab on the website. We look forward to working with you and solving the mystery of what happened to Caroline Chadwick.**

# FOUR

W HEN THE SEPARATISTS set out to establish a fishing village in Virginia, they didn't have the funds necessary to set it up on their own, so they entered into an agreement with investors. The investors would offer passage for the colonists and supply them with tools, clothing, and other necessities. In return, the colonists would work for the investors, sending natural resources such as fish, timber, and furs back to England. All assets, including the land and the Pilgrims' houses, belonged to the investors until the end of seven years when they were divided among investors and colonists.

It's a system that's been around forever, and yet it's still not perfect. Especially when one bites off more than one can chew and has no way to swallow. Nana left her house to me. I owned it fair and square — lock, stock, and barrel. Greg didn't contest it in the divorce. I was home free. I was Unveiled!

Then I decided to move on with my life by pulling my equity out of the house and opening a café. I had no qualms. When my personal life fell apart, I always kept things progressing professionally. Promotions, bonuses, crisp, clean uniforms — those were my Xanax. I found the perfect location, one block from the ocean.

I'm in love with the sea. I used to go to the beach and imagine my mother walking out of the waves like a mermaid. "I've been here this whole time, love," she would say, holding her arms wide while the peach, gauzy nightgown I used to love to lay my cheek against clung to her wet skin. Once the realtor showed me the space on Sandpiper Street, I would have done anything to have it. My world was so off-kilter, so unbalanced, and it was only when I settled into Sandpiper and took a big gulp of sea air that I felt my scales calibrate. A life spent preparing new recipes, keeping my business structured and thriving, organizing, and cleaning my industrial kitchen every day until it sparkled and shined—nothing sounded better.

Monday morning, after the breakfast rush, I pull out the local business book and look for foreclosure attorneys. I have no idea what I'm looking for. Is one any different from another? All the attorneys are lumped together, but only a handful specialize in real estate, as far as I can tell. Some are in Savannah, and some are as far away as Shanning's Bay. I prefer someone closer. I flip page after page, circling the few that mention real estate, eventually reaching the end of the alphabet and settling on one at the bottom of the page with a small, unassuming ad, hoping he'll be less expensive. No photo, no colored, glossy pages — just J. Scott Warner, Esq. Attorney At Law. Real Estate, Estate Planning, Business Law. Bonus: he's nearby in Flannery Cove.

Mr. Warner is not in, so I leave a message with his receptionist. A stumbling, long-winded message about a bitter divorce and a charming, sentimental family home.

A new email from Helena has arrived, taunting me with its bold text in the subject line. Her words are brief though. She's thanked me again for reconsidering, assuring me she will pay my deposit by four o'clock this afternoon and has attached files containing what information she has. I click on the attachment and spend the next hour pouring over my mother's past life. Obviously, my father has given this information to her. There's my mother's original birth certificate, my mother and father's marriage certificate, and a few grainy photos, none adequately showing my mom's shining blue eyes, her smooth skin, her high cheekbones, or her wide smile. I've never seen a picture of my mother that zeroes in on her sculpted bone structure or shows the aura she carries. The newspaper article detailing the accident that supposedly killed my mother is in a separate attachment, and I read it as if hearing it all for the first time. I absently and mindlessly scratch away at my wrists. I look down and see bumps forming, and try to soothe the hives with a lighter touch, a delicate rubbing while wondering if I can find anything that seems to prove my mother died in that accident.

Flipping through the things I've printed from Helena's email is mentally exhausting. I have looked through this stuff dozens of times. From years eight through fifteen of my life I studied them daily, trying to remember my mother's tiny laugh and the way she twirled nervously at the ends of her hair. I remember how I searched for pictures that showed the twinkle in her eyes or the pucker of her lips.

I pick up the phone on my desk once again.

"Mary, how come I could never find any good pictures of you? Did you ever face the camera head-on, even once?"

I hear the resignation, the long sigh. Going over this repeatedly is not her favorite subject, and I tried to put it to rest years ago, but Helena has woken it. I've got to go over all this again, have it fresh in my mind and know what I'm up against.

"That day after the crash." She pauses, trying to think how best to explain her erratic behavior to me yet again. "I went to the house, planted the train ticket receipt, and took all the pictures that identified me clearly, in case the police opened an investigation. And I didn't relish the thought of a photo obituary."

"I imagine not," I say with disdain. "But didn't you think that raised suspicions?"

"Not really, there weren't that many photos. Your dad and I hadn't documented that much. Our wedding had been at the courthouse. We didn't take trips or do things that needed to be remembered. His life centered around Flannery Cove."

"So you've said."

She plods on. "The only pictures I ever took were of you, and I felt those were mine to keep. Honestly, I figured your dad... well, I don't know what I figured. But, your grandmother... well, never mind."

I'm not sure where she was going with that one, but I digress. "So tell me again," I say. "You left the house to go for a walk all the way in Shanning's Bay and think about what you were going to do."

"Yes... For goodness' sake, Amy, yes! I wanted to go with Ian. I was sick of living in that small town, suffocating in that stuffy country club."

I've heard this before. Mom has told me how she wasn't cut out for tea parties and Junior League meetings. She wasn't doing right by me she'd said, as if leaving me was a better solution. She had told me all of this and more about her life with my father and me, as if I were a trusted girlfriend, not the little girl she had left behind with the "dull" dad.

"So Ian had called it off with Cassandra and re-entered my life. I tried to resist him, Ames. I really did."

I picture Ian calling my mom on the phone after years of being gone from her life. Years in which she had thought of nothing but him. I picture her surprise as she heard his playfully mischievous voice bellowing through the phone lines as if no time had passed, as if he hadn't left her standing at an altar years earlier and run off with another woman. I picture her fingers twisting the ends of her hair as she looked across the room at me and made her decision, and I wonder what ran through her mind as she pinned her dreams on such a faraway, foreign destination with no going back.

I already knew the ending of the story by heart. Mom had gone for a long walk by the river to sort things in her mind. She'd met up with Ian there, and they'd seen the train derail. While everyone else stood in horror as the passenger cars slipped off the tracks and into the deep water below, Ian had seen an opportunity. My mother never came home that night. My dad kept telling me she had gone to a friend's house and was staying the night. Even years later, I would wonder if he suspected she wasn't returning. I've tried to ask, but he changes the subject. My father is not one to be tied down to heart-to-heart conversations — certainly not uncomfortable ones. But I've wondered if he knew what friend she was visiting and was making excuses for her. He couldn't have feared yet that she was dead, none of us would even hear about the train until the next morning over breakfast when the morning news came on.

I had gone to school, and Dad had gone to work. It was just another day in our routine lives. No connection between that train and my mom had been made yet. I'd assumed I would get off the bus that afternoon and run into my mother's arms, and she would evade my questions of where she had been the night before and pretend to be interested in my school papers and how Mary Ellen Donovan's mother had shown up at the school with birthday cupcakes for everyone.

47

But that's not what happened. I got off the bus that afternoon, and two police cars were in our driveway. My nana and my dad were sitting in the kitchen with the officers. Mom still wasn't home. Dad had found a receipt for a train ticket on the floor of her closet. The date and time stamp matched the details the newscasters kept repeating: The train had left the Savannah depot and derailed in Shanning's Bay where the Savannah River meets the ocean and the tracks take a sudden turn. My mother had been on the train that plummeted to the bottom of the river the night before, I was told.

THE FIRST THING I notice is a little guy who has seemingly just returned from a safari.

He's sitting at the counter, dressed in head-to-toe tan, a Wallaroo canvas drawstring hat perched on his head and binoculars draped around his neck, as if rhinos or cheetahs could stampede by at any time. He is licking maple glaze off of his little fingers and studying each digit intently as if trying to figure out how the glaze and the fingers got there.

"Hi Paulus," I say and Margo pivots her stool toward me. Her surprise settles into a comfortable countenance when she sees me.

"Amethyst." Paulus stops licking and assesses me. There's no familiarity or warmth to his tone. He goes back to licking.

"Paulus, could you please go wash your hands?" His mother gently pulls an index finger from his lips, creating a sucking sound.

For a few seconds, he looks at her with no expression, and I brace myself. The blank stare looks like he's stunned, ready to explode. But he extends his little lace-up boots until his toes find the floor and slide from the stool. He holds the binoculars up to his eyes and turns his head back and forth until he spots the restrooms and drops them back to his chest. Hoisting his shoulders back he sets out for the twenty-step trek to the door marked "Men" as if he'll be gone for weeks.

"Thank you for being so kind to him," says Margo, as we both watch him on his expedition.

"Of course." I turn back to her. "He's a doll."

Is that the right description to use for an elementary school-aged boy? *Maybe not,* I think as Margo smiles at me with her mouth twisted in a way that makes her appear to be sizing me up. *Maybe he's a sport? A gem?*

"Not everyone is. Kind, I mean." Margo flattens her lips. Short, dark bangs are brushed to the side and blend in with the wisps that tuck behind her ears. She is dressed professionally, but with little adornment. Her face is sweet, soft, and feminine, but void of make-up, aside from a quick sweep of mascara and a light pink gloss on her thin lips. I can see the lines that fan out from her tired eyes and the threads of silver weaving themselves in with her chestnut strands, but they only add to her features.

"It is time for the class to begin." Madame Bienve bellows from the landing, looking down on the café and tapping at the little watch strapped to her thin wrist. Three little ballerinas scramble from a booth behind us, their mothers shooing them off with promises to be right there when the hour is up.

"I love it that this café is so close to Paulus' new school. I hope this one works out," Margo says.

"Huh? *This café?*"

"This new school. He started there after Christmas. The old one wasn't… well, it didn't work out well. This new one is close to my office, so I can take my last client at two o'clock and pick Paulus up."

"Good plan." I nod my head and sound like I'd helped her come up with it. "What does Paulus' dad do?" Paulus returns from the bathroom, and I expect to drop the subject.

"My ex-husband tried this for two years and three months. Haven't heard from him since he took a promotion in Chicago, aside from the check he *does* faithfully deposit every month."

"That's fortunate."

"My brother sees to it," she says quickly. I imagine a bear of a man casting hulking shadows over a cringing mouse of a man.

"Oh. Um, so where's your office?"

"Over on Beachwood Drive." She points in the direction of the school. "Five minutes from here. Sundale Speech Therapy."

"Ah. I think I pass it on my way home. How's the new school so far?"

She shrugs, no optimism. "Hard to say yet."

Paulus crouches below the stool next to Margo, spinning the seat, slowing it down, spinning it again, trying to see how the mechanics of it work. He doesn't appear to be paying any attention to our conversation.

"Paulus is an eccentric kid," she murmurs. I glance down at his determined scowl. "My brother," she begins, then stammers and begins again. "My brother would like to see me put Paulus in a school over in Savannah, but I don't think…"

"Savannahs only twenty minutes."

"Yes, but it's not the right place for Paulus. My brother wants to slap a label on Paulus and put him in a school that fits the label." Again she says Paulus is "just eccentric." It reminds me of how I always insist my house is eclectic, while realtors want to slap uncomplimentary labels like "loud" and "unique" on it. I don't care. I like loud and unique.

I pat Margo's outstretched hand. "I like eccentric."

D EATON AND MADAME Bienve pass each other coming and going that afternoon. He on his way in, she on her way out. "Whatcha got going on tonight?" He asks me.

"We've been summoned to my dad's for Hailey's birthday." Just what I want to do: face my two backstabbers and make nice with them.

Jenna backs toward the door, flipping the open sign over. I walk over and open my office door then return to the seating area.

"Fun," Deaton says. I can't tell if it's sincere or sarcastic. He pushes his glasses up the bridge of his nose. "Hey, I meant what I said."

I search my memory. *Brunettes? Big knees?*

"I'd like to read your book."

I study my fingernails. "Yeah, I'll have to dig that out one of these days."

"Please do," Deaton says, as Otis wanders out into the café. Deaton's arm is hanging to the side of the booth, toward the floor. Otis' snout runs smack into his hand and nudges, and Deaton flinches then pulls it away.

"Not a dog person?" I laugh, as he wipes his hand on a napkin then walks to the bar to get a few more.

"Not really an animal person," he says. "Just cats. And goldfish."

"Ah." I tilt my head back. "Not a good combination, I hear."

Deaton returns with a handful of napkins. Probably a few dollars' worth.

"So, I agreed to meet up with Marvin F."

*"You did?"* his brows shoot up in surprise.

"Yes. And the *F* is for Feegan, by the way."

"Feegan," he says, rolling the word around in his mouth, feeling it out. "Amy Feegan."

"It sounds like he has really big front teeth."

Deaton laughs. "Ha! How so?"

"I dunno. I guess it's those two side-by-side *e's*, like in teeth, a big bunny-toothed smile."

"Nooo," Deaton says, as if our discussion is of utmost importance. "I'm not getting that. I'm thinking more like a skinny, emaciated hippie type. Lives off the land, bathes once a week."

"How are *you* coming up with *that?*"

Otis grunts and drops onto the floor and lays his head on his outstretched front paws, uninterested in Deaton's answer.

"I dunno. Starvin' Marvin. Vegan Feegan."

My eyes blink, "You must have been a joy in grade school."

"I was," he says. "Still am."

"Not sold." I pick up my dishcloth and return to my work.

AROUND SEVEN O'CLOCK in the evening, Hailey and I ring the doorbell to Dad's new condo. This is another thing that's irritating me, though I guess I have no right. Until last year, Dad still lived in my childhood home. I still had a bedroom decorated in teen heartthrob posters and a kitchen I felt comfortable making a grilled cheese sandwich in. Mrs. Ryder next door still called out to me every time I visited and filled me in on everything that was going on with neighbors. And even that stain on the wall in the master bedroom, that awful stain that revealed so much if you knew to look beyond the center of it, beyond the eye of the storm to the outer fringes where all the debris lay in heaps waiting to be sorted — even that stain was something I still missed.

Now, I have to visit Dad in a one-bedroom condo on the fourth floor and be escorted by a man that pushes the buttons in the elevator. I know none of his neighbors, not even sure if he does.

Most of everything we had when I was growing up has been given to charity since there's no room for it in his new place. Helena has filled his condo with items that mean nothing to me or Hailey and are as unfamiliar to me as discretion had been to Mrs. Ryder.

Except for the dishes. We dine on takeout from Grille Dumon and eat it off my mother's antique Noritake Rosemont dishes, while Helena nonchalantly tells us all about her recent inquiry to a private investigator and Dad shakes his head in agreement and keeps his mouth full of salmon and rice pilaf.

*"A private investigator?"* I ask incredulously, scattering my silverware while Hailey looks down and straightens it and places it back beside my plate as carefully as she would a baby in a bassinet. I imagine a future judge looking down from his bench at me. *"This! This is the moment you should have weighed your loyalties, young lady."*

"Why are you doing this?" I finally ask, and though nothing, absolutely nothing, is said about a proposal, much is said about the life insurance.

"So you never cashed it in?" I turn to Dad, who seems to be urging me with his eyes to please not let this fragile vase he keeps his relationship with Helena in crash to the floor.

"He couldn't," she answers for him. "He didn't have proof that she died."

The overhead vent blows my hair. I tuck it behind my ears. "But the train ticket." I hold up my hands and look around the room as if to say, *"And she's not here."*

"Yes." Helena reaches across the table and gently takes hold of my wrist. "We all know she's gone." She keeps her hand on me. "Legally, she is considered dead. But your father has never felt entirely comfortable with the police investigation and wants proof."

I look back at Dad. Funny how he has never wanted proof before. He's barely even wanted to acknowledge Caroline Chadwick ever existed, as if I miraculously appeared in his living room one evening and he'd agreed to make sure I stayed alive.

"So proof will release the funds?" I ask, and Helena lets go of my wrist and leans back. I feel certain that there was enough "proof" in that ticket receipt. She was declared dead. Proof or not. I wish I could warn her. This proof she wants to solidify things enough to persuade my father to have the funds released will have the opposite effect. On both the money and the availability of the groom.

"Think about it, Amy." she folds her hands on the table. "Those funds could do a lot for *all* of you." She stresses the word "all." *So Dad has told her.*

I have not told dad everything about my financial problems, and I certainly haven't told him I'm about to lose Nana's house. But I have told him I'm struggling with the café. That's no secret — every beachside business is struggling right now if they signed their lease agreements when that was the popular place to be. Thank God I hadn't told him everything — I don't want all of that shared with Helena, nor do I want to bring it to Hailey's attention yet.

"Hailey will be going away to school soon," she reminds all of us while turning to smile sweetly at Hailey, who nervously smiles back, "Business at the restaurant will slow down even more after the tourists leave."

I raise my sleeve a bit and scratch at the itching skin, then pull it back down and finally nod and rub at my chin as if I have conceded. Of course, we should prove my mother is dead, even if we have to dive to the bottom of the river and haul her body up.

After they get all that pesky business out of the way, Dad and Helena are ready for the evening to end. I can see it in their body language, the way Helena starts to clear the table, the way Dad yawns, and the way the conversation dies down to almost nothing.

On the way out the door, Dad hands Hailey a card with a twenty-five- dollar gift card to Claire's Boutique in the mall. "For some nice, new earrings," he says, while Hailey rubs at her bare right lobe that has never been pierced — never will be pierced. I would have thought that he, of all people, would know that, would remember why. But I guess he has forgotten even more than I thought.

"I accepted the job," I say in the dark car on the way home.

"I knew you would," Hailey says. This tone I can read: *Duh! Like you're going to betray your own mother by not staying by her side in life and in death.* "I knew there was no way you were going to let someone else dig Grandma up," she says. She gives me half a smile, sympathetic in its simplicity, knowing there was no burial. "You should tell them, Mom. Just tell them you're the investigator and help them get whatever proof they need."

"Not on my mother's grave."

# *FIVE*

THE FOLLOWING SATURDAY after I close the café I make a trip to Atlanta.

"Are you sure you can't get away to visit Aunt Mary?" I ask Hailey, but she's just learned she got the lead in the school's rendition of *"The Butterfly Queen"* and has to start rehearsals.

"No Jarod!" I remind her on my way out the door. I need a Mrs. Ryder next door. I never would have been able to entertain any boys at home when I was in school, wouldn't have even been able to entertain the thought. Unfortunately, I did entertain a persistent Greg Hollander in the back seat of his car, so what was the point of it all anyway?

I use the four-hour trip to sort things in my mind. I've not thought about the whole thing with Mom in so long, my details on the deception are fuzzy. Sometimes I can't even remember what I'm supposed to know or not know and what's common knowledge or bald-faced lies.

Ian is home and helps me get bags inside. "Mary has the guest room all made up for you," he says, pulling me into a hug.

It's not hard to see how Mom was torn, how she never got over Ian. He's a charming, good-looking man with rugged olive skin and a full head of dark hair that has only begun to gray. His dark eyes look straight at you when he speaks that eloquent Irish brogue, and often he takes you by the wrist and holds on to your hand making you feel like the most important person he's ever met. He has charisma down to an exact science. The thing is, I can see right through him like I'm watching a play and I can predict what he's gonna say and do. Mary is the leading lady that never got a copy of the script. She's going with it, improvising.

I'd like to say she's enjoying the ride, but she's not. She would disagree, but a woman who depends on anti-anxiety medication and has a hundred nervous habits and never settles into her true self is not enjoying anything — I know this firsthand.

After dinner, we settle into the living room for after-dinner cognacs and some dessert I can't even pronounce. Ian and Mary are not rich, but Ian prefers to live like they are. "Nothing but the finest for my love," he is fond of saying. She smiles a rosy lipsticked smile. I have stayed the weekend with Mary and Ian lots of times and have never seen her in a ratty pair of pajamas with no make-up on or flattened, dirty hair.

They sit in the teal armchairs opposite me, and I settle into the corner of the gray suede sofa and adjust a beaded pillow behind my back. I stare at the oil painting of a gondola in Venice until it becomes one big blur.

I'm not uncomfortable talking in front of Ian. We've done it before. I think he enjoys the retelling of the whole story as much as some men enjoy talking about the big fish that almost got away.

I reach for the notebook I keep in my purse. "I have a few questions."

Mom fingers the locket at her throat and looks around the room. Her polished toes push into the soft fibers of the fake Persian rug. "I'll try to answer them," she finally says with resignation.

"It's the least you could do," I'd like to reply. Instead, I smile — my nice, tight, not-a-smile smile.

"I remember you snuck back with the ticket receipt."

"And took her photos," Ian says, ignoring what I said about the ticket.

"Yes, and took the photos. By the way, do you have any of those old photos?"

"No," Mom says. "Ian burned all of that stuff. I couldn't have it around."

I'm not sure if she means it was too risky or too sad, but I don't ask. There are some things I don't want to know.

"So, where did you go again? How exactly did you pull it off?" I need to hear some details again if I'm to hide them effectively.

Ian takes over the telling of the story as if reliving a great adventure. "After your mum left your home that afternoon, the day after the crash, we met back up at Penwood Park," he says. "We made it here to Atlanta that same afternoon and took the four o'clock flight out."

I glance at Mom, trying to decipher if she had been giddy or sickened to get on that flight.

"My cousin Raibert met us at the gate when we finally landed in Glasgow," he continues. "We drove to Kircaldy and found a sublet that same day." He laughs. "After all the money it took to make everything happen, we didn't have two dimes left to rub together, but we lucked out all right, and then I got the job as a chef at La Pasana." He tells the story as if it were the greatest love story ever. "Remember that squat, love?"

My mom blinks.

"We had a nice life in Kircaldy," he says, thinking back over the years.

I wonder if he and Mom had been living in the same place, sharing the same life. She doesn't look like she recalls it all with the fondness he does.

"Your mum always missed you, of course," he says.

I lean forward and set the beaded pillow that's digging into my back on the rug beside the couch.

"And then came the opportunity to move back to Atlanta," Mom finally speaks up, her voice a mound of cotton.

"And that's when I saw it," I say, "When I found out the truth." And she finally smiles.

I'm supposed to leave Sunday afternoon, but Ian has gone to work at the restaurant, and Mom's friend Rhoda comes over from the apartment across the lake. The three of us end up laughing the day away, never realizing the sun has gone down.

"Oh, come on, one more night," Rhoda says, as she rings for pizza delivery, and since I haven't even repacked my bags, I agree to it after Cory says he can hold down the fort for an hour or so. I can get on the road by five A.M. and be at the café the next morning before it gets too busy.

"Five A.M.," I declare. "No later. I have a ton of things to do this week, and I'm already pushing Monday Morning Staff Meeting back to Monday *Mid-Morning* Staff Meeting."

Rhoda is Mary's best friend, her only friend aside from me. She has lived directly across from Mary and Ian since the day they moved to Atlanta and into #19 Colonial Plantation. She knows everything about my mom and Ian's relationship, except for their biggest secret. To Rhoda, I am the former student of Mary's that loves her dearly.

We share a large pizza and drink a full bottle of wine, and when Rhoda finally unfolds her legs and rises from her position at the coffee table, it's almost midnight.

The next morning I rise early and pass Ian and Mary's bedroom on the way to the kitchen. Their bed has not been slept in. Mom is on the couch awake, holding tight to a pillow she keeps clutched to her chest.

"Sometimes he closes late and sleeps in a cot in his office," she explains a few minutes later, eyeing me over the rim of her coffee cup, even though I haven't asked.

I AGREE TO MEET Marvin Feegan one night that week for dinner. We're supposed to meet at the new seafood restaurant on the docks and go see a movie.

Marvin calls about thirty minutes before the scheduled time. "Hey, I need to stop at the Walmart over by Second and Balsam Street. Wanna meet me there?"

"Er... okay," I say.

"I'll be in housewares. Wearing a green shirt."

I find him right away. Marvin is not wasting away from starvation, quite the contrary. There's a hint of the person I'd seen online in his face, but somehow between then and now he has ballooned and grown an extra chin. He does not have long, dirty hair as Deaton predicted and his teeth are very adequately sized, but his features have all the excitement of a boiled egg. He's bent over a stack of plastic bins pulling them out and trying to read the small print on the label.

"Hey, do you think this might hold about fifteen board games?" He says when he spots me. It's like we've known each other for ages and I'm equally invested in the tote.

"Um, I guess so."

"I'm trying to clean out my hallway closet and get some things organized," he says, grimacing like the decision between large and extra-large physically hurts.

Forty-five minutes later Marvin has decided on the red colored bin that's wider instead of taller, and I have helped a little old lady named Betty reach something on a top shelf and heard her life story, from age five to present, through two marriages, from Florida to Delaware and then to Georgia. My stomach is rumbling. I follow Marvin to the cash register, and he realizes he has forgotten the lid. He asks if I'd mind running back to get it, and I have to detour around cosmetics and take the long way to avoid running back into Betty who is now in the garden department sizing up water hoses.

By the time we leave Walmart, Marvin asks if I want to just go to the Waffle House across the street.

We sit at the Waffle House trying to decide between breakfast and dinner. There is something stuck in Marvin's nostrils that is causing him to whistle with every intake of breath. He doesn't seem to notice. By the fifth trill, I'm beginning to put together a little melody.

By the time we leave Waffle House, Marvin informs me that the movie — *whistle* — has already been playing — *whistle* — for over half an hour — *whistle*.

By the time we get back to our cars in the Walmart parking lot, I have decided I would rather date the Pope than Marvin Feegan.

Strike one.

"SO IT WASN'T love at first sight?" Deaton asks, laughing while I pick at the invisible lint on my jeans.

"I'm not sure what it was at first sight. His head was in a plastic storage bin." I close my eyes, exasperated. Atticus strides past and looks up at me the same way Madame Bienve does.

"Well, you can cross it off your bucket list," Deaton guffaws.

"Ha. Funny! So what were you telling me about your aunt?" I ask, changing the conversation, closing the door on relationship talk.

"Oh yeah. So Tommy Mobley, the contractor, has started on the house, and..." his cell phone dings, and he pulls it from his pocket.

"Well, whaddya know," he says. "She said yes."

I snap to attention.

"Who said yes? Yes to what?"

He smiles as if he has a secret then leans forward and shows me his phone screen. He scrolls back up to where the text communication started so I can follow the dialog.

I glance at him warily. "She saw you on Potion#9?"

"Yup. We're going to a barbecue at her cousin's house Saturday," he says.

He goes to the register area and returns with his laptop and brings up her profile. Her name is Kristlyn Solidan. A bright smile beams from the screen. She's a devout flosser, most likely. She looks perfect for Deaton. Sweet, honest, beautiful.

One of us got lucky, at least.

*Even as the sweet fragrance of love wafted through the air, she feared it would never find her again. She was destined to be alone, a spinster, a forgotten recluse. And while the rest of the world laughed and celebrated, she would have to be content to watch from the sidelines. Alone.*

THURSDAY MORNING, JUST after I serve table number five their salmon and avocado omelets with tomato grits, the foreclosure attorney finally returns my phone call.

"My office," I mouth and motion to Cory, leaving him and Jenna to take care of things out front.

"So I haven't actually received any kind of formal notice yet," I say, "I guess we're still in the *pre*-foreclosure stage."

"Start from the beginning," he says in a soft and encouraging lawyerly voice.

I begin with Nana dying and leaving her house to me. I take him through the divorce and the notion of how nice it would be to have a little café on the beach and how I had found the perfect location and cleverly named it. And once I had such a perfect name and location I had to follow through on it, so I took out a second mortgage on Nana's house. Now, with Flannery Cove expanding in the wrong direction, I couldn't pay it back and was six months behind on the payment and kept getting notices from the bank.

When I finally finish he's silent.

"Are you still there?" I ask, expecting the line to buzz and all my rambling to have been for naught.

"Yes," he answers, "Just trying to scribble all this down, but my hand isn't that fast."

"Sorry if I threw in too much unnecessary stuff."

"No, no. It's all part of your story. Now let me ask the obvious. Have you tried to sell it?"

That takes me through another series of events about how I'd listed the house with two different realtors and no wonder it didn't sell because neither realtor had appreciated its individuality and marketed it properly.

"Mm-hmm." I can hear him thinking this through as if every single word is important, worth documenting.

"So. Amy," he says, and I can tell by the hesitation he's had to rifle through some pages to find my name. "Have you been served a Notice of Default?"

"Um, I don't think so. Would I know?"

"I think you would," he says. I detect a smile in his voice, "Let me do some courthouse searching, and I'll get back to you."

"Thank you so much, Mr. Warner," I say, the relief apparent in my voice.

"Call me Scott. And Amy, try not to panic."

**From: Unveiled@officeweb.com**
**To: Helena1098@myFCcourier.com**
**Subject: Investigation**

**Ms. Delgado, I will be the investigator working your case. Over the weekend I did quite a bit of work familiarizing myself with the case. I will be in touch soon. Thank you.**

I'm pleasantly surprised to find a little boy dressed for a proper day of croquet sitting at my counter eating a Pumpkin Maple Muffin when I emerge from my office. Paulus wears an oxford pullover with knee shorts, saddle shoes, a bow tie, and a bowler hat. He and Margo are a welcome respite from the stress of spending the last hour telling a complete stranger how badly I've messed up, and from emailing Helena.

"I am delighted to see you today, Amethyst," Paulus says upon catching sight of me mid-spin on his stool. "I come bearing news."

Margo seems upbeat as well. I assume this news is good.

"I have procured a comrade for myself. His name is Tyler, and his hair is styled in a Mohican fashion, named after the Mohican tribe but more closely resembling the style worn by the Pawnee Indians. Historically the hair was plucked out rather than shaved, but I don't believe that's the way Tyler acquired it."

"That's wonderful." I look to Margo for confirmation that this is indeed wonderful. She seems very pleased.

Paulus moseys over to the coffee counter and begins lining up packets of sugar.

"This is good," I say to Margo. "It sounds like the new school may be working out."

"I think so," she says. "It's hard to make these decisions myself and not know if they're the right ones or not."

I tap my fingernail on the countertop. "Is there no support system?"

"I have my brother, but we disagree on things regarding Paulus." She twists her napkin in her fingers. "He insists on things I don't feel are in Paulus' best interest. Trust issues, I guess." She rolls her eyes self-deprecatingly.

I nod. Trust issues, I understand.

*You understand because you know what a person is truly capable of. You know the people who trust you shouldn't.*

I pat her hand and try to smile with bright eyes, closing the shades on the windows to my soul, "I get it."

# *Six*

AT 8:45 FRIDAY morning, I spot Helena and Buffy Barrington seated at the booth with the ripped vinyl upholstery that's been temporarily taped over. I have an order in for a replacement, but of course, those two have to come in before it's arrived.

I stumble like the police are sitting at the table, and I've been counting money from the bank I recently robbed.

"Amy, dear," Helena motions me over, "I woke up this morning craving one of your omelets."

Buffy keeps her eyes on her menu. "Amy, how are you?"

"I'm fine, Mrs. Barrington. You?"

She flattens her lips in response, saying nothing more. I can only suppose that means fine.

*My mother said your husband brushed up against her and touched her.* That night the stain appeared. I'd heard her. *"And that sleazy Hal Barrington,"* she'd yelled to my father.

I thank Helena again for a lovely birthday dinner for Hailey and excuse myself to do a "mountain of work," but I'm afraid to do any investigation-related work or even think about it with Helena in such close proximity. I've no idea how this is ever going to work.

The foreclosure attorney calls me just before lunch. "Amy." He uses my name as if we've known each other for years.

"Mr. Warner."

"I wanted to let you know there is no formal Notice of Default filed yet, so you have time. Any chance you might still be able to bring your mortgage current?"

I've tried to think of every way possible to do that. I always come up with nothing. The price of produce and eggs and milk, it all continues to rise as business lags.

"Tell me again about the divorce," he says.

"The whole thing or just the judge's decision?"

"Whatever you like. Whatever you feel is relevant, important. I have my pen ready this time."

"We settled amicably," I begin. "Greg didn't try to get any part of the house. He agreed that Hailey was to stay with me and see him whenever she wanted, and I had no problem with that." Mr. Warner doesn't interrupt, so I keep going. "He paid child support until Hailey's eighteenth birthday a few weeks ago, and still does assist with whatever she needs, but he's never paid alimony since I own a house outright and have a way to make a living."

"That's par for the course in Georgia," he says.

Our conversation turns to divorce. Mr. Warner was married briefly years ago, he tells me.

"Yeah… that didn't go over so well. I can't say I wasn't warned. My family saw all the red flags, but I turned away from them and refused to look."

I wonder why he never remarried. He's probably a stuffy old curmudgeon, set in his ways, smoking pipes and filing legal briefs simultaneously. But then again he's so easy to talk to, so inviting. Maybe he's more of a sappy old man who finds joy and meaning in his profession and a handful of nieces and nephews.

He fills in the blanks. "I'm pretty gun shy after all that. Adrienne was a master manipulator. She simply could not tell the truth. It wasn't in her."

"I understand that. 'I'm working late' became the worst phrase ever," I admit, recalling Greg's lies that led me to where I'm at now. "But I heard it almost daily."

Before I realize it we've segued into the worst phrases ever from childhood to adulthood. This is the strangest lawyer/client dynamic ever. The lawyer who helped me when I purchased the café never said two unrelated words to me. It was all documents and drafts and signatures. Maybe I'm Mr. Warner's only client. No wonder he didn't have a full-page glossy ad.

"Eat your dinner. Explain this grade. It's past midnight," he recalls.

"We need to talk. You're fired. Watch out for that tree!" I match him phrase for phrase.

"Watch out for that tree?"

"Day after I got my license and my first car. Followed immediately by 'too late'."

"You have to retake the bar exam," he says.

"Your mother's gone," I say

When we finally hang up, two hours have passed. Dear God, I've whiled away the morning with this nonsense. At least my lawyer finds me interesting and kind. Maybe he'll work extra hard for me. My stomach is growling from a missed lunch. I do a little work on Helena's case, which basically consists of holding the newspaper article from the train derailment in my hands and chanting, "Think, think, think!"

The café is still fairly quiet before the afternooners show up. Madame Bienve taps up above me adding to my already pounding head, my nerves, my itching arms. I go over the following week's schedules, renew my ad in the Restaurant Round-Up, and place an online order for paper goods.

I type in Scott Warner and am given a long list to choose from. I find J. Scott Warner's social media page and click on it. It's not a business page. The page is set to private, and I can't see anything but a small profile picture of the scales of justice.

I haven't checked my personal email in a few weeks, but I need to get back in the habit. I've pulled *A Maiden's Voyage* out from under my bed, tweaked a few things, and sent it back out to five more literary agents. Still no response from any of them, but it was a good, creative diversion — attempting to infiltrate myself into others' lives, even if they *were* fictitious, and manipulate them to happy endings tied up in a big bow, all problems solved.

Actually, it was an incoherent mess.

A knock at my office door startles me. Cory and Jenna don't usually knock, they just fling open. If I'm needed out in the café, there's no time for manners. I hope it's not Madame Bienve coming to ask, or rather tell me to please try to keep my customers' voices under control. "They interfere with the rela-jon-zhip of music to dance," she's fond of saying.

There is a pirate at my door.

"Hello, Amethyst," he says when I open it.

He looks up at me with the one eye that doesn't have a black patch over it. I'm not taken aback to see Paulus wearing black pants and boots, a long, red jacket, and a black hat. I wouldn't even be surprised to see him waving a sword or carrying a parrot on his shoulder.

I join him and Margo briefly at the counter while Paulus tells me about Tyler's broken arm, though I have to prod most of the information out of him. He isn't enthusiastic in the telling of his new friend's fall on the soccer field, and oddly there's no history lesson of how Plaster of Paris came to be used for making surgical molds, or anything of the like.

I walk Margo and Paulus to the door after Paulus finishes the usual routine of licking each finger and being sent to the restroom to wash.

"Wait here a second," I say.

I run back to the counter and ask Cory to box up two Pumpkin Maple Muffins.

"To get you through the weekend," I say to Margo, as I hand them to the four-foot buccaneer who yawns wide and rubs at his unpatched eye. Tired, bored, an average eight-year-old boy, like any other.

"HEY, WAIT. I'M coming over in a sec," I holler across the street.

I run back to my office and open the bottom drawer. I draw in a breath, asking myself one last time if I'm sure I want to do this.

"Don't forget to flip the sign and lock the door," I yell to Cory, waving my keys in the air to show him I can get back in.

I tap on the glass bookstore door and Deaton motions me in. "It's not locked," he yells over the hum of the vacuum.

I settle myself into a chair while he finishes vacuuming and start the small talk while he wraps the cord up and wheels it back into the storage closet.

"When's the big date?"

"Two weeks," he says. "Any last-minute advice?" He runs a hand through his hair. "And before you say to get a haircut, I'm getting one in the morning."

"I wasn't going to say anything of the kind. Your hair is more styled than a mannequin's."

"So, I guess you've been busy. Haven't seen ya in a few days," Deaton says. He sits down and adjusts his glasses. "Whatcha been up to?"

The story pours out of me because I'm drowning, and I need a lifeline. I'm itching to death and my lies are growing legs, and it's starting to show on my washed-out face and in the dead look of my eyes. I tell Deaton everything. Well, *almost* everything. I tell him about a mother that died, not about one that lives in Atlanta under another name. I'm wiping tears from my eyes as I talk about the tragedy that rocked my childhood. "Still... so hard... I miss her so much."

"And so let me get this straight," he finally says, his elbows resting on his knees and his hands holding on to the sides of his head as if thinking about everything I've told him physically hurts. "You own an investigation agency and your future step-mother has hired you to prove that your *real* mother died in a train accident twenty-something years ago?"

Hearing someone say it out loud makes my heart speed up even more, and my hives wake up and start tingling. I sound stupid. Who runs an investigation agency? It's like I'm Nancy Drew. And a mother that died so tragically? It sounds like a big lie.

*Well....*

Deaton shakes his head and stares at the border on the area rug he's placed in front of the reading chairs.

"And you're not supposed to know your dad even proposed, and they don't have any idea that they've hired *you*, but they do know that *you* know they've hired *someone*?"

"Yes, they told Hailey and me at her birthday dinner. Apparently, there was a life insurance policy. My dad never..." I let the sentence hang.

"Ah." Deaton gently nods his head.

"I don't think it's only that. I just. I think Helena..." I honestly don't know what Helena thinks, or suspects, or what her motives are. They don't seem selfish so much as cautious and concerned. But what would I know about any of that?

"And it was a train that derailed? You were eight? They never found her body?"

"Yes, yes, and no," I answer. I want to move on from this subject. Hovering over it is like sitting in an uncomfortable chair with coils poking out.

The two of us sit side-by-side staring off into space, lost in our deep thoughts. Around us, the room grows darker, and the world grows quieter.

I finally break the silence. "I have to go."

Deaton rises from his chair but only nods, still trying to comprehend my tragedy and my mess. His hair is standing up at the crown, and his eyes look a bit glazed.

I start to make my way to the door but remember something. I turn around and walk back to the chair I'd been sitting in. Reaching under it, I produce a box and hold it out to him.

"My manuscript of *A Maiden's Voyage*," I say. "Hope you enjoy it."

# SEVEN

"APPARENTLY SHE HASN'T been keeping up with her mammograms. They say it's estrogen-related."

"She lost her health insurance when they got divorced and wasn't able to go to the doctor until she married Heath."

I know from snatches of previous conversations that the fair-haired, brown-eyed Nikki, the one dance-mom that works full-time as a hairdresser and part-time at a jewelry store to pay for her daughter's ballet lessons with Madame Bienve, met her new husband Heath on Potion#9. That's where I got the idea to join myself. But that's all I knew about her until recently. I don't do dance moms.

Now, I've taken to sitting with some of the other dance moms when they come in, for the first five minutes or so, to get updates on their friend's condition. She's been diagnosed with breast cancer.

They're not all a half-bad bunch. Not the crowd I'm used to socializing with, but not bad. Nikki is scheduled for surgery the following week.

I introduce some of the little ballerinas to Paulus, but trying to make any kind of connection there is like trying to mend a frayed electric cord while it's plugged into an outlet, and the result might be as catastrophic.

I wave to Deaton each morning when he passes by the window. We're on two entirely different time schedules. He's beginning his morning run when I'm already thinking about the lunch menu.

It's Friday that everything seems to happen all at once. Mr. Warner calls and checks to see how my week has gone.

"No notices of anything yet?" he asks.

Hearing his voice, my heart seems to find a slower pattern, and my stress declines, which is ironic because he's a reminder of what a mess I've created. I guess it's comforting to be handing it off to him, letting him take it over since there's no way I can look my dad in the face and ask for advice, sympathy, help, encouragement, or anything else right now.

"I have a few things I'd like you to look over," he says. "When can we meet up?"

I imagine I'm going to need to sign a contract, pony up a big deposit. Jenna is out sick, and things are quite chaotic. "I can't get away anytime soon. Any chance you could stop by my café?"

"Be there this afternoon," he says breezily.

At three o'clock Margo and Paulus enter the café. Paulus is a simple businessman today. A three-piece suit, dress shoes, a handkerchief tucked into his breast pocket, even a little briefcase in his tight grip.

As soon as he enters, he stops in his tracks. I follow his gaze to another young boy sitting nearby with his father, leaning over slurping chowder from his bowl. He has a mohawk, a Ridley Elementary shirt on, and a cast on his arm.

*Tyler.*

Tyler looks up and sees Paulus and rolls his eyes. I can see by Margo's expression that she has already made the connection, but she clearly hasn't seen the roll of the eyes or the disgusted expression on Tyler's face.

"You must be Tyler," she moves forward, holding tight to Paulus' hand, pulling him along. She wears an expression of pure delight. "Look, Paulus, it's your friend, Tyler."

Tyler doesn't bother lifting his head from his bowl, but he does lift his eyes. "I'm not friends with that freak!"

Tyler's dad swats lightly at the hand that's holding the spoon and mumbles some inadequate warning.

Margo stops short, as if she's been crossing a quiet street and a semi-trailer has appeared in front of her going a hundred miles an hour. She can't quite think what to do.

I motion to Cory. "Pumpkin Muffins. Quick!" As if I can sedate the situation with a shot of sugar.

Cory bends down and reaches into the pastry display. He looks back up, pale-faced, hands upturned. "We're out of Pumpkin Maple" he says, sprinting toward us, "But look, Paul, I brought you a cinnamon raisin bagel."

"My name is not Paul, it's Paulus! The Egyptians used cinnamon as a perfuming agent during the embalming process," Paulus screams. "I don't want cinnamon!" He throws himself on the wood floor of the café, kicking his heels. His briefcase hits with a thud and slides under a nearby booth.

Tyler and his dad get up from their booth, throw a few bucks on the table, and head hurriedly toward the door. Everyone else in the café is horrified, mesmerized by the scene unfolding in front of them, but I imagine Tyler has seen it played out a few times before at school.

"Bye Polly," he mumbles on his way out, looking like he might kick at him if everyone weren't watching. I get the feeling Tyler probably throws cats in creeks, pokes babies in their eye sockets, and starts fires with his mind. He's like a Stephen King novel. I would run out and tackle him on the sidewalk if I weren't preoccupied with picking Paulus up off the floor. Paulus has now realized the other end of his body may bring more satisfaction in its revolt than his feet. I catch him just as his head lifts off the floor.

"Please, don't hurt yourself." I hold him tight and cradle his little, freckled face in my arms.

Margo pulls at her skirt and bends down, but she keeps trying to apologize to everyone else in the room. To every pair of feet that walks past she mumbles. "Sorry... so sorry... sorry... sorry... sorry."

We get him calmed down, and he stands back up as if surprised to find himself lying on the floor in the first place. Or at least that's the assessment I'm inclined to make when there's no hint of embarrassment.

"We're going to go," Margo says, her eyes lowered, her face filled with despair.

"I promise to never run out of them again," I vow to her on their way out. It's the only promise I can make, even though pastries are the least of her worries.

"Bake a batch of Pumpkin Muffins and find an address for Margo Proverton, please." I turn to Cory when the door shuts behind them, with the urgency of an ER doctor in a medical drama. *Muffins, stat!*

The café conversation returns to its normal banter. The door chimes continuously with patrons entering and exiting, and Hailey finally shows up to help. My phone dings in my pocket with a text from Mr. Warner.

"Be there in a few minutes."

I've just put in a request for my lunch. I check on Cory in the kitchen and hurry back to the front, smiling sincerely at the older man in the trench coat who walks through the door, looking around. His little tuft of blonde hair is blown to the side, the roots slightly bent back, his cheeks are flushed, and his eyes are kind and twinkly. He's as comforting looking as I imagined.

I walk out from behind the counter ready to greet him.

"Amy?" Someone says behind me. I turn and lock eyes with a man I've never seen before. He looks to be in his early forties. He has wavy, dark hair, a slight stubble across the lower half of his face, dark brown eyes, thick eyebrows, and a wide smile of straight, white teeth that line up obediently like soldiers.

"Yes?" I turn toward him, quite intrigued.

He stands, and I take in the full length, from head to toe.

"I'm Scott," he says, extending a hand.

I look back at the doorway. The man in the trench coat has located the person he was meeting up with, and the two of them are walking toward a booth, engrossed in conversation. Looking back to Scott, I reach for his outstretched hand and notice the contrast: trim, manicured nails with rough, calloused skin.

I slide into the booth and flip through the pamphlets he slides across to me. They explain the foreclosure process, short sales, and reverse mortgages.

"Not sure if any of this can help," he says. "I know you're nervous, but foreclosure is a long process. A lot can happen before the bank gets around to filing and following through."

71

I nod politely. I don't think so, but I nod.

Hailey wipes the booth behind Scott and raises her eyebrows at me. She delivers two glasses of water, a cup of coffee, and my BLT to the table so she can get a better look at my visitor.

"Mr. Er, Scott, this is my daughter, Hailey." I stare exaggeratedly at her as he turns away from me and greets her.

Cory calls her from the kitchen, and she rushes away. "Great to meet you," she calls over her shoulder.

"Eat, please." Scott nods at my plate. My BLT is sliced perfectly. The lettuce is crisp and green, and a touch of ranch dressing is peeking out. I'm ravenous. I slide the plate closer and pick up a triangle and return to the brochures.

"Can I offer you anything? On the house?"

He takes a sip of his coffee and swallows. "No. This is fine. Although you are quite an advertisement for that sandwich." He smiles and touches the side of his lip.

"Oh." I've been chewing and reading, or pretending to read anyway, and I try to think back. *Did I inhale my food? Do I look like a horse at a trough?* I wipe at my own lip with my napkin, and he smiles like I'm amusing. It's a smile that leads me to believe he finds life itself quite amusing.

"Next time I want that," he says pointedly.

I chuckle, covering my nerves. I'm still trying to get my bearings, adjusting to the fact that my lawyer is nothing like I imagined. I ate too fast, most definitely a horse at a trough. The sandwich is rumbling around. I decide to conquer the feeling of shyness that has overcome me. I study him for a second while unwrapping my straw. I point the straw at him. "You know, you're nothing like I imagined on the phone."

"You're exactly what I imagined."

I draw in a breath and take a sip of water to busy myself. *Think! What would be the charming comeback?* I've got nothing.

"Welp, I should run. Traffic on the highway gets backed up this time of day, and I need to be in Savannah by six." He pushes his mug to the side.

"Do I need to pay a deposit? Sign any papers?"

"No need to worry about that now," he says reassuringly. "I haven't done anything yet." His smile reaches his eyes, crinkling the faint lines that stretch from their sides.

I walk him to the door. "Thanks for bringing these by," I say, holding the pamphlets up in my hand.

"No problem." He turns and begins to walk away. As an afterthought he turns back toward me and calls out, "She's not here right now."

My forehead wrinkles. "Sorry?"

"Another worst phrase ever!" He explains, referring to our prior phone conversation. "I came by looking to give you those once before," he says, nodding toward the pamphlets I hold in my hand. "That almost topped the 'You need to retake the bar exam' one." He grins and turns away, then strolls into the late afternoon shadows.

The café has emptied. I hadn't even noticed. Cory and Hailey both stand at the counter, staring at me.

I twist the necklace at my throat. *My mother's daughter.* I'm feeling giddy and anxious. So that I don't look like someone who just met a new boy from another state who showed up in homeroom, I resort to business mode and point at them. "Can one of you make sure those muffins get to Margo and Paulus this evening on your way home, please?"

DEATON HAS BEEN on his date with the lovely Kristlyn. I've been too busy to sit down and actually talk to him in a few weeks, but we speak through hand signals — waves, shrugs, thumbs-up, thumbs-down, big smiles, dramatic frowns.

I stand at the door of the café and raise my hands in question the Monday after they've been on their first date, while he runs by in his Nikes, running shorts, and sleeveless tee shirt. Spring has arrived, as Mr. Kent has said it would, and everyone has shed clothes as trees grow new leaves and clouds fill the sky above us. Deaton gives me a thumbs-up this morning, accompanied by a big, toothy grin.

Hours later, I cross the street hoping to have some armchair time. Maybe I will tell Deaton I had my insides flip over today. But how to explain who Scott Warner is and why I need his services? I'd rather not go down that road yet, and hopefully I'll never have to. I press my forehead to the glass door of the bookstore, cupping my hands to the side to see better. The store is dark, clean, tucked away for the night. Atticus is nowhere to be seen.

I text: "Where R U?"

My phone dings in response immediately: "Upstairs.

Wait a sec."

I stand on the sidewalk, looking over at my storefront, assessing it, seeing that it could use a good pressure wash. I wave goodbye to Mr. Kent as he leaves for the evening.

Deaton appears downstairs and lets me in.

"C'mon," he gestures for me to follow, while he runs back toward the stairs that lead to his apartment. A chicken breast is simmering in a pan on the stovetop in some sort of creamy sauce, pungent with paprika.

"I'm back, Mom," he says. "Amy's here."

A woman's voice fills the little kitchen area while Deaton strides to the refrigerator, pulls another chicken breast from a package, holds it up, and raises his eyebrows at me.

"Sure," I shrug. "If you have enough."

"Hello, Amy." Deaton's mother's voice bellows from a phone sitting on the counter.

"Hello, Mrs. Dunklin. Nice to meet you."

Deaton seasons the other chicken breast and adds it to the saucepan.

"Oh, it's nice to meet you as well," she says. "I hear you make a great cup of coffee. So anyway, Deats. L.J. is going to marry Alyson, and Patty doubts she's even going to be invited to the wedding if you can imagine such craziness," Mrs. Dunklin continues. "I'd never thought I'd see the day. Listen, honey, I need to run and go water my flowers before it gets dark. You have yourself a nice night, and I'll talk to you tomorrow. And remember what I said." With that she's off, tending to the next item on her list.

"My mom says I work too much. Says I need a project." He rolls his eyes, and I try to picture him rebuilding an engine, even though my imagination doesn't go far on this one because I have no idea how an engine looks outside of a car's hood, scattered in pieces. "She obviously does not understand what goes into setting up a new business."

We eat in silence for a while watching the news on the large screen mounted on the wall across the room.

"So the date was good?"

He wipes a napkin across his lips.

"Oh yeah, real good."

The overhead vent blows air down at the table. I weigh my napkin down with my fork, saying nothing.

"Kris is great," he says.

I smile sincerely. "You seem to have hit it off quickly."

"Her family was all there, you know, at the barbecue, and everyone seemed really nice."

*Family*! I nod and frown, wishing I had some nice, big family I could pull out of my own bag of tricks. If I ever meet someone they're going to think I'm so lame. My daughter out on her own, my father remarried, my mother dead. Just me and my dog.

*My mother dead!* I'd lied to my own husband. While he lied, I lied. And I wondered why we didn't make it. I blamed everything and everyone, except myself.

"Listen, Ames," Deaton says. "I've been thinking. I want to help you find out the truth about your mom."

I swallow. I reach for my glass and take a long sip of water and swallow again. My stomach gurgles with saffron rice and guilt.

"Oh no." I wave a hand at him. "You don't have to do that."

"I know I don't *have* to. I said I *want* to."

"This chicken is delicious. What's it sautéed in?"

"Paprika and coconut milk. Stop avoiding."

I lay down my fork again and look toward the television. I refold the napkin in my lap and take a deep breath.

"Deaton, I *know* the truth about my mother. She is gone and having to prove it is ridiculous. There's nothing to find. Really, there isn't. I'm going to tell Helena that."

*Shut up! Shut up! Shut up! Stop with the mother!* The very word, "mother" is souring in my stomach.

He looks toward the television for a moment then back at me like he doesn't believe I will.

"Really," I say, smiling with plastic confidence. "I'm going to do that soon."

I GET A TEXT from Rhoda: "Worried about Mary. Ian's been gone for a few days. I think she's taking too many of those pills of hers. She's been jittery. Wanted

to give you a heads-up in case you call her and she

seems out of it."

I settle into bed that night, troubled and restless, dreaming craziness. I'm on the railroad tracks, a bluish, blustery night. I'm a detective on serious business. A train is coming straight at me. I can see Hailey, Deaton, my father, and the Asian lady from the corner dry cleaners through the front window. They're all yelling at me to get out of the way, but I stand there. Just as suddenly, I'm outside of my dream and overseeing it, yelling at myself, but the dream me is oblivious to the danger I'm putting myself in. I won't listen or heed my own warnings.

I wake early in the morning before the light has even begun to stretch across the horizon.

*She laid there contemplating her future with a cast of characters designed to bring her world to an abrupt halt.*

*Quirk!* I imagine a masked man dressed in a black cape, kind of like The Hamburgler. He blurts the one word out to me, then vanishes. I'm not sure if I'm dreaming again or just imagining. The lines between the two are so blurred. Maybe I'm hungry....

*Or going nuts....*

I roll back over and close my eyes, desperate for the sleep that will close the curtain on any and all mental images and wayward thoughts. And warning bells.

# EIGHT

"SO WHO WAS he?" Hailey asks me over Cheerios Sunday morning.

"He's an attorney, Hailey."

She sits silently, buttering her toast.

"Oh, still divorce stuff," she finally says, taking a bite.

"No. Now that I'm past that and handled it all so well, the universe has decided to hand me some more."

She looks up from the magazine she's been skimming.

"Hailey, I've messed up big-time."

"What? Mom? You're scaring me." She swallows down her toast and takes a sip of juice.

"Honey, I might lose the house," I tell her, filling her in on the whole fiasco.

She sits and absorbs it. Hailey's a good absorber — a slow simmerer. But I can see from the shadows that cross her face that the possibility of our not having this beloved home is hitting her hard, penetrating with unwelcome emotion.

"Can't you borrow more money?"

"Well, no. That would be like an alcoholic taking a keg to an AA get-together. And anyway, the bank won't give me more. I'm tainted now." I smile crookedly trying to falsely reassure her things will be okay. Still able to make a self-deprecating joke. "I've borrowed on my credit card, so I have an emergency stash. But that will not bail me out of foreclosure."

"Whatever happens, we'll be okay," she finally says. "As long as we have each other, right?"

"Of course."

"I'll be going off to school soon anyway, and you might want to downsize when I'm gone," she says, making me feel even more miserable, more ancient, more alone. "You could move in with Chappy if you have to. Chappy and Helena, I mean."

"That sounds lovely, Hailey. Thank you for solving that for me."

After she leaves I lie around unproductively on the couch in my pajamas, moving my arm back and forth slowly over the edge, my fingertips grazing the carpet like I'm drifting off to sea in a little rowboat. I've got to get myself out of this funk and pull off an amazing feat — a few of them, actually.

On top of everything else I'm going through, I must be premenopausal. A few nights ago I met up with some of my old Starbucks buddies and sat there staring into space, paying no attention to anything anyone was saying. I tried to create three new recipes last week, and each bombed and ended up down the drain. Even the task of organizing my pantry and bringing some order to my life does nothing to thrill me, although I imagine it would feel so good to take control of something — anything!

I've decided I absolutely cannot lose my house. I have got to do something. Scott Warner has to do something. *Someone, somehow, something!* There are so many memories tied up in this house: baths in the old claw foot tub (that sadly, no longer lives here because of the big crack that formed down the middle when the shelf that held all the shampoos and toiletries fell on it.) The antique bed with the covers that always smelled of lavender and a hint of mustiness. Susan and I playing with Barbies, acting out our ideal lives with intact families. Getting ready for my wedding and my dad coming to pick me up in a classic, old Ford Thunderbird he'd borrowed to take me to the church, and me getting my heel stuck between the bricks on the walkway.

I'm beginning to feel entirely differently about my mom. I am angered, and it's like I'm seeing it for the first time in its actuality. Well of course, now that I'm seeing it outside of myself, looking at the whole, huge, sordid picture. I've kept this at bay for so long, but I shut it down and keep it at bay once more because I don't want to think any differently about her, won't allow myself to. I want to hold on to the same love I felt for her as a five-year-old.

I muster the strength to walk to the table and log on to my Potion#9 page. One guy wants to know if I would be interested in going away for the weekend with him to his company's sales conference in Orlando. Another sleazeball wants to know if I'm into evenings with more than one companion.

*Only if their names are Ben and Jerry, and said evening includes many cartons of Chunky Monkey!*

I log onto Unveiled's email and debate about what to say to Helena. I stare at the screen for close to thirty minutes, finally settling on, "Making great strides on your case," and pushing send. Afterward, I panic and retreat to the sofa, my rowboat. I'm imagining the waves churning in a dark, angry sea, myself bobbing along, crouching down low, drifting away.

And I wish it were true.

MARGO BRUSHES IMAGINARY crumbs from her lap. "I want to thank you for the way you helped me handle Paulus."

Paulus stands nearby, dressed in a little white cotton lab coat over a pair of dark blue pants and sparkling white tennis shoes.

"So obviously this new school isn't working out any better." She clenches her jaw.

It must be so difficult for her to come into this café every afternoon and be surrounded by prancing ballerinas, while her son is something different every day.

"No. No, I guess it isn't." I frown.

Margo studies me. Her eyes have lost some of their wariness, the emotions she held in when I first met her. I want to be a friend to her. I realize I'm reeling this woman into my orbit. I also realize my orbit should have yellow hazard tape all around it.

SCOTT WARNER CALLS. It's the first time since we met. I'm unsure how to react to him. There was a flirtation. *Wasn't there?*

But he's back to business mode. "I'm sending a new realtor your way. Don't feel obligated to use her, but she sold my receptionist's house in two weeks."

"Send away!" I say, knowing I have to follow through the motions, but praying something will happen to keep this home in my name, in my family.

Sheila Thomas from Sandy Shores Realty meets me at the house the following afternoon.

She frowns when Otis follows me into the house as if he's going to give her the tour. She frowns even more when she sees my charming array of colors, my vintage art décor, my two master suites — one up, one down — my white carpeting, my lack of garage space, and my empty koi pond outside the back door instead of a lap pool.

"It's going to take a unique individual, you recognize that right?" She says, shuffling through her bag.

There was a time I would have thought "unique" was a lovely adjective to bestow upon a person. Now I know it means strange and psychotic.

I sign on the dotted line and agree to let her list my beloved home, knowing that "beloved" is not one of the adjectives she'll be using in her description to potential clients, and planning to rip up the contract in her face soon anyway.

*Someone, somehow, something.* I have to believe it will happen.

"SO THEY SAID there were no allergies, right?"

"Right," I answer Deaton, while we attempt to work together in my little kitchen at home without constantly running into each other.

"Where do you keep your coriander?" He asks.

"At the grocery store," I answer quickly. "Ran out last week trying to create the perfect paratha and forgot to restock."

He twists his lips, thinking of what he can use as a substitute.

"I have cumin and cardamom. I can make it work," I say.

"Okay," he dictates to me like a drill sergeant. "We're going to do ten dishes for them. I've brought everything we need."

"Except for the coriander," I point out.

He ignores the barb and tries to act like he's the chef in the house. "We need to set up a system here. I've got twelve disposable pans with lids, so we'll stack them up and deliver them when it's all assembled and Vicki's husband can freeze them and pull them out to bake when they need them. On days when things are particularly bad."

"Nikki's."

He checks the paper in his hand where he's written his instructions down. "Right. Nikki's."

I roll my eyes. "Zhu speaking my a love language," I say in my best French chef accent, which isn't good at all. Just trying to lighten the heaviness of our task.

I'd decided to do this when I first heard about the situation, but I've been so preoccupied this is the first chance I've had. I still barely know the woman, but I feel responsible for my café patrons. Like Margo and Paulus. Some might say I'm trying to make family where family doesn't exist. Some might be on to something.

Hailey is taking the SAT all day, so I've roped Deaton into helping me. He has reluctantly agreed and now taken over the whole project like it's his, and I'm his lowly assistant. We work side-by-side all afternoon, splattering red sauce on my tile backsplash and spilling seasonings on my floors. When we finally finish our last casserole, I have a pot of coffee ready.

"I wanted to tell you I finished, *A Maiden's Voyage*." He blows on his cup, not meeting my eyes.

"And?"

He settles back in his chair.

"Your research was impressive," he begins. "Your dialog, your scenes. All *very, very* good. And the story is pretty intriguing, actually. I was a bit surprised, ya know, I mean… *pilgrims*. But it hooked me." He seems to struggle with how to tell me something. I can't figure out what it can possibly be if my scenes and my dialogue are so good.

"It's the characters, Ames. I don't feel anything for them. I couldn't have cared less if they ended up together or not."

I stare at him, my mouth open. How can anyone not care about Eleanor and Samuel?

"I know you love them. But you created them. I have to tell you from someone who doesn't know any more about them than what you've revealed, I can't love them like you do."

It would have been less shocking if he'd nailed my fingers to the kitchen counter.

"Do you think I can add to their character? Can I make readers care?"

He holds up his palms. "I don't know. I think it's worth a try. If you can, you might have a great story there." He hesitates, wanting to put the subject behind us. "So when are we going to get busy with the case?" His eyes search mine over his cup.

I stir in my seat. "Deaton, really, you don't need to do this with me."

"Amy, I'm doing this. I'm going to help you with this. What kind of friend would I be if I let you go through this alone? Your own mother, for God's sake. It's going to be so hard. *So hard*," he reiterates sympathetically.

I run my fingers through the fringe on the placemat in front of me, then concentrate on brushing it all straight. I begin to scratch. First the fingers, then the wrists, then the forearms.

*Please go be with this new girlfriend. Leave me alone. If this is what it takes to have friends, I don't want them!*

"Deaton. Listen…"

"This is going to take a toll on you, Amy. You may not think it will, but it will. My gosh, you have to relive and prove your own mother's death!"

I consider him working alongside me on such a futile mission. I'd have to act the entire time as if I thought differently, living a bald-faced lie. I can't do it.

But then again, it would allow me to see if a novice, a person without all the knowledge of my mom and her true fate, would ever be able to find her. All things I need to know, because my mother can never be found. Ever! Not after I've kept her dead this long in the minds of the people I love most.

*But the wrongness of it all… the law…*

"*La la la… the law,*" I imagine my mother saying, with her fingers plugging her ears. "*You're much too conscientious for your own good, Amy.*"

My phone dings with a text. I check and see that it's from

Rhoda. "Ian back home. Mary happy again!"

I roll my lips together and sigh. Ian is what it takes to make her happy. Just Ian. I catch Deaton's eye and curve my lips slightly, trying to give him a half-smile.

"Good news?" Deaton asks.

"Just something about Mary," I answer.

"Mary?"

"Have I told you about my former English teacher, Mary, who lives in Atlanta? We're very close."

"No. Tell me more about her."

And that's where the trail of deceit forks off and takes a turn for the worse, ensnaring yet another person.

# nine

W HEN I WAS sixteen, I got a card in the mail from my mom. "Sweet sixteen, to my baby girl," it read and was filled with sweet sentiments.

"P.S: Don't forget to burn this," was the last line on the card.

And I faithfully burned it. I'd committed her loopy handwriting to memory — the way her letters would start out slanting to the left and end up slanted to the right. The way her cursive *"I"* looked like a sailboat bobbing along next to the other letters. I used to have miniature bonfires in the fireplace of our old house when I was home alone. I'd run home from the post office while Dad was still at work and watch flames char any remnants of my mother from existence. Poof, she'd disappear again.

*Your mother was on the train. Your mother is gone.*

And once: *Your mother has left us. You must learn to go on without her.*

My father had such strange ways of putting his thoughts into words. No experience in comforting me, little willingness to figure out how when it came to the subject of my mom.

And that is the man my mother had left behind when she chose to be a crash victim, chose to leave behind that receipt, and chose to run to Scotland with Ian.

"I wrote you so many letters from Scotland. So very many," She told me years later. "But I always ripped them up afterward."

And then when I was fifteen there came that school field trip to Atlanta. My class was going to tour the CNN building. Dad signed the permission slip and told me he hoped I had a really good time, that I deserved a bit of fun after all my hard work and good grades. Realistically, I had made a *D* in English that year and was on the verge of failing Algebra, but my dad left that kind of stuff up to me, in all my adolescent wisdom.

It was outside the hotel. All of us checked in, and Mrs. Wentworth asked if some of us girls would like to take a taxi ride around the city before it got dark. We were waiting on the curb, and I saw the man on the bench with the newspaper folded beside him. There was space on the seat, and I was so tired after that long bus drive. I sat down beside him and glanced down. My mother's face, just the way I remembered it, looked back at me.

The taxi pulled up to the curb, and everyone got in, except for me.

"Amy, dear," Mrs. Wentworth called from the front passenger window.

"C'mon, Amy." Becky held on to the door and patted the space beside her on the back seat.

I laid my backpack on the newspaper and lifted it all in one fell swoop, stealing the man's newspaper and making a run for the back seat. I threw myself in and shut the door, and the cab pulled away from the curb as I shoved it into my backpack.

That night, after we got back to the room, I was able to pull it out and look into the eyes of my mother again, for the first time in years.

**Mr. and Mrs. Arthur Van Pelt attend the opening evening of *Birds of Paradise* at the Mortimer Theater. Ian Guthry, owner of Fins and Feathers Bistro, and his wife Mary can be seen in the background.**

There was an accompanying article and a picture that showed a clear image of Mr. and Mrs. Arthur Van Pelt and a shadowed, hazy image of the couple the city of Atlanta knew as Ian and Mary Guthry. No one else from home would have caught it, had they seen it. But a girl who had spent infancy gazing into the eyes of Atlanta's "Mary", a girl who had spent her childhood smiling up at Mary's proud expression – that girl knew.

O N A CRISP, clear Wednesday night, Deaton and I head to the Flannery Cove Public Library to scan the microfilm for old newspaper articles. It's hard to believe we have to do this to find everything, but the Flannery Cove Courier hadn't yet been digitized in the early nineties, so these things aren't all available online. I pretend to have zero knowledge of anything other than, "My mother went out one evening, and I never saw her again."

We talk about other things as we scan the machine that whirls by so fast I feel like I'm on a train myself.

"So, I dropped all the meals off at Nikki's," I say. "She said to thank you."

"Mmm."

"How's Aunt Patty and L.J.?" I ask.

"Same. Tommy Mobley's gettin' the house all fixed up plumb purty, though."

I smile. "Good for him. Good for her."

"Paul doing any better in school?"

"Paulus! And no, not last I heard. The kids are brutal to him and the teachers aren't much better, I think.

I start to say something about wanting to help him, but, in light of my recent charitable endeavors to reach out to the Dance Moms, I'll look like a sympathy show-off.

"Got something," Deaton says suddenly and stops the machine on a black-and-white photograph of the train accident. He scrolls a little further, and an article detailing the crash is next to it. He reads out loud to me, and I nod thoughtfully. Confirming this lines up with what I already know. He pushes print and keeps scrolling. More news articles appear throughout the next few day's editions.

He mumbles silently, reading an account of the investigation in an article written two weeks after the accident. I hear him suck in his breath. "Amy, come listen to this."

I glance up and he reads aloud. "There were two *unidentified* female bodies recovered from the river."

All the way back to the café, where I've left my car parked, Deaton rambles on and on about the newspaper article while I sit silently looking out at the night sky. I'm so depressed, unearthing all of these memories. I have to keep reminding myself that my mother is Mary, who lives four hours away from me and speaks to me by phone almost every day. But it's hard to shake the image of her on that train, plummeting into the river, her mouth opened wide mid-scream, her eyes huge with shock. It's hard because that is the concocted image that was stuck in my head for so many years of my youth.

"So how can we find out who these women were, do you think?" I finally take my thoughts away from the crash and focus on the investigation before us.

"Well, that's your job, isn't it?"

I pause. "Indeed it is."

I didn't mean to sound snarky, but it came out that way. Deaton takes his eyes off the road and glances at me. "I mean, however you go about this process, I'm here for you one hundred percent."

*How do I go about this process?*

"I'll make an appointment to talk with the lead detective who was assigned to this case," I say. "As the daughter of one of the victims, *not* an investigator. How's your schedule look next week?"

He blows a wisp of hair off his forehead and flicks his turn signal. As we sit at the red light, he mentally reviews his calendar.

"Kristlyn comes back into town Monday, and we're supposed to meet for dinner that night then go to an exhibit Wednesday evening and a movie Friday night. Otherwise, I'm all yours."

"Oh! I didn't realize. So, gosh, y'all are hitting it off quickly. Good for you!" I say exaggeratedly like a therapist congratulating someone for addressing their feelings — moving past all their anger. "We don't have to keep. I mean, I can manage this…"

"Yeah," says Deaton, interrupting me. "About Kris." The interior of the car is dark, but I can make out his jawline, his upturned lips. It rained lightly while we were in the library, and every time a car comes from the opposite direction their lights bounce off the wet pavement. "I haven't been honest about how I met her."

I hold on to the door as we turn.

"Remember I told you I had been dating a girl back home and that I hadn't dated since I came out here?"

*Again with the coming out!*

He doesn't wait for me to respond.

"Well, that's true, but not entirely true. Kristlyn is the girl from back home. We were dating, but it wasn't really serious. It was headed that way, but it never got the chance." He veers to the left and passes a silver sedan. "She moved out here to be closer to her family and took a job with the gallery in Savannah." He pauses, allowing me to absorb this much before continuing. "I flew out with her initially to help her look for a place, but we fell apart after that. After she left, I gave it some thought. I'd been passed over for the Braxton promotion, and I've always wanted to open a bookstore. Never thought much about a small, coastal town in Georgia, but when Kristlyn moved out here, I packed up and followed. I mean, not stalkerish or anything. I just liked the area."

"Okay," I say, unsure how he expects me to respond. "You don't have to explain…"

He interrupts me. "She was overwhelmed to find me here. Her words," he says, smiling, his eyes intent on the road. "And then I opened the bookstore and got busy and kinda thought…" He looks at me, a quick flash like he's going to reveal something, but he shakes his head and chuckles like I'd never believe it anyway.

I let the moment pass without prodding as if I hadn't noticed.

"Well, anyway." He waves his hand, none of that being important obviously in light of this new turn of events.

"But you said she saw you on Potion#9."

"Yes, she did. That is true!" He takes his eyes off the road and looks at me with his eyebrows raised and nods his head earnestly. "*She* looked *me* up," he says, thumping his chest boisterously. "My Potion profile came up in her search, and she contacted me. She said — again her words, not mine — that she had been *overwhelmed*," he pronounces this like I might need to look the meaning up later, "with moving out here and then realizing I came too. But now that she's settling in and missing me she was thrilled that I'm here and still available."

He glances at me, and I nod. *Okay. You can stop telling me all this now.*

"I didn't 'follow' her out here," he says, putting the word in air quotes. "I really did fall in love with the quaintness of Flannery Cove. It's a perfect location for me."

I chew my thumbnail. "Mm-hmm. Not buying that one, but whatever."

"It's like no time at all passed." He's gone from unsure how to tell his story to elated to tell his story, and I can't shut him up. "We still get along as great as we did. There's really something there between us. I knew there was," he says, nodding his head, tapping his steering wheel, confirming it to himself.

I recognize a wave of jealousy. My one prospect from the whole dating site was horrendous, and here's Deaton reconnecting with a girl he had already fallen for. I hate losing, but I'm not even in the game. I'm stuck in the dugout, and no one is calling my name to play. I sigh and pick at little threads my sweater has left on my jeans.

But there's something else I'm feeling — something that comforts me that I can't quite identify. And then it hits me. Deaton just handed me a gift, beautifully wrapped with a big bow. Inside was justification. Justification that assuages my guilt a fraction, even though in terms of comparison his deceit is a two and mine is off the charts. I pat my leg with finality. "Well." I smile some big, over-the-top grin. "That's great. Happy for ya."

"So try to set up a meeting with the detective for Tuesday, late afternoon," he says.

I log onto my profile page that same evening and sift through all the weirdos — my new relaxation technique. Out of nine messages, only one sounds like we live on the same planet.

> **Hi. I am new to this website and saw your profile. I am 37 years old and single (never married.) I am an investment banker for Seraxus International. The attached picture is the real me, scouts honor. I like movie nights at home, lazy Sunday mornings, and roads that lead to nowhere. I know I'm up against guys who like to bungee jump off of cliffs and swim with sharks. I'm not that guy. I'm just average old Bradley, and when I'm feeling adventurous, I'll answer to Brad. If this sounds like someone you'd like to meet, please respond.**

Bradley sounds nothing like anyone I'd ever seek out, but he sounds nice and safe. He actually sounds dorky, but whatever. It's hard to imagine this guy sidling up to a girl in a bar when he has another girl waiting at home and asking her if she'd like to get a room somewhere. And since that's what I look for in a man now, I respond. He says he needs new lounge chairs for his deck area. I agree to meet him Saturday afternoon at the outdoor furniture store and give my input and hope it's more exciting than shopping for storage bins at Wal-Mart.

# *Ten*

"YOU NEED TO get more sleep." Madame Bienve lifts the spectacles she keeps on a chain around her neck and rubs a thumb across the skin under my eyes. "And you must moisturize." She inspects my pores and then pirouettes and ascends the stairs, her work done.

"Wow." Margo turns on her stool and examines me from head to toe. "She forgot to mention your lackluster hair."

I roll my eyes, stroking my split ends. Paulus has taken to wiping the windows in the café down for me each afternoon, after finishing his muffin. He's extremely diligent in his work, wiping in little circles with his napkin and ensuring not a single fiber of lint remains on the glass.

"How are you doing today, Margo?" Her mind seems far away, occupied.

"Not great." She shrugs. "I need to make some decisions regarding Paulus. I think I need to make some changes in his life, but I don't know which ones to make." She taps a knuckle against her teeth.

I look off to where he stands working. Today Paulus is a 1920's newsboy in his knickers and a button-down shirt with suspenders and a driving hat. The little knee socks that rise from his saddle shoes bag around his ankles.

"I'm not sure how to help you there. I mean, I don't know much about anything but the regular public school, but if you need someone to attend a meeting to be a second set of ears and try to figure out what to do, I'd be happy to do that."

It's not my place, but sometimes when I fall into bed at night and try to focus on everything I need to be worrying about, Paulus' face floats across my thoughts. The homeless beggar on the corner haunts me as well. So does global warming, worldwide famine, and faulty train brakes. I'm fairly certain they call all of this avoidance. Anything to keep my mind off the things I need to wrap it around.

"I don't know what I need," she says, exasperated. "My brother attends all Paulus' meetings with me, but we butt heads so much when it comes to his care. He doesn't have kids of his own, and I know Paulus means the world to him, but he wants him in a special school, and I think he needs to stay mainstreamed. Paulus needs other personalities and characteristics opposite of his own to emulate."

"That sounds reasonable. It sounds like he's a great one to have to confer with. I'd give anything to have a sibling."

*Susan, why'd you leave?*

"Are you talking about Uncle Jeremy?"

I haven't even noticed that Paulus has finished the windows and stands behind us.

"You're lonely," Paulus says, looking at me as if he's been thinking about this for a while and has finally determined that something must be said. No sense ignoring the obvious, that's not getting anyone anywhere. "God said it is not good for man to be alone, so I will make him a helper."

"We tried parochial school once," Margo says. "Saint Andrew's Episcopal."

"Uncle Jeremy needs a helper."

THE INSIDE OF a police station is exactly the way it's depicted on television. It's grimy and busy, and everyone yells over each other with no consideration of manners or language. I've been expecting to be greeted by an overweight man with a comb-over, smoking a cigar. Instead, petite Detective Sharonda Keller with the swinging corn-row braids escorts us into a small office and kicks the door behind us shut with her boot.

"Coffee?" She asks while rifling through her desk.

"No thank you," I say at the same time Deaton turns his phone off.

Finally, she folds her hands on her desk and leans forward to give us her undivided attention. Her phone rings and she holds up an index finger to us and answers it.

"Keller." She leans back and holds the phone to her ear with one hand while continuing to rifle through her desk drawers with the other. "Yup. No, it was Carlson. Two o'clock, I think."

I glance around the office, but there's nothing to look at: beige walls with coffee dripped down the left one, painted concrete floor, and a fluorescent light overhead with only one bulb still burning.

"He needs to get that car and go through it with a fine-toothed comb," she says. She hangs up the phone without saying bye and returns her attention to us. "Now, where were we?"

"I am here to try to find out more about a case that was handled by a…" I open my notebook and check the name. "A Detective McCarthy. Back in 1988. A train derailed and plunged into the river, killing everyone on board."

Detective Keller nods, taking it in, not horrified or surprised. This is her life: crimes, accidents, tragedies. "Detective McCarthy died in…" She leans back, her lips twisted in thought. "1997?"

"Amy's mother was on board that train," Deaton says.

"She was never identified," I explain. "I just want, I don't know, some sort of closure."

Thompson nods. "No body, no burial. I get it. Gotta warn ya, though, it's gonna be tough. Old and cold always is. But I'll look into it — try, anyway."

I sit with my folder in my lap, staring at the coffee drip. Deaton reaches over and takes the folder and hands it to Thompson. "Here's everything we've found out so far on our own."

"Care if I make copies?" Thompson asks.

"I already made them," Deaton answers.

I GET BACK TO the café in time to help Jenna close. I'm exhausted from facing the detective, talking about the train accident, saying my mother's name over and over, tracing the path of that coffee stain.

I want to call Becky, but I just can't. *What's new with me? Well, Dad proposed to Helena and I'm making fools of both of them and doing my mother's bidding as I've always done.* Becky has never been on board with keeping my mother a secret. Even at fifteen, she was wary of such a huge load.

So, I'm avoiding Becky right now. Another casualty of the tornado.

I check in with Helena via email and tell her that we at Unveiled have been doing some extensive research, we're making great strides, all the things I'm supposed to say. I check my personal email. I'd asked Deaton for my manuscript back and tried to work on it a little, but I couldn't seem to make very many changes. My little brain grew arms and stood before the barbells, but I couldn't seem to get them off the ground, too mentally exhausted. I can no longer see the story with a discerning eye, and I'm only writing now to avoid doing other things. Even I realize that. I have written an entire chapter where Eleanor has to confess an enormous secret to Samuel, and he is okay with it. I delete it, of course. It is pure nonsense, wishful thinking. I've sent *A Maiden's Voyage* out to two new agents anyway, and one of them has already replied.

> **Dear Author,**
>
> **Thank you for your email, and for giving me a look at your material. Unfortunately, I'm afraid I must pass, as it is not the right fit for me. I hope you will accept my best wishes for your future success.**
>
> **Sincerely,**
> **Marilyn Eden**
> **Eden Literary Agency**

I'm letting Eleanor and Samuel down, along with everyone else in my life. I have not been able to convey their passion, their characteristics, their sentiments. I sigh imagining them, he in his breeches and doublet, she in her stay, waistcoat, and petticoat. They both stand side-by-side, scowling at me, so disappointed.

"AMY, IT'S BEEN so long. You look wonderful." Fiona Bienve, Madame's daughter, jumps up from the booth and runs to hug me as soon as I walk through the door early the next morning.

"Don't let your mother hear you saying that. She'll have you at the optometrist's office before lunchtime." I return her hug. "What brings you to town?"

"Mother has been needing some help with things. And I need a bit of a break from New York City."

"I love the new do." I touch my hand to Fiona's cropped, black strands. She has cheeks like little, pink posies, porcelain skin, and dark, bushy eyebrows that she somehow manages to turn into an enviable feature. Fiona dresses like a New Yorker, in the latest colors and styles. Fiona is also petite and about ninety-eight pounds. The kind of girl who makes other girls feel big-boned.

"Your cell," Cory calls to me from the counter.

"Excuse me, Fiona." I place a hand to her arm, which hides beneath her red trench coat's sleeve. The body of the coat is cinched at her waist, tighter than the watch on my wrist. I grab my phone off the counter. She waves and goes upstairs to her mother's studio.

"Hello, this is Amy," I say while reaching for my freshly washed apron on the hook behind the counter.

"Amy. Scott Warner." His voice is as warm and gooey as a chocolate chip cookie. "Just checking in to see how the new agent is working out."

I step into my office and kick the door shut behind me, closing off the noise of the café, entering the space where I can become someone other than Amy the waitress, barista, boss, orphan, victim, whatever. "She's holding an open house this weekend," I say.

"Good. That's good. I know it's no consolation, but so many are in this situation right now. Job security for me, I guess."

I say nothing. I smile, but of course, he can't see that.

"It's the economy. And divorce. Dadgum divorce leaves so many stranded with mortgages they can't handle alone. So unfair."

It's on the tip of my tongue to remind him it was only after my divorce that I had gotten myself in over my head. "Dadgum divorce," I agree. We sound like old-time men that complain about the world while spitting tobacco.

Per our usual, we stray way off the conversational course of our business with each other. I picture him there in his office, with his earnest expression and slight stubble.

"Did you all try counseling?" He asks.

"Once, but Greg wasn't into it. It was a lost cause."

He remains silent, probably rubbing a hand across that sexy scruff of his. Someone should tell him that if he included a head-shot in his advertising, no words would be needed.

"I tried everything I could think of to keep Greg from straying, but it was futile. The world is full of too many beautiful women, and I couldn't pay them all to stay away from him," I say.

Scott sniffs then makes a slight "hmph" sound with his throat. Kind of a laugh, kind of an observation, a realization.

"Tried everything? What exactly did you try?" He asks. "It wasn't your job to keep him from breaking his vows... No. I'm sorry. This is none of my business. You'll forgive me? I have a strong dislike for that sort of thing. I don't do family law because I can't stomach it."

I remain silent. The question was rhetorical.

"But seriously the guy's a fool. Did you ever try just getting him to look deep into your green eyes and see what he was walking away from?"

I swallow, pause, and glance around the room, feeling a bit off-kilter. "What good would that do?" I finally ask. "I told you there are way too many beautiful women in the world. My algae-colored eyes weren't gonna matter."

"First off, I saw more of a lovely brilliant sea-glass shade, not algae. And obviously, you don't know your own power. Nor do you know how to accept a compliment."

Not the first time I've heard that I don't know how to accept a compliment. I sit in my office thinking about Scott Warner and those very words long after we hang up. That's another quirk, I guess. Most females know how to smile and bat their eyes and lap up flattery, but not me. Maybe that's something a mother teaches a daughter during the formative years. Once I told a teacher who gave me an "A" on my cotton gin report and announced to the class what an excellent job I had done researching, that Eli Whitney was my great, great, great, great grandfather's cousin, so it didn't really count.

I sit in my office and work on the next week's menu as the sun moves behind me, and I make a mental note to pick up some cortisol cream while I think about Helena and rake away at my arms.

TWO DAYS LATER Sheila Thomas, the new real estate agent, finally shows up and plants the open house sign in the yard before I've left for the morning.

She rings the doorbell, and I throw open the door like today is the day, let's go ahead and celebrate. One look at the skies ruins that mood. I glance at the dark clouds and back to my white carpet.

"Let me grab a bucket or something to put here in the foyer," I say.

"What for?" She lays flyers and notebooks out on my dining room table and gathers my placemats into a pile. "Where can we stuff these?" She asks, turning and looking for a place.

I take them from her and go back to the kitchen and shove them in a drawer. "The carpet," I say, pointing. "We can't have people walking through mud and onto the carpet." I grab a towel and try to arrange it nicely at the entryway.

All of a sudden, I remember something. Me, only six years old or so, coming home from the beach to Nana's house and standing at the door while she toweled me off. Susan was inside, sitting on the couch. *Why hadn't she gone to the beach with me?* She looked toward me with an expectant smile but didn't say anything until I went over to the sofa and sat by her. I remember Nana said something about her being in time-out and she wasn't able to play that day. I had to play by myself.

"I think it'll just get all wrinkled," Sheila says, pointing to the towel I've smoothed out on the floor. "It's not a good idea to point out how high maintenance that carpet is. People already know they have to come in and paint and re-tile. You don't want to keep reminding them of things to add to the list."

I puff my cheeks and blow out the air.

I WORK THE BREAKFAST shift at the café, clean out the refrigerator, and start on a grocery list before I notice the time. Around eleven Hailey relieves me.

Just before noon, I get to Sunshine Patio Store and Bradley is waiting outside on the sidewalk for me like he's the valet. I recognize him immediately. I'd looked at his picture dozens of times dreading the possibilities of what he might surprise me with, but there he is dressed in jeans and tennis shoes, mid-thirties, all teeth intact. His jeans aren't very form-fitting, they're a tad big, droopy in the rear, puckered at the waist where his belt is on the last notch, and his green and blue plaid button-down is a little wrinkled, especially in the button area. Not clothes I would have selected for him if I were his wife and did his shopping. Then again who wants a man who can't pick out his own clothes, even if they aren't the crispest, the most complimentary? He's smiling like I'm a sight for sore eyes.

I pull into a parking spot and sprint toward him. "Sorry, I'm a bit late. I'm having an open house today, and the agent, and work, and the traffic." As I say this, I wave a hand to encompass all I'd endured getting across town.

Bradley rocks on his heels, his hands in his pockets, like he's sizing me up. He holds out his hand to shake mine. "Hey," he says.

I dump my keys into my purse and free my hand so I can take his. He nods his head toward the showroom. "Wanna go in?"

We spend about an hour in the showroom. I follow Bradley around giving my opinion on the comfort of various loungers. He sits in them all, asking about the stain resistance of the fabrics and scrutinizing the flammability factor on the tags.

"I like this one," I say, sitting on the dark wicker with aqua cushions.

"I'm not sure that would match my other stuff," he says sucking air through clenched teeth like he's afraid I might force it on him.

"It's whatever you like," I answer breezily.

Bradley pays and arranges to have it all delivered to his house the following week.

"Let me treat you to lunch?"

"I'd like that."

I follow him to a sandwich shop nearby.

"Did you want something nicer?" he asks. "We could get something nicer." He cranes his neck, looking up and down the street as if he needs to find something better before I dart away.

"This is fine, Bradley."

"Order whatever you like." He spots the cookies wrapped in cellophane near the register. "You could even have a cookie." He holds them up like prizes, something no other man has surely ever been able to offer.

He chews methodically. He asks me all about my daughter, my business, my life, and when I get a word in, I ask him about his.

"Never been married," he says, wiping a napkin across his mouth. "Came close to asking once, but glad I didn't." He shakes his head as if he's shaken the thought away. "Stocks, that's my thing. I'm a numbers guy. I like financial security. I like showing people their growing portfolios, watching the line on the graph increase." He moves his fingers in an upward motion while he chews, then takes a sip of his drink. "What about you?"

I picture my house falling into the sea and being swallowed up as the graph line plummets downward off the chart... like a runaway train. I've barely known Bradley a full day, and already I'm a disappointment to all he holds important.

"Yeah, those are good things," I agree.

When we part company outside the sandwich shop he walks me to my car. "I'd like to call you again, Amy."

"Um Sure. I'd like to get that call." I grin and toss my keys and thankfully catch them.

So nice to spend time with someone not harassing me about a corpse.

# *ELEVEN*

THE OPENING EVENING of *The Butterfly Queen* is a success. I'm the first to arrive, trying to put something on every chair in our aisle to hold them. Dad and Helena arrive shortly afterward and then Greg and Sherri.

"How 'bout that girl of ours, Ames." Greg pulls me into a hug. Somehow I manage — *mostly* — to separate Greg the failure of a husband from Greg the dad to my daughter. They're two different people to me.

Sheri leans over and taps me on the shoulder. I turn and smile. It's hard not to like Sheri Rhymlich. She's a skinny, little wisp of a thing. Her brown hair hangs straight, her features are fairly non-descript. She wears sensible outfits and comfortable shoes. I have no idea how she ended up with Greg or what she sees in him.

"Raleigh!" Greg notices my father sitting on the other side of me and reaches across the back of my neck, cupping a hand around my dad's shoulders. Dad looks up from his program and smiles. Whatever transpired between Greg and me has been set aside by my Dad. He can see Greg in town and sit down and have lunch with the man. Jarod waves from a seat a few rows ahead of us, and the lights start to dim.

Everyone starts to shuffle around, and I look up to see what the commotion is about. Deaton stands at the end of the row, trying to squeeze in next to Helena. "Nice to meet you," he says to her. "I've heard a *lot* about you."

We're thrust into darkness, and the production begins.

BRADLEY STOPS BY the café the next morning with an invitation to a co-worker's house for dinner Thursday evening. I agree to go and ask him to pick me up at my house.

When he arrives I open the door and invite him in. "Just let me grab my shoes," I say, greeting him.

"Hey," he says. It seems to be his favorite word. Bradley does that thing he does with his hands in his pockets, rocking on his heels, a big grin on his face. He watches me walk back toward my room and never says a word about the house like he hasn't even noticed he's not outside anymore.

Julia and Thom Weston live in the east end of Flannery Cove, in a little starter home — a 1940s type bungalow, flat roof, bay window, the thickest, greenest grass I've ever seen. Bradley rings the doorbell then opens the door to let himself in.

"Bradley, my man!" Thom sprints across the floor like they live in a sprawling mansion, meeting us at the door. "You must be Amy."

Julia comes out of the kitchen, an apron over her blue dress, high heels tapping across oak floors.

"Bradley." She hugs him with one arm, holding her wine glass in the other. "Amy, we've heard so much about you."

I smile timidly. I've only been on one date with Bradley and haven't mentioned it to anybody. What can he possibly have said about me based on one date? That I sure knew how to pick an excellent set of patio furniture?

The four of us eat in the small dining area, which is part of the living room, set off in the corner. Throughout conversations about summers in Georgia and Julia and Thom's wedding two years earlier the DOW and the NASDAQ are continuously weaved in and out, like two toddlers whom everyone adores and can't bring themselves to keep in their rooms or at the kid's table, out of the way.

"Nabisco's up by ten points," Thom says while scooping out more Caesar salad. "Shoulda bought into that last week." He picks up his fork and stabs as much as he can on it.

Bradley nods and runs a flat palm over his cowlick. .It sprouts from the back center of his head like a rooster's tail feathers. The class ring he wears looks like a big marble on his finger. I have a class ring somewhere, maybe in an old shoebox or my sock drawer. I'm not sure. Haven't worn it in twenty years.

I smile and nod as the NASDAQ numbers are discussed between the three of them like I know what the heck they're talking about. I'm hoping I don't get called on it, but if I do, I'll say something about Oreos or Nutter Butter since that's the extent of my Nabisco knowledge. I've studied business, administration, and analytics — the organizational stuff. If there's a lull in the conversation maybe I can weave in some ledgers and credits and debits — that's my language. But there's not.

My mind wanders to Scott Warner, and I wonder if he has stocks and bonds. Probably. He likely invests wisely and has a good intuition about the world of trading. He probably thinks I'm extremely unsophisticated to have made the decisions I did that led our paths to cross. I wonder how many ignorant people he has to help dig out of their messes, how many fragile hands he has to hold, and how many women he has to spend time on the phone with, building their trust by developing a rapport after divorce and deceit have left them skittish and wary.

*Obviously, you don't know your own power.*

How I wish he could know the real me, the person I was before all this happened. The me who can make a gourmet meal out of five random ingredients. The me who people used to say could sell ice skates to an amputee. The woman in control of everything — her organized closets, her labeled containers, her detailed records, and her finite double lines on ledgers that ended with plus signs.

"What about you, Amy? Ready to call it a night?" Bradley looks at his watch on his left wrist and places his napkin on the table with his right, signaling that he's ready. It's 8:35.

I nod and stifle a yawn.

THE END OF April brings bright blue skies.

My house sits on the market, the sale sign leaning sideways in my front yard, tired of all the effort. I'm both troubled and relieved. I wave to my neighbors — so many I've known since I was born. I love them all dearly, particularly the Westfields, who live diagonally from me. They depend on me to reboot their modem when their internet goes down, change their air filters and smoke alarms every six months, and bring over the spare key every time Mr. Westfield locks himself out of the house. Now I come home in the evenings and reminisce about one day after another in this house, and the recollections nearly kill me.

Becky couldn't believe it when we found out I had a house — *an actual house!* — waiting for me. The plan had been for the two of us to move into it together. I would be downstairs, she would be up, and there would be a steady stream of good-looking men lined up at the door.

And then I announced I'd be marrying Greg Hollander and moving him in with me.

The wedding, what a day that had been. Becky was my maid of honor. I had two other girls from my senior class stand with me as well — Maria Cross and Shannon Bass. I'd have had Susan, but I'd already lost her by then. How or why Dad managed to throw together a nice wedding for me on such short notice was beyond me, but to his credit he did.

The five of us girls had gotten ready in the very room I now sleep in. My bridesmaid's dresses were billowing, flowing things the color of orange sherbet. I remember thinking they looked like satin bedspreads and would be as wide if taken apart at the seam. Becky had made a cassette tape of recorded songs to play, so that day is forever known as the Captain and Tennille day in my mind. We'd rewound and replayed "Love Will Keep Us Together" over and over. Greg's ring sat nearby, glistening in its little beige box atop the antique dresser that had belonged to Nana's mother, deceiving me with sparkling promises of magnificence and richness of life, full circles with no end, thick bands not easily severed.

And then Dad had arrived to escort me to the church. I'd been in the bathroom straddling the toilet and thinking to myself, *it's my last night as a little girl in this house. Now, I will be the mistress of it.* That had sounded so grown-up, so alluring. Becky had come ripping into the room, taking no notice of my embarrassing stance. "I made you an emergency kit," she'd said. "It doubles as your something old."

Once we managed to get my dress back down, she handed me a little, beaded purse on a long chain that I'd admired at a thrift store but hadn't bought. Inside were various items she thought I might need: clear nail polish — *"In case your pantyhose run."* Breath mints — *"You chose salmon as your main course!"* Tissue — *"In case you get sniffly."* Tampons — *"Yeah, I thought about that one later. Duh!"* Tylenol — *"You're marrying Greg Hollander."*

When Dad knocked, I opened the front door. My father took one look at me and I had to open the little purse and hand him the tissue. "If only your mother could see you," he'd said.

THE END OF April brings wind and rain. Standard form rejection letters continue to appear in my inbox. Samuel and Eleanor's voices grow louder in my mind. But I'm too preoccupied to try to sharpen their dialog or make them more relatable. They are who they are. And in my head, Helena's moaning and whining are quickly drowning theirs out anyway.

I don't hear from Scott Warner, which means nothing has been filed yet. But I wonder why he doesn't call to tell me nothing has been filed, or to see if I've noticed all the butterflies emerging from their cocoons lately, if I saw the rainbow over the bridge last evening, or to tell me what's going on in the world of law… *anything.*

Other than business stuff, my phone remains relatively silent. Until one evening at Deaton's.

Kristlyn's job still hasn't transferred her completely to Georgia, and she flies back to Des Moines often. I met her a few weeks earlier. She had just come back from a run with Deaton, and I was outside sweeping the front walk. They ran over and he introduced me as his, "best buddy I've been telling you all about." I'd smiled and made small talk, and after a reasonable length of time had passed and I could slide my gaze down toward her knees, I took in her tanned legs and the seamless structure. The thigh blended toward the calf beautifully. I'd gazed back up at her golden halo of hair. He's chosen someone nothing like me after all.

Tonight Kristlyn is in Fresno at a conference on The Evolution of Visual Art in the Modern Era. Deaton is making grilled cheese sandwiches and tomato soup for the two of us in his little loft kitchen, and I'm sprawled out on his very stiff and unyielding sofa, trying to get comfortable and working on the New York Times crossword puzzle.

"Fourteen letter word meaning canine term for a broad head with a short muzzle," I holler across the back of the sofa.

"Told ya, I'm not an animal person," Deaton hollers back. "You could ask me what a five-letter word for something meant to be slipped around the neck for walking your dog is, and I would struggle."

"You're a..." my phone rings beside me. I sit up and rifle through my purse, throwing things onto the coffee table to get to it before it stops ringing.

The call is coming in from the Flannery Cove Police Department.

# TWELVE

W HEN HAILEY WAS young and Greg was out partying at night, I would towel her off after her bath and slip nightgowns adorned with Disney princesses over her head. I would snuggle under the blankets with her and read her bedtime stories. A favorite was Dr. Seuss, *Are You My Mother?*

"Read it again," Hailey would say over and over, until she knew by heart the story of the just-hatched bird whose mother has left the nest in search of food, not knowing he would choose that time to enter the world, and how he goes off in search of her, asking various animals and even a boat and a plane along the way if they are his mother.

"Are you my mother?" Hailey used to ask the flowers in the yard, the dishes on the table, the toothbrush I placed in her mouth.

"This is Detective Keller," The woman on the other end of the phone says.

Deaton stands nearby, gesturing for me to put her on speaker-phone, and I pretend not to see him until it becomes unreasonable to believe. I place the phone on the coffee table in the middle of my purse's inventory and click the button that allows her voice to fill the air.

"Detective Keller," I greet her. "Deaton and I are both here."

"What have you been able to find out, Detective?" Deaton wipes his hands on a dishtowel and sits down next to me on the sofa. He's all seriousness — prepared to find out my mother died all over again. I stiffen and brace myself for news I know I will not hear.

"One of the unidentified women in the train was Mexican," she says. "Her identity still has not been uncovered to this day. We assume she was an undocumented worker. It was tourist season, and the hotels in Savannah used to hire many maids without papers and pay them under the table."

I swallow, and Deaton squeezes my arm. "And the other passenger?"

"Caucasian. Late twenties, early thirties," she says. "Two months pregnant."

Later, after we've managed to pick at dinner, Deaton turns to me. We've been sitting side-by-side on the sofa like we're at a bus stop bench, as darkness has fallen and neither one of us has noticed. Finally, he reaches over and flicks a lamp on the side table. "Do you think your mom could have been pregnant?"

I'm not sure how I'll answer this. My mom could not have been pregnant. Her tubes were tied after my birth, her one accidental pregnancy. I don't have to reveal this to Deaton. I could let this second woman be my mom, mourn her all over again and close this case.

*Can you be my mother?* I wonder, in the same tone Hailey used to ask, hoping there is some way I could turn this woman into the pretense of her. If I don't tell the truth, Deaton will find it out on his own. And if not, Helena and her next investigator will. Anyone who thinks it through enough would automatically know that Caroline Chadwick would have had obstetrical care. She would not have been unidentified. "I don't believe my mother was pregnant," I say, without turning my head to look at him. "Unless maybe she didn't know."

Ten minutes pass in silence. Deaton sighs and grabs my wrist. "You realize what this means, Amy?"

I glance at his face. I don't ask, but my silence and my expression do.

"Your mother may not have been on that train. Your mother may be alive."

I shake my arm loose. "Don't you think my mother would have come home if she were alive?"

"I don't know." He bites his lower lip as if that's the part he's struggling with. "There may be another reason she never made it home that night. Maybe she couldn't and still can't." After a few more seconds of silence, he stares straight ahead and mumbles a promise. "I'm gonna find out for you, though."

THE PHONE TRILLS urgently, but goes unanswered. It takes Becky so many hours to get back to me, the urgency has faded by the time she does, and I'm breathing again. Maybe I would have confessed, sought advice. Most likely not, but that was my intention, at least to dip my toe in the water and feel the temperature.

"Beck," I start, but I don't have the energy. I can't keep it all straight anymore — who knows what or suspects what and how much, and what's still secret and from whom. It boggles the mind. Between trying to make the café thrive again and figuring out how to run an investigation in reverse, I'm exhausted. And feeling the pressure to publish something just because it was written is about to push me over the edge.

"I just called to check on how you're doing," I say, and listen for the next half hour about Bryan's workload and how difficult it is to take care of everything when he's gone.

"Preachin' to the choir," I remind her. Although my ex's apparent workload was a different thing. "I've met an interesting guy," I say, although once I've said it, I wonder if interesting is the right word to describe Bradley. I imagine him waving a denying hand at anyone who paints him with such a brush. "I'm just Bradley," he would say. "A numbers guy."

"He's a numbers guy," I tell Becky, but in a different tone than Bradley uses. Mine hints at numbers as something glamorous and mysterious. "He's never been married."

I can't think of anything else to say. *He just got new patio furniture…. He could use a few new outfits….* "He's the nicest guy."

"Nice is good," she says hesitantly, "It beats the alternative."

"Yeah. I'm counting on that."

"TELL ME WHAT'S going through your mind right now," I say to Bradley one evening later that week over shrimp and hush puppies at a restaurant down by the dock.

He pauses, his hand halfway between his mouth and his plate.

"No planning. You have to tell me what you were thinking when I asked. And go!" I prod, pointing with my fork.

"Um, I was thinking about a speech I gave in high school once for the debate team. Small school," he says while chewing, owning up to the truth that he hadn't debated at Harvard or anything remotely close. I almost point out that he shouldn't downplay everything, but I think about my own inability to gracefully accept a compliment.

*"She certainly is quirky,"* My mother and father say to each other over my newborn form in a cradle sleeping peacefully. They smooth the blanket over my knees, more cute little golf balls than baseballs at that point in my life. *"I think I'll leave her to you to take care of,"* my mom says and my dad nods agreeably. *"Ok, whatever you think is best."*

"Only fifty in my graduating class." Bradley's voice brings me back from my dreaming. "About a hundred fifty in the high school and we all pretty much had the same opinions on everything, having been raised in such a small town. But that day I had to *pretend,*" he stresses the word as if it's a talent he had gained after so much practice, "that I believed that the death penalty should be abolished."

The mind is a constantly spinning slot machine, and what it lands on is often quite random. I know if I were put on the spot like that, there's no telling what would be flashing on my mental screen. The difference between Bradley and me is that I would say, "I was just thinking of rainbows and butterflies and a few of my favorite things. You know, the usual stuff." But Bradley is an earnest and open book, God bless him, and he's anything but sinister. Otherwise, this honest answer would give me pause.

*Should the death penalty be abolished?* I don't know. I'm sure I can think of arguments for both sides. Maybe if I want to know the truth I should ask Scott Warner what he thinks of the death penalty. He is an attorney after all. His opinion would be the correct one. And the funny thing is I could probably blurt out such a strange question to him between sentences about principal and interest and negative equity, and we could go off in that direction without it being the least bit awkward.

If he would call.

"So you don't think it should be abolished?" I ask, not really caring anymore.

Bradley cocks his head and looks at me, considering. "Well, no. I've always been told that if a person killed another, their life should be taken as well."

"But that was your parent's opinion. The one that formed your early one." I rest my forearms on the table and lean in, garnering a bit more interest again.

Bradley shrugs. "Yeah, I guess."

"Have your own thoughts not evolved since? What if a person is innocent, and they are convicted and sent to death row anyway?" My voice is rising a bit as if Bradley is debating with me, but he's just sitting there with his mouth twisted in confusion.

"Well, I wouldn't want that person to be executed, obviously."

"But they will be if capital punishment is in effect!" I'm trying to drive home a point, but I'm not real sure what the point is.

"So it should be eliminated." He smiles, placating me, and picks up the dessert menu.

"But what about the hard-core, evil people of the world that do kill violently?" I shake my hands in front of me as if all of humanity going forward hinges on this age-old dilemma being solved right here and now, by the two of us.

"Well, *that's* what I was saying."

"But Bradley," I whisper through clenched teeth. I'm getting frustrated, but my voice lowers even more. "This isn't just a one-dimensional issue. It's complex. You *have* to have many thoughts on it. You *have* to be passionate about it!" I feel myself going a little off-kilter. It's unexplainable. Why does he have to be passionate about the death penalty? It's not like I'm on trial for it, and I imagine telling both Becky and Deaton next week we broke up before we even got off the ground because Bradley didn't know where he stood on capital punishment. I almost laugh at my madness, imagining Deaton saying something like, "Are you planning to run for district attorney soon?"

Bradley sighs and folds the dessert menu and lays it back on the table. His face takes on the appearance of someone who's deep in concentration like he's thinking this whole issue through, but I imagine he's actually trying to determine what it is I want him to say. This blasé appeasing approach to things — I'm not sure I can

live like this, or allow him to continue to. A person has to have...
I search my mind for a word. *Gumption*!

"I'm sticking with not abolishing it," he finally says, his lips
pressed into a thin line, conveying finality.

"But why?" I can't help it. I have to pull something out of him.
Despite the lack of people in line behind him vying for position
with me, Bradley's attentiveness and willingness to conform can
be stifling. His flip-flop convictions strike me as weak.

"Because of what I said before. And..." He raises his eyebrows
in earnest. You'd think we were in the throes of foreplay, the way
I lean in, anticipating. "Life imprisonment costs the American
taxpayers over forty grand a year per prisoner."

"That's it?" I finally say deflated, after looking at him for a
full twenty seconds. "That's your argument?"

"I wasn't arguing," he says, looking around to see if anyone
nearby thought we were. Everyone at the nearby tables is engrossed
in their own conversations.

"Everyone thinks death is the ultimate punishment," I say like I'm
so disappointed in him. "But it's not. Life imprisonment is no piece
of cake. You have no idea!" I declare as if I've known many lifers.

"I have a vague idea," he raises his brows. "I've been in this
restaurant with you for about an hour now and it's beginning to
feel kinda like that."

I pause with my finger pointed in the air, insulted but relieved.
It feels like I'm a detective who's been searching all night finally
hollering, "We got something over here," just before daybreak.
There's hope. Bradley has gumption potential.

We leave the restaurant, hand in hand. All talk of legisla-
tive punishment is left behind. "Want to walk on the beach for a
bit?" I ask.

He pats a hand to his scalp. "I'd never get this darn thing to
lay down for the night if I did that."

I'm not sure if he's joking or not, so I laugh softly, hesitantly,
and walk toward the steps that lead down to the beach. I roll up
my jeans and slip off my shoes. Bradley follows, but he keeps his
shoes on. His arms hang at his sides as if they're being weighed
down by heavy suitcases clutched in his hands. It makes it hard for
me to relax. It seems as if I'm enjoying the pleasure of the stroll
and he's alongside to monitor me, like a security guard who's not
supposed to fraternize too closely with the subject.

If this were me and Greg he'd be yelling, "Come on, Chadwick. Load up, we're leaving." Or he might say something like, "You want to be near the water? Well, here you go," and pick me up and toss me in. I look over at Bradley, just clomping along, sand kicking up behind him as he sinks with each step. He's studying me, trying to make sure he keeps up and doesn't lose me on this empty stretch of beach. The fact that he's only out here in the wind getting his shoes full of sand for me is not lost on me.

"We can go," I holler over the waves.

If it were a test I was giving him, I suppose he passed. *Close enough.*

The supposing part might be a problem if there weren't so many bigger ones to dwell on.

M Y FATHER AND Helena are seated near the door of the café, holding hands and speaking softly to each other, waiting patiently. Cory points them out to me. "Said he wanted his daughter to seat them."

"Dad!" I'm excited to see him until I remember I'm actually horrified and nervous. "Helena." I nod — barely, uncertainly, rather unpleasantly I'm sure.

"Sparkle!" Dad rises from the bench and Helena smiles and does the same. She doesn't seem to have noticed my reservation, my rudeness.

"I know," she says, patting the top of her hair. "It's awful."

I can hear her going on and on about her new hairdo as I lead them to a booth. Along the way, I grab a few menus, then I turn to face her, trying to appear interested.

"But Delores was out sick, so I had to schedule an appointment with someone new. Well, that turned out to be the worst thing I've ever done," she proclaims. There's laughter in her words as if recalling a hilarious story for me. Maybe she is. I can't fully concentrate on it. "Fresh out of beauty school. Using my head as a practice scalp for some new developer she kept talking about, probably racking up points or bonuses of some sort for how many people she uses it on. So this is the result," she says, sliding into the booth as I place a menu in front of her. "Curls so tight I have a perpetual headache."

With a tilt of my head, I assess her and see she's had a bit of bad luck at the hands of this new hairdresser. Her hair looks like my heart feels — constricted, tight, relentless.

"It looks good." I widen my smile and try to make the brightness reach my eyes, but the only way I know to do that is to continually blink and re-open them wide, which may look as though I have an undiagnosed neurological condition. "Really good."

Helena adjusts her reading glasses and looks over the top of them at me. "You're a good liar. Isn't she a good liar, Raleigh?"

"She is no such thing," my dad says. "That's my daughter you're speaking of." He smiles at Helena and winks at me.

I laugh nervously. Blink. Open wide. Smile. Helena laughs and swats at dad with her menu as if this is their usual banter. They've got the routine down: foot in mouth, scold, wink, and chuckle.

"How's your, um, investigation thing going?" I ask later when I've made the rounds again and inquired how they liked their Gruyere macaroni and balsamic mushroom meatloaf sandwiches. I try to make the investigation sound minor, a hobby Helena has taken up temporarily and might replace the following week with ceramics or scrapbooking.

It's my dad that answers before she can. "Helena is making great strides," he says proudly, as if she is the one doing the investigating herself instead of just paying someone else and barking out theories and attaching documents.

I smirk and look off to the side. I'm sure my face reveals that I'm still not reconciled with this. I'm hoping it does, anyway. I need my expression to speak for me. I look back at both of them like there's something I want to say, and I'm thinking how best to phrase it. They both look at me, then look at each other. They simultaneously blink and look back at me. *"Yes?"* they both seem to be saying with their expressions. *"What is it? Let's lay this out on the table."*

I glide my lips together, moistening them. "Well, thank God for Helena," I finally say. "My mother deserves to rest in peace, and the rest of us deserve to live in peace." I deliver that last line right as I reach for their dirty silverware. Then I pivot and walk away from them.

I T'S AN IMPULSIVE decision — an effort to take charge of
something I might be able to wrap my head around, something
I might be able to organize into a nice folder labeled complete. I'd
obtained Margo's address the time I had the muffins delivered.
The house is on Sinclair Avenue, the section of town that's gone
through major transformations in the last few years. I park in front
of a beige Spanish-style house, thickly stuccoed like a heavily frosted
cake, and knock on the richly stained front door. Two quick raps.

The door is opened by a lifeguard. Paulus has on a red and
white striped tank top over bright white swimming trunks that
reach to his knees. Water shoes with slip-resistant soles are on his
feet, and a pair of binoculars hang around his neck. I remember
the binoculars from a previous outfit, but I can't remember which
one. He is holding them to his face and looks through them at my
feet then lifts his head to my face, still peering through the lenses.

"Amethyst," he says without surprise, as if I show up every
day at his door. He leaves the door open and walks away, back to
whatever he had been doing.

I step hesitantly into a foyer. Backpacks and jackets, umbrellas,
and capes hang from the hooks. The house is clean and smelling
of disinfectant, but messy with newspapers, folders, and unpacked
shopping bags littering the counter space. An empty box blocks my
path from the foyer to the living area, where an ironing board is set
up and a dozen or more outfits are folded over the back of the sofa.

"Margo?" I holler across the house, rooted to my spot. I follow
her response down another hallway and into a room. She's tucking a fitted sheet around the mattress of a twin bed. The room is
painted light blue, and everything in it matches. Margo straightens,
surprised to see me in her home. She looks down at her housecoat
and smooths a hand over it. It's four o'clock in the afternoon, so
I imagine she hasn't changed out of it all day.

I lay the cardboard box of muffins on a simple wood dresser
next to a book on Greek mythology. "I was in the neighborhood." I
smile meekly, reaching down to tuck the opposite side of the fitted
sheet in. Together we make the little bed, smoothing and tucking,
making small talk as we go.

Afterward, we move to the living room, where Margo resumes
her ironing and I pick at clutter. I take it upon myself to straighten
papers, fluff pillows, and hang the ironed clothes. It's as if we've
become some kind of tag team, digging in and accomplishing

what so obviously needs to be accomplished. In just a few hours, I have her house whipped into shape, and I feel like I've had a full afternoon of therapy.

At six o'clock Margo comes right out and asks me to start frying the hamburgers that are thawing in the refrigerator, and I march right into the adjoining kitchen and locate what I need as if I had organized the cabinets and drawers myself.

The three of us sit at the table over hamburgers and canned black-eyed peas and fruit punch poured into plastic happy meal cups. It's the most unorthodox meal I've ever seen, and yet it's so humble I bow my head in thanks when Paulus starts to pray.

"Our Father, Who does art in heaven," he begins. Ten minutes later he's finally done and I bite into a cold piece of meat and take a sip of the warm beverage.

Margo and I are working side-by-side, her washing, me drying, when the phone rings at seven.

"That'll be my brother checking on us."

I hear snatches of the conversation. It doesn't sound confrontational. "I have a friend over," I hear her say. "I have to go."

"My brother," she says returning to the kitchen. "Checking in."

Paulus strolls back into the room. His binoculars are stuck to his face. "You need to be a helper to my uncle Jeremy," he says to me. I remember Paulus telling me about the sixth day of creation or something like that, and I imagine this Uncle Jeremy and myself cloaked in fig leaves standing in a blinding light.

"Where does this Uncle Jeremy live, Paulus?"

"3985 Briarwood Lane. Flannery Cove, Georgia 45689."

"And what does Uncle Jeremy do?"

"He's a counselor."

I look to Margo. "Kid might be on to something. I could use a counselor."

She starts to open her mouth but is interrupted by Paulus. "Recreational bather in trouble. I'll be performing an emergency water rescue."

"Please don't fill the bathtub up, Paulus," his mother yells, exhaustion wearing down her every word, as her son scurries back into another part of the house.

"I better get going." I glance at the clock on the wall. It's stuck on 11:40.

I can hear the bathtub water running down the hall. "Grab on to the lifeline," Paulus is hollering to an imaginary victim. "I'm coming in."

H AILEY IS THE one who gets the mail the day it finally comes. I can tell she's deflated. She's sitting out back on the bench swing that my grandpa hung some forty-odd years ago on the large branch of the gigantic oak we've always called Atlas, because it carries the weight of the swing and, metaphorically, our lives. Solid teak, sturdy and stable, this swing is. And discreet. This swing has held me, comforted me, and kept all my confidences. From my mother sitting beside me reading *B is for Betsy* as I mouthed the words I'd memorized, to Becky, Susan, and I playing on it like we were on a ride at Disney — *"All aboard. Buckle up. We are not, we repeat not, responsible for cameras and personal devices."* — to sitting and pondering where my husband was so many evenings and where my marriage was headed.

Hailey's eyes are red. The tip of her nose is as well. She says nothing, just hands me the envelope.

The bank intends to file foreclosure.

"Okay," Scott breathes a heavy sigh, "So, now we begin."

The way he says it, it's as if the two of us are belted into a seat on a roller coaster track that reaches upward, the little car that holds us climbing and chugging along, slowly running out of energy and speed. Despite the grim picture, I'm not altogether disheartened by it if the car holds the two of us snuggly and comfortably — and lands softly.

"We have thirty days to contest this," he says. "We can buy some time."

I start to ask about all my options, what grounds I can contest on.

"I'm due in court in thirty minutes, Amy. I'm going to have to let you go, but I'll get my secretary on this first thing in the morning."

I hang up more dejected than when I'd first dialed the phone. The little car on the roller coaster flies off the track.

From: Helena1098@myFCcourier.com
To: UnveiledI@officeweb.com
Subject: Investigation

**It is now May. Please report something. A phone call from you would be nice at this point. I have some questions.**

Above my head, Madame Bienve taps out my torment. *One, two three, four. You must do more! Five, six, seven, eight. It is getting late!*

I pick up the phone and dial Dad. He answers on the second ring. "Sparkle."

"Dad." I run my hand over the surface of my desk and take a deep breath. "I was wondering. I just wanted." My head is throbbing, but I plunder on. "I would like to have Mom's old dishes."

"Mom's old dishes? Your mother's?"

"Yes. My mother's." I say through clenched teeth. "I have very little of hers."

"I thought you had some jewelry," he says as if the few pieces of broken chains and mismatched clip-on earrings should account for something, should be enough to satisfy me.

Silence fills the space between us.

"I'll check with Helena."

I hang up on him. *Dear God*, I've hung up on Dad, just silenced him mid-conversation. I'm going to lose my dad just like my home if I don't get my head in the game. *Not a game, Amy. That might be the problem. You need to get that straight in your head.*

I lost my dad once when I was nine. I thought it was the end of life as I knew it — something very akin to my current feeling. Becky and I had been at the Carroll County Fair with Dad. It was a warm Sunday afternoon, the final day of the carnival. We'd been walking around together in the livestock tent, but somewhere along the way Dad stopped to talk to someone, and Becky and I kept on walking. We didn't wander far, just over to where the 4H kids were gathered. We'd stopped and tasted the sample of peach currant, and I began to look for Dad since I knew he liked peach. But he was nowhere to be found. The drop in my heart was like an untethered elevator going from the twenty-first floor to the basement.

In the twenty-five minutes it took to locate my dad, standing by the sign reading Revolutionary Row, transfixed by the woman weaving a basket, I was an orphan. Becky kept muttering, "He's here. The fair will be gone tomorrow," as if we just had to wait for the grounds to empty and we'd be able to locate the lone man surrounded by desolation. That was over twelve hours away. Even I, in my panic, put that together. Orphan: nowhere to go, no one who would love me. No one in the world who would even know me.

In twenty-five minutes, at the tender age of nine, I realized what it meant to really know someone. To this day, no one knows me like my father. No one has traveled inside of my heart all my days. No one has carried me inside of theirs. Just my father — the one I basically just took scissors to and cut out of the family portrait.

I listen to the crowd outside my office door. It sounds like there are more than usual for so late in the afternoon, but I don't have the patience to deal with anyone right now.

I return to my spreadsheet: the status of sales, historical versus projected. It's far less demanding than Helena's hysterics, but I still hear Helena in my head. I'll call her when I feel like it. Which will be never!

An hour later I take Otis out the back door for a quick walk then start to clean my office. Afterward, I unload boxes with determination, thinking about the reality of placing a call to Helena. *How?* I fluff the flattened pillow Otis has been lying on as I stand in the middle of my office and wonder how to keep track of this stuff without proper storage and then my cell phone vibrates. Scott Warner's name appears on the display. I'm not sure I have the patience or energy to deal with this mess right now either. *So many messes!*

"I have a plan." He gets right to the point. "We're going to apply for a modification program for you. It's doubtful we'll get anywhere with it at the end of the day," he warns me, "but it will buy more time."

I'm agreeable to anything, but he hears the exasperation, me not rising to the challenge.

"Will you do me a favor, Amy?"

"Okay," I say warily.

117

"I volunteer at Habitat for Humanity. We have a frame-in this Saturday. I want you to come."

"I don't know," I stammer. "I mean, I—"

"It's part of your bill. I require it."

"Ha. Where and what time?"

"Hold on a sec." He puts the phone down and I hear some sort of whimpering in the background.

*He's got a baby?*

"Sorry. New puppy. Got him from the pound yesterday."

"Aww. You like dogs?"

"And cats, and pigs, and horses, and cows. Grew up on a farm. I would've become a veterinarian if my dad hadn't lost the farm to foreclosure and ignited a different fire in me."

"Scott," I say, reaching into my purse and finding it folded up, just where I left it. "Do you know a fourteen-letter word meaning," I clear my throat and continue, "canine term for a broad head with a short muzzle?"

"Brachycephalic," he says as if everyone knows that, as if it weren't the most random question ever. "B-r-a-c-h-y-c-e-p-h-a-l-i-c."

I pencil it in, and it works perfectly with ten down and three across.

"What'd you name him?" My voice is raspy with sentiment.

*So what? The man likes dogs and knows vocabulary.*

I am absolutely not going to lose my composure and swoon over my lawyer. Not happening. The likelihood on a scale of one to ten? Zero!

Realistically, a four.

Eight and a half, tops.

"Patere." He sounds out the word with an emphasis on the last syllable, rhyming it with the word fear. "P-a-t-e-r-e."

"Patere? Huh? Does he look French?"

"He kind of does," Scott says in a *now that you mention it* tone. "Nah," he chuckles. "Just like to say this is my pup, Patere. Corny. I know."

I laugh immediately, remembering a wooden dog with four strings that Susan and I used to play with. One pull of the right string could make him stand up, hike up a back leg, or sprawl out with all four paws to the side. Nana had given it to me as an end-of-school-year treat and had given Susan… I don't remember what Susan had been given, but we both played with that dog and pretended he was a show dog and we were his handlers.

"You could have named him Peeve. Like, meet my pet, Peeve."

"I could've," he agrees. I can tell he's awed, either by the fact that I'm playing the game or that my name was actually better. "If I had a lion, I'd name him Dandy. Meet my dandy lion."

"My panda, Monium. My cat, Scan."

"If I had a chicken, I'd name him Magnet and take him to all the hottest clubs," he says. "That way I'd always have my chick, Magnet."

"And I'd say, 'Move along and take your bull, Malarkey.'"

"I'll see you Saturday after you close the café, Amy." He ends our banter with a soft goodbye.

Best phrase ever: *"I'll see you Saturday."* Worst phrase ever: *"I doubt we'll get anywhere."*

# THIRTEEN

THE FLANNERY COVE High School graduation ceremony is held on Friday night. We take up two rows. Dad and Helena sit beside Deaton again, who has brought Kristlyn. Bradley and I sit behind them while I lean forward trying to monitor their conversation. Five minutes before the graduates march down the aisle, Greg and Sherri slip in beside us. Greg seats himself right beside Bradley and crosses one leg over the other at the knee.

Greg folds up his program into a coil and reaches across Bradley, tapping me on the knee with it, then turns his attention to Bradley. "Greg Hollander." He holds out a large, tanned hand. Bradley reaches for it. The dark, curly hairs on Bradley's knuckles seem excessive. A ridiculous thought. What's wrong with me? *So shallow!*

I wish I had paid more attention to his white shirt and suggested something that would have brought out more color in his face. A nice salmon could have changed his hair color from its dishwater hue to a rich golden oak. Greg isn't a tall man, but he has perfected the larger-than-life presence that diminishes everyone around him. It's all I can do not to jab Bradley's side and whisper to sit up straighter.

*At least he used hair gel and made a bit of an effort* I think to myself as the lights dim, and Bradley reaches for my hand.

When the ceremony is over, Greg slaps a flattened palm on my father's back. "Ralls, my man. We know how to grow 'em, eh Buddy?"

"How 'bout our girl, Ames?" Greg says to me.

"She's a gem. Just like her mother," I say pointedly.

"Pardon the pun, Amethyst," Bradley says, leading us straight up to the joke and introducing us all to it, instead of just letting it stand on its own.

Greg cocks one eyebrow at me but doesn't comment.

"Whatta you do, Brad-lee?" He pronounces his name like it's two put together. It makes Bradley sound like a martial arts expert. Maybe he can karate chop Greg's head right off his shoulders.

I turn to Bradley and look him over. His hair gel has dried, and his cowlick stands straight up, stiff as the peak of a whipped egg white.

"I'm in investing," Bradley says. "Stocks, bonds, portfolios, all that stuff other people find boring." Bradley just can't help himself. He just can't play it up.

*Please don't say numbers guy.*

"Numbers guy."

Greg tilts his head back, looking at Bradley with an analytical eye. "Raleigh, you all feel like a late celebration dinner at the Ale House?"

"He's a bit of a narcissist, is he not?" Bradley says to me on the way to the Ale House.

"A bit," I say, not wanting to talk about it.

"I can't imagine what you ever saw in him."

*Flash, flair, danger and drive, excitement, exhilaration, and passion,* I want to shout, but I imagine Bradley would shake his head, purse his lips, and compare it to a risky investment. *Fine mess all that got you in, just like all those clients of Bernie Madoff's.*

I stare ahead at the darkness spread out before us. I'm agitated, and he knows it. Bradley grips the wheel tightly, his eyes focused straight ahead. He takes his eyes off the road momentarily, patting my hand lying on the seat between us. "I'll never hurt you the way he did, Amy."

*Whoa!* My mind skitters all over the place. I've known Bradley for a brief time. He is a date, nothing more. And his words are comforting, but he doesn't even know how Greg hurt me. He doesn't question or concern himself, he just accepts that it happened. He's a numbers man, not a details man, after all. But for all he knows I called it quits because my husband trimmed the hedges too short.

*Comforting.* Do I really feel comforted by Bradley? Is it my dad I long to feel comforted by and can't be because of my own doing, my own fears about being around him? My fears of slipping, of being found out — my fears of destroying him?

*No. Of course not.* Bradley *is* comforting. He *is* manly. He is… I purse my lips, concentrating, but I can't think of any more descriptions. And why am I even thinking about my father anyway when I'm on a date?

*Because I'm thinking of my father every second of every day.*

Time with Bradley is easy, uncomplicated, at least for the most part. There's no one else in my life I can honestly say that about at the moment. *Don't rock the boat,* I constantly remind myself. *Don't overthink it. Just go with it.*

C ORY OFFERED TO take over Saturday morning, so I leave a sleeping Hailey in a heap under her floral quilt and head to a part of town that's already fully awake, maybe never fully went to sleep. The sun is starting to rise, but I can already tell its brightness will never completely illuminate over the cracked, dingy sidewalks, peeling paint, and overgrown yards strewn with debris, toys, and broken-down cars.

"Sleep well?" Scott asks.

"Yup."

"Good. You'll need your energy for what I have planned for you." Scott turns and heads toward the concrete slab where people are standing looking at blueprints.

*Wait. Was that suggestive?*

He turns and winks at me as if he's read my mind and is answering.

"Everyone, this is Amy. Amy, this is Mike, Colin, Beverly, Pat, Sammy, and Debbie." He points everyone out, and I give one wave.

Scott puts me with Debbie and hands both of us hammers. We work side-by-side companionably, Debbie singing along to the radio, dancing while she hammers in rhythm. I use the peaceful time to practice an impending phone conversation with Helena regarding the investigation. I keep tossing her bits and pieces, but she's made it clear she wants more, and soon. By mid-morning, another woman, three kids in tow, shows up to join us.

"Wanda, I want you to help Amy and Debbie," Scott says. "Blake, Sarah, and Tony follow me." He points to the three kids.

Debbie is up on a ladder when she turns and sees Wanda. She squeals and jumps down from it. "Girl. How is it? You gotta tell me all about it."

"It's the best thing since cinnamon met apple pie. Better than Motown music on a Saturday night."

"Is it better than an afternoon nap during a summer rainstorm? A good man that loves a house full of kids?"

"It's good, but I don't know if it's as good as all that," Wanda says, and they double over in laughter. Must be some private joke between them or something, but I stand there grinning like I understand it, like a dimwit that just smiles at everything.

"Seriously," Wanda says, "it's the best thing to ever happen to us. My babies go to bed every night — *a real bed* — I ain't just talkin' 'bout no pallet on the floor."

"Can't wait," Debbie whispers, more to herself than anyone else. "This one's mine," she says running her hand over bare wood.

Blake, Sara, and Tony are disheartened to find they aren't leaving to go back to their new air-conditioned home with the swing set in the backyard right after lunch.

"Mo-om," Sara, the little five-year-old with braided hair and tennis shoes that light up with every stomp of her foot, says. "I'm soooo tired." Her brothers join in the protest too.

It's not just Wanda that chastises them for their lack of enthusiasm. There's a team spirit, a camaraderie among everyone. It's as if they've been part of a group for a long time, and they're comfortable with each other. It takes a village, they say.

Scott turns to Blake, who's probably six. Blake is hanging off of his mom's arms, literally pulling at her like she's a lever. "What'd I tell you about that whining last weekend?"

Blake stops to think. "That you'd fire me from the job, and I wouldn't get no more grape Slurpees?"

"That's right. Now run along and finish up what you were doing earlier, then we'll take a trip to the store."

All three kids run back to their tasks. Scott grabs a toolbox and turns to take it back to his truck. I follow along and plop myself down on the tailgate. He grabs two bottles of water from a cooler nearby and moves the toolbox he's just set down so he can join me. He's wearing a short-sleeve shirt and the muscles in his forearms strain. I glance toward them. "I thought you said you didn't work out."

"I said I don't go to the gym." He wipes the sweat on his forehead with a bandanna from his back pocket. "I work out by doing things that have a purpose. "He reaches over and takes hold of a strand of my hair that's come loose from my braid. "Paint. The ends of your hair are dipped in white paint." He wipes it with his bandana and tucks it behind my ear. He stares at me, and I at him. "Definitely sea-glass green," he says, looking in my eyes, then running an index finger down the bridge of my nose. "On your nose too. There's more paint on you than on the wall." He takes a deep breath, wipes his finger on his bandana, and takes a swig of his water.

"So you make all your clients work on Habitat Houses?"

"No. Just you. The rest of 'em I squeeze enough money out of to keep the lights on."

I look down at the dirt on the ground. "You wanted me to hear their stories. To realize how fortunate I am."

"I just wanted you to pay your bill. Pull your weight. If you got something else out of it, then it sounds like that's a bonus."

He grabs a ball cap from the back pocket of his jeans, whips it into shape, and places it on his head.

"You're a regular magician. What else you got back there?"

The muscles on his tanned arms flinch again as he picks up a ladder propped against a tree. "Tricks of the trade, Home Girl. Just tricks of the trade." He winks and walks away.

Wanda and Debbie both call out to me. "Amy, over here. We need your help." I hold my head up as I stride back toward them imagining I'm the newest member of the village.

D EATON DOESN'T SEEM to know what to do with his energy lately. He bounces from foot to foot like he's standing on hot pavement.

I'm just back from a spin class — thirsty, sticky, smelly. I just want to open the café, get things going, and run home for a quick shower then return.

"Amy," he says, sprinting over before I can open the café door. His eyes are wide and sparkly, and his face is flushed with color.

I stare at him.

"You were born here, right?"

"Yeeessss," I say, drawing the word out, unsure of whether to be honest or not.

"That means your mother had an obstetrician here in Flannery Cove. I know privacy laws have changed and stuff, but that doctor would know if your mom was pregnant again," he says. "We just need to find that doctor."

I study him. He's caught the investigative bug, and I know what that's like. You do things you wouldn't normally do for the sake of the case.

"I, um, I think I'm going to have to just drop this, Deaton. Drop the whole thing and let Helena find someone else to prove my mother's fate to her."

He blinks as if I've come for his eyes with my fingernails. He finally speaks. "What are you saying? This is *your* responsibility. This is *your* prerogative."

"Helena wants a phone call," I tell him. "She'll know my voice. I can't call and discuss this with her. It's over."

He looks to the side, considering. "She said this?"

"Yes, in her latest email. It's not an unusual request," I say. "At some point, most people do want to speak. If not face to face, then at least on the phone. People know the nature of my business is best kept anonymous, but I get it… at least a phone call."

"Who does Helena think Unveiled Investigations is?" He asks.

"A team. A company." I wave my hands to try to come up with words. "Just you know… a group." I'm honestly amazed I've been able to keep her placated this long. The extreme anonymity thing is mostly for the general public, not my own clients. Except when they're Helena.

He's silent for a moment, aside from a few exhales and throat murmurs, as thoughts speed through his head like the microfiche reel. "I guess I could call her. It's just…well, I'd need to look over your previous correspondence. I'd need to be very familiar with everything she knows so far, everything you know."

"Yes," I say. "I suppose. But Deaton, this is getting out of hand." I blow my bangs with my breath, exasperated.

"Well, we're in it now, Ames. And it's my fault. I talked you into this when you wanted to turn it down. I guess I bear some responsibility here." He makes a final determination. "I'll make the call."

"There's no chance she'll recognize your voice?"

"I don't think so. There was so much noise in the theater the other night. We could barely hear each other. Geez, Ames, I can't believe I'm saying this. Who does this kind of crazy stuff?"

"Investigators," I say. "It's all in a day's work," I add like it's common practice among the best of the best. "But just for the record, I'm not in favor of this."

He's already started walking back across the street, but I call out, *"Remember that!"*

# *FOURTEEN*

"**I** CAN'T SAY I wasn't warned. Mary saw it in him straight away, but I wouldn't listen." I pull my legs up off the floor and cross them in my chair as I pat the space across the booth. "Come sit down. Take five minutes."

Hailey finishes wiping the tabletop then sits across from me.

"Daddy never met Mary though, did he?"

"No." I remember all the times I wanted Greg to make the trip to Atlanta for a visit with my supposed former English teacher. How much fun I thought the four of us would have together, Greg and Ian being very similar in their views and their manner, their cockiness. But Greg always used the weekends I went away as an opportunity to kick back with the other guys at the fire department. "No, they never actually met, but Mary just knew. She saw his pictures, heard enough about him from me." I shrug and continue, "Saw right through the whole thing."

"So she tried to warn you? I mean, like how?"

I'm trying to think back. It was all so long ago, it seems like a lifetime to me now. "I'd guess the fact that he never came with me to meet her said something. She frowned a lot when I talked about him."

I glance away from Hailey's questioning gaze, and mine settles more comfortably on the booth's upholstery next to her. Just plain, red vinyl, not the face of the daughter I love. It helps me remember with more clarity.

There had been a bit of a blow-up that last visit before our wedding. Mary had turned her mouth down at everything I said and wiped at tears when she flipped through our engagement pictures. I'd finally laid them all aside and turned to her.

"Are you not happy for me?" I asked. The question caught her off guard. I don't think she realized she'd been crying. She twisted the chain at her neck and tried to form a smile.

"I'm just..." She never finished the sentence.

Ian had tossed down the newspaper he'd been reading. "Not this again," he said to her, not yelling, but quite stern. "Let the girl marry the bloke if that's what makes her happy. People should be happy. End of story."

There was a palpable undercurrent, like this was a conversation they'd had before but not necessarily about Greg and me.

"She's just so young. I'm not sure you can know what makes you happy when you're so young," Mom answered him.

"Hello, I'm right here." I waved my hands between the two of them, so they'd stop having a conversation about me that didn't include my input. I leaned forward on the sofa and patted Mary's hand reassuringly. "I do know."

"So there ya have it," Ian said, picking the paper back up and shaking it out.

Mary just nodded and stared out the living room window, over the rooftop of the building behind theirs. "I hope you do," she said, then slid her eyes over toward Ian who was fully engrossed in the news in front of him by then. "But if you decide even at the very last minute that this isn't it, promise me you'll run in the opposite direction."

I didn't answer. I didn't think it required an answer. I figured Mary was just saying one of those things mothers say before a wedding, and I knew she was feeling especially sentimental since the only part she could partake of in the entire ceremony was flipping through the photos after the fact.

"Promise me," she said again, insistently.

Ian stood up about that time and headed toward the coat rack by the front door. "It's settled then," he said. "Let's all go round to the pub for a pint and a toast."

Mary and I followed behind before he slammed out the door without us, never getting back to the subject at hand. Except for when we were sitting at the booth in the pub and Ian was talking with some guys and Mary and I had reached a lull in our conversation. She and I were watching a young couple sitting at a booth across the aisle. "She's my best friend for God's sake, Darryl," we overheard the woman say. "I never knew you found her so attractive."

Mary had leaned into me and whispered, "Remember this — marry the guy who never even notices there are other women in the world."

I think about my daughter. The only advice I've ever felt qualified to give her on the subject was, "Marry a man with a family tendency toward narrow shoulders. You'll thank me when you're in the throes of childbirth."

I realize Hailey is still waiting for my answer. I meet her eyes again and think about how best to summarize the memory I've just revisited.

"I think she tried to warn me of the end of the story before it began," I tell her. "But I refused to listen."

My phone begins to ring in my back pocket. I reach back and pull it out, squinting at the screen. Hailey looks at her phone, checking the time. "Breaks over, I guess. Slave driver," she mumbles back to me, and I swat her on the butt.

"Only a few more weeks and you're done with me."

I press the button to answer my phone before it stops ringing.

"Amy!" A voice bellows down the line as if he's pronouncing me the winner of something.

"Mr. Warner!" I match his enthusiasm, but I'm trying to keep it professional, emphasizing the "Mister." Wondering if he'll correct me, or if we're just attorney and client.

"Mr. Warner?" he laughs. "Surely I'm at least Scott to you. I'm just checking in. Any bites on the house?"

"Slow season." I mimic the nasally business tone of my new agent.

"Well, we've got the loan modification paperwork ready, so that'll buy a little time."

I nod, even though he can't see me.

"Amy, have you come to terms with this? I mean, do you have a plan if we can't save or sell the house?"

"Honestly? No. And no. This was my Nana's house, Scott. *My Nana's!*"

"I'm working on it." He exhales a long sigh. "If we can stall it long enough for it to sell then at least you'd have the money to…" His sentence trails off. He knows that's a positive outcome, but not the desired one.

I feel ridiculous. This man is my lawyer. I shouldn't be whining to him. Surely he doesn't care whose house it is or was or how old it is or how many memories it holds. He doesn't know or care about Mighty Atlas and the teak swing, the Westfields and their air filters, the cobblestone that the rubber tip of my heel broke off in. He doesn't know that my identity, my ability to keep breathing, is all tied up in that house — particularly the closet wall in Hailey's room where I scribbled in crayon at five years of age words that somewhat resembled "I love my family," beside drawn stick figures of us all together, holding hands. No one would understand that closet wall is the only family portrait I have.

Except Scott does seem to care about all those things. I can hear in his voice the concern, the desire to do more and make it all right for me. "Thank you for all you've done. I need to pay you some sort of retainer or something." I politely try to bring the conversation back to the business at hand.

"I suppose we should discuss that at some point and sign some paperwork."

"I can get with you right away and do that," I say eagerly, as if I've been looking for something to do with all my money.

"I'm out of town the rest of the week and next week is full too. Let me check my schedule." He begins to mumble to himself, "Due in court Wednesday, appointments all day Thursday, Monday no, Tuesday… hmm, no. Any chance you could meet me next Saturday to review things?"

I'm supposed to work the café next Saturday morning. "Um," I stammer. "Let me check *my* schedule. Open café Saturday morning. How about that afternoon, four-ish?"

"I'm kinda booked up that afternoon," he says, clearing his throat. "I'm free that evening."

*That evening?*

"Barrister's on Caldwell Street? Seven o'clock?"

"Um. Okay… I can do that."

"To sign some papers," he reiterates.
"To sign some papers, yes."

W ITH SHAKY HANDS, I email Helena and set up a conference call with "the investigator working her case." Deaton
has one day to review everything in the files and all the notes I've
jotted down, and Thursday evening after work I walk over to the
book store at the arranged time, and he dials the phone and puts
the speaker on. After three rings, it's my father who answers.

"Hello." His voice lifts at the end of the word. He's cheerful,
expectant.

"Yes, er, this is um." Deaton looks at me, and I know what he's
thinking. He didn't create an actual name for himself. "I'm looking
for a Helena Delgado," he finally says.

"This is Helena," Helena chimes in from the background. "We
have you on speakerphone. My... Mrs. Chadwick's husband... er,
former husband... he is here as well."

"Raulerson Chadwick," my father says.

I feel sick. And my arms — Dear God, the itch is so severe it's
amazing its path doesn't show on my skin like the lines on a map.

"Yes, this is Unveiled Investigations calling, Mrs. Delgado,"
Deaton says. "As planned. Remember?"

I roll my eyes at him and he shrugs, then swats me away so
he can focus on the task at hand. He begins to rifle through his
notes. "So, Mrs. Delgado. Mr. Chadwick. First, let me say I'm so
sorry for your loss."

There is complete silence on the other end. They're wondering
if he's telling them he found a body. Besides the fact that it's not
protocol to tell fiancé number two you're sorry for the loss of wife
number one.

He rifles through papers like he's looking for something.
Probably a way out of this. Sweat is beading on his brow. "Um.
So. This is where we're at," he begins. "We've ruled out one
unidentified female passenger on the train that evening. We
are working on ruling out or confirming the second. She was a
white female, same age group as your um, wife, Mr. Chadwick
and she was pregnant."

There is an intake of breath. It's Helena's.

"Pregnant?" My father says. "No. That can't be. Caroline couldn't have been pregnant."

There's a bit of murmuring on their end and I hear Helena say to him, "We don't know what's truth or fiction anymore. Maybe she only told you she did that."

Deaton doesn't even seem to register she's talking. "So, we're following that lead and, well, we're just gonna keep following all these leads, and we're gonna find out what we need to know here because that's what we do," he says nervously.

I close my eyes and shake my head. This is going downhill fast. There's so much awkward silence. None of them know how to keep this ball rolling.

"Oh! And we've located the wife of the deceased engineer who was driving that night."

I whip my head up.

My dad and Helena remain quiet. Well, what's there to say? The wife of a dead engineer has nothing to do with anything. What can they possibly ask Deaton about her when she wasn't even there?

"So, yeah. We're working that angle as well," Deaton says. I slice my hand across my neck. *Cease! Desist!*

I can't bear this anymore. I want to just say, "Daddy, it's me. Can you come get me?" But, of course, I can't. He's not standing tranquilly at the fair being mesmerized by a woman and her talented hands at work, waiting on me. And I'm not his innocent little girl, lost.

"Mister," Helena begins, and immediately Deaton interrupts her.

"Yes, I'm here," he says. "I thought I had accidentally lost you. A bit of a bad connection. I want you to know, Mrs. Delgado and Mr. Chadwick, that we are working this case and uncovering a lot of things. Very interesting things," he reiterates. "We're going to have a breakthrough soon, I'm sure."

As soon as the call is ended, I jump off the couch and begin pacing frantically. Deaton is practically green with fear. His shirt is soaked with perspiration. The tips of his hair are even damp.

"I'm sorry, Amy," he says. "I totally screwed that up one side and down the other. I needed to say something, and I couldn't think of anything. I think that was the worst thing I've ever done in my life." He drops his head into his hands, shaking it back and forth.

I'm still pacing, biting at my clenched fist.

Finally, he looks up. "I was like a deer in the headlights. This just shows how little we've accomplished here."

I have nothing to say in response, and we both stay in our fraught positions for a few moments.

"We're so out of our league—" I finally start to try to pull some coherent thoughts together and form a sentence.

"We need to get busy and make some serious headway on this," He interrupts, not exactly with exuberance, not exactly with defeat.

BALLERINA BELLA'S MOM, Nikki, has come through surgery successfully and is set to start eight weeks of radiation next week, so Deaton and I meet at the café early Sunday morning and the two of us, along with Kristlyn, Hailey, Jarod, and three other dance moms, form an assembly line, following recipes and assembling more casseroles to be frozen and delivered.

Midway through, Bradley shows up unexpectedly. It momentarily throws me. Bradley acts like we're a couple and have been for twenty-some-odd-years, already well past the intensity and excitement of being so. But then I look at Deaton and Kristlyn and try to muster my enthusiasm to match theirs. Coupling is good, it's what we set out to accomplish. Checked, and off the to-do list.

*Barristers at seven o'clock? Obviously, you don't know your own power.*

I file Scott Warner away, to be taken out later and mulled over. I scurry around like I can't think, can't hear, can't process anything anyone's asking me. Too busy for chit-chat. "Busy, busy, busy," I even chant once when Deaton is heading my way, and I do a complete circle back to the kitchen.

When the last casserole is stacked in the freezer and everyone else has dispersed, Kristlyn excuses herself to use the restroom. Bradley is washing dishes, and I walk to my office to get the mop. I scoot boxes out of the way, grab the mop, and turn around and run into Deaton standing right behind me.

"Oh, dear God." I hold a hand to my heart. "I need that supply closet space so I'll have somewhere to store stuff like this," I say, holding up the mangled yarn mop like a puppet. I know what Deaton's going to ask me about, and I don't want to discuss it. I'm so done with this!

He ignores the mop. "Have you found out anything more about your mother? Whether she could have been pregnant?"

I look beyond his shoulder, reminding him we don't have time for this discussion at the moment. At some point I know I'm going to have to put some meat on the bones I've been tossing his way, but the whole point of letting him assist me was to see how far someone could get in the investigation on their own. This truth will find its way to him though; it doesn't require much digging. I'd spoken to Mary right after Detective Thompson had informed us of the second unidentified woman's pregnancy.

"I had my tubes tied after I had you," She'd whispered down the phone line, trying to soften her harsh answer to my unvoiced question. I couldn't help picturing my young, tormented mother lying in a hospital bed, grabbing a night nurse by the collar, and begging her to help make sure nothing like me ever happened to her again.

"Did Dad know?" I'd said strongly as if that image didn't affect me in the least.

"Not right away. Later, yes. We had a big blow-up about it before... before I left."

I thought back to the argument I'd heard late one night, just a day or two before the accident. I'd woken up to use the bathroom and stood in my bedroom doorway hearing random words and then the crash that had sent me scurrying back to my covers. The next morning there were shards of glass on the carpet of my parent's bedroom and a red wine stain dribbled in a thin line down to the baseboard and pooled there like a large exclamation point. That stain still showed through the new coat of paint that had been brushed over it later, a reminder of things that were never covered up properly.

"My mother could not have been pregnant. *That* I know for certain," I whisper through clenched teeth to Deaton at the same time I clutch my mop and brush past him. I pause in the doorway and turn back around to him. "It wasn't her," I announce before he can confirm what this means. And then I turn around and leave him to connect the dots by himself.

Forty-five minutes later, Bradley and I stand at the café door and usher Deaton and Kristlyn out. I still cling to my upturned mop, occupying my hands. It stands between Bradley and me like a very tall sheepdog. "Thank you so much," I say to both of them and Bradley shakes his head in agreement, thoroughly invested in the endeavor. We look like some old, boring parents the kids stopped by to help before going back to their busy, exciting lives and leaving us to stay behind and mop.

And that's what we do. We stand there silently watching them as Deaton puts his arm around Kristlyn and she leans into him. She must have said something funny because he throws his head back and laughs and she stops and looks at him and starts laughing too. They laugh all the way across the street and into the bookstore, and I imagine they laugh up the stairs to the loft and right on into each other's arms.

"Welp." Bradley finally turns away, rocks back on his heels, and clasps his hands to indicate we've stared long enough. "Let's finish up here and go back to my place," he says. I wonder if the two of us can find something to laugh that hard about. Can Bradley put his arm around me and throw his head back? Can I make him lose himself in me and delight in the process?

"Okay," I say, determined to try. Determined to beat Deaton at this dating thing.

I'VE BEEN TO Bradley's house before. Today though, I'm looking at it more critically. I think it's because Scott asked me if I had a plan, a place to go if or when my own house is taken from me. Bradley's house could be my plan B, I suppose. It's all I've got. *An awful thought.*

But Bradley doesn't even know yet that my house might be foreclosed on. He knows it's for sale, but I imagine he thinks it's a strategic move on my part to capitalize on the equity he assumes I have in it. Equity I did have before I gambled on it.

Bradley's house is a typical spec house in a typical newer neighborhood. All the trees were cut down when the land was cleared and graded, so the yards are comprised of matching small shrubs and mulch. There are no old brick walkways, only smooth white concrete drives with minivans and mid-sized sedans parked up and down the street. No trees with names, no growth chart measurements beside the utility room door, no lingering scents of family dinners, and celebratory bouquets, and baby shampoo — the fragrances of family life. Inside Bradley's home, the décor is sparse and the air is odorless. I try to mentally place my eggplant-colored sectional in the room and imagine my curtains in place of the vinyl blinds that hang there now. I'm unable to figure out how we're going to work the sectional into this room, but if we have to flip ourselves over the back of it every time we get on or off of it, that'll have to do.

"Those blinds would be happier in an uptown office," I say.

"What?" Bradley calls back to me from the kitchen. "Lemon in your tea?"

"Sure," I say, not repeating my statement. He doesn't notice. There is a picture of Bradley's mom and dad in a frame on top of the shelf above the TV that his stereo sits on, and another picture of Bradley and a few guys — I recognize his friend Thom — on skis in the snow.

I pick up another frame with a very attractive couple in it. "Who is this?

"Came with the frame," he says, laughing.

*Aha! A laugh. I can work with this. Say something to make it funnier, and we could get mileage out of it for hours.* But I just smile and place the frame back on the shelf. What can be said about a simple, gold frame?

Bradley assembles everything he needs to grill hamburgers and carries them outside to his backyard. There is a small patio slab poured just outside the kitchen nook with his new patio furniture and a small grill set up. He spends a few minutes cleaning the racks on the grill and gives me a thumbs-up through the window when he's done. I smile and point in the direction of the bathroom down the hall. "Be right back," I mouth.

Instead of using the half bath down the hall, I venture into the one in Bradley's bedroom. After putting the toilet seat down and doing what I came to do, I stand at the sink and wash my hands with the little sliver of soap that's laid out like a miniature surfboard on the dish. I splash at the little whiskers collected in the pool of water around the drain then turn and see Bradley's shower behind me. I'm curious about what products he uses, and I want to pull back the curtain and see what it looks like in there.

What if he has a camera in here? *Well, if I'm dating a man that has a camera in his bathroom then I've got bigger problems than his seeing me look inside his shower.*

Still, I make a big deal out of looking at my hands and pretending to find the sliver of soap inadequate. I look around as if I might find a better piece somewhere else... *hmmm... where?* And then I spot the shower and act as if an idea has occurred to me. I'm like a mime with dirty hands.

I pull back the white, vinyl curtain and take in the nondescript black-and-white label on a bottle of green shampoo: generic Prell. There is nothing else in the shower, aside from the bar of deodorant soap which I lift from the puddle it sits in and wash my hands once again before placing it back and pulling the curtain just like it was. I slap my hands against each other as if I'm pleased with their cleanliness now and turn away from the mirror.

But there's a medicine cabinet, the next best thing to an open diary. *There's only room for one chameleon in every relationship,* I tell myself while making a show of looking down at my index finger and examining something on it and sucking on it like it's sore and requires a bandage.

There are no bandages. Likewise, there are no prescription medicines, no scandalous remedies for shameful ailments, no creams for mysterious rashes. I'm almost disappointed. There is a toothbrush lying on one shelf all by itself and a roll of toothpaste lying flat as a sunbather on another. There's the razor as well as a nose hair trimmer standing in a plastic cup on another shelf, and some clear silicone-looking pieces in sealed plastic, which I pick up to examine after exaggeratedly sucking once more on the imaginary sore on my finger. I know immediately what this is, thanks to my father.

I close the door to the medicine cabinet and scowl that I haven't found the much-needed bandage, then turn toward the door. I turn off the bathroom light, close the door, and turn my eyes toward Bradley's nightstand. There it is, just as I suspected after I found the clear silicone fittings, sitting innocently on the wooden surface at the right of his king-sized bed. And I wonder how in the world I am ever going to spend the evening with Bradley, dressed seductively in a black, lacy negligee while he lies beside me with sleep apnea, hooked up to the hose of a CPAP machine like an elephant that escaped from the circus.

*My life!* I pause a moment and give its demise the rightful moment of solitude.

I make my way back to the patio where Bradley is taking the burgers off the grill, and I open the back door to let him come in and grab the potato salad from the refrigerator.

"Chips?" He offers the bag to me. I smile thanks and shake my finger like I have a sore on it.

"Paper cut or something," I mumble.

We eat in companionable silence, the chime of fork tines against ceramic and ice cubes against glass filling the air. "Ya know," I finally say, shaking my fork as if I've said this a million times before. "We could liven up your space here."

Bradley looks at his unoccupied photo frames, his few brown throw pillows lined up obediently one behind the other.

"Liven it up?" he twists his lips, unsure what I mean.

"You know, just add some splashes of color." I regret the word "splashes" immediately, imagining Bradley thinks I'm going to haul in some lime green paint and throw it at the wall. "I mean, like," I wave my hand in the air as if all this is coming to me in spurts, "hang some curtains over those vinyl blinds. Put a few things on the wall and maybe a rug on the floor. Put a picture of us in the frame that still has the models in it."

Bradley swallows a fork full of potato salad and takes a sip of tea. "We could do that," he agrees with indifference.

Bradley reminds me of a much-needed blanket on a cold night. If he weren't here, I suppose I'd be freezing. Rare is the man who doesn't have any shameful secrets in his medicine cabinet or his life, just sleep apnea and generic shampoo. Good. Safe. Bradley.

Occasionally I have the uncomfortable awareness I'd had that night in the restaurant when I'd tried so hard to coax some passionate thoughts from him. I recognize that and I distance myself, sometimes for days, other times for weeks. Bradley sulks, not helping his cause. But then I return, cognizant of my feelings as well as my lack of them. *Passing the time*, I think. Not unlike watching a movie because it won awards but not becoming invested enough in it to convey its plot.

My day ends with my hands hovering over the keyboards of my computer like sparrows in flight looking for a place to land. What do I write? I'm irate that Deaton had to bring this back to the forefront of my mind.

**To: Helena1098@myFCcourier.com**
**From: Unveiled@officeweb.com**
**Subject: Investigation**

**Dear Ms. Delgado, As discussed, we're following the lead on the second unidentified woman from the accident. She was pregnant. We will be following up with Caroline's obstetrician from her first pregnancy to see if he can, or will, verify anything regarding that. However, if you wish to pursue the investigation into her identity, we may need your fiancé to pursue that lead, due to patient confidentiality. There are quite a few other things we are working on for you and will be in contact when we have definitive news.**

I scroll through social media and start to log off my laptop, but I see a new email has arrived in the last few minutes, so I click back on my inbox.

**To: Unveiled@officeweb.com**
**From: Helena1098@myFCcourier.com**
**Subject: Investigation**

**Caroline Chadwick had her tubes tied after the birth of her first child, so she could not have been pregnant. Thank you for your diligence in pursuing the truth. I believe we are getting closer, and it will emerge soon.**

# FIFTEEN

W HEN SAMUEL TOLD Eleanor he would be gone for a few days on a hunting trip, she looked forward to his homecoming and their lovemaking. At the time I wrote that storyline I imagined I might one day do the same with someone. But when Deaton tells me he'll be taking Kristlyn to Iowa, a trip "home" he calls it, my envy surprises me. I'm happy he has found someone, so why does this produce such a feeling of emptiness in me?

*It's not them I'm jealous of,* I tell myself. It's Mrs. Dunklin and Cousin Patty, even Larry Sr. and L.J. People to break bread and commiserate with or kick their hind ends to the county line, whatever the case may be. Home, family, loyalties, and love.

I watch them load Deaton's car early Monday morning, waving from the sidewalk as I sweep the walkway and they drive away. It's seven A.M. and already ninety degrees. My bangs are jumbled and plastered to my forehead. Deaton taps the horn. Two quick beeps, a friendly farewell, and they're off. Instead of focusing on the desolation I feel, I look forward to a whole week without Deaton's expectant face and endless inquiries.

Five days before my meet-up with Scott and I'm not sure what to do with myself. The week is a blank slate, full of possibilities, if only I could think of any. The café just passed its annual health department inspection with flying colors, and I wish I had it in me to savor that celebration a bit, but it's quite overshadowed right now. I should tell Bradley what I'm going through. I haven't told him Deaton and I are teaming up to try to find out more about my mom's death. He'll ask questions, and I've created enough chaos already.

As it is now I have to constantly remind myself who knows what. Mom, Hailey, Becky, and now Deaton know I'm Unveiled Investigations, but only Becky knows my mother is alive and living in Atlanta under the name Mary Guthry. But Becky still does not know Helena has unknowingly hired me to find out what happened to my mother. She'd slap a straitjacket on me and haul me to the loony bin if she got wind of that one. She's always thought the whole fiasco was a bit demented anyway, and the older we get the more I tend to agree.

*And Bradley.* So many things this man doesn't know, things I don't have the energy or the wherewithal to bring up. But how can we grow close if I don't turn to him? How can I get past my reservations if I don't give the guy a fair chance? And does anyone have a fair chance next to Scott Warner?

*No, but Scott Warner is not dating me.*

I haven't even told Bradley that I have a side gig. I just don't feel like it. I'm not sure what I feel like doing, aside from getting in my car and tapping my own horn while rounding the corner on my way to somewhere. *I have people I can visit too, Deaton. Just watch!*

"What's your week look like?" I ask Cory. "Any chance you and Jenna could handle the café by yourselves for two days if I outline everything, make sure we're well-stocked, and am only a phone call away?"

He puckers his lips and looks to the side, thinking about his plans. Finally, he nods. "I think so. I have to be somewhere Wednesday night at six, though."

I decide then and there, on the spot, even though a part of me wonders why I keep being pulled in her direction, further into her web. "I'll make it a day and a half, and be back Wednesday afternoon. I have a friend in Atlanta. We're like family, and I'd like Hailey to have a chance to visit with her before she leaves for school in August. I'll make absolutely certain I've left nothing here undone," I promise.

Hailey hears her name and stops behind me on her way to a booth, her arms straining under the weight of a platter full of pastries and drinks. "Really? Aunt Mary's?" She smiles and nods eagerly, and I'm comforted that she's so fond of Mary, that they share a special bond even if it's all built on a falsehood.

*A lie,* something inside of me shouts, but I hush it. *I prefer falsehood, thank you.*

On Tuesday morning, we load Otis into the back seat, along with a bulky, outdated suitcase we both share, and back out of the driveway onto Kindler Street. The morning air is muggy. Two young mothers dressed in the suburban uniform of black leggings, sports bra, and ponytail are pushing high-tech strollers down the sidewalk, jogging at a brisk pace. A group of bicyclists form a line on the side of the road, and I slow and try to swerve far away from them. They resemble a swarm of mosquitos with their shiny helmets, their intense focus, and determination. I beep twice and make the turn that leads to the freeway, and Otis grumbles and settles into his pillow.

We ride along for a while holding a Madonna concert, until Hailey turns down the music and folds her legs in the seat. "So, getting back to our conversation from the other day. What did Aunt Mary say when you and Dad broke up?"

I wonder why this sudden interest in the marriage problems Greg and I had. "She just cried along with me. No 'I told you so' or anything like that."

She nods, thinking this over.

"Don't scowl," I say. "You'll get worry lines." I point to my forehead.

"So you don't think Aunt Mary is happy with her life? With Ian?"

I hesitate to answer this. I don't know how much to say, and it's getting harder to keep track of this story too. Hailey knows Mary knew Ian when she was younger and they broke up. She knows they reconnected years later and moved to Scotland before coming back to America. What gets sticky is when she was supposedly my teacher. It has to fit in after moving back to America, but before settling in Atlanta, and Mary and I have never actually sat down and plotted out our time frames to solidify our story. It's not exactly the best mother/daughter bonding activity.

"I imagine Mary is happy for the most part," I say. "But I also imagine she has her share of regrets. Like all of us."

"But Ian's so fun," Hailey says as if that's all it takes to have a life full of promise.

"He is that."

*I've heard people in homeless shelters and prisons say*
Mary has been watching for us out the windows, an,
I park she heads to Hailey's side of the car holding her arn.
"Oh, I'm so glad to see you, Sweetheart. Oh, your hair .
gotten longer. And so skinny. Too skinny. You must be starving.
Let me take something. Come in."

The sun is high in the sky, glistening off her champagne-colored
strands. My mother is a well-kept woman. She wears her hair in a
sleek shoulder-length style and enjoys monthly visits to the salon
for a precise trim, root touch-up, deep conditioning treatment,
and brow waxing. Mary is the type of woman who can wear
oversized sunglasses and big hats or scarves wrapped and tied
as headbands without looking like a caricature of herself or a
mental patient. Her pearl polished fingernails grab Hailey at
the shoulders and hold on before clasping behind her back in a
hug, and I glance at my frayed hangnail and the red spot next
to my thumbnail where a piece of skin was loose and I ripped it
with my teeth, and wonder if I've really found the right woman.
How can this be my mother?

Ian is still at the pub, but Mary says he's promised to head home
early and take us all out for a big dinner. "So, I thought we'd just
nibble for lunch," she says strolling into the kitchen and handing
me a tray of cheese, crackers, and some sliced veggies.

I carry it into the living room and place it on the coffee table,
while Hailey wanders around the room with her hands clasped
behind her back, studying the paintings on the wall and the col-
lection of crystal figurines on the credenza. She does this every
time we visit, adoring her Aunt Mary's taste, admiring her selec-
tions, absorbing her every move. The room is so unlike our house,
decorated in grays and blues and whispering of solitude and class,
and yet something about it feels so lonely to me. The gray walls
make me feel like I'm underwater, breaking through the surface.
Beautiful, but lonely feeling.

"Come sit and tell me all about your plans." Mary pats the seat
beside her and Hailey kicks off her shoes and leaps into the space.
She lays her head on Mary's shoulder, and Mary strokes her hair
while they talk about SAT scores and GPA's, dorms and sororities,
and Shakespeare's influence on modern theater. I curl up in the
mid-century modern accent chair as best I can, stuffing pillows

between the walnut frame and myself, and fall asleep until Ian's voice booms across the room.

"Ah, my three lovely lassies."

I sit up and turn toward the front door. Ian is at his best, agreeable and enthusiastic, eager to be the one responsible for showing us a good time. He hangs up his jacket and strolls into the room and Mary rises, straightening her fitted white blouse over her navy blue capris. She fits herself right into him and he kisses the top of her head.

The air has filled with a charge. My head is not groggy like it usually is from an afternoon nap. The muted colors of the room seem to have intensified, and for the first time I notice the music that's been playing softly in another room. Hailey hugs Ian and returns to the sofa, but she's no longer sedate and dreamy. She sits forward, her elbows resting on her knees, and watches Ian pour himself a whiskey and sit down in the chair beside mine. He crosses one leg over another, and Hailey jiggles her legs in anticipation of what's coming now that Ian is here, which is always a bit nerve-wracking. Ian can get caught up in a story and get carried away with the details, and I constantly have to steer it back to the mundane. Mary slips into her loafers, crosses her ankles, and positions her legs to the side, and I correct my posture and sit up straight with my hands on the arms of the chair and my feet planted on the plush carpet in front of me.

Ian's cell phone rings and he checks the display and takes the call in another room. When he returns to the living room, his mood is a little less exuberant, but he's trying to cover it.

Mary is standing at the mirror in the entryway touching up her lipstick. She spots him behind her in the reflection and sees the change in demeanor. "Something wrong, darling?"

"No, no," Ian says, brushing away the thought with a wave of his hand. "Just a bit knackered after a long day. But I'll be grand once again when I get me some fish and chips." He holds a hand out to Hailey as if they're going to dance, and when she takes it he does give her a twirl and then holds the other hand out to me.

The four of us climb into his little sports car, and Ian has hit thirty before we've left the parking lot. He maneuvers with precision, his hand resting on the gearshift as he weaves in and out of traffic. Mary's hand rests on his leg. They appear the picture of the American dream, defying age, boredom, and misery of any sort.

"Aren't we going to the restaurant?"

"Thought we'd throw some notes around T̶. tonight," Ian says, taking his hand off the gearshift and hand over hers. "I've been at the restaurant all day."

She continues to stare at him, saying nothing, and in the back seat I tense and look out my window as if I'm not listening to them.

"Never hurts to check the competition," he says, and she nods and twists in her seat to smile at Hailey and me as Ian pulls into the Nag's Head parking lot.

I'm almost finished with my roast beef when an older couple walks past us and gets seated two tables away from us. Ian has been telling us about a woman that rides a bicycle around town and stops often at *Fins and Feathers* for tea. The week before she had come in for dinner dressed in an evening gown and sure enough when they saw her leave she was on the bicycle with the dress hiked up. "Bit soft in the head perhaps," Ian says with his fork ready to slide into his mouth, but then he stops and studies the couple quickly — so quickly I'm not sure anyone else noticed he skipped a beat.

He is silent for the remainder of the meal, even with Hailey who can usually bring out his animation and wicked sense of humor. A few bites later he turns to Mary, "I'm sorry, love. I just fancy an evening at home. Would you mind?"

"Of course not," she says, though I can see she's surprised. Hailey and I are still eating, but we both lay down our forks and nod in agreement, although the whole discussion is strange.

I glance around to see if the waitress is anywhere nearby, and I see the older couple watching us. She is whispering to her husband, and he is nodding as if he's realizing something.

"Check please," Ian says to the girl that's walking through with a tray of drinks, even though she's not our waitress.

Five minutes or so go by, and Ian gets up and says we'll just go up front and get the check. We file out of our booth, and I see the man from the booth behind us rise. In two steps he's upon us, extending his hand.

"Ian?" he says, smiling. His wife has turned in the booth to watch us, but she's not joining him in his greeting. She's craning her neck over the waitress, who blocks her view.

Ian turns as if he's just noticed the man. "Henry Blodger!" He shakes the man's extended hand with gusto, all traces of his not feeling well completely disappeared. "Fancy running into you here, mate."

"Fancy running into *you*," Mr. Blodger says. "Don't you *own* the *Fins and Feathers*?"

"Like right I do," Ian says. "We've come to check the competition." He turns to the three of us standing there. "Henry, this is Mary, Amy, and Hailey Hollander." He slips the different surname onto the end as if all three of us share it. It's all delivered in a way as if we're just along helping Ian assess the competition, as he says.

Mr. Blodger cocks his head and says, "Shame Eliza couldn't check the competition with you."

"Shame indeed," Ian says as if it truly is. "She's a good one for spotting things. A prize, that one is." He glances at his watch. "So good to see you, Henry. Mrs. Blodger." He turns and waves to the woman seated in the booth. "We have to get back to things." He brushes an arm around us as if he's sweeping us all up, and the three of us allow him to, smiling at the man still standing in the middle of the aisle. We pay at the register and leave the restaurant.

"Who's Eliza?" Hailey says once she's buckled in the back seat. I draw in my breath. I don't want to know who Eliza is.

"Hostess at the pub," Ian says, turning to look behind him and winking at Hailey before he pulls out of the parking spot. "Bit odd for the lad to say she should dine with us, but I believe he was a bit battered," he says, pulling into the traffic and accelerating.

We return to the apartment, and Ian has found his strength, humor, and charm once more. He and I have an in-depth discussion on menus reflecting brand and then the three of us stay up late playing cards until Ian slips an arm around Mary. "Call it a day, love?"

I glance at the clock: 1:32 A.M. We've been having so much fun no one noticed the evening had turned into a new day.

Hailey yawns and throws down her cards. I remember my afternoon nap most likely sustained me, but I imagine she's dead on her feet. We leave our glasses and plates on the table and stumble to our bedrooms, mumbling goodnights. The apartment is only a two-bedroom, so Hailey and I walk toward the guest room across the hall from the master.

"Sleep well, darling," Mary says over her shoulder, and Ian turns at the doorway.

"I'll most likely be gone in the morn," he says. He hugs us both. There's so much I want to say: *Take care of her for me. Keep her happy. Don't let her slip.*

And the next morning when Hailey and I set out under an early morning's sunrise, Ian is indeed already gone. "Make sure Ian takes care of you. Make sure he keeps you happy," I say to my mother after we've hugged three times and I've gotten into the car and rolled down the window to prolong our departure.

"Of course," she says, smiling. "You make sure Bradley does the same. And bring him next time," I hear her yelling after me as we roll forward, away from Atlanta.

"Onward to Flannery Cove," I say, about ten miles down the road.

Hailey pulls the headphones from her ears. "And back to the search for Grandma's body." She gives me a lopsided, sympathetic half-smile.

I ring Mary to let her know we've made it home and then check the messages on my answering machine. My father's voice speaks to me in an uplifted tone, not an ounce of tension. "Amy? Are you there? Helena and I want you to have those dishes," he says, as if I never asked and they just thought of it themselves. "Can you come by after work? Amy? Call me back."

Then Deaton's voice, in a whispery kind of voice, "Hey. I tried your cell, but couldn't get through. I need you to call me."

I pick up my cell. It hasn't rung or chimed in two days. I hadn't thought much of it because I'd checked in with Cory numerous times. I try to call it from the house phone, but get a message that the number isn't in service.

*Aargh! I didn't pay the bill.*

I dial Deaton from my eBay princess phone, and he answers on the second ring.

"Ames, what in the world? Where've you been?"

"I went to Atlanta. To visit my friend Mary. Aren't you in Iowa?"

"Yes," he whispers. I'm imagining Mrs. Dunklin and Cousin Patty and Kristlyn all sitting in the living room on the tweed sofa with a gingham valance blowing and the ceiling fan whirring above them. They're laughing so hard they don't notice Deaton has slipped off to the bathroom and disappeared.

"I only have a second," Deaton says. "There was some guy. Mickey Connelly. He was arrested on counterfeiting and forgery charges shortly after the train wreck." I feel my heart quicken.

147

I'm trying to think how to counteract his words before he even gets them out. "You said your dad found the receipt from your mom's train ticket."

"Yes," I mumble, even though it wasn't a question.

"I need that receipt, Amy."

"I'll find it," I promise, with all the enthusiasm I can muster. "My gosh, Deaton, do you think..." I let my sentence linger.

"I do," he answers. "I really do."

I FOLLOW A BIG car with two little heads bobbing in the back seat most of the way to Dad's. Right before I turn left into Whisper Winds Condominiums, the other car turns right.

I exit the elevator and knock twice, and Helena opens the door. "Amy, dear." She kisses me on the cheek, and I take in the smell of her: gardenias and Oil of Olay. My father is in the kitchen stirring something at the stove, which seems very out of character for him.

"Sparkle." He taps the wooden spoon on the side of the pot. "I'm perfecting my signature red sauce."

"Didn't know you had a signature red sauce," I say, dropping my purse in the nearest chair.

Helena catches my eye and winks. "No restaurants to review tonight, so it's Raleigh's turn to cook."

"Ahh."

Helena has been tidying up, running the heavy old Hoover across the beige carpet. That vacuum is one of the few things Dad kept from the old house, but it doesn't hold any memories of my mother. I'm unable to recall her ever pushing it. As I watch her wind the cord around the two hooks in the back of it I wonder briefly what life would have been like if Dad had met Helena when I was younger. I inhale the smell of pine and disinfectant and compare it to my mother's house where surfaces are wiped with natural cleaners and vinegar leaving behind a meek freshness reminiscent of a dill pickle. This pine and lemony stuff smells like something that would have welcomed me home nicely from school each day, along with chocolate chip cookies and the perfected red sauce. I'm curious if Helena would have helped me with homework and made sure I didn't entertain boys in my bedroom and allowed Mrs. Ryder to take her eyes off of me and tend to her own household. Or maybe she would have spent my childhood yelling that Caroline Chadwick wasn't on that train and wanting to know what my ten-year-old self knew about it.

"My heavens, you need a license to operate that old thing." Helena wheels it into the front closet and collapses in the chair on the other side of the table. "Oh, the dishes!" She pops back up and scurries to the front hall closet where she just put the vacuum cleaner away. She reaches to the shelf above, and Dad puts the spoon in the sink and rushes to help her.

"I can get them," I say, and the two of them move to the side and let me handle the three boxes of dishes. I stack them near the front door.

Helena moves back to the kitchen, and I go in to retrieve my purse and see she's set three places for dinner. "Tell your dad his sauce is better than anything you've had in the finest Italian restaurants," she whispers to me while dad strains pasta through a colander.

"I haven't been to many fine Italian restaurants lately, but okay," I whisper back.

"Hailey tells me the two of you went to visit Mary," Dad says to me while twirling noodles around his fork. "Amy's former English teacher who lives in Atlanta," he reminds Helena, and she nods while twirling as well.

They're twirlers. I'm a cutter. I glance up briefly and nod, but look back down quickly, intent on slicing my noodles into little bite-sized pieces. I'm concentrating and scowling as if the side of my fork isn't quite sharp enough to penetrate cooked pasta.

The silence stretches. I've got to say something. I glance up from my determined cutting, and they're both chewing and looking at me. "It was fun. We didn't really do anything. We went out to eat and played cards and just talked and then left early this morning. Just got home. Do you all ever play cards at the club? You know Hailey's pretty good at it. Good sauce, Dad. Better than anything I've had in the finest Italian restaurants. What'd you put in it?"

I finally stop for a sip of water, while Dad recounts his trials and tribulations in the kitchen. "First, I put in three teaspoons of oregano," he says. "Which was *way* too much."

Helena grimaces as if she can still taste the overpowering herb. "I think you put in three *tablespoons*," she says. She turns to me. "The tablespoon was in the dishwasher, not the teaspoon."

The two of them continue, recalling mixed up tablespoons and teaspoons, and oregano versus marjoram, and how much better fresh garlic is than store-bought. I whip my head from one to the other and every once in a while I say something like, *"Marjoram? Really?"*

"And you'll never guess," dad says, his eyes beaming with anticipation.

"What?"

"The ingredient we finally found to make it perfect. You'll never guess."

He and Helena both seem to be sitting on edge. "Pumpkin," he announces before I can begin guessing. "Just regular canned pumpkin. Tasteless, but tones down anything overpowering."

I'm actually the one who had told him this, but I nod in amazement.

"And adds fiber," Helena reminds him.

*"Really?* Well, it's delicious." I gather up a bunch of sliced noodles on my fork and they stack there like firewood.

Dad starts rifling through kitchen drawers. "I wrote down the final recipe. I'll copy it down for you if I can find some notepaper."

"Pumpkin. Wow." I shake my head as if they've just told me dad discovered The Declaration of Independence rolled up in the linen closet when he moved into the condo. *"Oh*, Pumpkin!" I think of another avenue to steer the conversation down. "Have you had my pumpkin muffins at the café?"

"I have." Helena raises an index finger. "Scrumptious!"

And that allows me to lead us into a discussion of Paulus and his school problems and his love of my pumpkin muffins, while Dad continues trying to locate writing paper. "I'm not even sure he's learning anything where he is now. I wish his mom could find a school he could thrive in," I say. "I wish he had a single friend."

"The right environment is key," Helena agrees, as she gathers the dishes from the table and carries them to the sink.

"Key!" Dad says, snapping his fingers, and giving up on the paper. "Do you still have that desk that used to be in the old house?"

"Of course I do."

*I'm not one to discard family heirlooms so easily, Dad.*

"I think I found the key to that top drawer. Let me grab it and I'll help you get those boxes out to your car."

"Bye Amy," Helena hollers over her shoulder. "I'd
my hands." She lifts her hands out of the water and sh.
suds that cover them and drip back into the sink. "I'll ema.
I turn suddenly at the door. "What? Email me?"
"Your dad's recipe," she hollers. I hear her say something else
I can't quite catch and then, "And I can update you on the investigation if you like." All this is being broadcast while Dad comes out
of his bedroom holding up a little, brass key, and I imagine life
as I know it being devoured by flames as devastating as Atlanta's
fire of 1864.

# SIXTEEN

SHEILA THOMAS RINGS my doorbell at seven o'clock the next morning. I'm dressed and ready to head out the door, but the sink is full of dirty dishes, the beds are unmade, and unread newspapers are piled at my front door like I've already abandoned the place. The Amy of last year would not even recognize this defeated sloth of a person who hadn't washed and dried every dish and wiped a smidgen of buffing paste over the sink to shine it up before turning in the night before.

"Amy, this is Kevin and Amanda Schware," she says when I open the door. She holds a briefcase at her side and a flier with the information on my house.

"Imagine it all updated." Sheila begins her spiel with her hands held up fanning the room, and I excuse myself to go load my dishwasher.

Kevin says, "Oh no, I like it so far. How 'bout you, Mandy?"

Amanda nods her approval.

I position myself in the dining room with another cup of coffee, so I can hear what's being said from any downstairs room they go in. Sheila changes her tactic to point out the original materials, the eclectic fixtures, and the *"funky vibe"* — her words she came up with right there on the spot.

I can hear Kevin and Amanda discussing the white carpeting. "We'll put down our big, brown area rug over it," she says. They come into the dining room where I'm sitting and Amanda asks if he likes the paint color.

"Prob'ly turn this into a homeschooling room," Kevin says, shrugging. "Color don't matter. Walls gonna end up scribbled on anyway."

I imagine Nana lifting the lid of her coffin and snapping to attention.

"Oh, it'd be perfect for that," Sheila exclaims. "How old are the kids?"

Amanda counts on her fingers. "Josiah's fourteen, Julia's ten, Justin's eight, and the twins Jasper and Jensen are six."

"Let me show you the upstairs," Sheila says. "Now you know it's only two bedrooms? One master up and another down."

"There goes that," I say to Otis, who lays curled at my feet under the dining room table.

I can hear Kevin and Amanda on the landing talking about partitions and bunk beds and sharing and character building and Jensen, who could use a good life lesson on what it means to love your brother.

The three of them descend the stairs and head into the kitchen. Amanda wants to measure the actual countertops and is saying things like, "dehydrate" and "soaking kefir."

"No, you're right. They just don't make 'em like they used to," I hear Sheila say, then the little trio heads into my bedroom, and I lose them. I imagine them looking at my big, comfortable bed and trying to think of more names that could begin with *J. This is where we'll make Jessie.*

"Well it's certainly one to add to the list," Sheila is saying when they come out of the bedroom. Amanda and Kevin agree, but apparently there's another house over on Greenbriar Street that's got a fenced-in back yard and a trampoline the owners are leaving behind. "And space for goats and chickens," she reminds her husband, and he nods as if that's right up there with indoor plumbing. I want to mention that I think goats might eat trampolines, but it's none of my business.

"Thank you for letting us in, Amy," Sheila says, and Amanda and Kevin both shake my hand. Their car is blocking mine in the driveway, and I can't leave until they do. I watch them through the kitchen window as they walk through the backyard. Amanda is standing under the generous shade of Atlas gesturing wildly with her hands and Kevin keeps a fist at his chin, rubbing and pondering, and Sheila just smiles and bobs her head up and down as if she's been trying to tell everyone of my home's amazing potential and now finally someone gets it. I can tell Amanda's talking about a fence and I think trimming Atlas back, then Kevin gets out a tape measure and they stretch it as far as it'll go, maybe considering space for the goats and chickens, which I'm sure aren't allowed in the city limits.

I settle Otis into the office later and drop my bags and head out front. I'm watering the geraniums in the window box when I see Kristlyn come out of the bookstore and head toward her car. She's rolling her suitcase. She puts it into the trunk of her car. We wave to each other, and then she heads over to my sidewalk.

"Hey, how was the trip?" I realize I'm watering the concrete and hoist the hose back up to the flowers.

"Fabulous," Kristlyn says. "Quite a few degrees cooler than it is here right now." She wipes a hand across her forehead and brushes her hair off her face.

"How was Deaton's mom?" I ask as if Mrs. Dunklin and I are old friends.

"Good. Much better than she was this time last year."

Apparently, she and Mrs. Dunklin *are* old friends. I nod, pretending to know what she's referring to.

"Oh, and Patty!" She holds her hands up excitedly. "Her house turned out fabulous. And, she and Tommy Mobley have rekindled some old high school romance."

"The contractor?"

"Yeah. Tommy. Tommy Mobley," she says as if these people live and breathe right under my nose every day.

I lay the hose down and turn off the spigot. "Well take that, Loser Larry!"

"Exactly!" Kristlyn shifts her weight and pulls at the overnight bag she's still carrying on her shoulder. "I'm due across town for a meeting in thirty minutes. Better run."

"Want a coffee for the road?"

"That'd be great." She smiles, showing a set of gleaming, straight teeth.

I run back inside and make a cup for her. While I pour I think about these faceless people. Patty and Tommy and Mrs.

Dunklin and the various aunts and uncles and cousins. I think about having someone one day with a kinship like that. Someone whose mom might ask me to help her organize her old photo albums and clean out her closets and say, "Take whatever you want, dear. That's why I asked you to come." Someone who might say, "Oh you should have Amy help you with the house, she's got an eye for those things." A wayward member like L.J. who'd see me in the grocery store and turn down the other aisle to avoid me because I'm *one of them*. An entire clan that might take me into their chambers and never let me go.

Kristlyn settles into the driver's seat and pulls her seat belt over her dress, and I hand her the cup.

"Thanks," she holds it up before placing it in the cup holder beside her.

"Anytime."

My head is throbbing from the non-stop clattering of dishes, the heat that keeps rising from my feet straight up to my eyeballs, the tapping of Madame Bienve's stick, and the dance-mom chatter. After letting Otis out, I settle myself in my chair and massage my temples. It's Thursday, and I've heard nothing from Scott Warner. I wonder if he remembers our meeting, or if I should try to think of a reason to call him so he can remind me about it and I can say something like, "Oh yes. I'm so glad you reminded me of that." I wonder if his receptionist might call me in the next two days and cancel the meeting altogether.

While I'm wondering all this, I reach into my wallet and retrieve the desk key Dad gave me. It slides right into the lock on the drawer I haven't been able to open since I brought the desk here, but the door still doesn't budge. I have to jimmy it back and forth and finally open the drawer beneath it and pound up under it before it opens. After that, I begin to lift items out and place them one by one on my desktop: an old phone book, some stationery and book of postage stamps, scattered pencils and pens, paperclips, and a stack of menus from takeout restaurants. Stuck inside one of the menus is Mom's fraudulent receipt for the train ticket.

Holding this ticket is like reading my diary from seventh grade. *Bobby Flared asked me to the dance. Maria Jelvonicho sat by me at lunch and wants to know if I'll spend the night Friday. Dad rented a movie, but we ended up talking for hours about how I was faring without Mom and never watched it.* Lies, all of it — figments of an imagination on overdrive.

I know all about this receipt, I made Mom tell me everything that day I found her. I'd gotten into the taxi with the newspaper article shoved in my backpack. I'd toured downtown Atlanta that afternoon with Mrs. Wentworth and my friends and spent that evening back at the hotel squinting at the hazy image of my mother in the background of that photo, and I'd made my decision.

"I think it's food poisoning," I said the next morning when everyone was in line to get on the bus that would take them to the CNN building. I'd crumbled up the cookies Becky handed me and threw them in the toilet and stuck my finger down my throat to retch. Mrs. Wentworth stood in the doorway of the hotel room bathroom and wrung her hands. I looked up with my teary eyes and red face and brushed my damp bangs off my forehead, murmuring that I had to go lay back down.

I flung myself back on the twin bed and could hear Mrs. Wentworth and Mr. Davis out in the hallway. "We have to get going. We're going to be late. Should someone stay with her? We won't have enough chaperones for this group. It's Amy Chadwick. She's never been in any trouble. The hotel workers will be here."

And so it was decided that I would lie in bed all day, and they'd be back around four o'clock. "She's already asleep," Mrs. Wentworth said, laying a hand across my forehead before they all turned and marched down the hallway to the waiting bus.

My room overlooked the parking lot, and as soon as I saw the bus pull away from the curb I grabbed my room key and took the elevator down to the lobby, out the revolving door, and hailed a taxi. "Fins and Feathers restaurant," I said as if I was a little heiress, an experienced traveler. The taxi driver was a middle-aged, bald man with a black mustache and a long face. He barreled through the morning traffic, taking turns on two wheels and weaving in and out of lanes before he pulled into a parking lot outside a brick building. Only three cars were in the lot.

He turned around to face me. I sat still with my feet planted firmly on the floor and my hands folded in my lap. "Is this the place?" He asked.

I looked out the window and nodded, seeing the Fins and Feathers logo written in gold on a black backdrop. I couldn't see inside the restaurant, but it looked dark.

"Meter's runnin', Miss." The taxi driver seemed reluctant to leave me there, but there was a little radio attached to his dashboard that kept speaking and crackling. I think he had people waiting on him.

I handed over a bunch of dollars and put my hand on the door handle. The taxi driver hurriedly opened his door and ran around the back of the car and opened mine from the outside. He extended a hand to help me out, and I took it reluctantly. I stood with the car door still open, and he mumbled something I didn't hear then opened the front passenger door and rummaged around until he found a scrap of paper and a pen. "Names Jim," he said, holding the paper up against the car and jotting a phone number on it. "My taxi is number 45780." He thrust the paper into my hand, but I remained still, my legs barely holding me up and my hands shaking. "You call me if you need me to pick you back up, ya hear?"

I nodded, but I didn't move.

"Oh jeez," Jim said, turning in a circle and looking around. He spotted a bench just outside the restaurant door. He took me by the arm and led me to it. "Jim. 45780," he repeated. Then he frowned and walked back to his cab still idling nearby and slowly drove away.

I sat on the bench for what seemed like hours, never getting up and looking in the door or windows of the restaurant. Instead, I just sat on the bench and swung my tennis shoes back and forth and counted the little boomerang-shaped cigarettes ground out in the nearby bucket of sand.

A silver car roared into the lot and a tall man in a suit and a long, black coat got out of it. He approached, carrying a briefcase in one hand and reading some papers he was holding in the other. The man almost didn't see me, but just when he started to open the front door he looked to his left. "Well, hello there," he said in an accent very different from anyone I knew. He shoved the papers into the briefcase and turned his attention to me.

I said nothing. I just looked down at the tennis shoes I kept swinging back and forth.

He knelt beside the bench, and I swung my head to the side and looked into dark, captivating eyes.

"Are you alone?" he said, and I nodded.

He stood back up and looked across the empty parking lot. He extended a hand. "We don't open till four, but come in and let's round you up a nibble."

I followed him into the restaurant and even at my young age, I recognized the soft carpets, the expensive multi-grained woods. This was the kind of restaurant most people reserved for special occasions. He ushered me into a booth, and I sank into a soft, leather seat and stared at my chewed fingernails.

"Tammy," he said.

I jerked my head up thinking he'd said my name and realized he was speaking to a woman that was coming in from a back room.

"Can you get this young girl a sandwich, please? What would you like, little one?"

"I want my mom," I said, finally breaking my silence. He pulled his head back, just a bit like I'd slapped him with a weak hand — and then his handsome features changed.

"Your mum?"

I looked into his eyes and stared. I reached into my pocket and pulled out the newspaper photo and unfolded it, flattening it on the table.

"Caroline?"

"My mom. Caroline." I began to cry softly.

Tammy came back with a sandwich, grilled bread with some kind of cheese inside I'd never tasted before. Despite sticking my finger down my throat a few hours earlier and the memory of cookie chunks in toilet water, I was ravenously hungry. I picked it up and began to chew while tears still rolled down my face.

"Caroline is teaching right now." I wasn't sure if this man was saying this to himself or me, or maybe to Tammy, who still stood by the table. "Stay with her," he had said to Tammy, pointing at me. "I'm going to call the school." He'd patted my hand and started to walk away, but then he'd turned back around as Tammy was taking his place in the booth across from me. "Her name is Amy."

The train receipt slips from my fingers and falls to the floor. I lean down and pick it up, and when I sit back up I hear a small knock on my door. I'm not even sure I really heard it, but Otis is holding his head up looking at the door, confirming it.

I shove the receipt back into the drawer and sit up straight. "Come in."

Paulus settles his gaze on the wall behind me. "I'll be starting a new school, but it's still not the school I should probably be at, that's what Uncle Jeremy told my mother, but my mother said I need to be mainstreamed. Mainstreaming results in higher academic achievement, higher self-esteem, and better social skills, but my mother says even with skills it's still difficult for a boy not involved in sports to gain popularity on the social ladder."

"And what does your uncle say about that?" I say, walking toward him.

"He says, 'And you think that's all that's standing in his way, Margo?' "

I smile, but Paulus stands there as deadpan as ever, the joke lost on him. His eyes determinedly fix on my right ear. I'm beginning to hope this uncle gets through to Margo one day. He just might have some valid points.

But I've got my own worries.

BY FRIDAY, I still have heard nothing from the realtor or from Scott Warner. I'd charged two months of cell phone service on my credit card, so I know there isn't anything technical interfering with correspondence. I don't have a lot of time to dwell on it because Hailey has her bags packed and ready to drive to Columbia to check into her dorm.

"I'm officially an old woman," I say with my bottom lip pouted out, as she brings the last bag down the stairs that morning.

She reaches over and stretches my eyes tight and pretends to analyze with the practiced eye of a surgeon. I suck in my cheeks and pucker my lips. "I see traces of youth still there," she says. "It's not a lost cause, but I'm going to prescribe some good moisturizer and some wine coolers and lots of laughing. No tears!"

"Actually, laughing contorts the face into unnatural positions and causes more wrinkles."

"Okay. Suit yourself. Sit here and remain stoic."

As soon as she pulls out of the driveway, I turn to Otis. "You heard her. No tears—*stoic*!"

I stand in my dining room and turn in a full circle. The house certainly isn't loud or overwhelming now. Everything is quiet, solemn. The only movement comes from the dust floating through the air where the sun shines through the back windows. Just me, Otis, and the dust now, the only life forms inhabiting the space.

THE CAFÉ IS busy. Deaton pops in, but we barely have time to talk. He has to stand at the café door and keep an eye on his shop in case anyone ventures in, but he does manage to elaborate a little on Mickey Connelly, the counterfeiter, and hand me an old article he'd printed out from the Flannery Cove Courier on the arrest. I read it while he watches me.

## THOUSANDS OF DOLLARS AND DOCUMENTS. ALL FAKE.

**Police in Savannah confiscated computers, printers, ink, and official documents and stamps Wednesday. The items are believed to have been used in an elaborate and ongoing scheme that investigators say is part of a cross-country counterfeiting and fraud operation. "I want to congratulate the tireless work of the detectives and the U.S. Postal Service for their efforts in bringing this case to a closure," Savannah Sheriff Neil Kapertuno said.**

**The scheme was discovered when Savannah police traced counterfeit bills flooding the area to 56-year-old Michael Connelly of Flannery Cove.**

**Connelly was apprehended at his home early Wednesday, where the printing of fake bills and documents allegedly took place over nine months. Investigators say Connelly took in orders and mailed out stacks of fake money and documents as quickly as he could print them.**

**"Mr. Connelly shipped over 1,200 packages of counterfeit currency in nine months along with fraudulent documents linked to multiple states," Kapertuno said. Customers that paid by credit card are still being investigated, but detectives admit that cash clients will be nearly impossible to track.**
**Investigators call it one of the most sophisticated and lucrative operations they've seen.**

When I'm done, I look up. Deaton is standing close, waiting for my reaction.

"You think this is related to the train crash?" I squint, as if I don't make the connection, but I know it is. I've always thought the detectives investigating my mother's disappearance hadn't done a very thorough job, but I certainly couldn't fault them for not connecting this counterfeiting operation with her. She was presumed dead, her body somewhere in the ocean. Only someone who knew for certain she wasn't would dig this deep, and even then I wasn't sure they would latch on to this. But Deaton's working overtime in his attempt to bring me closure... *or bring me my mother.*

"Don't you see?" he says. "Look at the date. This sting all went down a few weeks after the crash. Your mother wasn't on that train, Amy." He lays a hand on my arm. "She had a receipt for it for some reason, but she wasn't on it."

I turn my head and glance off to the side. Deaton exhales and stammers a bit then draws me into his arms and pats my back as if I'm about to cry. When he finally lets me go, I dab at my eyes.

"It's connected, Ames. I know it is. You say you saw the receipt?"

I nod. I had told him I saw the receipt a long time ago as proof that my mother had been on the train, so he knows it exists.

"Find that receipt," he says. "I'm working on finding Mickey Connelly."

I'm nearly weak when I finally get to my office. I've seen my daughter off to the biggest milestone in her life so far, texted back and forth with her all afternoon, worked the busiest shift of the day, stacked numerous boxes of inventory that arrived into a toppling pyramid, let Otis out three times so far in just the last two hours — *what did he eat last night?* — held my breath for two phone calls that still haven't come, had to ask Madame Bienve to turn down her "phonograph" so I could hear myself think — if I call it anything else, she pretends not to know what I'm talking about — and listened to Deaton tell me that the mother I've kept hidden for years is most likely alive and he's hot on her trail.

An email greeting from Helena on my personal account with my dad's sauce recipe attached is in my inbox, pulsing like a heartbeat. It's now August. I've got to update her. I think of this woman that truly seems to be bringing something out in my dad — but then again, she's wreaking such havoc on our lives — but then again she seems to genuinely care about me — but then again, my dad doesn't even have opinions of his own anymore without being fed hers. My mind wanders to the image of him standing at the stove with that sauce splattering out of the pot like minnows in a bucket, all smiles and pride that he'd perfected what he set out to create, and back to Helena, dressed in a comfortable house dress, her fingers dripping suds as she happily scrubbed at the pots and pans Dad had stacked up beside the stove, and wiping at the blobs of sauce dotting the countertops.

And then I think of my mother. The way she'd come running into that restaurant before Tammy had even had a chance to clear away the plate in front of me. She'd grabbed onto Ian's arm for support and looked all around until she spotted me there in that booth, and she'd run to me. Her knees had buckled just once, but she'd caught herself and continued. Grabbing me into her arms she whispered into my hair, "Amethyst, my dear, dear, Amethyst. Amy." Her bright blue eyes had shone with tears. She'd sat beside me that entire afternoon, never leaving that booth, until she and Ian drove me back to the block my hotel was on and watched me walk to it in time to get back into my bed before my classmates returned. She had turned to me before I got out of the car and given me her phone number. "You are to call me, Amy, as soon as you can. Whatever time it is, I will answer. I need a little time to think about what I'm going to do, but I promise you that one way or another you and I will never lose each other again."

And even though my heart leaps into my throat, my gut twists, and my nerves sizzle, I sit down in front of my laptop and do it anyway.

**To: Helena1098@myFCcourier.com**
**From: Unveiled@officeweb.com**

**Subject: Investigation**

**After intensive investigation, we have discovered that there may have been more passengers on the train than was initially reported. If that is the case, Caroline Chadwick is most likely amongst the deceased, as speculated. You mentioned a receipt for her purchased train ticket. To investigate further along these lines, we need to have that receipt analyzed and verified. It is of vital importance to your case. Please let me know when you would be able to produce that, and I will provide my post office box. I look forward to hearing from you. Unveiled Investigation Agency.**

After hitting send, I reach into my pocket and look at the receipt stub one last time. And then I walk across the room, plug in my shredder, and toss it in.

I'm supposed to cook a gourmet dinner for Bradley at my house that evening, but I stop and pick up a pizza instead. Not even a good pizza with five different kinds of cheeses. A five-dollar thing on a crust so thick it's like eating three bagels at once. I barely say a word while the two of us sit at the bistro table, me in my chair and him in Hailey's.

He pats my hand and gives me a sad, sympathetic smile. "She's only two-and-a-half hours away. She'll be home often."

I start to cry. I'm missing Hailey already. Every time I glance at the staircase I see her flying down it, her hair in a loose, sloppy ponytail, her cheeks flushed with the excitement of wherever she's headed, late as always. I think about how she'd feel about what I did earlier, what I've been doing her entire life: deceiving, covering up. It's been the only way to have my mother, and once I had Hailey, it was the only way for her to have her grandmother. Everything I've done, I've done for us. And yet at the same time, I'd berated Greg for his deceit and raised Hailey in a zero-tolerance for lying household. She asked me once if it was okay to tell Suzanna Whilette that she liked her awful, new haircut so she didn't hurt her feelings. I'd considered it and suggested maybe telling Suzanna she liked her hair longer, but that was just her opinion, and besides her eyes were so pretty no one even looked at her hair. That was true. Suzanna Whilette did have eyes like a Siamese cat.

But I'm not even sure that how a person is raised has that much effect on whom they turn out to be. Maybe it's just innate. Either you're lovely and moral, or you're hypocritical and disgusting. I'd been raised not to lie too, and yet look at me, the master of the trade. Once I told my fourth-grade teacher that my mother was not dead, she was just out in California helping her cousin Linda Ronstadt with her concerts. I didn't even know who Linda Ronstadt was really. I only knew it was a name that wouldn't arouse as much suspicion as if I'd said Cher. Mrs. Hamilton called my dad, and when she didn't hear back from him she called Nana and suggested I might benefit from some counseling. After that, I remember standing at the sink in what is now my master bathroom and having my mouth washed with soap while Susan stood in line behind me to get hers washed for something too — *supporting my claim?* No, that couldn't be right, Susan didn't even go to the same school as I did.

Bradley pats harder at my hand and then scoots his chair closer and moves his hand to the top of my head and pats there until it becomes downright annoying. The rhythm of the pats sounds like a train bumping along on the tracks.

Finally, he sighs and says, "I've got an early morning," in a tone that indicates if it weren't for that he'd carry me to my bed and hold me until I don't have a tear left in me. I wonder if he suspects I don't want to be carried to bed, or if he doesn't want to carry me there… *which came first, the chicken or the egg?*

I nod my understanding then stand at the door and wave as he drives away.

I leave the empty pizza box on the table and toss the cups in the sink. I try to brush my teeth without looking at my devious self in the mirror. I cover up the DVD player and my alarm clock light, turn on my sound machine, and lie in the dark.

*She was overcome with the guilt that pierced her soul. A sharp pain unlike any other that left her bleeding and raw.*

I fall asleep and dream that I'm laid out on a sterile table in an otherwise empty room. Helena is vacuuming my insides with the hose from the old Hoover, and my dad is rubbing his hands together. "Perfect," he keeps saying over and over. My mom stands in the background holding her train ticket receipt. It's being sucked out of her hand toward the vacuum, but she clings tightly to it. Deaton points to a big, black mass near my heart and tells Helena she missed a spot, and she repositions her vacuum hose to try to get it.

Hailey appears and she and Deaton both say they can't even look at me anymore. They open the door to leave, and a bell chimes. Then they walk out and the door slams shut, but the bell keeps chiming insistently. I realize it's my phone beside me ringing, and I sit up and knock the battery cover off the clock. It's six A.M.

*Hailey!*

"Hello." My voice is scratchy, uncertain.

"Hi, Home Girl."

*Scott Warner!*

"Sorry I'm calling so early, but I knew you'd be up since you said you were opening the café this morning."

I spring to a sitting position, throwing the covers off.

"I just wanted to confirm Barristers at seven tonight."

I've nearly made myself sick with blame and regret, and I'm not a pretty picture to behold. This I know. But my heart instantly leaps with joy.

"I'll be there."

"Great. I'm headed to Habitat. Got a paintbrush with my name on it."

"That sounds fun," I say, scrambling out of my bed while holding the phone between my ear and my shoulder.

"I'd reserve one for you if you weren't working."

I try to think what to say while tossing my clothes on the bed, but Scott picks back up.

"Amy?"

"Yes, I'm here. I'm just…"

"I feel terrible having you *meet* me at Barristers, but it's a business meeting, you see, and an attorney can't…"

"I understand," I say quickly. Too quickly. I should have let him finish, because do I understand? Was he trying to explain something or make sure I realize that I am his client and *only* his client.?

"Okay," he says. His voice is cautious, his tone uncertain. I interrupted, and now I have no clues. "See you tonight."

I barely have time to brush my hair and throw on clothes in my mad dash to get to the café, but it's slow anyway. I've only had five customers between seven and eleven, and I make the executive decision to close at one instead of two.

Scott has given me an idea. I still haven't heard anything from my realtor about Kevin and Amanda Schware. They probably left my house the other morning like everyone else who looks at it, declaring that they must immediately wash their eyes out with some kind of chemical to rid themselves of the sight.

I head to the hardware store and walk directly to the paint department. There are hundreds, maybe thousands, of paint swatches. The oranges are so vivid, like a tangerine that's just been sliced open. The blues are bright as peacock feathers, the greens are blades of grass on a freshly mowed, summer lawn. But I'm there to find the blandest of the bland beige, like Bradley's rooms.

*Like Bradley's life!*

I reprimand myself for that thought. There's a woman next to me holding up swatches to match them to a pillow, and I turn to her and say, "Which of these do you think is the blandest?"

She smiles like I'm kidding then squints and looks at the card in my hand that ranges from empty space beige to skin that's never seen the sun beige. After a moment she chooses the one in the middle, and I nod my approval. "I'll take two gallons," I say to the man behind the counter.

I return to my empty house, imagining Hailey at the kitchen sink scolding me for leaving pizza boxes open on the counter all night, but before she can finish her lecture, she's vanished from my mind.

I've put Samuel and Eleanor back on the shelf. My mind skitters around for any delusion or fictitious plot it can grab onto and run with — ignoring reality and everything my reality encompasses right now. Imaginary Hailey comes and goes like a vapor, a distraction akin to the eye of the hurricane. *This isn't healthy,* I tell myself as I absentmindedly scrape away at the flesh on my arms. *The backside of this hurricane is going to be worse than the front.*

I open the door to my bedroom. My covers are twisted like an old yarn mop in the middle of my bed. I continue into my bathroom. Six hours until I have to be at the restaurant. *What to do with my hair,* I wonder. My bangs are too long, not enough volume, so I lift them and trim them just a bit. I look through my make-up, wondering if it has expiration dates on it. I can't remember purchasing any of this stuff. Afterward, I go back into the bedroom and open the blinds, flooding the room with light, and assess the walls covered in a mossy green, the color of ferns in the forest.

I open one gallon with the little tool the guy at the store gave me and pour it into the tray, then roll the applicator into the creamy mixture, and without any hesitation, I swipe it across the wall from the ceiling to the baseboard. The green underneath is still visible so I roll and swipe three more times. My phone rings, so I put the roller back down in the tray and reach for it.

It's Rhoda, Mary's neighbor. Unusual — not entirely unheard of — but unusual.

"Rhoda? How are you?" I ask in an upbeat voice, warding off negative energy.

"He's gone, Amy," she says.

"Gone? Ian?" I've been through this countless times over the years. He comes, he goes, she medicates.

"He's moved his stuff out. He's with someone else."

Pent-up stress escapes my lips. "How is she?" I know my mother. I know how she is. She's curled up in a heap on the floor.

"She needs you."

This is all *I* need on top of everything else.

My dinner. Scott's boisterous laugh and the sparkle in his eye that accompanies it. The green dress that matches my eyes and makes me look like I've had a touch of sun. The possibilities... they all float through my mind and disintegrate like the petals of a dandelion. Every time this happens to me it's always because of her.

I take a moment to consider my way out of this. To Hades and back with this sympathy! It's gone on long enough and drained so much out of me.

"I'm on my way."

I leave the roller saturated with flesh-colored fluid and go to my bathroom to grab a few things. While there, I throw my hair back in a top knot. A few pieces of my newly trimmed strands don't make it in and fall forward like a thick comma across my forehead. My suitcase is still packed and sitting in the corner of my room, and I grab it and throw a few more things in, rouse Otis from his pillow, lock the door, and head to the car. I check the rearview mirror while backing out of the driveway and once again I find myself on the road, heading toward a mother who headed away from me when I needed her most.

As soon as I get to a place with less traffic, I call. He answers on the fourth ring.

"Canceling on me already?" His tone is light, jovial.

I try to explain the situation, but where to even begin. "She's like a second mom to me. She's not the strongest person. I'm afraid this is going to destroy her."

He's silent for a few seconds. "She doesn't have any children?" he says — of all the things.

I hesitate for a moment. "No. No children. I'm all she's got."

"Okay then. Well, I'm disappointed, but of course, you have to go."

"I'll get with you as soon as I get back. I'm so sorry, Scott. I was looking forward… I wanted…" I'm not sure what to say without seeing his expression. I'm still unsure what he was trying to convey to me that morning.

"Go take care of your friend."

A few minutes later my vision begins to splotch. Big, psychedelic blobs form, float, and disintegrate in front of me. *I can't see anything! Why can't I see anything?*

I go through my usual mental list of things that might be killing me, feeling more panicky and faint by the second. This could be a brain tumor. It could also be extreme anger. Then I realize I haven't eaten a thing all day. I've been so nervous with anticipation over my dinner plans.

It's not quite evening when I arrive, but the living room is dark. Maybe it's just that my eyes haven't adjusted from being outside, but I can hardly see to walk to the bedroom. The sweet smell of tobacco still lingers in the air. Mom always says she can't smell it, must be immune to it, but it's like a ghost in the room, subtly weaving in and out. "She's lying down in there," Rhoda whispers. "It's bad this time."

I lie down beside her and lay my head across her chest. Her window blinds are open enough to allow just a smidgen of the sunset across the room, and it diminishes as it grows darker. Rhoda tiptoes out and leaves us like that, and we lay there not saying a word until the room is black.

"He's engaged," Mom finally says.

I lift my head and look at her, even though I can't see her eyes. "*Engaged?* I just saw him three days ago. We went to dinner," I say as if she hadn't been there. Immediately I know what her next words are going to be.

"Her name's Eliza. She's a hostess at the restaurant."

"I don't understand."

"That makes two of us."

The nightlight in the bathroom is on a timer, and it comes on. I can see her lying so small, way over on the side like she's used to in this big bed with a multitude of big, fluffy pillows, and thick, layered quilts. A lot can happen in three days — she looks at least ten pounds lighter. Her skin is not glowing from the sheen of pricey creams, and she's not wearing her usual silk pajamas. She's dressed in an oversized, plain white t-shirt and her skin looks pale and sallow. It resembles a piece of wax paper that's been folded and flattened back out.

She gets up and walks to the closet and opens it to show me the rod that holds nothing, as if she needed to prove to me he was gone. Maybe she did because I still keep expecting him to open that front door anytime now and announce he's home — *Pour the spirits and let the party begin.* How sly this man's character is. Even after everything, I still sometimes think of him as the man who rescued me from that bench outside the restaurant rather than the man who stole my mom away, the man who came into my house and changed the course of my life.

I spend the next day with her. We have no concept of time. Eggs are scrambled after midnight, coffee is steeped in the evening. Sleep comes in small spurts. "She's pregnant," she tells me. "He's marrying her." I have no words, only nods and sighs, and inadequate pats and strokes. I'm not sure if it's a good idea or not, but I finally go out to my car and bring in the three boxes that have been there for days and offer them much in the way a small child presents a crayon drawing. *Is it good? Does it make it all better?*

It's hard to tell, honestly. Mary reaches for the Noritake dish and turns it over, rubbing her hand over the surface and fingering the rim. She doesn't cry, but if she smiles I miss it.

"Grilled cheese sandwiches," she finally says.

"Pardon?"

"I sat at the table with you the day before I left, and we ate grilled cheese sandwiches and brownies off of the good plates and celebrated the "*A*" on your science test."

"How fish turn into fossils," I say, remembering bits and pieces of that day that ended with the wine glass being thrown at the wall that evening. I remember coming home from school the next day, and wondering why everyone was talking in whispers. My nana was there and the police too, and Mrs. Ryder rang the doorbell to tell me she had just taken some cookies out of the oven and did I want to come over and have some. She kept leaning in and trying to look behind Nana into the kitchen where the police were sitting with Dad, but Nana said that would be great and ushered me out the door real quickly to go next door.

"That day," I tell her, "I had to go to Mrs. Ryder's while the police told Dad and Nana that you were on the train. She'd made these cookies — they were like little vanilla things with cranberry jelly or something weird in the middle. I nibbled at one, and when she turned away, I spit it in a napkin and shoved it in her couch cushions."

Mom pats my hand as if that's the worst I'd had to endure that day. "You hated science so much. I'd helped you study for that test, and you were so proud of that grade. We both were," she says. "The next week you were supposed to be tested on plant fossils, and I always wondered how you did on that one."

"I don't remember," I say, but I do. I remember that huge, red *F* slashed across the page. The *F*'s pretty much stayed with me for the rest of the year.

I want to continue this discussion. I've thought of so many more questions to ask since the last time I was here and we talked about it. Over and over I've relived that day Mom and Ian took me back to the hotel in Atlanta and she'd given me her phone number. She'd slipped it into my hands and whispered to me, but she'd looked across at Ian in the front seat and he'd shaken his head and turned to stare out his window. I could tell he was saying he'd warned her this wasn't a good idea.

I want to ask her all about how she came up with the idea of opening a post office box in Flannery Cove for me and how she went about it. About the first time I'd called her and she'd given me all the instructions about how I was to walk to the post office after school one day, and Ian would be waiting outside with a key to give me. How she told me that this was how we would communicate for now, and I was to always burn her letters and never write her address on paper — it must be ingrained in my brain only, she'd said — and how I had memorized that address over and over for years, absolutely terrified I'd wake up one day and it'd vanish from my mind. Would she think it was cute or sad that I used to say my prayers out loud every night in my bed way past my middle school years, "Dear Lord, Please take care of my mother in heaven," I'd say very clearly in case my dad could hear me, but I was thinking, *Dear Lord, please take care of my mother at 8900 Colonial Plantation Road, Apartment #19, Atlanta, Georgia 30312.*

But I say none of this because my mother is fragile enough right now without reminders of all her failings. I'm going to have to leave her soon, and I don't want to add any water to the sea of sorrow she's swimming in. This is not the time. My deadline of February is five months away, so I still have time to dissect through this when she's stronger if I can keep Deaton's newfound enthusiasm tempered, stop him from wanting to pick up his sword and slay dragons every time he walks out the door. She has to go back to school in three weeks, she's already told me, so she has to get stronger. She's acknowledged that.

It's the morning before I have to head home and leave her to find that strength, that my own buckles and gets away from me like it's just strapped on roller skates for the first time. It was doing so well, staying close, keeping me clutched in its tight grip, and then bam! It came barreling out of me with outstretched arms, desperately trying to regain balance and composure before plowing into the wall and crumbling at my feet. All because of Deaton's text.

> "I found the last known address for Mickey Connelly. He was living in the same house before his arrest and when he got out of prison he went back to it. Very possibly still there! We have a visit to pay."

# SEVENTEEN

**M**Y STRENGTH SHAKES itself off, regains its composure, and returns to me, assuring me Deaton is no match for my webs. If he knocks one down, I can rebuild. Practice makes perfect and all. Ironically it happens right after Sheila Thomas calls to tell me that Kevin and Amanda Schware are ready to present me with an offer on the house.

"I have exciting news," she says, with as much enthusiasm as someone calling to tell me the tree outside my door has grown a new leaf. "An offer. Can I come by your café and have you sign it?"

"Um. Yes?" I question it. The author inside of me screams. *This isn't the way it's supposed to be turning out. Girl can't lose family home on top of everything else! Girl needs something in her life to hold on to.*

*Well, I'll still have the café...*

Bradley doesn't even enter my mind.

I want to ask everything about it. *How much? What are the conditions? Do I have to remodel the whole thing before we close?* But I stay cool — just another offer — yawn.

She arrives around four o'clock that afternoon, just as Margo and Paulus are leaving. I've told everyone my first offer is coming. Everyone except Scott that is. I've tried to call, but his secretary says he's out and won't return to the office until next week.

*"Pick up the phone when it's ringing or you might not get a call back."*

172

We sit in the corner booth, the most private one in the café. She hands me the papers with a promising smile. "It's a good offer, I think," she says, rummaging through her purse and laying out items on the table's surface: pen, phone, glasses.

I scan it over cautiously like a test I haven't prepared for, but there's so much fine print. *Blah, Blah, Blah... where's the bottom line?* I find it on page three. The Schwares are offering me three thousand less than my asking price — the figure that, to the penny, would have paid off my debt to the bank and allowed me to walk away penniless but mortgage-free and right side up.

Sheila Thomas drones on and on about what's next: inspection, appraisal, title company. "The Schwares would like to close by late October."

While she talks, I focus on her eyes and her mouth, as if I'm paying very close attention. Her lids are brushed in a taupe color. There is a little smidgen of mustard in the right corner of her lips.

I think about my very meager bank account going down even more and my thermostat going up to stay in the high, inexpensive digits. Thank God it's almost fall again, only that means we're getting closer to February. *Helena.*

*One issue at a time.*

I'm remembering sitting in the living room watching Old Yeller on the big old console TV when I was around six years old. I've even been told Pappy used to rock me to sleep sometimes in that living room, but of course, I don't remember that. I think about Susan and me, playing restaurant in the black-and-white-tiled kitchen, and I think about Hailey — crawling, walking, running, skipping, and leaving. I even think about Greg carrying me over the threshold and asking if I was sure I wasn't carrying triplets, and I smile at the memory. And I remember how Nana used to tell me the story about how she had a crib in the living room for me when I was a baby and I'd turn myself sideways and get my little legs stuck between the slats and cry for her to come align me again. I'm so off-kilter now, I wish my Nana could set me straight and put me at peace.

And then my thoughts turn to the five Schware kids lined up in my dining room, holding crayons and scribbling on my golden dining room walls, which brings me back to the mustard blob.

"Sorry?" I say, raising my eyebrows in polite and earnest interest.

"Aren't you elated?" Sheila sits back against the booth proudly and repeats her question.

"Of course. Elated." I pick up the pen and scribble an illegible signature — a downward, wavering, defeated line with a few loops.

"**S**O HOW EXACTLY did you find him?" Deaton and I are in his car headed to the house I pray has burned down in the last few days. An image of a house taken from the internet sits on his lap and he's driving slowly, looking past me out the passenger side window, comparing each house we pass to the one in the picture.

"Detective Keller." We stop at a stop sign and a boy walks in front of us, carrying a skateboard. The boy has thin, white wires coming out of his ears and his eyes stay focused on his shoes. He's back on his board and weaving in and out of parked cars and garbage cans pulled to the curb before we accelerate again. "She put me in touch with Connelly's parole officer. He hasn't seen him in five years, but his last visit to him was at this house."

He must think I'm the worst investigator ever, and I wish so badly I could show how good I actually am at this, *or was*. I haven't spoken to Detective Keller since she told us the second unidentified woman was pregnant. Deaton's talking to detectives and parole officers and printing out pictures of the very house my mother may have stood in when her fake documents were created. It's easy to solve a case, but it's nearly impossible to know where to begin when you're purposely trying to make a case unsolvable. I remember when I was in Deaton's kitchen that day and his mom was talking to him on the phone. "You need a project," he said she'd told him.

*Well, Mrs. Dunklin, he has one now!*

Deaton stops in front of a blue house. Its wood siding is mildewed, and the blue is faded. The grass is patchy, and the screen door hangs open. "This is it," he says backing up a bit, so he's not blocking the walkway that leads up to the front door. He rubs his hands together like he's bracing for something and opens his door.

"Deaton." I grab onto his arm, but I don't know what else to say.

He quickly places his hand over mine and scrunches his nose to position his glasses. "It'll be okay, Ames. I'll do the talking so you don't have to."

I follow slowly behind him up the front walk. He stands on the top step and gives the door three quick knocks as I remain on the walkway, three steps down from him, looking around the neighborhood. A toddler next door is sitting on his walkway wearing only a diaper and drawing with chalk, oblivious to us.

"Coming." A voice comes from inside the house, and I can hear footsteps pounding the floor, getting closer. The lock seems to be a bit of a pain, but then the door opens and there stands a girl around twenty, maybe twenty-five. Her hair looks like she's just been dying it jet-black when we interrupted her. It's long, parted in the middle, and hanging down the sides of her face like she's peeking through a heavy theater curtain. She's dressed in a flannel shirt that's untucked from a pair of denim shorts that I assume, judging from the frays that hang from them like moss from the oaks in my yard, she took the scissors to and cut up herself. Her eyes are big and innocent and her lashes are also black and enviably long.

"Uh, yeah?" She says, looking past us and up and down the street like she's checking for someone else, maybe Mickey. Deaton looks back at me to see if I want to do the talking, but I give a slight nod.

"We're trying to locate a Mickey Connelly who used to live at this address," he says, showing her the image of her own house. She glances at the photo in his hand and back to his face.

"Never heard of 'im." She keeps a hand on the door, turning the knob back and forth. The repetitive gesture is annoying, and I want to reach up and put my hand over hers to stop it.

Deaton looks back at me. I scowl, disappointed, and start to thank her for her time.

"Do you mind me asking how long you've lived here?" he says.

She takes in a breath and looks him up and down quickly. "Bout three years. Three years in January."

"Never got any mail for a Mickey Connelly? Nothing?" Deaton asks her.

"Nope."

There doesn't seem to be anything left to say. I'm wondering if Deaton's going to leave our contact information with her, but it's pretty unlikely she's going to hear something about Mr. Connelly anytime soon if she hasn't heard it yet, and even more unlikely she'd do anything with our information besides toss it in the garbage. "Well, thanks for talking to us," Deaton says reluctantly, stepping down one step. A man comes outside next door, picks up the boy from the sidewalk, and lifts the garage door. I turn and watch them like I'm thinking about what we can do now, then I feel Deaton tap my hand to guide me back down the walkway. Glancing back at this girl, whose name we never even got, I smile my thanks.

*Her world, which was toppling, righted itself and she went on her way with a spring in her step and a…*

"Wait!" We're almost to the car when I hear the screen door slam shut. "You might try asking this man," she says, holding out a piece of paper to us. "Frank Wasserman. My landlord."

"**H**OW DO I look?" I ask Bradley. We're going to try to catch the nine o'clock movie, and we need to hurry.

"Great as always," he says, without looking up from his phone to confirm it. Apparently not as great as those confusing charts he's always admiring. I look him over quickly before we head out the door. He's dedicated, that's for sure, all furrowed brow and pursed lips.

We sit through one hour and forty-five minutes of some movie about a couple shipwrecked on an island — time I use to think about Frank Wasserman and what he might say and how I can counteract it — then walk across the street for a late-night snack. "I've been thinking about your café," Bradley says, as he taps the straw on the table to break the paper it's wrapped in.

"My café? What about it?"

"We might want to think about expanding it. I think it could be bigger maybe, bring in more profits."

*We?* I pull my head back.

"Just thinking of your bottom line." He holds his hands in the air, don't-shoot-me style.

"I don't want a bigger café. More work. More hours. More dance moms." *More funding!*

I've been dating Bradley for five months now. When he talks about my bottom line, it should not have anything to do with my finances.

I lay my hand on his and interrupt him softly. "Bradley, I don't have a net worth. I'm selling my house for three thousand dollars less than I owe on it, and I'm barely scraping by."

Two creases appear between his eyebrows. "I thought the house was your grandmother's. I thought she left it to you."

I lay it all on the table, telling my numbers guy that I had a bunch of numbers, but I threw them all in the blender with a few other things and what came out wasn't good. I've ruined all my numbers in the process. "It was either a house or a business," I say. "Turns out I can't have both."

Bradley leans back against his booth and lets out a puff of air, exasperated with me and my ruining of numbers. He smooths down his cowlick as if that will help him think more clearly. "Well," he finally says. "It may not happen this year, maybe not even next. But you'll get back on your feet and bring that portfolio back up."

*Back up? Portfolio?* I have a vague idea of what a portfolio is, but I've never had one — up or down. But it's a sweet sentiment, a vote of confidence.

"Bradley, would you notice if my best friend were attractive?" I ask, remembering my mother's long-ago advice.

"What? Who's your best friend? Deaton?"

I wave my hand. *Just kidding, never mind.*

"Amy. I don't have eyes for anyone but you. Certainly not Deaton. You can put money on that!"

"If I had any." I smile meekly and say at the same time he proclaims, "If you had any!"

We leave the restaurant and decide to call it a night. I yawn as we pull into my driveway and give him my tired face. "Oh gosh, so exhausted," I say in case he didn't get the message from the exaggerated sigh, the stretching of my back, or the rubbing of my eyes.

"Walk you to the door?"

"No, that's okay. I'll find my way." I recite my standard lines. We're a comfortable, predictable pair, one that goes separate ways every single time we're together. Every single time!

*Good, safe Bradley!*

We kiss goodnight. I sweep my negative thoughts of him from my mind and make out with him a bit, biting his lip playfully and pulling back to look intensely into his eyes. Sure enough, the only thing that results from our tussle is his unruly sprig of hair springing to life. I draw back as if fighting a passionate internal struggle.

*To be continued...*

I open the door, get out, and softly close it back staying in the disappointed, but oh so tired mood we've conjured and perfected.

The Hailey of my wishful thinking is on the landing looking at her watch and tapping her foot. *It's not even midnight yet,* I think. Her fleeting image dissipates.

*Reality, schmality.*

I grab my laptop and a blanket and head for the sofa to work on my sales reports. Helena has emailed to tell me she has been turning the house upside down trying to find that train ticket receipt.

> **Raulerson says he hasn't seen it in years but is sure it's packed away somewhere. We will find it! I have made another deposit in your account. Please bear with me and thank you so much for your continued endeavors and your patience.**

*Dear God!*

I exit and go to my Potion#9 profile, which I haven't looked at in months. Breezing through a few of my responses from potential dates, I'm so relieved I found Bradley before I met up with any of these men. Relieved I'm not still out there sitting through boring conversations and feeling nothing hopeful.

*But you are.* Hailey is back. The one person never afraid to tell it like it is. I ignore her imaginary nudge.

Then I try to find Deaton's profile, but he's taken it down. Same with Bradley. I look over my own and do the same — delete.

IT'S SATURDAY AFTERNOON, and I debate whether to do it, but I can't seem to help myself. I'm just going to drive by and check it out, but they've probably moved on to another project.

Only they haven't. They're all there inside the now constructed Habitat House. I can see them through the front window. Wanda and Debbie are both painting, which reminds me I should be home doing that myself. I slow down, but I keep driving past, then I circle the block and return. I'm not seeing Scott's truck, but I'm dressed in running pants and tennis shoes, ready to work, and I think Wanda and Debbie will be glad to see me again, glad to have me help. The front door is open to allow ventilation, and I walk in and clear my throat to get their attention. There are a few people in the kitchen working on something, and someone crosses the hallway and glances my way. They all turn and smile and resume their tasks, but Wanda and Debbie both turn and immediately lay down their paintbrushes.

"Girl, we thought we'd scared you off," Wanda says.

I wave toward the kitchen where a few faces I recognize are looking at me. A man — Dave something or other if I remember correctly — comes down from his ladder and lays his caulk gun on the countertop. "Amy. Great to have you back."

"Great to be back."

I'm not seeing Scott anywhere in the crowd. I head toward the front room with Wanda and Debbie. "Is Scott here?" I whisper to them, woman to woman.

"Scott Warner? He's in Honduras," Debbie says loudly. The newly built house, void of any furnishings, intensifies her voice. "Won't be back for another week I think."

I stare at her.

"El Cayo Campo," Wanda says. "Drilling wells for the village to have clean water supplies. People been drinking from the river. Always having stomachaches and catching diseases."

I nod as if I know all about it.

"Scott sponsors a well somewhere twice a year and goes to help drill it."

I pick up my roller. I'm on my third wall, rolling away, watching the bare drywall soak up the stark white primer when my phone rings. I pull it from my pocket and try to answer it without getting any paint on it, holding it between my shoulder and my ear, but before I can say anything Deaton's voice takes over. "Amy. Listen. Frank Wasserman lives over in Hinesville. I got hold of his wife, Margie, this morning. Frank wasn't there, but she said he'll be home on Tuesday morning."

"Tuesday morning?" My voice is too loud in this vacant house. Debbie stops rolling and looks at me. She and Wanda decide to take a break and leave the room. "Tuesday morning," I repeat softly.

"I've got a guy coming in a few mornings a week to help me in the shop, and he said he could start this week. We gotta be there by ten, Margie said. Frank has a doctor's appointment at twelve-thirty."

# EIGHTEEN

THE LINE CRACKLES, and it's hard to hear everything. Scott is calling from Honduras. His voice sounds upbeat as he says my name, like this is not a business call. He isn't in his office wearing a dark suit shuffling through papers. He's in a third-world country with a shovel, but he's stopped digging to call me. I imagine all the people of the village hovering nearby waiting breathlessly for the first sight of water and him saying it'll be a little while longer because there's a girl in Georgia.

"I message called."

I'm only getting every third word or so he says.

"Thing ok?"

"I just wanted to let you know Sheila brought me a contract. It's uh, a good one." I shout so he can hear me all the way in Honduras.

There's silence. Either he's stopped talking or I'm not hearing him. Then it picks back up. "Sounds when bank close not you."

"I'm not getting what you're saying. Bad connection."

No response from his end. "I'll come by next week and pay my bill," I finally say.

"Not sale for almost good," he replies.

T HE CAFÉ OPENS Tuesday morning, and I keep a careful eye on the clock. Cory comes in around nine and takes over so I can go to my office and change into something nicer to wear to Hinesville. I'm trying to zip the back of my blouse when he opens my office door and slides a box in. "Package for ya just arrived," he says. I stoop down and pick the box up off the floor. It's heavy. I find a pair of scissors to rip through the tape and open the flaps and lift out the contents. Wrapped in layers of padding and paper is a ceramic house, an island-type cottage, purple with green shutters, and a crooked wood sign hanging over the front door that says, "Welcome." There's a slit in the roof to put change through and I can hear coins clanging around inside. A note is taped to the back that I unfold and read.

**Save all your pennies. Love, Bradley.**

I clutch a hand to my heart — a gesture to show the world. *See! What a good man! I told you all!* Although it's not really all that sweet. It's more like a command. Well, it could be taken either way, I suppose. Men never speak clearly enough to be understood.

I glance at the clock, ten minutes to ten. I'll have to hurry and get over to the bookstore, so I holler to Cory on my way out and run across the street. Deaton's giving the new guy last-minute instructions. "Amy, this is Weston," he says as I stand off to the side waiting. "Amy owns the café across the street."

"Cool," Weston says. His dark hair hangs in his eyes, but he tosses his head and flings them aside to look at me.

Deaton claps his palms together. "We gotta get going. You sure you got everything?" Weston nods, not seeming concerned either way. "You can call my cell with any questions. *Anything*," Deaton stresses while grabbing his keys from under the counter.

"Nice meeting you, Weston," I call over my shoulder. He flings his bangs again and waves.

Deaton's passenger seat smells sweet and feminine like cotton candy. I tell him about the Schwares and their offer and Bradley's gift that just arrived. I'm still trying to decipher the intention behind the gesture, thinking more about that than Frank Wasserman and what he might say. Surely he didn't keep up with his past tenants.

"So it's going well with the two of you?" Deaton says, as he shifts into high gear and merges onto the interstate. He's practically fizzling and crackling with tension and excitement, trying to have a normal conversation, but not totally focused on my reply.

I smile and nod and turn to watch the scenery whiz by. "Sure."

The sun is hot through the window, and I lay my head back and close my eyes and try to think about Bradley, but other things keep kicking him out of my head. We pass by the dirt road that leads to the strawberry farm where Dad took Becky and Susan and me to pick. We'd emerged dripping in red like we'd been working in a haunted house, and full as ticks on a bloodhound.

"We're here."

I feel the car come to a stop and look up at the brick house. We pull into the driveway and the front door opens eagerly. A woman with brown, tightly curled hair stands in the doorway and comes out on the porch holding a dishtowel.

"I've just made some chicken salad sandwiches. And Frank's home," she announces as if she was afraid he might take off even though she'd told Deaton he'd be there. "I'm Margie."

It's dark and cluttered inside the house. Newspapers pile beside the recliner and on the table in front of it. The mantle is crowded with collectible teapots and clocks, and the walls are covered in framed certificates, gold coins, and antique magazine covers. Smells of old books and damp wood permeate.

The door opens in and has to be shoved to glide back over the old carpet. Mr. Wasserman doesn't turn around and greet us. He's sitting in his recliner watching the news, which is turned up very loud. Margie walks us around in front of him and shouts over the voice of the commentator that's reporting on the jobless rate in America. "Frank, this is the man I told you was coming to ask about the house," she says, and then turns to me, "I'm sorry, dear, I didn't catch your name."

"Amy." I smile at her and hope my eyes will adjust to the dark interior soon. I can hardly see to walk any further, and I can't hear anything being said. Deaton is saying something to Frank, but I've no idea what.

"Now, I've made some sandwiches for us," Margie says as we follow her into the kitchen like we're on a tour and this is the first stop. The kitchen is separated from the living area by a swinging door. All three of us enter, and Margie goes straight to the refrigerator and takes out a bowl that's loosely covered with flapping plastic wrap. I stare at the collectible cookie jars cluttered on the counter and on the shelf built above the upper cabinets and around the perimeter of the room.

"Sit down and make yourselves comfortable," she says pulling the chairs out from the table for us. "I've made some chicken salad," she repeats for the third time.

"What can I do to help?" I join her at the counter and hold out my hands for the cups she's lifting down from the cabinet.

"Oh no. You sit tight. I'll get all this." She opens another cabinet and pulls out half a loaf of bread and begins to spoon the contents of the Tupperware bowl onto the thin, white slices, humming while spooning.

Deaton taps his fingers on the little, chipped, enamel table. "How long have you all lived here, Mrs. Wasserman?"

"Oh, call me Margie. We've been here forever and a day." She sets the sandwiches in front of us on paper towels and shakes some chips out of a bag. "Raised four kids in this house. Used to be a nicer neighborhood. Frank's uncle left him five rent houses when he died, and we decided to stay put, keep them rented, and let Frank take early retirement from the factory." She shakes the last of the broken chips onto her paper towel. "Frank, lunch!" She cracks open the swinging door and hollers at her husband.

Frank comes through the door, but he keeps the swinging door propped open with the loud television blaring in. "So which house y'all interested in renting?" he finally asks with his mouth full. "I got one vacant now and two more coming up." I lift my sandwich to my lips and look at Mr. Wasserman now that I can finally see him. He's not a large man, but his stomach is quite protruding. His dark hair is sparse and oiled down with something, and his nose has somehow mushroomed over the years, overtaking his other features. On his cheeks is a web of broken veins like the smaller lines on a map, his face a permanent sunburn.

Margie's chicken salad is swimming in mayonnaise and has soaked through the thinly sliced bread in the middle, which now looks like raw dough. Deaton looks at me. I look down at my paper towel and press my index finger to pick up pieces of potato chips. "Well actually, Mr. Wasserman, we're trying to locate one of your past tenants. A Mickey Connelly that lived in a house you own in Flannery Cove," he says.

"Mickey Connelly," Margie says, shaking her head slightly. "Oh, dear! I never thought we should have let him back in that house. Left with two months of unpaid rent." This is obviously a sore subject that's been hashed and rehashed.

Frank shoots her a look. "And just what do you suggest I should have done? The house was sitting empty not paying for its lawn care and utilities." He glances at Deaton. "Can't help ya," he says as he turns his eyes back to the doorway and the TV. "Crazy politicians," he mumbles in reference to whatever the newscaster has said, and Margie smiles nervously at me. "That house is rented right now," he says, still looking at the TV. "Under lease till..." he rolls his eyes upward, thinking, "June, I think."

"Mr. Wasserman," I finally speak up. "We're not interested in the house. We're interested in finding Mickey Connelly.

"Whatcha want with that scumbag?" Frank says, wiping his sleeve across his mouth. "What's he done now?"

"We think he might have some things that belong to me," I say. "We—"

"Money," Frank interrupts me. "Mr. Connelly owes quite a few people money. We'll add you to the list." He finally takes his eyes off the TV. "I've no idea where the man is. If I did, I'd have *my* money already."

"Any chance you still have any papers he filled out when he rented the house?" Deaton scoots closer to the table. I notice he hasn't touched his lunch. His eyes dart back and forth between all of us. "Do you know if he had any family or close friends nearby? Maybe someone he used as a reference?"

"Oh, we would have thrown all of that away a long time ago," Margie says worriedly, her two months unpaid rent slipping out of her hands again. She looks at the clock on the wall. "Frank." she nods toward it. "The doctor."

Frank scoots back, his chair screeching on the floor. "Guy moved into that house back in, oh I dunno, eighty-eight, eighty-nine," he says, wrapping his hands around his big stomach. "He got arrested and left that place full of crap. Some reporter showed up wanting papers and willing to pay for 'em, but the rest of it I had to pay someone else to haul away, so it was a wash."

Margie inhales. Frank's blood pressure probably can't handle this trip down memory lane.

"When Mickey showed back up years later, the house was empty and in need of repairs, and he promised to do 'em for me. I'd just had that back surgery," he says, looking at Margie. She nods affirmation. "He stayed for about six months. Never did a dad-burned thing, then left me with two month's rent and an electric bill I had to settle before the next tenant could get hooked up."

I know before he says it what Deaton's next question is going to be and that I should beat him to it, show I'm at least a fraction of the investigator he, the novice, is.

The words are out of his mouth before my brain has formulated them into a sentence. "You said a reporter wanted his papers?" Deaton leans in, elbows on the table.

Margie glances at the clock on the wall again and rises from her chair. She places the loose saran wrap back over the Tupperware container. "I just have to get this back in the icebox," she says.

"Yeah." Frank wads up his paper towel into a ball. He tosses it back on the table. "Wanted to do a story on the arrest or something, I guess." He shrugs his shoulder. "I tried to get him to take everything in the house, but he only wanted certain things. I helped him box up paperwork and some stamps, I think. Buncha junk."

I finally pipe in. "Any chance you still remember his name?"

Frank chuckles. "How'd I know you were gonna ask that?" He shrugs. "Something Monterey. Monterey something or other." He continues to shake his head. "I dunno. All I got's Monterey." He turns back to the TV.

"Frank. The time," Margie says. Frank looks over his shoulder at the clock on the wall. Deaton and I both stand. Our time is up. "Let me pack you kids a cola or something cool for the road." She opens the refrigerator again and looks at me.

"I'd bet money you'll never find Mickey Connelly," Frank says. "But if you ever do, you tell him he owes Frank Wasserman a hundred thirty-eight dollars for electric and six-fifty for two month's rent." He turns back around at the doorway. "And if we're dead, he owes it to our kids."

Margie places two cold cans of root beer in my hands, despite my protests. She ushers us back through the living room, past the news show turned up to full volume. "I hope you find your man," she says to us as she waves from the front porch.

I close my door and Deaton reverses out of the driveway.

"I hope we find our *woman*," I say, on the verge of tears.

Deaton stares straight ahead and exhales all the personal responsibility he feels. "I know this is hard for you, Ames. I don't mind doing all the legwork on this. Just keep your eye on the end goal."

I can't even remember the supposed end goal. Dead mother? Mother in a coma? Stranded on an island mother?

Cory is scheduled to work till closing, so I shut myself in my office for most of the afternoon to tend to my business. I'm compelled to tell Helena something, so I write various things out, delete them, and start over again. I do this about ten times and give up. My mom needs to stay dead as far as Helena and my dad are concerned, and Deaton, and Hailey, and now Bradley and Scott Walker — *everyone in my life* — and there's just no way to spin it anymore. Her grave gets shallower with the passing of each day.

I call Bradley on the way home and tell him his package made it to me. "I mean it, Amy," he says. "You'll get back on track." Everything always seems to have a train connotation.

When I pull into my driveway Dad is sitting in his car at the curb waiting for me. "Uh, I'll have to call you back, Bradley," I say, turning off my engine. Dad's face is covered by the newspaper, and he hasn't seen me pull in, nor is he aware that I've approached him until I rap on his driver's side window.

He jumps in his seat. "Like ta give me a heart attack, Sparkle." I'm happy to see him but worried about what an unexpected visit means. I lean into him as he gets out of his car, inhaling the familiar smell of cinnamon tic-tacs and spray starch. *My Dad!*

There's a "for sale" sign in my yard with a "sale pending" banner that's been attached to it. Surely he's spotted it, but he says nothing about it.

I lay my takeout salad and the black sea bass I'd picked up earlier and planned on broiling on the kitchen counter and head to the laundry room to feed Otis. "Make yourself at home," I holler over my shoulder. When I return to the kitchen, Dad is standing in front of an open cabinet, pulling out a glass.

"Care if I have a glass of something?" He shuts the cabinet, and I take the glass from him and fill it with ice. "Where're the dishes?" He nods his head at my upper cabinets.

"Dishes? They're in the cabinet. Oh, *those* dishes. Well, they're still packed." I busy myself with my salad, pouring it into a bigger bowl, leaning into my refrigerator to find the right dressing. I've decided not to bother with my fish. Too much standing at the counter sprinkling seasonings and waiting on it to broil. I need to keep my hands and my mouth busy. "Help yourself to whatever you'd like to drink. I have sweet tea, cucumber lemonade, water."

He chooses tea and joins me at the bistro table, sitting in Hailey's chair. "You like The Green Room?" He watches me eat and points to my salad. I feel as if I'm being quizzed, under very close scrutiny.

"Oh, well. It's a salad. I would have brought one home from the café, but Cory cleaned everything up before I had a chance."

"Helena and I don't care for it so much, The Green Room. Haven't had lunch there, but she did a dinner review. Don't get the Broccoli Chicken Bake." I nod and wonder if his opinion ever varies from Helena's. If it does, I haven't heard tell of it. It's always "Helena and I think this," or "Helena and I don't like, do like whatever."

"So, I guess you saw the sign in the yard," I say. "Looks like I've sold the house."

"I didn't notice it, but that's good. That's what you wanted."

His enthusiasm is genuine, but I think if I told Dad I was selling everything to move to Amish Country and teach school his reaction would be the same. Whatever decision I make in life is good, no flak from him. God, what I'd give for some dad flak some days, but he keeps sipping at his tea, asking no details about who's going to be living in Nana's house, how I did on the sale, when's the closing, where I'm going. All my life I've wanted so badly to delve deep with him instead of always gliding surfaces, avoiding potholes, steering clear of any detours.

"I'm glad you came by to visit, Dad. It gets lonely here without Hailey."

"I bet. That's why it's good that you're selling it. I'm wondering if during your packing you might have come across anything."

I look around me. Nothing is even packed yet.

"Anything? Like what?"

"Well, Helena and I have been trying to find something. The private investigator she, *uh, we* hired..."

I nod between bites and wipe at the vinaigrette on my lip. "Uh-huh. How's that going?" I keep eating, seemingly only vaguely interested in his response.

"So far, it's not. Helena is a bit discouraged with the investigator, but then there just doesn't seem to be much to go on. We've hit a bit of a standstill if you will, and we're looking for a receipt for the train ticket your mother purchased. Can't seem to find it anywhere."

I lay down my fork. I have to be interested in this or it will seem strange. "Why would you think it might be here? Why do you even need that? I mean, I don't know, Dad. I'm very confused about this whole thing."

Dad pauses before answering me then holds up his glass. "Can I have more?"

I take the glass and go back to the refrigerator, and he wipes at the condensation on the table with his napkin. "I'm not sure what Helena wants to accomplish, but I need to support her. She's got it in her head that your mother may not have been on that train."

I place the glass back down on the table a bit heavily. I want to shout *What about supporting me? What about how this is affecting me? What about saying 'my wife' instead of 'your mother'?*

Shouting any of this would make no difference. Dad would find a way to pacify me, and we'd be on to another topic before I even realized it, and I can't get the words past my deceitful lips anyway. "So why is a receipt important?"

He takes a sip of the tea. "I'm not really sure. For some reason, the investigation is stalled without that receipt. Verification, I suppose. New technology possibly."

"Well, I haven't seen any receipt."

We sit in silence for a few seconds then he says, "Amy, there's something I should tell you."

He's going to tell me about the unidentified women on the train and how he always assumed one was Mom, and he now knows it wasn't, and that he's lost Mom. He turned his back and lost her. I look straight at him and prepare myself for this talk. How would I normally react if I had no inside knowledge? Instead, he moistens his lips and leans forward. He pats my hand and says, "I'm glad you have a buyer for the house. It's a good thing for you. I worry about you."

I've finished what I can of my salad and toss the rest in the garbage, feeling sick. Dad rises from the table and tosses the ice from his glass into the sink. "If I find," I start to say, but I'm interrupted by the ringing of the phone. I hold up a finger to Dad and grab the receiver.

He stands by for a few minutes, waiting for me to see him out. "Um, hold on just a second," I say into the receiver and hold it to my chest while I kiss Dad on the cheek. "It's Mary."

This is the closest I'll ever get to having my mom and dad both in the room with me, one in person and the other on the receiving end of a phone line. But the comparison momentarily jaunts me. One so inexhaustibly emotionally complex and the other only requiring the barest of fundamental needs from me: walk me, feed me, toss me the occasional bone, and I'll love you forever, I promise.

He smiles and holds up a hand. "I'll see myself out." He walks to the front door and turns to look at me again before he leaves. In his view he's had a nice visit with me, he's going home to a nice, new condominium — maybe a visit from his girlfriend that he apparently sees eye to eye with on everything, and things have turned out for me like he thinks I wanted them to. All is well with his world.

"I'm back," I murmur into the phone. I am not feeling charitable toward my mother right now. I'm sorry she's hurting, and I'm worried about her, but I just had a conversation with my father about her death. When I look in a mirror, a liar looks back at me because of her. She hears the weariness in my tone, my aloofness.

"What is it?" She says, rather impatiently, and I have an immediate epiphany. If I have a problem, then we can spend time dissecting that instead of her problems. Her problems never get solved anyway. We just go over and over them and let them keep dragging us down.

"I'm sad about the house, Mom. Have you not been paying attention to my life at all?"

"Mary."

I ignore the correction and plod on, and my fears and heartaches pour out. "Nana's house. God, I never thought it would end up like this. I thought Hailey's kids would hunt Easter eggs in this yard one day, bake Christmas cookies with me."

"I know. I know." Mom's voice is soft, reassuring — not the desperate breathlessness I've heard non-stop for the last few weeks. A real Mom voice. "But, isn't it hard to be there without Hailey? Don't the memories just kill you?"

*Yes. No.*

"I don't know. I'm just... I have so much right now with this investigation. I can't...I'm scared."

I hear her voice in the background of my own. "Don't worry about that. Ian covered my tracks well."

"It's more than just covering tracks. You don't ever seem to get past that, to the heart of the matter. And the house selling. I've let my family down. This isn't what Nana intended." I take a second to breathe and continue. "And with Dad selling our old house this is all I had left. This was the only house I have memories of you in."

"Me? I don't... What memories do you have of *me* there?"

I try to think. I'm sure I have memories of my mom here, but I can't put my finger on them. *Thanksgiving? Christmas?* No. I'm only able to picture us at the house by the country club on holidays. "Well, I know this is where you came to find me before you left." It's all I can think of on the spur of the moment, but I really don't know. She's told me she never meant to leave me. She said I was supposed to be at Nana's that afternoon, and she was going to slip in and grab me. Only when she got here we weren't around, so they got the receipt made for the train ticket, and she snuck back into our house to place it. Ian told her there wasn't any time to waste — their plane was leaving in a few hours.

"How were you going to just slip in and take me from Nana's?" I ask, changing courses on the conversation.

"Good God, Amy. I've told you this. It was a half-day of school that day. She was supposed to pick you up and take you to her house." Her voice is high as if she's justifying herself. "How was I supposed to know she'd take you shopping instead of straight home? The normal routine was to park you in the living room while she went into her bedroom to watch her stories. Her soap operas."

Something about this doesn't seem right. I've never questioned it before, but now I wonder. "But she was in charge of me. Weren't you the least bit afraid that she might be even more devastated and get in serious trouble with the law if I was taken while in her care? My God, she could have been arrested for neglect or something. Did you ever think about that, *Mary?*" My voice is rising, as this occurs to me. How could my mother have come up with a plan that could have very possibly implicated my grandmother in something she had nothing to do with? To make these decisions for her own life was one thing, but to put Nana in that situation was another. "Well, did it?" I practically scream.

She is silent on her end. The silence lasts a bit too long, and I wonder if she's hung up. But then I hear her again, loud and clear, with some sort of determination in her tone. "I not only thought about it," she says through clenched teeth. "I hoped for it."

# *Nineteen*

"YOU HOPED FOR it?" I shriek into the phone. "What is that supposed to mean?"

My mother exhales as if she's coming to terms with something. "Amy, listen."

"I'm all ears."

"It's time I clear up a few fuzzy memories for you."

The space in front of me seems to go dark, dizzying. I tighten my grip on the phone with one hand and steady myself with the other.

"First, I want you to know that home... home is not a building. Take it from me, home is where the ones you love are. Selling a house doesn't take that away. Leaving and turning your back on them does." She chokes on the last words, but I hear them. I'm so sick of her choking on her own words, her own doings. I don't feel sorry for her anymore.

"I've told you I wanted to come back for you when I wasn't able to take you with me that day. But we had a flight to catch, and when we got to Scotland Ian told me I was literally dead to you all. I just... I feared... I couldn't." She is crying openly now. "When Ian's dad died and we got to come back to Atlanta to take over the restaurant, I was full of such hope. The thought of being that close to you. The hope that I could see you, even if it was across a park

191

or five rows behind you in a movie theater. I never in my wildest dreams imagined it would be *you* who found *me*."

"I'm getting impatient with the trip down memory lane, Mom," I say, with annoyance.

"Wait. I." She's demanding to be heard. "I never meant to leave you. *Never!* I could not stay married to your dad. I could not live that life any longer. I wanted Ian. But I always wanted you too. Leaving you was not my plan. My plan was to take you and that foster child, Susan, with me."

"*Susan!?*" I'm thoroughly confused. Why would my mother take a foster child to Scotland? *Kidnap her?* "I don't understand," I say, warily.

"Amy. Your memories of your Nana and that home are not accurate. You were so young, you don't remember. Maybe you didn't even notice."

There's that dizzying array of strobes again, that heat fanning out from my core. What is she talking about? My nana was a wonderful woman. She loved me so much. She took in an orphan, for God's sake. She was a saint.

"Susan would have been better off with us in Scotland. It was part of the deal. Ian promised me we'd never be found, and Susan would be happier."

This is absolute garbage. My mother and her insane drama! "Happy?" I scream. "What are you talking about? Susan was happy!"

"Your grandmother was not the loving person you remember her being," Mary says softly, practically, as if she's making sense. "She was loving to you, sure. You were her flesh and blood. But, she was awful to Susan. She was… well… powerful, always lording that power."

"Now wait a minute. You can't say…"

"I tried to stop it. God knows I tried, Amy. Your father would not acknowledge it, and it was another source of contention between us. I tried so hard to…"

I feel it then, the slight crack that's appeared in a fragile family heirloom. I slam down the phone, cutting off her vile words, putting more distance in the miles between us than there's been in a long time. My nana was a pillar of the community. She had friends and acquaintances up and down the Georgia Coast. She organized the annual orphanage fundraising dinner every year at the country club, raising tens of thousands of dollars in donations. I cannot hear another word of this blasphemous talk against her.

SCOTT WALKER HAS gone cold again. I've heard nothing, no talk of meet-ups or mortgages. I've been moping around all morning, depressed and downright angry. My mother has me irritated and ornery like a horsefly has landed on my scalp. I'm so mad, I could spit darts, and I feel certain that Scott Warner is a predator that casts magic spells on all his female clients and should be reported to the Georgia bar.

But when Bradley shows up unexpectedly to have lunch with me at the café, I glance up and my eyes take him in, delighted. He's dressed in a way I've never seen him before: Khaki pants that fit tightly, a blue buttoned shirt that seems to either be brand new or recently dry cleaned. He's wearing a coral and white striped tie. He looks good!

"Hey," he says.

I walk away from the booth and greet him across the room. He kisses me quickly on the lips in front of everyone, and I'm proud of him. I'm proud of Bradley. Well, I'm shallow and fickle, that's what I am. But at the moment, I'm proud.

*Attention everyone, I have a man I'm proud of here!*

"What brings you to this side of town?"

"Hoping you're free for lunch," he says, taking off his sunglasses. They're attached to a Croakie that loops around his neck. I actually shake my head in wonder, he's just so cool and successful looking.

We head to the booth in the far corner and Jenna rushes over with a menu for him.

"Sooo." I draw the word out and lean in, placing my face on my palms, my elbows on the table.

"Sooo," he says right back.

Madame Bienve taps above us. She's all over the floor today like she's outlining a dot-to-dot picture. Bradley never even seems to notice. He doesn't seem to notice anything but me, just like my mom once said it should be.

After lunch, I retreat to my office to get some paperwork done. I grow bored and achy sitting in my chair so I dial the familiar number, just to check in. Not because a newly spiffed-up Bradley made me think of an always spiffed-up Scott — *no, definitely not.*

"Scott Warner's office," his receptionist says. *Tamra*, I think her name is.

"Hi. Um, this is Amy Hollander. I'm a client of Mr. Walker's. Was. I was a client."

"Hello, Amy," she says. Her voice is crisp, professional, and friendly. "What can I do for you?"

"I was wondering if he's in. I think I have a bill to pay. I need to know how to go about taking care of that."

"Hold just a moment, please. Let me check for you."

I hold, listening to music until she comes back on the line.

"Amy, Mr. Warner is not here, but I've located your file. There is no balance due at this time."

I chew at my lip. He's never in anymore. I wonder if he's back from his trip. "I, um. If that changes could you please let me know? And could you please make sure Mr. Warner knows my house is under contract?"

"That's wonderful news. I will certainly tell him that for you. Have a good day, Amy."

Some thirty minutes or so later I walk out of my office and smack dab into Paulus. He's in the same century with the rest of us today, dressed in tan shorts and a dark blue shirt. I'm immediately caught off guard. I know Paulus' clothing choices follow his mood. If he's not extravagant with his fashion, then he's most likely feeling depressed. "Paulus," I say, acting as if I haven't even noticed. "How nice to see you. Have you had your muffin already?"

He looks behind me and speaks as if someone's plastered to the wall. "My educational goals are being met to my mother's satisfaction at my new school, but the faculty is not meeting my other needs and my peers are less than genial." Paulus shows no emotion when he speaks, but I think I'm beginning to see a slight frown, perhaps a weariness, in his body when he discusses school-related matters. Even he has grown tired of his dilemma.

"Oh, Paulus." I hug him to me. It's an automatic impulse, but probably not one he'll appreciate. I loosen my arms and let him go, ready to apologize, but he stays smushed up against me. His arms hang limp at his sides, but he does not move. We stand like that until I return my hand to the back of his head and stroke the little wisp of hair that curls into a ducktail at the nape of his neck.

"Where do you think you would like to go to school, Paulus? Do you have any ideas?"

"My mother says we will go to the drawing board. Apparently, I've been there before, but I have no recollection of it."

Deaton waltzes in ten minutes later. "Socialite Special before you clean the coffers, please."

"I've told you, you're using that word the wrong way. Coffers means... nevermind." I reach for a Styrofoam cup and fill it up for him. "You can put all your silly, frilly stuff in it yourself." I nod toward the creams and sugars.

He pumps his flavor into the cup. "I have news."

I know what his news is going to be. I'm a step ahead of him this time. I figured this out days ago but never said anything — obviously. I'd hoped he would never make this seemingly impossible connection. He's good... very good.

"So this Monterey guy Mr. Wasserman spoke of." He looks around for a stir stick and decides on a straw instead. He stirs for a second, saying nothing, then continues. "I kept looking for someone with the last name Monterey. Been digging for days. Couldn't find a thing." He takes a sip of his coffee. "So then I came across an article in the Monterey County Herald. *Monterey, California,*" he enunciates, smiling with glee.

I nod and raise my eyebrows, letting him believe he's impressed me. "Go on."

"So this article was about a guy named Joe Mulligan. Better known as Monterey Joe."

"Monterey Joe," I repeat the name.

"Article said Monterey Joe was retiring. It was a year after the train accident. Guess where Ol' Joe was retiring to?"

"Georgia?"

"Savannah."

"You've found him?"

"Of course," he says, ever the dedicated investigator.

*Of course.*

"We have an appointment?"

"No, actually," he says, chewing on the stir stick. He takes it out of his mouth and talks with it pointed at me. "I found his last known address, but no phone number. We're gonna have to show up at Joe's unexpected."

I HAVEN'T SPOKEN WITH Mary since I slammed the phone down mid-conversation a few nights ago. We remain silent, disconnected. My mind keeps playing tricks on me. She's put some ideas into it, and now it won't let them go.

There was a night Nana made a big dinner. We all sat at a large, oblong table filled with crispy golden fried chicken, creamy mashed potatoes, slick ears of corn with pats of butter sliding off them, and little green peas piled high in a white bowl that was spidered with hairline cracks. Dad said a blessing, and we all got ready to pass the plates around the table. I sat next to my mother. Susan sat on the other side of me. Before the tray of chicken reached Susan, Nana scurried back into the kitchen and returned with a small bowl of something that looked like cold, coagulated gravy. It seems like my mother said something about it and Nana said Susan had been having some stomach trouble lately and the doctor had told her she needed to eat the stuff in the bowl.

I'd watched her touch her spoon to it and the surface broke, like a rock hitting pond scum. There was a lot of arguing back and forth between my mom and my dad and my grandmother, and Susan had sat there eating the whole bowl of the thick, brown gunk while my mother pleaded with my father to open his eyes and see what was going on. I recall my father being very distressed, but it seems like he agreed with both Mom and with Nana, placating them both.

My memory is fuzzy on a lot of the details, but I am clear on one. After Susan finished her goop and all the surrounding adults were arguing, she softly said, "Excuse me," then stood up and threw every bit of it back up on the plush, beige carpet. Nana had grabbed her by the elbow and pushed her up the stairs to her little bedroom and stayed up there with her for a long time. Taking care of her, I assumed.

When Nana finally came back down the carpet had been cleaned and no one would have known the whole thing happened, except for the tension. My mother grabbed me and told my father we were leaving. By then I was confused and crying, though I do remember my father then telling Nana to pack a bag for Susan because he was taking her home with us. I remember that because

I couldn't reconcile why we would take her to spend the night if she was sick.

Other things like that keep popping into my mind, and it's trying to twist them into something other than what they were. So when she finally calls me on Thursday, I'm apprehensive to get back into anything with her. I don't want to remember these things.

"Amy," she says. "Can you come up? I need you." And just like I told Deaton way back when we filled out those stupid online profiles, I'm a sucker when someone is kind or vulnerable, even if they've ticked me off to a likely point of no return. This holds especially true for my mother, as it's most likely where it originates from.

"I'm really not in the mood for this," I say, but I look at the calendar taped to the side of my refrigerator anyway. I notice the appraisal is scheduled for later the following week. I pinch the bridge of my nose and consider. "I suppose I could meet you halfway Monday afternoon. I'll go to a rest area. I am not coming all the way to Atlanta."

"I'm teaching until two."

"I control the conversation.," I say.

"Fine. Just please come."

"I have to leave by six to come on back home, so it's gonna be quick."

D EATON AND I decide to drive to Savannah to see Monterey Joe on Saturday. Kristlyn is in town, but she's shopping with a friend that morning. "I'd like to be back by two if possible," Deaton says when I meet him out in my driveway and throw my bag in his back seat. I nod in agreement — I have mountains of receipts on my desk to weed through. It's a crisp, clear morning like the outdoors is being air-conditioned. Little Matthew Splindle is riding his tricycle up and down his driveway across the street while his mom sits on her porch talking on her cell phone. I turn to Deaton with a smile. "Let's do this."

I'm beginning to convince myself all these loose threads will never amount to any sort of recognizable garment. A landlord here… a reporter there… put it all together and you've got a landlord and a reporter — nothing more.

We drive to Savannah with the windows down. Deaton says he hopes Monterey Joe is friendlier than Frank Wasserman. I remind him we promised Frank we'd track down his two-month's rent. "Add that to the list," I shout over the wind and the sound of traffic. Anyone looking at a photo of us would think we're on a carefree jaunt down the coast. Deaton almost misses our exit and veers off quickly.

The town of Savannah is enjoying the temperature change, and the farmer's market at Forsyth Park is crowded. Deaton's GPS leads us right up to the curb of the two-story house. It's as bright as a lemon and sparkles like it's been freshly cleaned with one. The shutters are white, and the sun bounces off the windows. Joe Mulligan's home looks like that of a man who has his life in order. My loose threads threaten to merge and strengthen. A coat of many colors blows in the breeze on the outer edges of my mind, but I grab scissors and slash it. I take Deaton's hand and haul myself out of the low bucket seat of his car and follow behind as he sprints to the white French door with the fall wreath attached to it.

As always I hang behind a bit and allow Deaton to ring the doorbell. I can see through the glass in the door: shiny, light oak floors, and walls the color of a cloudless sky. A young boy, maybe three, comes barreling down the hallway off to the right, his mother hollering behind him, "Wait for me to open the door, Nicholas."

He gets to the door and stands there staring at us suspiciously. Deaton waves, but he doesn't wave back. His mother reaches the door and pulls it open, and he hides behind her legs, staring out at us. She's young, beautiful, fortunate with this house and this darling child, the kind of woman that holds the world in her hands. "Hello," she says, her mouth pulled wide. "How can I help you?"

Deaton glances back at me before speaking to her. "We're looking for Joe Mulligan," he says. "This was the last known address for him."

Her smile fades just slightly and is replaced with a bit of wariness. She doesn't pull the door open any further, but she reaches over to the right of her and drops her keys on an entry table. I hadn't noticed she was holding keys, but now I take in the sunglasses pushed up on her forehead, the cranberry-colored jeans and denim button-down blouse, the tan boots, and the touch of gloss on her lips. She must have been on her way out when we interrupted her. "What do you need with him?" she says, as she unfurls the boy's chubby hands from her thighs and tells him to go play for a minute.

"We were hoping he might have some information on a case we're working on," I say before Deaton can — an attempt to make myself noticed and look like I have something to do here besides ride shotgun while Deaton unearths my deeply buried family secrets.

Her facial muscles relax and she opens the door a bit further. "Oh, a case. Maybe I could put you in touch with someone else."

Deaton produces the folder full of information he's gathered so far and thrusts it toward her. "Do you know Joe?"

"He's my father," she answers him, a bit reluctantly. She takes the folder but doesn't open it. "But I'm not sure. Well, he…" Her sentence trails.

"Oh," Deaton says and looks back at me. I smile warily and try to appear as if this is going well. "Deaton Dunklin." He holds out his hand to her.

"Amy Hollander," I say, copying his gesture.

She shakes our outstretched hands. "Alexa Kendrick. Alexa *Mulligan* Kendrick. Just a second." She leaves the door open and steps back a few steps to look down the hallway, checking on Nicholas I assume. Satisfied, she returns to us and opens the file Deaton has given her.

He continues talking. "Amy and I are investigating a train accident. Derailment, actually. Happened in 1988. There are some, uh, questions as to who may have been on board, and we're trying to uncover the identity of some of them."

She looks up from the files she's scanning. "The train?"

"Yes," he confirms, a bit bewildered. It's as if they've both reached the same page in the file at the same time, hers literally in front of her and his tucked safely in his mind. "We think there may be some connection to your dad and a counterfeiter that was arrested around that time."

I wince. He's giving out too much information. I don't want the rest of the world connecting these threads and making full garments. I can't go around slashing them all if that happens.

A dawning comes over her features. If possible, her sparkly eyes intensify and her rosy cheeks flush even more, like little posies. "I've been waiting for you," she says as she finally opens the door wide.

# TWENTY

"SO YOUR FATHER knew?" Deaton is sitting in the over-sized club chair to the right of the fireplace. I am in the matching one across the room, diagonal from him, but I can see his face. He's excited, and I try my best to appear so as well. Deaton is leaning back in his chair, his legs outstretched, his hands wrapped around a glass of lemonade that Alexa has brought to him. My lemonade remains untouched, and I am perched on the edge of my chair, eager to hear every word said. Alexa is seated between us on the leather sofa. Her legs are crossed, the picture of composure.

"Well, like I said. We had to put Dad in a nursing home last November. He just got too bad." She frowns at the memory. I frown with her, but Deaton forgets to appear sympathetic. He keeps nodding his head like an eager dog, following her trail, waiting for the conclusion. "Before the Alzheimer's he had been researching a few different cases. He retired out here to be with us, you know." Deaton nods his head as if Joe himself had told him all about it before he packed up and left California.

"He became interested in a few cases that caught his attention and wanted to spend his retirement years solving them. 'Keep the ol' noggin strong' he used to say." She shrugs at her father's logic that didn't work. "Anyway, the train derailment was one of them.

200

He was determined to find out everything about it. I remember he said there was a disappearance of a local woman at the same time. There was apparently only a small write-up about her disappearance, and then she was listed as one of the victims of the accident, but he said something about two other unidentified women."

She knits her brow. "I don't know. I can't remember everything. Dad knew things other people didn't necessarily know because he had contacts and sources everywhere. He'd tell us things he'd found out sometimes at the dinner table. He lived with us about five years or so before we had to put him in a home, but..." She shakes her head, trying to recall. "Dad felt like the two things might not be as separate as the media or the police led everyone to believe. He too thought there was something to the counterfeiter's arrest."

"He met the counterfeiter, Mickey Connelly?" Deaton asks, looking for a coaster to place his glass on.

"No. No, I don't believe so." Alexa hands him one that was in a wooden box on the marble-topped coffee table in front of her. "He only purchased some of his things. Paperwork Mr. Connelly had left behind at a house he had been renting before his arrest."

I hate to do it, but it's inevitable, so again I beat Deaton to it. "Is there any way we could see those things?" Surely they were tossed when Joe moved to the nursing home, I pray.

Alexa uncrosses her legs. She glances at the diamond-encrusted watch strapped to her thin wrist. "I would love to show you those things, but they are in a storage facility across town. I have to be somewhere soon, so I can't open it for you today. Would one day next week work for you? Perhaps Thursday morning?"

Alexa's little boy comes toddling into the room pulling a blanket behind him. He crawls up in her lap and sticks a thumb in his mouth. She gently pulls it out and whispers, "Don't you fall asleep just yet. We'll be in the car soon," while she kisses the top of his blond head.

"That would be wonderful," Deaton says. He drains the last of his lemonade and places the empty glass back on the coaster. "I hope it's not too much of an inconvenience. We need this information. You just have no idea." He drones on and on, way overboard.

And then Alexa stands and says the worst possible thing she could say to him. More fuel to blow this fire he's started sky high. "This case really dogged my father. I would love to see someone solve it for his legacy. As I said, I've been waiting for you. Well, for someone."

201

Deaton rises, towering well over her. He acts like he's about to salute something and take an oath. "I would love that as well," he says. "We will see you next Thursday."

J ENNA SHOWS UP Monday late in the morning to relieve me but stands outside the front door talking to Deaton's new helper, Weston. I suspect these two have gotten to know each other a bit and like what they know so far. I've heard they've joined forces to help Mr. Kent figure out his new mobile phone — his first-ever foray into technology. When she finally comes in I grab my purse and run out the back, hollering my thanks to her for taking over. "Call if you need me, and don't forget Otis." I'm on the road leading out of town before noon.

Mary calls me when I'm on the interstate. "Could we meet at a restaurant? I should be able to get out of here early afternoon," she says. "There's a little place in Macon. The Back Porch. Good food. Never crowded."

"That'll be fine," I say and hang up.

I'm nervous about meeting her. We haven't spoken since she tried to do whatever she was doing with all that talk about Nana. We've never had anything like this between us before, thanks to me. I never question, never challenge her — *a lot like my dad maybe, after all* — at least I never had before slamming the phone down on her words the other evening. In my defense, how could I? An adolescent girl isn't going to challenge the mother she's been longing for and finally reconnected with. And once I'd let her ultimate betrayal slide, what was there left to argue? I was fifteen and desperate when it started and then I had no way out. She was my mom, and I took what I could get and she knew it. We both did.

A hostess seats me at a booth. The restaurant is brightly lit, but unlike Mom said it's not empty and private, it's bustling and busy, especially for a Monday afternoon.

"I'm expecting one more." I smile at the waitress as she hands me a menu. She takes my drink order and returns with one more menu. I'm waiting on my drink and checking the time when Mom breezes through the door.

She looks around at all the people and settles herself into the other side of the booth. She drops her dark sunglasses into her large designer purse and reaches for my hand that's resting on the table. Her eyes are clear and alert. Thank God she has rent to pay, a lifestyle of sorts to maintain, roots to bleach, and a career to fund it all. Thank God she's taking her medications. "How are you, Amy?"

I pull my hand away.

"Amy," she starts, but the waitress appears, interrupting her. She reluctantly takes her eyes off of me and orders. "Water with lemon, please. And a turkey club, no mayo."

The waitress looks at me. "The same." I wave a hand. It doesn't matter what I eat.

Mom returns to the conversation she started. "Listen. I may not have been as diplomatic as I could have been."

I look at her. She will not apologize for her words, only for the manner in which they'd been said. I can't believe this! I put up a hand to stop her. Something in my brain shifts into a slot labeled fed-up.

"I can't. I can't listen to this talk about Nana. She was the one who stayed. She raised me, for God's sake, when you didn't." Feelings I've kept at bay for so long break through and embolden me. I'm like a can of soda that's been shaken for too long, and now it's been opened and spewing everywhere. "All my life you've treated family like some holiday retreat you can make a reservation for when you feel like it. You live it up, soak up all the sun and goodness, then you check out again and mope and wallow in your restlessness."

She leans back in the booth.

There's a silence that stretches. It's so peaceful I'd like to just curl up and rest in it, like a cat on a window sill. I'm so exhausted, so done with everything. I don't even care if I've cut her heart out with my sharp tongue.

"I deserve that," she finally says and picks up her napkin to dab at her eyes. "Amy, listen."

"No, Mom. *You* listen!"

She clamps her mouth shut then opens it just long enough to correct me. "Mary."

"Mary," I sigh while rifling through my purse for an aspirin. "Whatever." There is so much noise in this little restaurant. The waitress keeps walking past us and asking if we're good, telling us our food will be out shortly, and the surrounding booths are all filled with people talking and laughing and clinking their forks on their plates. "I said I was going to control the conversation, and I meant it. It's just that ever since you said those things the other night, I'm having these flashbacks on things and they're all weird. Not the way I remembered at all."

She leans forward.

"Like things with Susan. Food she was served that was different from ours."

She nods as if this is accurate.

"Times she got in trouble, only I can't think what she did."

We sit in silence for a bit. The waitress delivers our food. It has no taste, no color, no smell. I just lift it to my lips and chew it because I'm supposed to, but my lips feel rubbery and my stomach threatens to toss it all back up.

Mom leaves her food untouched on her plate. "That's right," she says softly. "I don't want to go into details, but Susan was a prop for your grandmother to solidify her charitable standing in the community. Do you understand what I'm saying?"

I set my jaw determinedly. "No, I do not."

"She was not treated well, and it made me sick. I tried." She clears her throat and continues, "I tried to stop it. I tried to get your father to stop it, but he refused to see it. His mother could do no wrong, not even the wrong that was happening right in front of his face. Well, it was subtle," she admits, "but it was definitely there. A blind man could have seen." She pats my hand. "We don't have to talk about it anymore. No use. What's done is done."

"That's another reason I wanted to hold on to the house." I wad up my napkin and toss it over my half-eaten lunch. "I always thought Susan would show back up one day looking for Nana, and I'd be there to tell her she was gone. I thought she'd be crushed."

Mom frowns sympathetically then says, "Honey, if Susan showed back up looking for your Nana that's the last place I'd want to be."

I contemplate this for a moment. "Let me ask you about something else then. Did you know a Mickey Connelly?"

She flattens her lips and thinks. "Doesn't ring a bell."

"He was arrested shortly after the train accident. He faked documents for people. I think..." I hesitate, then continue. "I think he did yours."

"Oh," she says. "Possibly." Like I've suggested he may have been the guy that bagged her groceries.

"He rented a house," I say this like it has anything to do with anything.

"Amy, don't worry. Really. You have enough on your plate. I'm telling you, no one's going to track me down after all this time. No one cares."

"Helena does. *I'm* telling *you*, Mom!" My voice gets higher.

"Mary!"

"Mary, whatever! Helena is going to find you. One way or another. Dead or alive. She wants to marry your husband! Did Mickey Connelly do your paperwork for you?"

She exhales. "I don't know, Amy. Possibly." She shakes her head and shrugs nonchalantly. "That morning I dyed my hair and packed my things." I try to catch her eyes, but she's looking off to the side, remembering. "I went to get you, and when that didn't work out I met Ian over by the train station to leave my car. We had to park a bit away because the police were everywhere around there." She moistens her lips and continues. "We went somewhere." She holds out a hand, palm up. "I don't know the man's name. He owed Ian a favor, and he made it all top priority. It was fast, and it was convincing."

I feel the bile rise in my throat.

"He made up a receipt for a train ticket to make it look like I'd been on the train then he took my picture. Told me to pick a common name that wouldn't stand out, and I chose Mary then I attached it to Guthry, thinking, *hoping,* that Ian would eventually marry me. The man, whoever he was, had me sign things. Printed. Laminated. I don't know. We had to hurry. Had a plane to catch." She narrows her eyes and shakes her head like she's fluffing her hair, or trying to shake this heaviness off. "All of my documentation is top-notch. I can assure you of that."

"Do you remember where he lived?"

"No idea," she says. "I wasn't in the right frame of mind. Not sure I ever have been."

She expects me to join in her little joke, but I remain stoic as her story comes to life in my head.

It's just before we leave that I hear it. I'm glancing at my watch, and Mom knows I have to get on the road. Enough has been said about Nana and Mr. Connelly, and we've moved on to other safer subjects for now — weather, rush hour traffic, sugar versus Splenda. I'm barely engaged, but Mom talks enough to fill the silence.

The voice comes just behind me, as I'm getting out of the booth. Mom's already standing in the aisle, rummaging through her purse for her keys.

"If I've said it once, I've said it a thousand times."

I freeze. I'd know that voice and that expression anywhere. A pulse, and then that quickening of the heart I've become so familiar with lately overtakes me.

Mom keeps rummaging. I rise and try to reach for her arm, but she stands firm. "Do you see my keys?" she asks me.

I stare at the floor and mumble. She stops rummaging. "What's wrong with you *now*?"

I glance up and meet the eyes of the girl in the booth behind me. "Amy!" she says, surprised. I smile meekly and give a weak wave. My mother hears and looks up, just as I'm acknowledging Leeza Ryder. "Mom," Leeza reaches across the table and takes her mother-in-law's hand. "Behind you. It's Amy Chadwick," she says, using my maiden name. And then her mother-in-law, the nosiest woman in all of Flannery Cove, the woman that lived next door to me since the day I was born in my mom's and dad's former home — Mrs. Ryder — turns around in her seat pleasantly surprised as well.

Her eyes shift left and right and then settle on me. "Amy, dear." She starts to get up from her booth, but Leeza rises instead and places a hand on her mother-in-law to keep her in place. I bend down and hug her as she stays seated.

My mother turns away from us and continues rummaging, and Leeza begins to ask all about my dad's new condominium and my café. "I have got to get over there sometime," she says. "Mom, we *have* to do that." Mrs. Ryder nods and wants to know all about how my dad is doing and if he's still dating Helena.

My mom, still turned away from us, begins to walk away. Leeza is talking about her job as a manager at the Seascape Inn. She stops mid-sentence before Mom can walk away. "I'm sorry. How rude of us. Please introduce us to your friend." She reaches out to touch my mom's sleeve and begins to introduce herself, despite just asking me to do it. I watch the whole thing unfold like it's happening in slow motion, as Mom turns back to pull her sleeve away and Leeza says, "Hi, I'm Leeza Ryder and this is Deidre Ryder." She waves a hand toward her mother-in-law, still seated in the booth and staring into the middle of our grouping.

My mother doesn't say anything for a moment. The silence is lingering and awkward, until Leeza finally says, "Amy grew up next door to Deidre."

Still, Mom says nothing, but I manage a murmured, "This is my friend, Mary."

Leeza smiles broadly and begins to address her. "How nice you..." But Mary just nods an acknowledgment and turns and walks away.

"She's just had some terrible news," I attempt to explain.

Mrs. Ryder's eyes find mine again and bore deep into them, into my soul. "Oh, dreadful," she says. "Is she a friend from home?"

Sweat has formed in my hairline, my neck, and my hands. "Um, yes. Well, she used to live in Flannery Cove. She taught me in school and we became close, but she moved to Atlanta, and I still try to get up here and see her from time to time." I'm rambling on, trying to change the direction of any route Mrs. Ryder's mind might be on.

Mrs. Ryder seems even more interested now. "Which school did she teach in? Perhaps Leeza had her as well." She says this without even averting her gaze toward Leeza, which is extremely intimidating.

"Oh! I don't... I don't think so. She was only at Northwood for a short time, but we grew close. She was very helpful to me." Her stare continues to focus so intently on me that I add, "It was during a difficult time."

"Of course it was," Mrs. Ryder says sympathetically. "Oh, you poor dear, Amy. I think of you and your lovely father every day."

"The Broxton's have added on to your dad's old house," Leeza says. "You should see it. The garage is huge. So out of proportion."

"Distasteful," Mrs. Ryder agrees, but she still keeps studying me, looking right through me.

I make a point of looking at my watch. "Oh gosh. I have to go. It was so nice to see you all. So nice."

"Oh, you too," Mrs. Ryder says.

Leeza says something similar, but I don't catch it. I'm locked in a staredown with her mother-in-law. She wins. I fix my focus elsewhere.

I hug them both and begin to walk down the aisle away from them when I hear Mrs. Ryder say something about the restroom. *What if Mary's in there hiding out?*

I pivot and think I might go to the restroom too, just in case, to run interference. I change my mind, going back and forth a few times like a squirrel crossing in front of an oncoming car. I can't. The walls of this place are closing in on me.

My hands are shaking so badly I'm not sure I trust myself to drive when I reach the car. The space inside my head is roaring, the stale air is dizzying, and my heart is beating out of rhythm. I lay my head in my hands and sob — huge, gulping sobs that wrack my whole body. It's amazing how many thoughts can fit in one's head in the space of seconds: My mom, my grandmother, Helena, my faithful dad, my sweet Hailey, dragon-slaying Deaton, even the elusive Scott Warner. They all collide in my mind.

I'm startled by the rapping on my window. I jolt and look up to find Leeza standing there, tapping with her key. She seems surprised to find me crying, embarrassed to be invading my privacy.

I have to turn my key to roll down my window. I wipe a fist across my cheeks and look at Leeza. "My friend. She got some really bad news today. Remember I told you? I'm just so upset for her."

She wrinkles her forehead in concern. "I'm so sorry. Is there anything I can do?"

"No. No." I wave my hand as if I've blown it out of proportion. "But it was so nice to see you both," I say again and try for a bright smile. I've gone from sixty down to zero in seconds.

"Well, I'm so sorry to interrupt," she says, clutching her keys in her fist, trying to figure me out. "Mom asked me if I would try to catch you before you left. She wanted to know if you could stop by and visit her one day next week."

I hesitate, and she jumps back in with an explanation. "She wanted to talk to you about something important."

"Oh." I sniff and reach over to my glove compartment and grab a tissue. "I'll have to see what day I can get away. The café keeps me so busy."

"Okay. Well, please do." She reaches into her purse and pulls out a piece of notepaper that Mrs. Ryder's phone number is written on. "Mom's number isn't listed anymore." She hands me the paper, and I take it and put it on the seat beside me.

"I have to get on the road."

Leeza nods. "Us too. Long trip home."

We sit in silence for a second, both unsure what else to say.

"Okay." She slaps a palm on my car door. "Better go. Drive safe. And Amy," she says before turning around. "Don't forget about Mom."

# TWENTY-ONE

THE APPRAISER WALKS the perimeter of my backyard with a measurement roller and stands back to look at the roof. He sees me through the window sitting at the bistro table eating my breakfast and waves. Thirty minutes or so later he rings the doorbell, and when I open it for him he wipes his shoes, glances at the white carpet in the living room, and decides to slip them off and leave them at the door.

"Mike Handell." He hands me his business card. "Just need to take a few measurements and get in the attic."

I follow him from room to room for a while, but then I return to the kitchen table and my magazine.

"Is that water heater new?" He ducks his head around the corner, holding his clipboard out in front of him.

"No. Maybe five, six years old. Oh, and I'll be fixing the paint on that wall in the master bedroom."

"Okay. I'll be pulling down the stairs in the laundry room and checking out a few things in the attic. Then I'll get out of your hair."

I go back to my magazine and five minutes later I hear the wood access door slam shut, and he reappears.

"That was fast."

"Yes, ma'am. Thanks for letting me in. I'll probably have this ready by Friday."

"Okay." I walk him to the door. "Will you be mailing it to me, or can I pick it up?"

"No. It's the property of the bank. You may be able to get a copy from them if you want one." He wipes a hand across his brow. There are little beads of sweat lined up across it, and his starched shirt has sagged and surrendered its pride. I can't even read the name of his company across his pocket anymore.

He turns to walk back to his truck then pivots to look up at the roof one more time. "Nice place," he says, shielding his eyes from the sun. "I can tell it's been taken care of." He looks back down at the clipboard. "Grow up here?"

"My grandmother left it to me when she died." I twist the doorknob with the hand that's holding the door open and start to say something about the memories I'm leaving behind, but stop myself.

*Maybe they're better left behind?*

Instead, I softly close the door. The click of it is loud in the quiet space. Such a quiet, empty space.

"Congratulations on the sale! Hope your friend is doing better. I have some business out of town, but I'll be back in a few weeks. I would like to meet up with you then and talk to you. Yes?"

I've read Scott's text at least ten times in two hours, trying to read between the lines. Where was he when he wrote it? How long did he take to decide what he would write? What does "talk to me" mean? Does it mean present me with my bill?

I write numerous replies and delete them all, finally settling on a simple: "Yes!"

I toss and turn all night Wednesday. I have no energy to continue this treasure hunt, where my mother's corpse is supposed to be the treasure. To be fair, Deaton's idea of a treasure would be to find her lying in a hospital somewhere with amnesia where she's been all along and present her to me all spiffed up and ready to pick up where we left off.

I'm late meeting Deaton at the bookstore. It's pouring down rain, so I pull up to the front and beep and he runs out. Weston waves from the doorway.

"Guess he's working out okay?"

He folds his long legs into my small front seat area and reaches to move the seat. "He'll do."

The rest of the ride to Savannah is mostly silent, at least on my end. Deaton rattles on a bit about Kristlyn's job and how he can't wait for her trips back and forth to dwindle. I nod and smile during his pauses, but mostly keep my mind on where I'm going, what I'm doing, how to keep the world from closing in on me. Traffic is heavy and slow, and the rain is noisy. I'm gripping the wheel like a determined grandma.

We're supposed to meet Alexa at eleven-fifteen, but it's after eleven-thirty when I finally pull up to the storage facility. Deaton reaches into his wallet for the folded-up piece of paper that she wrote the code to open the gate on. It slides open with a screech and we head toward the back to unit 56.

A man is waiting in a silver Volvo wagon in front of the roll-up door. I pull up beside it and spot the empty toddler seat strapped in the back seat. He gets out and the three of us stand in the pouring rain. He's dressed for work in a white button-down shirt and Navy chinos and has an umbrella almost as large as the one over my backyard patio table. Deaton and I both huddle ineffectively under one I pulled out of my glove compartment. "Alexa forgot she was helping at Nicholas' pre-school this morning. I'm Geoffrey." He's yelling over the sound of the rain, and there's no time for handshakes and formalities. He lifts the door of the unit and all three of us run inside then Geoffrey goes back to the door and lowers it halfway against the blowing rain and finds the switch for the overhead light.

"I think it's one of those over there." He points toward the boxes and totes stacked up near the rear. Deaton nods and begins to unstack boxes that are piled high. Each box has the contents written across the top in magic marker. As he places them on the floor, I read them nervously. So far they are all the property of the Kendrick family: Kendrick-books. Kendrick-photos. Kendrick-baby clothes. Geoffrey stands toward the back of the unit, well away from the door and the spray of water, scrolling through his phone, paying no attention to us. When it rings he lifts the door, runs back to the safety of his car, gets in the front seat, and takes the call.

The rain has lightened up a bit, so I leave the door open. Deaton hands another cardboard box down to me and turns around to wipe his dirty hands on the front of his jeans. "I think this one might be it."

I stare at the box labeled Kendrick-Dad's research. He reaches into his pocket, removes a knife, and slices at the tape. Geoffrey is still talking inside his car. Two men are unloading a dining room set from the back of a pickup truck into a unit down the alley. They're trying to keep it covered with a tarp that keeps flapping and hitting their faces. I lean down and peer into the box with Deaton. Inside, the box is divided into categories. File folders that divide it are labeled: Patricia Snyder kidnapping. Samuel Stadler wrongful conviction. Mickey Connelly counterfeit ring.

*Dear God, it's hot in this building.*

Deaton's eyes meet my own. I'm shaking like an unbalanced washing machine. Geoffrey is still on the phone in his car. The two men down the alley have unloaded the last of the chairs and are inside their building. My world is spinning, and my heart beats so loudly I'm sure Deaton can hear it. He places a hand over mine. "It's okay," he says, trying to calm me. "This is a good thing."

I don't respond. Instead, I sit down on the floor of the unit and stare at the box. There is no right or wrong way to react when one is hot on the trail of a dead mother that's coming back to life. No one can say I acted strangely like something was off, like maybe I already knew.

*Can they?*

Deaton runs back to his car and returns with an empty box of his own. He gathers all the papers in the Mickey Connelly portion of the box and puts them in his box. Then he can't resist. He starts looking at them, even though Geoffrey Kendrick is clearly trying to conduct business out of the front seat of his car, and it's so uncomfortable in this storage unit.

"There's not a lot here." He frowns. The papers seem to be in some sort of chronological order. He pulls out a thin onion-skin paper and lays it right there on the concrete floor, and I hear him mumble, "Week of the accident," to himself. I'm still sitting and staring. *"In shock,"* I imagine Deaton telling people later. *"Poor thing was in complete shock."*

My eyes glance over to what he's reading. It's as if these papers have a heartbeat I'm connected to. There are five names jotted at the top of the page with a lot of writing I can't read underneath them. The five names stand out, though: Stephen P. Westland. Monique L. Brandt. S.P. Loganstein. Mary Guthry. B. Leventhal.

I begin to shake so hard my teeth are chattering, and no matter how hard I bite down I can't stop them. Deaton glances up and sees me. "Oh gosh. We can take these and look at them later," he says, just as Geoffrey starts up his car.

Deaton helps up off the floor and holds up the cardboard box letting Geoffrey know he's got what he needs. Geoffrey nods then rolls down his window. "Didn't mean to rush you. I needed to power up my phone."

"No. We're good," Deaton yells back and helps me into the passenger seat of my car before running back to close the storage unit door. Geoffrey gets out and locks it and the two of them stand there for a second, talking in the drizzle of rain that continues to fall. They shake hands and part. Deaton gets into the driver's seat and turns the defroster on full blast. "Let's get you some coffee somewhere," he says, rubbing his hands together. "We passed a drive-through on the way in. Around the corner."

We're back in Flannery Cove before the lunch crowd has completely thinned out. I can see inside the café windows when we pull up to the curb.

"I can't do this right now."

Deaton nods, understanding. He comes around to my door and opens it. He walks me across to the bookstore. Weston is sitting on a stool reading something. He gets up when we come in and the stool falls — a loud, obnoxious noise. A woman in the children's section quickly walks to the next aisle calling for her son.

"Hey, man. She okay?" Weston whips his hair so he can see clearly.

"She's okay," Deaton assures him. He keeps hold of my arm and leads me up the stairs to his apartment. The blinds are open, and the space is filled with light, but he strides across the room and shuts them so darkness envelops. Deaton leads me to the couch, and I lay down like the invalid I currently am while he props a pillow behind my head. He disappears for a bit and returns with a blanket he lays over me. "Try to rest," he attempts to whisper, but his voice is husky, deep with emotion over what he's experiencing. "I'll be downstairs if you need anything."

He softly closes the door behind him, and I'm left alone lying on Deaton's sofa, surrounded by his things. I lift my lids and roll my eyes around the space. His DVR light is on, recording something. There's a blender that's still half full of some green liquid on the counter. Yesterday's newspaper is sticking out of the top of the kitchen garbage can. I sit up and slip my fingers in the blinds and look out across the street at my café, thinking of all the work I'd like to be tackling. *Maybe I could just muster up the strength to walk...* but then I lie back down and close my eyes and don't wake until the early evening when Deaton shakes my shoulders.

"Ames. Ames, wake-up."

It takes me a moment to remember where I am. It's the blender on the counter that reminds me.

"Listen. Are you listening to me?"

My head is groggy, but I'm listening.

"I've been looking through everything in the box. There are five names of people that Connelly did things for in the days before the accident. I'm not sure if these names — if they're people's original names or new names."

I stare straight ahead at the bronze knob on the hallway linen closet, right into the very center of it, and gnaw at my knuckles, plugging my words and sobs.

*It's happening...*

"And that one. The Monique Brandt. There's a Monique Brandt in Bowling Green, Kentucky. She's fifty-nine years old, so she claims. She owns a hair salon. She resembles you, Amy."

I sit up straighter and look at him, raising a hand to my tangled strands.

*My mother owns a hair salon? My mother lives in Kentucky?* It doesn't take me long to optimistically pick up this thread and run it through a steel needle and begin to sew with it.

"Do you think? Could it really be?" I hold tight to the blanket Deaton laid over me hours ago. I clutch it in my hands like I'm clutching my last bit of hope.

"I don't know. I do think there's something there. I think we're on the right trail. Whether this woman turns out to be someone or not…" he lets his sentence linger. "We'll keep an eye on her. Find out everything we can while we're researching the others too."

I nod and stare at the doorknob again. Maybe he'll think I'm envisioning my future — the one where I get off the plane in Kentucky and run into the arms of the mother who's been waiting for me. My eyes fill up with tears. The good and the bad, I suppose, is that I can cry conveniently and quickly in my corrupt deceit. But what does it say for someone who has such a stockpile of sadness always at the forefront, just one tight blink away? It occurs to me then that I should ask. "Can I see her?"

He reaches over to the side chair where he's dropped his laptop and reaches for it.

"Wait." I bite my lip and think for a minute. "I want to look at it alone. Will you send me the link to what you saw?" Of course, I would want my privacy for such an overwhelming thing.

He lays the laptop back down. "Amy, she might just be Monique Brandt from Kentucky."

"I know," I say. "But she might not be."

From: Helena1098@myFCcourier.com
To: Unveiled@officeweb.com
Subject: Investigation

**I am sorry to tell you I have been unable to locate the train ticket receipt. Raleigh had it at one point, and we have searched everywhere, to no avail. Hopefully, you will be able to continue the investigation without the missing piece of evidence. If not, please let me know as soon as possible, so I may hire someone else to take over since it is now October.**

I hope Helena hasn't already hired someone else because this message has been sitting in my inbox for a week, and I've had no inspiration on how to respond. She's probably putting big X's every day on calendar spaces at the stroke of midnight, exclaiming, "Another day gone by that your former wife laughs at this family from her castle abroad, Raleigh. I won't stand for this past February, I tell you."

From: Unveiled@officeweb.com
To: Helena1098@myFCcourier.com
Subject: investigation

**Dear Ms. Delgado,**

**We are so sorry to hear that the train receipt has not been located. This certainly stalls the investigation somewhat and makes it more difficult, but not impossible. We are following up on a very promising lead right now. Caroline Chadwick may be alive and living under an assumed name in Kentucky. If that is the case, it's seriously doubtful she will be forthcoming or want to be contacted, but at least we will know and can determine then how to proceed. We promise to let you know more as this unfolds. For now, please be patient and understanding. So much time has passed that some people have forgotten things. Others have died, relocated, etc. All of these factors make an investigation such as this even more challenging, but again, not impossible.**

**Thank you,**
**Unveiled Investigation Agency**

I'M DRIVING HOME early Monday evening when it occurs to me that if I take a left instead of a right on Franhauser and then veer off by the railroad tracks, I'll be in the old neighborhood.

Twenty minutes later I drive slowly past the remnants of my childhood. Vacant lots now have sprawling homes constructed on them. Old homes have been completely updated. Mr. Wilson still strolls in the afternoon with his miniature Doberman, now quite ancient, on a leash, and women push strollers past him and jog in place at the stop signs, waiting to hit their strides again.

I turn on to Winnipeg and can already see it up ahead. It looks a bit lopsided, just like Leeza said. The garage has a second story now, but the rest of the house is still the same. I wonder if the new owners ever found a stain-blocking paint that effectively covered that angry splash of wine — that final *screw-you-and-thi s-life-you've-chained-me-to* that my mother hurled at my father. I drive past, then turn around and pull up to the opposite curb.

I almost missed her there. Mrs. Ryder, dressed in a housecoat, is in her yard stooped over, watering her azaleas. A young woman I've never seen before is there, holding on to her free arm. She looks up and sees me there in my car watching and waves. I put my cell phone to my ear and pretend to be talking on it. She leans down and says something to Mrs. Ryder, and they both look back at me. Mrs. Ryder cranes her neck and peers intently, but she doesn't wave to me. *She knows what's going on and she's mad that I haven't come by so she can confront me.*

I drop the cell phone in the passenger seat and drive away from Winnipeg Avenue as fast as I can. When I get home, I can't make it to my bathtub fast enough.

*She peeled off every layer of clothing, leaving behind a trail that led to the healing waters and washed her despair down....*

No! Not now. I just want to lie here and empty my mind, not fill it with diversions, plots, and prose. I want to fill the tub and go under. Forget about everything that's driving me wacko.

While the tub fills with hot water, I run to the kitchen and grab a loaf of bread and a jar of peanut butter, along with a bottle of wine.

The water becomes unbearably hot before I can even lean over the side and make a sandwich, so I have to lift my foot and add some cold. I sit back and try to lose myself in suds and sips. The bread is too much trouble to deal with, the spreading takes too much energy. I manage a system: One lick of peanut butter for every swig of wine.

The water grows cold, so I have to add hotter. Then it's too hot, and I'm tense, and I can't empty my mind from these troubling thoughts. I'm having to swish the wine around like mouthwash to keep my jaws from sticking together. I'm getting sleepy too — or drunk. Yes, that might be a possibility. I just want my bed and my comforter.

An empty wine bottle is still sitting on the bath rug the next morning. The peanut butter jar is on the edge of the tub, a knife still sticking out of it. My computer is propped open on my bed and my bath towel is still wrapped around me under my blankets like a full body bandage. The phone can be heard ringing, a faraway and tunnel-like sound. I fumble around on my nightstand and knock the bedroom phone to the floor.

I hear Sheila Thomas's voice before I can get the receiver to my ear. "Amy? Are you there?"

"I'm here." I wake up, or sober up, immediately. My voice is instantly chipper like I've been awake for hours. "Sorry 'bout that."

"I'm so glad I caught you at home, Amy." Her voice is back to the condescending tone. I try to remember. *Weren't we on equal footing? Didn't I have money dangling in front of her she was trying to reach? Weren't we pretend friends last time I checked?*

"I'm afraid I have some bad news."

I say nothing. I rub a hand across my forehead trying to stimulate some coherent thoughts — something I could say on my end that would make sense.

"The appraisal came back late yesterday," Sheila says. Her voice is so nasally. It's like she's underwater.

*Afternoon delight.* Nana never let me sing that song, said it was not for respectable little girls. I thought it was about the space shuttle program. My mind skitters all over the place, warding off Sheila's bad news.

"The house didn't appraise well. I'm so sorry."

*Skyrockets...* I'm not sure I have the right tune. *Maybe it's more like...*

"Amy?"

"Yes. Um. What does that mean exactly?" I glance toward my laptop and run a finger across its touchpad. The screen brightens and a woman's big smile greets me. Monique Brandt.

Sheila blows out a puff of air, exasperated. I guess I'm expected to know all this stuff.

I remember when I first found out Nana had left me her house. Surely there was some mistake. Nana trusted me to cook on her stove? Pay the gas bill on time every month? Remember to lock the doors at night and not let the garbage overflow? At that time, culinary had not yet been added to my repertoire of skills, and I didn't even know how to bake a potato. The first week I was married, I tried to make one for Greg on his hour-long dinner break. It was taking forever and I had to boil it instead. It split open in the boiling water and made a mess that I then scooped out, strained, buttered, salted, and served. If I couldn't be trusted with potatoes, I surely couldn't handle a whole house. And sure enough, here I am years later, not handling it. Not even fully comprehending what a bad appraisal means for me and the ol' homestead.

"It means that the house is valued at twelve thousand, sorry actually twelve thousand six hundred, less than you're asking. The Schwares are getting a loan from the bank, and that's all the bank will loan them."

"But you thought this was a good asking price. *You* suggested it."

"I'm an agent, not an appraiser, Amy. I was hoping to get that price, but if it's not worth it, then it's simply not. Perhaps…"

I cut her off before she can suggest I take a pickax to the kitchen tile and a blowtorch to the carpet. "I need time to think about this."

"That's fine. The Schwares have been informed, of course."

"And?"

"Well, unless you can pitch in the money to pay off your loan, then the offer is off the table. You understand."

I walk into the café feeling an eerie sense of calm. Perhaps I need to take a lesson from my dad. Whatever happens in life, it's okay, all good. Wife dies in a train accident? Handled! Daughter gets impregnated at eighteen by a complete jerk? No problem! Future fiancé wants proof wife died or to find her if she didn't? Easy-peasy!

*Yes, I'm going to become like this too,* I think to myself as I walk to my office and stumble over the boxes that came in late yesterday after I left. *No office space? Madame Bienve taunting me with the practically empty one she owns? Whatever.* I won't think about the problems that loom and threaten to make my entire world go dark. Nor will I conjure up plot twists and characters to avoid them. I'll get a grip. I'll face facts. I'll meditate my way out of everything.

I am feeling quite proud of my new attitude. As I walk out, I refuse to look up at the closet I covet or across the street to where Deaton stands, talking to a customer. Zen people don't look adversity in the face. They find alternative, peaceful places to rest their eyes. I'm searching for that peaceful place when Leeza Ryder appears right in front of my face like a brick wall I've smashed into. My carefree approach to life lasted all of twenty minutes.

"Thank goodness I caught you," she says.

# TWENTY-TWO

"A NOSY MEDDLING BUSY-BODY." That's what my mom had called Mrs. Ryder. "Another thing I couldn't handle in that ridiculously small town."

But then later, when I said something about Mrs. Ryder, Mom said she knew I couldn't go too far off the rails with her on duty — like she was an asset to an absent mother.

Strangely, all my mind can question at the moment is why Mrs. Ryder's daughter-in-law is with her all the time lately. Kimberly Ryder went away to college in Arizona the week after she graduated from high school and settled there permanently. Paul Ryder married Leeza, and they live somewhere nearby, but why is Leeza suddenly escorting her mother-in-law everywhere she goes?

"You're an elusive one," she laughs. "Mom and I finally decided we'd just come to you."

I smile as if this is great and nervously tuck my hair behind my ears. "Oh. Good. Gosh, we're so busy." I look around at all the empty booths. "Well, you know… deliveries and all."

Leeza clears her throat. "We won't keep you long. Mom, um, she just wanted to tell you one thing."

"But." I glance backward toward my office.

"Please, Amy. Just a moment?" She's grown impatient with me on her mother-in-law's behalf.

I follow her over to the booth Mrs. Ryder is sitting in.

*I'll just deny it. She can swear to it, but there's no proof that was my mother. But then she'll tell people she saw us in Macon and someone will go search. She might call Helena, and then…*

"Hello, Mrs. Ryder. How are you doing today?"

She's sitting in the booth staring straight ahead, but at the sound of my voice, she turns her head toward me. Mrs. Ryder squints and her eyes veer to the right but settle on my own eyes and penetrate deeply once again.

"I'm sorry I haven't been able to make it by to see you this week." I clasp her hands that are outstretched like they're searching for something.

Her gaze is so intent. I imagine she's about to say that I did make it by and she saw me.

*I did not! You did! Did not!* I'm prepared to go the distance and stick to my guns.

"I'm sorry I behaved so strangely last week in Macon. I want to apologize to you and your friend," she says to me.

I glance at Leeza. She pats Deidre's hand that rests on the table.

"She must think I'm quite the dotty old woman," Mrs. Ryder continues with a little chortle.

"No. I don't think," I say, unsure of what to add. This is not the conversation I was preparing for.

"Tell her why we were in Macon," Leeza says. "She's got deliveries to put away."

"Yes," Mrs. Ryder says, getting back to her thoughts. "You know I have diabetes?" She turns back to the table and stares down at her folded hands as if she's confessing something.

This does sound familiar. I think I remember Father's Day shopping with her and Kimberly one year when Mrs. Ryder felt faint and had to find some crackers. "My diabetes," she had explained while Kimberly and I came out from the clothes rack we'd been hiding in to see what was wrong.

"I've developed some complications," she explains. "Leeza has been so good." Leeza smiles and looks down at her lap. Mrs. Ryder stays focused on her folded hands. "She's been taking me to my specialist in Atlanta. We always look forward to our lunch at that little diner on the way home."

A group of five people come in and walk the aisle behind me on their way to a booth. I have to scoot in to let them by, so I sit down beside Mrs. Ryder. She scoots over to make room for me, but her gaze never leaves her hands.

"I've developed diabetic retinopathy." She stumbles a bit over the words. I look at her then at Leeza quizzically. "I'm almost completely blind."

"Caroline was on the train," Nana had said to Mrs. Ryder when she walked me back home that evening after I had shoved the cookies down in the couch cushions and watched *Happy Days* with their family.

"Uh-hm. I see," Mrs. Ryder had replied while she rubbed her chin and narrowed her eyes. Then she seemed to remember the proper way to behave and put her hand to her mouth in shock and said things that made more sense, given the circumstances.

I remember thinking they were speaking in some kind of adult code I wasn't meant to understand. I'm still not sure I understand it, but I wonder. Mom said she dyed her hair and left the house to go get Susan and me. Later, Ian sneaked into the house and planted the receipt. *How much did Mrs. Ryder figure out?*

Mrs. Ryder reaches over and puts an arm around my shoulder and pulls me in close. "No tears for me, Amy. I'm gonna be just fine. I've seen more in my lifetime than most could ever imagine."

CHRIST COMMUNITY CHURCH has over five hundred followers online. One of them is Monique Brandt. I like the church's page then I friend request Monique. Thirty minutes later she has assumed she must know me from church, and she accepts my request. I see we already have one mutual friend: Deaton Dunklin.

Monique has been married for thirteen years to Barry Brandt. She is the owner of Thairapy Salon in Bowling Green and has a son who is around twelve and a daughter who's maybe five or six, along with two Chihuahuas and a cat, judging by the pictures. At this very moment, Monique is apparently at Melvin's Diner with two of her girlfriends, according to her latest post. I enlarge the picture she's just uploaded and study her features. I'm not seeing any resemblance to myself other than our hair color, but if Deaton wants to think he does, then I'll go along with it. I look into her eyes. Do I glimpse a secret in them? A sadness behind the smile? *Of course I do.*

"Who's that?" Bradley asks.

I click my phone off and look around the pier. It's a crisp Saturday afternoon, and vendors are set up under a tent selling homemade foods, clothing, and décor. People are eating at outdoor bistros and sipping coffee on park benches. On the other side lies the inlet where children play in the sand and adults sunbathe and swim.

I haven't spent much time with Bradley in the last few weeks. I've been preoccupied, feigning busyness and headaches. That's mostly been true, but it's also been mixed in with my reluctance, my overall uncertainty, about Bradley. I never planned to take this relationship to the level of exclusivity, and somehow I think we're there anyway. We just slipped into it, and I'm not sure how to dig out. Or if I should. I don't know what I want, and it's unfair to him. I realize that.

I wonder how much I should say now. Do I drag Bradley into this facade too? What if he runs into Deaton at the bank or something and Deaton says, "How 'bout Amy's mom? All this time right there in Kentucky. You think it might really be her?"

"Look at that dog." I point to a little white terrier sunning on the deck of a yacht that's headed out.

Bradley looks at me instead of being sidetracked. I can see his eyes through his dark sunglasses.

"Remember I told you about my mom?" I say while I clip my hair up off my neck.

"Your mom? You said your mom died in a train accident."

"Yes. Yes, she did." I can't do it. I decide to leave her in the river for now

"Thinking about her today?" He rubs a hand up and down my arm.

The bench is hard on my back, so I snuggle in closer and rest against him, trying to conjure up pleasant thoughts and intimacy of some sort. "There's just something about fall. This time of year is always hard."

I glance over to the water. Someone is waving, trying to get my attention. My first thought is someone is drowning, or perhaps a shark has been spotted. *Should I call an ambulance?* I squint into the distance and recognize the ball cap.

Scott Warner.

*This isn't just my wayward thoughts again, avoiding?*

But no, he's flesh and blood and walking toward me, and I feel trapped — like I used to feel walking around the mall on a Friday night with my dad, while everyone else my age hung out with friends. *The cool kids.*

I slide away from Bradley.

"Amy!" Scott calls out as he strides closer and closer.

I rise from the bench and go to meet him halfway.

"Home Girl! I've been gone. I was going to call you later." He beams from ear to ear and moves like he's going to put an arm around my shoulder in a half-hug greeting, but by that time Bradley has risen from the bench and positioned himself firmly at my side. I hold out my hand and Scott looks down, then back up at my face quickly, then back down. He finally shakes it, drawing back from me. The air between us fills with something so thick it's palpable.

"I got the message about the house," he says smiling gingerly. "That's great. And how is your friend?"

I look over to Bradley standing there, rocking on his heels. *How is he? I don't know. Strange question.* "I…"

"Mary," Scott says. "How's your Aunt Mary?"

"Oh! Um, yeah. Mary. She's better. Good. Fine. Well, she's not fine, but she's better. Yes, definitely better."

Scott and Bradley are both studying me. I scratch at my arm then drop it to my side. "Better," I say again, nodding my head with finality.

"Scott Warner," Scott says, extending a hand to Bradley.

Bradley reaches for Scott's hand, and I clasp a hand to my mouth. "Oh gosh, so sorry. This is Bradley… my um… Bradley. Bradley's an Investment Banker with Seraxus. And Mr. Warner," I say turning to Bradley "is, *was*, helping me with my foreclosure process."

Bradley nods, understanding. "Ahh."

"I'm Amy's boyfriend," Bradley says. "Nice to meet you, Scott." There's an intent in Bradley's tone, ownership in his words.

Scott looks from me to Bradley and back again, and backs up a step.

I need to consult with Scott on what's next for the house, but I don't want to do it with Bradley standing here. It's private lawyer/client stuff. Bradley has been introduced. He should retreat to the bench. But he doesn't. The three of us stand there talking about the beautiful day, and Scott gives us a fishing report, and I nod, fascinated, while Bradley looks around for a garbage can to toss his water bottle into. I point one out in the distance, but he just nods and stays rooted, eavesdropping.

He steps closer to me and puts an arm around my shoulders, and I'm mortified. I bend over coughing and move away. Scott never mentions any meetings, or papers, or exchange of money. Nothing. Bradley won't leave, and it's like the big kids can't talk comfortably in front of the little one. *God, I'm a snob. A genuine, real-life snob!*

The entire episode is so uncomfortable. Scott and I finally wrap it up. We've stood there and made the smallest of small talk and held our hands to our eyes while we gazed out at the water and predicted the weather for the impending days long enough.

"See ya around, Amy," he finally says. "Nice to meet you, Bradley."

Bradley rejoins the conversation instead of observing it as he's been doing and shakes Scott's hand again. "Sure was. You have a nice day."

And Scott walks away, back toward his fishing pole stuck in the sand, dragging in the water.

I stand rooted to my spot, watching him get smaller and smaller until he is only a speck on the horizon.

Worst phrase ever: *"See ya around."*

From: Benderfam@yahoo.com
To: Unveiled@officeweb.com
Subject: infidelity

**I am interested in acquiring your services. I've been married to my husband for eleven years. I believe he is having an affair, and I would like to know for certain before I go into labor with our third child in January. Please advise how this procedure works.**

FIONA BIENVE ALWAYS said Flannery Cove was the end of the earth. It's quite a village unto its own, I admit. When the inspector from the Department of Health came a few months ago to inspect the café, he ordered pastries and coffee and ate while he made notes. He wasn't Mr. Grimaldi. He was *Jimmy* — Jimmy from high school. We sat out front and talked for an hour about his marriage to Denise Thame and their kids and my divorce from Greg.

"I don't think I could stand it. I love staying hidden on the streets of my beloved New York," Fiona had said to me at the time.

"Here? You're moving here?" I say when she corners me by the flavored creamers. Fiona has floated down from upstairs, surprising me. She's dressed just like Madame, and all the little girls sitting with their mothers waiting for their lessons to begin run to her and hug her legs. She loses her balance for a second and laughs.

"Yes," she says, pulling them all in. "Mother is going to retire. I'm going to take over."

"Wait. What? When is this happening?"

I watch five little girls circle her thin, toned legs. I tighten the tie on my apron and pull in my knees like most women suck in their stomachs.

"Soon," Fiona says. "I've given notice on my apartment and my job." She pats a little blonde on the head. "You girls head up. I'll be right there."

"So. Gosh, this is such a surprise," I say. "But a good one. We'll see each other every day."

"Actually, no. Probably not. I've found studio space on the other side of town, by the library. Big space, good rent, and no hurricane shutters needed." She waves a hand at the nearby water, clearly not a fan.

"Oh. What about your um, the guy you were dating?"

She cocks her head and wrinkles her brow, trying to recall who she was dating.

"Remember? Tom? Tommy?"

"Tony?" she says with her nose scrunched like I've mentioned something unpleasant. "He's just a sometimes date. An arm for the theater or an event. Rather dull, actually." She rolls her eyes and laughs. "My friend Debbie compares him to bagged salad that's a week old, all pale iceberg browning at the edges. I can leave him behind," she assures me, her hands coming together in a sort of finality.

*Dull?* That particular description rubs me the wrong way for some reason. "Life can get awfully lonely without lettuce," I mumble defensively, but Fiona doesn't hear me.

"We'll see each other once a week," Fiona says to me — Tony already tossed out and forgotten. "For lunch. I won't go more than a week without your Tomato Basil Pie." She smiles, turns, and floats back up the stairs. Her backside is the mirror image of her mothers. One solid unwavering line.

E VER SINCE HELENA'S first email, I've been free-falling. Finding Monique Brandt was my parachute. Deaton has been trying to find some others on the list and half-heartedly trying to find other Monique Brandts, because let's face it, why would a woman in hiding have a presence online? But he seems unable to fathom that conclusion and is particularly fixated on this one — *our Monique* — my compass leading out of this mess.

I think he may have become like the little bird in the Dr. Seuss book. *Are you her mother? Yes, you are her mother because I've grown weary of this constant searching.* Nonetheless, I go with it. *Yes, she looks just like me. Yes, we are carbon copies of each other.*

"She likes dogs!" I text to him.

"Did you notice her excellent writing ability?" He texts to me.

"Look at what she's wearing today—she's very color-

ful!" I text to him.

"Just like someone else I know!" He texts back.

The vague similarities continue to mount and take on a sharpness.

I stalk her constantly online. If she sneezes, I know about it because that would be the normal reaction from a girl who's hoping, waiting, and praying. I'm studying every eyelash on her and wondering how I'm going to tell Deaton I don't want Hailey knowing any of this. Don't even want her knowing her own grandmother? Who's ever going to believe that?

*"She obviously doesn't want us. I don't want my daughter rejected,"* I mentally rehearse. Maybe he'll believe that — he'll have no choice. Thank God Hailey's gone off to school while all this is going on. Although school is kicking her butt, thanks to signing up for twelve credit hours right off the bat. Apparently "Aunt Mary" is helping her with her Identities and Differences in Literature class, so they talk daily.

I've no idea how I'm going to keep Monique on my computer and out of my real life. I can't get on a plane and go visit this woman.

*Well, I could, maybe.*

*Nope. Too far. Crazy out-of-control.*

*But to save myself? Dad? Hailey?*

She'd deny my existence, deny she's ever been anything but who she is now, and I'd leave town in tears with Deaton so hurt all over again by the mother who didn't welcome me.

That's never going to work. I cannot let it come to that!

I imagine my future conversations otherwise: *Oh my mom? She's in Kentucky. Owns a salon. No, I never made it out there to see her. I'm happy just knowing she's there.*

Obviously, that will not work either. *I need to carve out some time and think about which of these scenarios I'd be most likely to pull off,* I think to myself as I smother my arms in Cortisone.

From: Unveiled@officeweb.com
To: Benderfam@yahoo.com
Subject: Investigation

We are sorry to hear about your situation. We would be happy to take on your case. Please deposit into our account (link attached) and fill out a few forms for us (also attached.) We will need current photos, place of employment, etc. (all info in the attached forms.) Thank you.

B RADLEY IS THE first to arrive Thanksgiving morning, and I greet him holding mixing beaters clogged with mashed potatoes. Hailey arrived home late the night before, but she's already up and dressed, sitting on the kitchen counter with her feet dangling and hitting the cabinet with the beat of whatever she's listening to on her iPhone. She waves and pulls the buds from her ears.

"Happy Turkey Day." Bradley puts the bag of dinner rolls he's brought on the table and looks around admiringly. He's dressed in his new pair of tight jeans and a rugby-type pullover. I stop licking mashed potatoes off my fingers and go to him. I press my palm to his cowlick and pat it. He's had it cut recently and it only stands up a few inches, like the hair on Otis' back when he stands at the window barking at squirrels. I smile and kiss him full on the lips and sneak a look back at Hailey. She's got the buds back in her ears and isn't paying any attention to us, so I turn back around and glide my tongue over Bradley's lips, tasting mint mouthwash. He is my boyfriend, as he says. Scott Warner stepped away from me that day at the pier, both literally and figuratively. I saw it, and I felt it. And he's not coming back. I'm going to call and try to do what I can to make this offer with the Schwares work. And I'm never going to see Scott Warner again. Business over. Filed away. Done deal.

"Well," Bradley says, raising his brows and drawing the word out slyly. "That'll put a grin near the ol' chin."

It sounds so unnatural. This good-natured silliness and these lopsided grins aren't who he is. It's like watching a stiff, uptight man try to line dance at a family wedding. I want him to find his groove, but I'm not sure I can bear to watch. He's so in style these days I wonder if he misses his comfortable old jeans or his comfortable old self.

I don't.

We're interrupted by the doorbell. Jarod has arrived and has met up with Margo and Paulus in the driveway. All three of them have their arms full. "There's more in the car," Margo says as she comes in and carefully places a large glass baking dish on the counter. "We're doing dinner for my brother later, so as long as I was cooking I made double of a few things." Paulus is dressed in brown pants that are rolled up to show red socks and loafers. He has paired it with a tan, collared shirt. I'm grateful he went with the English attire and not the Wampanoag. I can't imagine him sitting at the table shirtless with a painted face and headdress asking for someone to pass the carrots.

"Who else is coming?" Hailey asks once everything has been brought in. Jarod and Bradley are sitting in the living room with a football game on the television. The women are in the kitchen lining up dishes, lifting tinfoil off of them, and finding serving spoons.

"Um… Just Aunt Mary. Becky and Bryan didn't make it in, and Deaton and Kristlyn went to her family, and of course, you know Chappy's gone."

Becky and Bryan and their two kids usually come to my house for Thanksgiving, en route to Becky's mom's house where they celebrate the day after. But when she found out Mary was coming, she wasn't having any part of it. "No way I'm going to sit beside your mother, who I remember very well and I'm sure she remembers me, and both of us — *all three of us* — lie to Hailey and everyone else, *but especially Hailey*, about who she is. So not doing that!"

"Well, when you put it that way," I'd said, to lighten the lecture.

"I didn't *put* it any way," she said. "It *is* that way."

I'd closed my eyes and allowed her to berate down the phone lines. "I know," I'd finally said. "I'm in too deep on this, Beck. And I'd honestly prefer you not drown with me. It's a rip-tide over here. It really is."

"Yeah, well you could have stopped this a long time ago," she'd said. But anytime I pressed her on that, she had no answers for how. How does a child stop a parent from reaching out to them? How does a child end their love?

Obviously not easily because here I am allowing her to squeeze her way into my home, my holiday.

Her face appears in the glass of my front door. Hailey runs to let her in. This is the first time my mother has been in this house since the day she fled. She stands in the entryway with an exaggerated, fixed smile. I watch as she tries to take it all in.

"Mary, these are my friends. Margo, Paulus, Bradley." I point them all out while she nods and smiles at each one. "And Hailey's boyfriend, Jarod." Bradley gets up from the couch and shakes her hand. Jarod nods his head and smiles.

"I can't believe Aunt Mary finally came here." Hailey is practically leaping around the kitchen while I line up glasses and put ice in them.

"Well, she's just always been with Ian for holidays. This one's going to be hard for her." The truth is we've tiptoed around this for weeks. I pitied the thought of her in that apartment all by herself or across the way with Rhoda and Harry and Rhoda's mom, Beatrice, talking about the outrageous price of oil and rising tensions in the Middle East over dried-out turkey and soggy stuffing.

She was dreading it, and the fact that she even considered coming was such a healthy step for her. It's not lost on me that while my own mental health declines, I'm building hers up.

Dad and Helena had flown to Helena's daughter's house in Maine days earlier. Deaton and Kristlyn are planning to be at her cousin's house in Savannah all day. Admittedly, there was no reason Mary couldn't join us for just one day. And since it's Thanksgiving, I'm making an effort to show grace.

It's almost two o'clock before the turkey is ready. Jarod is still engrossed in the football game. He keeps jumping off the couch and yelling with his fists in the air. Bradley looks up and smiles — a silent cheering partner — but he's not going to go all crazy about it. I can hear snatches of conversation from Margo and Mary. They're only on the other side of the kitchen, but with all the racket from the TV, I can't catch every word. Paulus is sitting in the dining room waiting patiently for dinner. I've offered to let him snack or help or watch the television in Hailey's room, or play in the backyard, take Otis outside, anything… but he just wants to make sure he doesn't lose the seat he's chosen to dine in.

"Well, it's really our last hope," Margo says. "He's been at so many schools. They promise so much, but they never work out."

"I've heard good things about that one," Mary says. I've never seen my mom using her professional voice, giving advice. I'm begrudgingly filled with pride. "I had a student with Asperger's once, and…"

*Oh dear God in heaven! Not the "A" word!*

I'm not sure Margo will take well to that. I drop the roasting pan on the stovetop, a little too hard. Neither one of them notice.

"That's what my brother says. Been saying it for years but I…"

"I think he's right. You'll see." Mom reaches for Margo's wrist and holds it for a moment. "Special needs children—"

"Lunchtime! Dinnertime! Supper... um, whatever. Turkey!" I flutter and flap around my kitchen like I'm imitating one instead of serving one.

Everyone except Paulus, who remains attached to the chair, gathers in the kitchen and forms a line, each piling their plate high and relocating to the dining area.

When everyone is seated, I rise and clink a fork to my glass. "If I could just have a few words." Margo looks up from cutting Paulus' turkey. Jarod sets his fork back on his plate. Bradley pats his newly cut hair and folds his napkin. Mom smiles uncertainly. Hailey rolls her eyes and slouches in her chair.

I clear my throat, stand up straight, and hold on to the back of my chair like I'm at the podium and begin. "In 1614 English explorers sailed home with a ship full of Indians destined for slavery. They fled an epidemic of smallpox, but by the time Pilgrims arrived in Massachusetts there was only one left." I look up and form the name carefully with my lips. "Squanto."

I pause for dramatic effect. Everyone is staring at me, hanging on to my words. I may not have a publisher, but I have a captive audience. "Squanto knew their language and taught them to grow corn and how to fish and live off the land. He negotiated a peace treaty between the Pilgrims and the Wampanoags, and at the end of the first year the Pilgrims held a feast to honor them."

Hailey picks up her fork as if that's the end of my tribute. Jarod yawns with his mouth closed like he's hiding marbles in there.

"But as word spread others began to arrive and seized the land."

Hailey's fork that is loaded with sweet potato casserole en route to her mouth drops and clatters on her plate.

"They began capturing some natives for slaves and killing others, but the Pequot Nation fought back. In 1637 several hundred members of their tribe gathered for their annual Green Corn Festival — which is *our* Thanksgiving Celebration." I look around at their faces to make sure they're comprehending. Most of them are looking at the napkins in their laps, except for Paulus. His mental recorder is turned on taking notes. "Before dawn, the sleeping Indians were surrounded and shot or clubbed to death. Others were burned alive."

I reach for a sip of my water, and while I'm swallowing Bradley begins to clap. Everyone else joins in hesitantly, then quickly they all grab their forks and dig in. The chewing and clinking are so loud I don't know how to talk over it, and then they all begin their own conversations. As I sit down, I mutter to no one in particular that I wasn't done. "The story has a good ending," I say, but no one hears me.

"This is a beautiful home you have," Margo says to me. Bradley pats my leg consolingly under the table.

"Thank you." I maneuver my corn over to the other side of my mouth. I let it go at that, not wanting to go into details, as I look at the surrounding rooms. My Marigold dining room walls now look like breastfed baby diarrhea. My Mexican tile looks like mud. *Seriously, what was I thinking?* Who wants mud floors with chicken feet marked in them?

I hate this house now as much as Susan must have hated it. Hopefully, I can work this out with the Schwares. They can have it! They can hang sheets down the middle of the rooms and scribble growth charts and math lessons or whatever they want all over it. I want out! I have to come up with over twelve thousand dollars to get out, but I'll think about that tomorrow. Today is supposed to be stress-free, a day of gratitude.

We're almost done with dinner. Forks are slowing down along with the conversation, as everyone gets full. Paulus has been telling us all about how the typewriter was invented when some man was looking to create a machine for transcribing letters either singly or progressively one after another. It's a boring story, but everyone seems far more interested in it than they had been in finding out what happened to the Indians. When that topic finally dies down I catch my mom wink at Margo and Margo smiles, comforted. I see something out of the corner of my eye and glance up. There's Deaton and Kristlyn standing outside the front door. She's behind him holding a pie plate in both hands, and he's got a cake platter in his.

My napkin lands in the middle of my green beans when I throw it on the table and run to the door. I open it then step out on the front stoop and close the door behind me. They both step back to make room for me and continue to stand there with their arms loaded down. "I thought you couldn't come to dinner," I say to Deaton.

"But we made it for dessert," he announces holding up the cake to show me. He looks over my shoulder and waves to everyone at the table. I turn around and glance that way, and all of them are turned around looking at us, smiling and waving.

*Bunch of busybodies.*

"Happy Thanksgiving, Amy," Kristlyn says with a big, toothy grin. She readjusts the pie plate in her hands.

"Uh-huh," I say back to her, dismissively. "Did you deliver the food to Nikki's family?" I look back at Deaton, accusingly.

"I did that early this morning" He shoves past me, and actually pushes me aside — lightly, but still. "This is getting heavy," he says as he opens the door.

"Happy Thanksgiving!" The crowd at my dining room table erupts.

*Do these people ever shut up?*

Hailey and Jarod begin to clear the dishes, and Bradley goes out to my utility room like he owns the place. He returns with two folding chairs, and everyone slides together to make room for them. Before my mom can say anything, Hailey goes around behind mom's chair and puts her arms around her shoulders. "This is Aunt Mary. She's here from Atlanta."

*Oh God, please don't tell her last name,* I think as I picture that piece of paper with the names Monterey Joe had in his files: *Stephen P. Westland. Monique L. Brandt. S.P. Loganstein. Mary Guthry. B. Leventhal.*

Kristlyn hasn't stopped smiling since she walked in. She reaches a hand across the table to my mom, and Deaton puts his hands on his waist and looks at her. "The famous Mary. It's so great to finally meet you."

"The famous Deaton," Mom says back to him. "It's great to finally meet you as well." She's a natural at this, maneuvering in and out of fake conversation as swiftly and smoothly as a Mercedes. Years of practice at play.

No one is ready for dessert, so we're forced to stand there making conversation, and I try to keep an ear tuned to every single person — rudely interrupting many of them before much of anything can be said.

The chair beside my mom ends up being the one that's left empty once everyone rearranges, and I nudge Hailey to scoot down and give me hers so Mom and I aren't some split-screen image for our guests to view and recognize similarities. "What?"

Hailey turns around sharply as if I've poked her with a steak knife. "Why?"

Now everyone is paying attention to us. "Um, because I'll be running back and forth to the kitchen, and it's easier from here," I say, laying a hand on her shoulder and squeezing quite hard.

"Ow!" She flinches again and exclaims. She scoots over one seat, and I plant myself between her and Jarod. I'm in one of the folding chairs now and it sits lower than the other chairs, so I feel like a child that's not behaving. And then I realize that there could be resemblances between Hailey and my mom if anyone looks close enough.

"Oh. Look. I've split you two up. And you have such little time together these days. Hailey, you switch places with Jarod and I'll move down."

Hailey has been whispering something to Mom, and she looks up and waves a hand. "It's fine." At the same time, Jarod rises and points out that he can just switch places with me and he'll be next to Hailey.

"No, this chair is low. Hailey, switch with Jarod. Now!" I demand.

We finally get settled. I look up to see Deaton staring at me, trying to figure out what I'm doing.

*He knows. He saw the resemblance. No. He couldn't have. I'm paranoid. The last time I thought someone was staring holes through me they turned out to be blind.*

"So you were Amy's teacher," Bradley says, as Jarod and Hailey and I all try to maneuver around each other in the tight corner. I can hear Hailey saying something to Jarod about my being weird, and I give her an evil eye.

"I can only imagine that job." Deaton guffaws and reclines down in his seat, stretching his legs out.

"What school did you teach at?" Kristlyn asks.

"Oh. Board games!" I jump up from my chair and try to slide between everyone seated on the left side of the table and the hutch behind them. Everyone scoots in as close as they can. I run to the cabinet under the television in the living room and return immediately holding up a box. "Apples to Apples!" Everyone groans and mumbles about relaxing, being full, maybe after dessert, blah-blah-blah.

"You were saying," Margo turns to Mom, and Mom launches into some story about my junior high years and how precocious I was.

"I remember I assigned the entire class a paper on life goals. Amy's was to travel the country on horseback encouraging people to get out and vote."

*This must be some other student she had. She's turned me into another student — a real one. Gosh, she's good.*

Everyone laughs and I say, "Well, it is important. In Plymouth, even a non-church member could vote, but then they started leaning away from political democracy and..."

"Did you bring pie?" Hailey turns to Deaton, rudely interrupting me. Suddenly everyone's starving again. They all shuffle back from the table and head for the dessert table in the kitchen.

"I told you my apple pie would be appreciated," I hear Deaton say to Kristlyn. "Bet ya they don't have another one in there."

"And if they do?"

"I lose the bet and wash all the dishes we left in the sink while you relax with a turkey sandwich later," he answers her.

I turn and sneak a glance at her and pretend to be counting people like we're on a field trip to the kitchen and I might have lost one en route. She seems to be considering his proposal. "And if you're right?"

"I'll think of something," he whispers to her.

He glances my way, and I roll my eyes. I go stand beside Bradley and take his arm, just as proprietarily as he had taken mine a few days earlier. He doesn't seem as perturbed as I had been.

Dessert is a less formal event than dinner. Hailey and Jarod go back to the dining table and join Mary, and I begin moving all the other chairs far away from the table and scattering them around other rooms. "Just gonna sweep under the table and stuff," I say, explaining my task.

Bradley takes his cake and coffee into the living room, and Kristlyn follows him.

"Before dawn, the sleeping Indians were surrounded and shot or clubbed to death. Others were burned alive," I hear Paulus saying to Deaton.

I take my time surveying the desserts before settling on a smidgen of pumpkin roll and an oatmeal cookie and turn back to grab my mug with my free hand. I take a sip of my coffee to test its flavor before I leave the kitchen and all the creamers behind.

Suddenly Deaton is behind me. He holds up his mug and whispers, "Toast to your mom."

My coffee is scalding. I spit it right back into the mug and widen my eyes at him. "*What?*"

"Monique," he says. "I know, I know. She might not be. But you gotta admit, Amy. I'm pretty sure..."

I think about my real mom, just minutes earlier how she'd turned another student into me. I watch her manicured hands gesticulating and weaving together some story — God only knows what — and I'm strangely comforted by it.

She's not lost. *That's* my mother.

"You gotta admit." I smile and clink my mug to his.

W HEN I WAS twelve, I really did write a paper on life goals. That must be a standard middle school assignment. I don't remember much about it, except that Susan and I were going to have a motor home and drive it around letting all the stray animals in town spend nights in it. Shortly after I wrote it the idea grew, and I started looking at the classifieds every week and calling about recreational vehicles for sale.

One afternoon after school a man I had called drove his dilapidated, old camper to my house to meet me and show it off, hoping to make a sale. I was sitting on the front steps outside, waiting for him. "Well, it's not exactly what I was looking for, but maybe," I'd said as I circled it, kicking the tires, looking underneath it, and wondering if pink and purple flowers painted on it would make it look any better. When he opened the door to show me inside the smell of mold made me leap back, right into the arms of Mrs. Ryder.

"I think you need to take your camper and leave," she had said to the man.

"But it was only five hundred dollars," I'd sobbed, as the man with the shirt that rode up on his belly and the greasy hair that had kept falling in his face backed up and drove over the curb on his way out.

"It was a piece of junk, Amy. What kind of vehicle costs five hundred dollars? If something seems too good to be true, it usually is."

I kept sniffling as I watched the camper round the corner, with something underneath dragging behind.

"You must have tomatoes for eyeballs, child. You'd buy a cat in a sack," she said, throwing up her hands at me.

I'd asked my teacher the next day what Mrs. Ryder meant by all that and she said she assumed it reiterated the earlier statement that if something sounded too good to be true, it was.

Idioms became my new favorite thing. Year twelve through thirteen I spoke using them more than normal language, driving everyone around me crazy. Eventually, I gave up on the camper idea and started dabbling in a more creative outlet, writing little stories full of analogies and making up new sayings. It was the beginning of my love of the written word. I remember my dad laughing one day when he came across my list: When you step in manure, don't be surprised that there's a horse nearby. Like a free ride on a bus with no wheels. And my all-time favorite: Like a crocheted blanket on a cold, winter night.

Somewhere along the line, I'd forgotten Mrs. Ryder's words and my own wariness from lessons learned the hard way. But when I logged on to check on Monique that evening and see how her Thanksgiving Day had gone it all came back to me. If something seems too good to be true, it's probably a nice, warm blanket full of holes.

# TWENTY-THREE

I CAN'T BELIEVE HOW something like this could have happened overnight. Monique's husband doesn't have any social media to speak of, nor do her kids. She had been the only one in the family I could examine, but apparently I hadn't scrolled back enough years in her news feed to get a clear picture. Her six-year-old daughter, Carly, has nephritis. It seems Carly was sick years before, but until recently she's been fine — in remission, living the life of a typical six-year-old. Now I scroll way back in her mom's news feed and see posts from long ago, explaining kidney disease and inflammation of the glomeruli and asking for prayers. The medication and treatment she was put on at that time seemed to have been the answer to those prayers.

But the day before Thanksgiving, Carly got very sick. There's a picture of her in her hospital bed with her family gathered around her on Thanksgiving Day. She's swollen and pale. There are comments from friends and family members wanting updates, asking what they can do, and promising to pray once again.

While I sit in the dentist's chair I scroll through my screen reading all of this, then I look up everything I can about nephritis and try to figure out how a little girl at horseback riding lessons four days ago is now lying in a hospital bed looking like she's at death's door. And then I think about the casseroles I've been stacking in my freezer for a woman I barely know. Deaton's going to expect me to have some fundraising carnival for these people, my supposed relatives!

"Do you grind your teeth at night?"

The doctor is back. I drop my phone in my lap as he tilts my head back again and sticks his gloved fingers in my mouth. I'm unable to verbally answer his question, so I move my eyes back and forth like I'm terrified of something and shrug.

*I dunno.*

He pulls back my upper lip to examine, and I lie there like a prized filly.

"You have Bruxism."

I rub a hand over my heart. "Bwuim?"

He removes his fingers from my mouth and pushes his glasses back up then looks over them at me. "You clench your teeth. It's wearing down your enamel. Stressed?" he asks, smiling.

I make a sound with my throat and pull down my sleeve to cover the scratch marks on my forearm.

"We'll get you a mouthguard. Enamel doesn't come back once it's gone."

He finishes up with me, and the receptionist guides me to the check-out counter. She hands me my bill and a plastic bag with a toothbrush, toothpaste, and floss. "Doctor Gilder said you'd get me a mouthguard too," I say, rummaging through the bag.

"I'll set up another appointment for you, so we can make one."

I look at the charge card in my hand. "How much *is* a mouthguard?"

The receptionist swivels around in her chair and reaches for a laminated sheet. "Three twenty-five," she says.

I pull my card back toward me. "I. I can't do that right now."

She nods and reaches for my card again. "Twenty-five for your co-pay." She looks around and says in a much lower voice, "You can buy yourself a mouth guard at the drug store."

I DECIDE NOT TO decorate the house for Christmas. "I'm not in the mood this year," I say to Deaton. "I'll just stick to the café stuff."

He nods understandingly, holding the other end of the garland while I tape it to the front of the counter. "You've got a lot on your plate."

"You don't know the half of it."

The Monday after Thanksgiving I'd called Sheila Thomas to tell her I wanted the Schwares to have the house. "Do you think they could meet me halfway on the difference? Maybe? Something?" I'd rambled on to cover the silence on the other end of the phone.

"The Schwares have already gone under contract on another place," she'd said. "I picked my sign up out of your yard this morning."

"Worried about Carly and Monique?" Deaton stretches the garland too tight and I tug it back so it'll swag.

I'd been thinking of the Brandt family as some fictional people on TV or something. With her daughter's illness, the family became real. "What's the latest? I haven't looked since early this morning."

"It's bad." He lets out a long sigh. "Her blood pressure is very high, and someone said something about fluid buildup in her tissue."

I drop the garland and go sit in a booth. My own blood pressure is surely on an upward spiral, and my stomach wires are all wrapped up in a knot. I look like I've been in a fight with an alley cat, and I have mental distractions and an imaginary world that's starting to overpower my real one — not sure if that's a curse or a blessing yet.

*Add to the list: medicate or hand myself over to mental psychotic ramblings?*

And now that Doctor Gilder has pointed it out, my teeth are constantly clenched. "I don't have the energy to finish this," I say, throwing the rest of my decorations back in the box.

Deaton pulls out his phone. He clicks a few buttons then puts a hand to his mouth. He pulls the hand slowly, taking his lips with it.

"What now?"

"Monique just updated. The doctors are talking about a kidney transplant." He leans over and hugs me. "I'm so sorry, Amy," he says as if this is my little sister I diapered and burped myself.

Tears form, my throat clenches, and I choke on culpability.

THERE ARE A wide variety of mouthguards at the drug store, ranging in price from ten dollars to fifty dollars. "Hmm. So many," I say to myself and to the woman standing next to me, reading the back of a mouthwash bottle. She looks up, gives me a small, tight smile, and turns away.

I choose the twenty-five-dollar one, pay for it, and return to my car just as my phone starts ringing.

"You love the beach, right?" Bradley asks.

"Uh, yeah."

"Good. You have a reservation on the beach in Hilton Head next weekend."

"Really? But the caf—" I stop. The café won't go under in one weekend. Cory knows the café inside out and always wants to work more hours, and it'd be so good to get away from all this mess for a day or two, spending some time with the one person in my orbit completely oblivious to most everything about me. Goodbye, Amy! Hello, alternate universe! And — perfect opportunity — I've got to get past all my reservations and make this thing with Bradley work.

*This thing. What exactly is this thing, and how does it work?*

A memory floats through my mind that I haven't thought about in so long. Bradley's profile on Potion#9: *"I like movie nights at home, lazy Sunday mornings, and roads that lead to nowhere."* Truer words were never spoken.

"Trader and Investment Summit," he says. "I signed up this morning and booked a room for us at the Grand on Pelican Point."

THERE'S AN EMPTY spot on the park bench next to him. My newest subject, Andrew Bender is unusually tall, with a long face and a full head of black curls. His two little boys play nearby in the sand with the bag of spoons and cups and little, metal trucks, and machines. I sit in the space and reach in my bag for my book. Andrew pays me no attention. "James, let your brother have a turn," he yells and the older boy throws the bulldozer down and runs for the big, wooden pirate ship in the middle of the playground. "Argh, no. Don't just leave him there." He starts to get up, but the little one seems fine with it, so he decides he is too.

243

I glance up from my book. "My sister used to do the same thing to me all the time."

He finally notices I've sat down. "Sorry? Oh yeah. It's a bit of a problem, his sharing."

I nod and smile. "Two's tough."

"Bout to add a third to the party, so he's going to need to learn quickly."

"Oh wow. You're going to have your hands full."

The littlest one decides he's tired and leaves all the toys scattered in the sand and comes to see his father. He toddles right up to his dad's knees and lays his sandy face on them. His dad ruffles his hair. "That's why I'm at the park on a miserable, cold day." He laughs. "My wife needs a break while she can still get one."

He reaches down and zips the little boy's jacket up tighter and checks the string at the top to make sure it's still tightly tied. "I like shoes," the little boy says to me.

"I like shoes too," I say to him. "Especially on a day like this."

"Your shoes," His dad points. "He likes *your* shoes." I look down at the wedged boots my jeans are tucked into. My legs are crossed and I hold the top boot out for inspection, turning it a bit.

"Why thank you, kind sir," I say to the little boy, but he's grown bored with me and has buried his face into his dad's knees. He's moving his runny nose back and forth on the fabric of his dad's jeans.

"I bet your wife does have her hands full." I shake my head in wonder. "Three! I can't imagine."

"I can't either," he says. "She's a saint."

The bigger boy joins them at the bench. "I wanna go, Dad."

Mr. Bender looks at the watch on his wrist. "Ten more minutes?" he says, asking permission from two miniature versions of himself covered in sand and snot.

Both boys begin to whine. "You said that ten minutes ago," the older one says.

"Yeah. Ten mens is a lot," the younger one says.

His dad looks at me and we share a smile. "Who wants hot chocolate before we head home?"

"Me. Me." The chorus is eager.

"Go grab all our stuff, and we'll head out pardners," he says to them. To me, he reiterates, "I *really* don't know how she does it."

I watch them leave the playground then scroll through my phone and take care of a loose thread.

**From: Unveiled@officeweb.com**
**To: Helena1098@myFCcourier.com**
**Subject: Investigation**
**We plan to make a trip to Kentucky soon and do some**
**digging around. We will obtain DNA at that time.**

My phone dings immediately with a reply:

**From: Helena1098@myFCcourier.com**
**To: Unveiled@officeweb.com**
**Subject: Caroline has been found!**
**This is wonderful! Please let me know if I need to**
**deposit more money into your account to cover those**
**expenses. Caroline's daughter can provide DNA as**
**well if we need a familial match. Keep me posted!**

Mr. Bender has managed to get both boys loaded into the
minivan, but he seems to be struggling with the straps of the toddler seat. He finally shuts the back door and gets in the driver's
seat. I run to my car and follow behind until he gets to Bresslyn's
Sundae Shop and parks right in front.

I SEE THE BLINKING light when I walk in the door. "Sparkle,
it's Dad. Call me when you can. Okay. That's all. Is this thing
working? Amy? I'm going to hang up now. So, okay bye."

It's too late to return his call, so instead, I reach into my purse
and scrutinize the directions for the mouth guard.

*You've got to be kidding me — a do-it-yourself kit.*

**Put guard in the microwave for one minute then mold**
**hot guard to teeth.**

I rip open the package and throw it in the middle of the
microwave, on the glass tray. As soon as it dings, I pick it up and
drop it on the floor. I have to rinse it off and do the whole thing
over again. This time I try to grab it with a paper towel. I try to
line it up in my mouth and bite down in the center. I watch the

clock and hold it there for two minutes. When I'm done it almost fits my teeth, but it's not tight. I open my mouth, and it falls off.

*What if I choke on it? What if it slips off during my sleep and I just inhale it on down my throat?*

I decide to wait and try it out the night I go away with Bradley. That way he can save me if I'm choking. It never crosses my mind how totally unsexy that would be. He'll have his CPAP and I'll have my mouthguard. We'll bond over our apparatuses, just like a couple in the nursing home together.

*Sweetie, can you roll my oxygen tank on over here? Yes, Button. Can you hand me my teeth?*

Thursday begins with an early morning call from Dad. "Sparkle, did you get my message? I just," he stammers. "I wanted to update you on the latest. Please don't hang up." For the next ten minutes, he fills me in on the last few months of my own life. How the investigator needed a copy of the train receipt, and he and Helena looked everywhere for it. He ends with, "I know how upsetting this is, but now the investigator thinks your mother may be alive. And Helena thinks... well, we don't know what to make of it all."

*What the heck am I doing to my family?* Every time I correspond with Helena, I set aside the fact that I'm essentially corresponding with my father. Hearing him retell it all brings it full circle, back to him. I burst out crying.

"I know. I know. It's shocking." He attempts to console me. "I wanted to tell you this in person, but you work so much. I can't ever catch you girls. Hailey's so busy at school and you're always running." He's rambling. I imagine Helena has made him call me. She's probably sitting right there pointing at him, demanding he stick to the subject. "Now, Amy we don't know anything for sure," he drones on.

Helena probably just narrowed her eyes at him. "*We do know for sure,*" she's most likely mouthing with her hands all up in the air like a crazy, out-of-control conductor. "*The investigator said!*"

"It's not true," I say. "I don't know what you and Helena are trying to do, Dad, but leave me and Hailey out of it. Don't you dare call and tell her this. My mother would not have abandoned me." I'm screaming at him. I've never screamed at my dad. He avoids emotion and passion of any kind at all costs, and I'm not sure he can handle it. It'll shock his happy-go-lucky, easy flowing, bumpy-free existence. I soften my tone. "I just... I can't hear this. I'm sorry. I have to go."

**P**AULUS IS HAPPY to fill me in on the Christian Bishop, Saint Nicholas, while he sits at the counter eating a muffin and kicking at the garland Deaton and I taped across there. "Eyes, Paulus," Margo says to him and he adjusts his gaze directly at my pupils. He's a different child ever since he started attending The Madeline Rinaldi School for Autism. When he's done explaining, he folds his hands in his lap and says, "Now it's your turn to share something with me."

I'm trying to think of something that might interest him when Deaton appears beside me.

"Oh! You scared me. I didn't see you come..."

"Margo. Paulus," he says impatiently. "Amy, can I talk to you for a minute? In your office?"

"Uh. Sure." I try to think what I've done. What tracks do I need to cover now?

*He's going to ask me more about Aunt Mary from Thanksgiving. I knew he caught on to something.*

"Deat," I say nervously, as he closes the door behind me. "You have to believe I..."

"Amy, listen. It's Carly."

I stop and listen.

"First of all, I've looked at everyone else on Joe's list. There are two I can't find anything on because I'm still trying to figure out their first names. The others, from what little I've found, don't seem to fit at all, but I don't know. Honestly, I'm not digging that deeply anymore. I just keep going back to Monique. There are too many similarities between you two." He rubs at his eyes, defeated.

"Uh-huh. But, what about Carly?"

*Dear God, don't let her be dead.*

"I think we need to go out to Kentucky and confront Monique. I mean if you want me to go with you."

"What? Are you crazy?" I shriek. I run my fingers through my hair and turn away from him.

"No. Hear me out," he puts a hand on my shoulder to pull me back.

"I won't! This is the *worst* possible time. Her daughter is deathly ill and you want me to show up and say, 'Hi, I'm the other daughter — the one you abandoned. I was just hoping I could squeeze in here and pray with y'all while I puree what's left of your nerves in my blender here.'" I curl my lip at him and clench my teeth. *"My enamel,"* I want to yell at him. *"It doesn't replace itself!"*

I do roll up my sleeve and reveal my inner arm. The skin is creamy and unblemished there and a few pale pink tracks take on an especially frightful appearance. Deaton doesn't even notice. *"Look what you've caused me to do,"* I almost say, but stop myself. Not because I don't want to pass blame, but because now is not the time. A few scratches pale in comparison to a life-threatening disease. At some later point, I can reveal my inner turmoil and my outward manifestations of it and let Deaton know he's driving me insane and I need to let this go. Maybe I can tell him my therapist insists. I should maybe call a therapist and get that ball rolling.

"Amy, the doctors have said Carly needs a kidney transplant. So far, no one in the family is a match."

I stop rubbing my skin and clutch a hand to my throat. "What are you saying?"

"They need you, Amy. This might be the best time to show up and introduce yourself."

I need to stall, to slow Deaton down. "Give me the weekend to think about it," I say.

**B**EFORE BRADLEY AND I leave early Friday morning, I run out and stick a "For Rent" sign in the yard in the same hole Sheila's sale sign had made in the grass. "We'll try this for a while. Maybe I can rent it out and catch up on my debt," I say to Bradley as I wiggle the stake deeper into the ground.

The drive up to Hilton Head is pleasant until Bradley looks over and sees me catching up on what Monique has been doing.

"Friend of yours?" He's had a silly grin on his face since he showed up at my door in the wee hours.

*Play it more cool and suave, dude.* Someone needs to help him out in the love department. *This Amy, she's a tough cookie to crack, which is probably why no one else really cares to try.*

"I hardly know her," I say with a shrug. And then for some insane reason I add, "But she could be my mother."

Bradley veers off to the shoulder of the highway and turns to me. "Wh-what?"

Staring out the side window away from him and in a monotone voice, I tell him bits and pieces, what seems pertinent to intimacy. The truth about Aunt Mary is left out. Nor do I tell him I'm the investigator Helena unknowingly hired, although I'm not sure why I decide to keep that nugget to myself. One thing at a time, I suppose. I just tell him Deaton's been sleuthing around and what we've uncovered. If I'm going to *finally* solidify this relationship and forgo all others, then I've got to let him know what's going on with me. How could I move in with him and then, weeks later, say, *"Oh I never told you I wasn't sure if my mom really died twenty-eight years ago? Well, I've been searching for her and Voila! There she was living in Kentucky. But enough about that. Do you want your eggs scrambled or fried?"*

"My God! No wonder!" Bradley says, shaking his head. "I couldn't figure out. I mean, I knew something was holding you... I mean you're so... but this... My God, Amy!"

I sigh and run a hand over my mouth, down my chin.

Bradley looks at his watch and exhales. His first assembly is in three hours. He reaches for me, and I allow him to hold me with my face shoved into his chest, my nose flattened against his shirt. I don't squirm or wiggle because he deserves this embrace, and I deserve to have my nose flattened, my air depleted. Finally, he puts the car in drive and merges back in with traffic, but he doesn't let the discussion go. As cars whiz by us and the traffic into the city grows heavier, he asks me a million questions, and I answer them like a robot until he pats my leg and acknowledges that he understands this is emotionally exhausting. "We'll talk more about it later."

Grand on Pelican Point is the poshest hotel I've ever been inside. Dad and I didn't vacation much when I was growing up. He and Nana took me to Stone Mountain once, but it wasn't much fun. Susan didn't go, and even though my dad had plenty of money, he let his frugal mother dictate what we could and couldn't afford.

We could afford the gas to get there, but we could not afford meals in restaurants. We could afford bread and sandwich meat to keep in the room's refrigerator, but no chips or sodas. We'd pulled up to our motel room and walked from the car to the door and even though the room was a set price, we still had to turn the air conditioning up once we got inside so we didn't use too much. I had never been inside a fancy hotel lobby until my fateful field trip to Atlanta.

The wheels of my suitcase bump along the grout lines in the tiled foyer. We get our luggage up to the room, and the first thing I do is push the button on the air conditioner to turn it way down.

"I have to run," Bradley says apologetically. "You'll be fine?"

"Of course." I wave him off. "Go. You'll be late."

I unpack and lie down on the bed to read my book, but five pages later I have no idea what I've read. There's a beautiful, white sand beach just steps outside my door, and yet here's me, not caring. It *is* quite cool out, though. Not exactly beach weather. Scott Warner thinks I've sold my house and that my problems are over. He's probably sitting right now at his desk with a content expression, his pen poised in his hand, working on other cases and pleased that Amy Hollander is filed away.

*But,* I think with unexpected glee, *Amy Hollander is not filed away. Amy Hollander needs her lawyer back.*

"Scott Warner, please," I say to his receptionist. My heart is thumping, and my throat feels dry.

"Mr. Warner is tied up at the moment," she says. "May I put you through to his voicemail?"

"Yes, please," I answer.

There is a moment of music followed by, "You have reached the voicemail of Scott Warner. I'm not in right now." My mind drifts back to the first time I ever met him. I had thought that old man that bustled through the café door was him, and then he'd called my name. I'd turned around and there he was with that gleam in his eyes, reminding me of someone. Later I'd realized it was a young Chuck Woolery — the man I used to come home and watch every afternoon on *Love Connection.*

"Oh. um, Scott. This is Amy. Amy Hollander. I, Um, the house. It didn't sell. Long story. The appraisal—"

Beep! My time is up.

I pick my book back up and try five more pages before I set it down and pick up the TV remote. I have to study it for a few minutes to find a button that powers the machine on. I flip through various channels, all in the high hundreds. There seems to be no way to get the thing down to the normal single-digit channels, so I flip through something about the mating habits of lions, then an infomercial about a power scrubber, then something with people throwing chairs at each other and yelling catches my attention.

"She's old enough to be his mother!" One woman in tight spandex and a bra yells at another who's shoved into a mini dress with a plunging neckline and the entire middle section cut out. My mind drifts to my upcoming birthday. *Thirty-seven!* At twelve years old I thought I'd have a motorhome and a successful animal shelter by now. Yet here I am running around tripping over lies and actually hoping — *hoping!* — that I'll be homeless soon and able to bring my bank account balance to a nice round zero, because that's my best-case scenario. I'm divorced. I bathe in lies. I've found out the grandmother I thought I had never even existed, and I'm frigid.

There — I've said it. Jerry Springer has just told the woman in the mini dress she needs to identify her situation, so I do too. I'm as frosty as a glacier. Greg Hollander has ruined me for life. "At least I don't have a house full of cats," I say to Jerry. "I'm not a spinster. I have a job. I have lots of friends." Jerry hasn't stopped talking to mini dress. "I have a dog that adores me!"

Two hours later Bradley finds me sitting cross-legged in the middle of the bed so engrossed in the impending DNA results Jerry's next guests are waiting on that I haven't even heard him come in. He grabs the remote and clicks off the TV.

"You shouldn't have done that," I say. "It took me an hour to figure out how to turn it on."

"Ha. Shouldn't fill your head with that junk."

*That? That's nothing compared to my real life!*

"How was your class?"

"Great." He nods his head emphatically. "Good stuff. I'm starving."

I realize I am too, but I've spent my entire afternoon watching families in crisis. I haven't taken a shower or anything.

Bradley opens the drapes and looks out the window. "There's a Smokehouse something or other just down the road."

"Sounds good." I grab my purse and we're out the door.

The shower is like a car wash. Water pulses at me from all angles. I can't see to shut any of the spouts off, so I'm getting hit in the face, the chest, the stomach, the back. I'm as exhausted as if I'd swum the English Channel by the time I tighten the robe around me and open the bathroom door. My hair is wrapped up in a towel, turban style, making me wobble a bit as I walk to the bed.

Bradley is already lying there under the spread. His chest is bare, and I wonder if he's got anything else on. All I can see is a cowlick and a smile. I prop my pillows and make a bit of a deal about arranging and fluffing them. When that gets awkward I try to settle in. The bedspread is heavy and the top sheet is pulled so tightly that my toes fold over, so I kick at the bottom of the sheet to untuck it.

"There." I fold my hands over the bedspread on my lap and turn to Bradley, balancing my turban on my head.

*You look like a nun!*

Well, this is new. My mind has now provided me with a new distraction who dresses like a hooker and yells out dating advice to me. I ignore her and hold my head high with my turban intact.

Bradley smiles at me. "I love you, Amy."

I'm caught off guard. I was not expecting love to be proclaimed. I forgot that was a part of normal adult relationships. *Love.* I wasn't bargaining for love.

I stare deep into his eyes and stroke a finger on his cheek. "You are just the nicest man ever," I whisper so seductively that it really does sound equal to his proclamation. Almost.

Bradley gets out of the bed, wearing a pair of boxers. They're beige, and at first I think they're bare skin but then I realize Bradley's mid-section would not pucker, wrinkle or sag like that unless he'd once been four hundred pounds, which I doubt. He walks around to the end of the bed and kisses my big toe that is hanging out. I pucker my lips and narrow my eyes in a sexy, sleepy way. He slips himself between me and the top sheet and slides his way up my body and over my terrycloth robe until his face is sticking out from the sheet, close to mine. The sheet has a ruffle at the top of it, and as it drapes over Bradley's head it looks like he has on a baby bonnet. He's a seductive little baby.

I bite my lip.

*Don't laugh! Dear God in heaven, please don't laugh! Children are starving in third-world countries. That toddler that was kidnapped from Massachusetts last year still hasn't been found. Mrs. Ryder is going blind. Do not laugh!*

It doesn't work. I burst out laughing. Bradley rolls over back to his side of the bed. I turn to him and place a hand on my turban so it doesn't fall off. I'm ready to be serious now. I can do this.

"Ahh. I'm sorry, Amy," he says.

*Oh.* "Sorry?"

"Your mom and all. It's too much for you. I should have known. You're not even in your right frame of mind."

"Well, yes. It's a lot. I hope you... well, understand."

*Frigid!*

We both sigh at the same time and lie there holding hands and staring straight ahead. I wonder if Bradley's going to pull out his CPAP machine. If I want to talk seriously to him, I should get it all done now because I know once he hooks up it'll be like he's underwater talking through a snorkel, and I'll think about sharks tearing into people's flesh or something like that and burst out laughing again because apparently, that's the real me.

But I have no words to say, so I just lie there. I ponder the phrase "Right frame of mind." I'd searched for mental imagery the week before — just wanted to ensure other people had these imaginary intrusions too, and I wasn't about to ask anyone.

Turns out others do — particularly people with PTSD. *Do I have PTSD?* There was an entire article about using guided imagery to reduce stress. Apparently, my mind has already been doing this for me, but I made an appointment to see a therapist anyway. I'm pretty sure therapists like to heal the whole person, not just bits and pieces, so I've no idea how this will work. How to come clean with the doctor while holding on to my mother's lies? Perhaps therapists have miracles up their sleeves, other than the standard, "Tell the truth." I'm seeing a female, hoping she will understand the mother/daughter relationship and all it encompasses, although I sincerely doubt anyone else's relationship has ever come close to encompassing what mine does.

Within an hour I hear Bradley snoring so loudly I wouldn't be surprised if the drapes next to him get inhaled. I have no idea if he packed the machine and planned to use it — no idea if he's allowed to sleep without it.

*Could he stop breathing and die in his sleep?*

I slide in my mouth guard I laid on the nightstand earlier. It slips around, but I clench my teeth tightly to keep it in, which

253

seems rather counterproductive. Every time I start to drift off I jolt myself awake. I have to keep an eye on Bradley. He's snoring, blissfully unaware of my concern for his airway.

I lean over and gaze lovingly at his peaceful countenance. This nice, patient man. Turning back and twisting my lips, I sort through my feelings. It looks doubtful, like I'm showing an audience the real truth: *She cares for him somewhat, but she's so conflicted. Why? How to get over it? Stay tuned!*

I open my eyes when I hear voices outside in the hallway. I had fallen asleep. It only seems like it was for a few minutes, but the sun is brightening the sky outside our window, and I'm still propped up in the bed with pillows behind my back. My robe is tied properly — and frigidly — at the waist and my legs are crossed at the ankles. The turban has slipped off my head and lies in a damp heap beside me. I lift a hand to my hair and feel it branching out in all directions.

I've ruined Bradley's seminar — our getaway. I'm an evil witch, a fluffed-up pillow stuffed full of sand spurs, a tall glass of lemonade that turned out to be a urine specimen.

"*Stop it,*" I imagine saying to my idiom-loving twelve-year-old self. "*Surely you've moved past such silliness.*

"*Ha! You're an almost thirty-seven-year-old novelist with no agent,*" she says back to me. "*Whadda you know?*"

*Oh my God! The seminar!*

"Shpradley, shwake up." I shake him. He was supposed to be in a meeting at six o'clock.

*Oh God! He's dead.* I fell asleep for just a minute, and Bradley choked on his own tongue or whatever happens when CPAP patients don't hook up to their sleep support.

He opens one eye and gives me a sad, tired smile. "I'm not going," he says.

"Shnot shgoing?"

I place my palm under my mouth and spit my mouth guard into it. "How can you not go? You have to go." I peer at the bedside clock. "It's eight-thirty!"

He shakes his head and sits up. "This." He waves a hand over the bed and stops it on me. "This is more important. I promised you a day in Hilton Head, and I want to be part of it."

"Well, okay then." I sit up straight and pull my robe tight at my neck. "You're sure?"

He doesn't answer. Instead, he just goes into the bathroom and emerges ten minutes later dressed for the day in a pair of tan jeans and a navy sweater. Bradley smells of mouthwash and hair gel and looks extremely well-rested.

I saunter to the bathroom myself. The lighting in the bathroom is harsh — *surely it's the lighting* — although I noticed a few weeks ago that I look every bit of my upcoming age. I've never attempted to ward it off, I just kind of thought I had some unspoken pact with God that I would defy loss of gravity when the time came, to make up for my big knees, maybe. I turn my face left and right and peer closer.

I pat my drugstore cream just like the lady at the beauty counter showed me "Gently, in an upwards motion," into the dark, puffy, half-moons under my eyes and the little line between my eyebrows. I throw my hair into a ponytail, put on a bit of make-up, and brush my teeth.

"I am ready to seize the day," I stride back into the bed area and announce in my royal knight voice.

Bradley is scrutinizing the bill that's been slipped under the door with the phone to his ear. He holds up a finger to me. "Charge the same credit card. Yes, I'll need a copy for my taxes."

"You don't have to tell her it's for your taxes." I roll my eyes and snicker good-naturedly, but then decide it's none of my business when Bradley scowls and waves a hand for me to stop talking. This time last week I imagined us rubbing salve on each other's mysterious bumps and bruises in our nineties, side-by-side in the nursing home, and now I'm reluctant to tease him about the shoe-box of receipts he keeps in the back seat of his car. Crazy what the impact of intimacy, or lack thereof, can do to a couple.

"How about pancakes?" He asks in a serious tone when he hangs up the phone.

"Fine with me, if it's fine with you."

"Well, do you want pancakes?"

"I do if you do."

"Well, I only do if you do."

The Pancake House is just across the street from the hotel, but since Bradley checked out we have to move out of the hotel's parking garage, so we drive over. Bradley's mood seems to have shifted since we first woke up. It's like something has occurred to him, like he's remembered he's mad and not talking to me.

The waitress takes our drink order and returns within seconds with a cup of coffee. It's strong and very hot. I occupy myself blowing over the rim.

"Did you sleep well?" I ask, like I don't already know the answer.

Bradley is scrutinizing his menu as closely as he would an important document. He's following text with his finger and mumbling to himself. "Fine. You?"

"Oh. Fine. I guess. I woke a lot during the night."

He says nothing.

"First time away from the kids," I say, after leaning back in my chair toward the couple seated behind us. "She's mad that he's not missing them as much as she is."

Bradley blinks. I remember that he doesn't appreciate my eavesdropping, or my ability to sum stranger's situations up within two minutes of the eavesdropping. If we can't run with this and get some giggles out of it, I've got nothing.

Our pancakes are delivered to the table. The waitress runs back to the kitchen to grab her next order before we can ask her for anything else.

"Amy?"

Bradley's talking to me again. I quit cutting and look up at him with the sweetest smile like I hadn't noticed the earlier tension. I can feel the softness flood my features. If only I'd started with the creams years ago I'd be the beautiful face of peace and harmony right now.

"Hmmm?"

"You *don't* love me. Do you?"

The pancake is a brick in my throat. I lay my fork down beside my plate. "Of course," I say with raised eyebrows and bright eyes — the same look I'd mastered when my dad used to ask me if I ate all my broccoli and studied for my French test. Instinctively I reach to pat his hand, but I pull back, knowing that would look like grandmotherly love.

He's not convinced.

"They're your children too. I just don't get how easily you can jump on a plane and not even ask about her allergies. Do you even know she has allergies?" The woman at the table behind me is talking through clenched teeth to her husband.

"Do you think you ever could? Ever will?" Bradley asks.

If he just hadn't asked. I begged him in my mind not to. Until that moment, I'd told myself I could, maybe one day. Maybe I could have looked our grandchildren in the eyes one day and told them the story about how I put my face and all my quirks up on a website and, after I had met quite a few freaks, their Grampy showed up and wooed me with his normalcy. "Dull and boring is quite underrated, dear," I might have said to my granddaughter, *"And it's safe!"*

*No.* I can't keep fooling myself or him. I don't love him. I likely never will, not the way he means. Once, early on in our relationship, he told me he was falling in love with me. I'd told myself that was just a phrase people said, meaning nothing, (and I still believe that was the case with Bradley) and I had shooed it away. "Probably not the wisest thing you could do," I'd told him. *True words, but cruel.*

But the way he'd accepted that response — no questioning, no pride. No gumption, after all.

Right there in the Pancake House, trying to subtly lick the syrup off my fingertips, I realize I've lived my entire life with two extremes. I'd spent my childhood with a man who was complacent in everything — a man who loved me indisputably and without challenge — a man who would have nodded and agreed to most anything. And after I'd left my father's care I'd married a man who was restless in everything, never complacent. And I've longed for the in-between — the man who would laugh at my funny jokes and roll his eyes at my dumb ones. The man who would call me out and one-up me, keep me on my toes and keep my tongue sharp. The man who would find the phrase *keep my tongue sharp* fodder for our own hilarious, very private joke. The man who would encourage and support me and hold my intense interest.

I look at Bradley. He's just not that man. I know that unquestionably now because I have met that man.

Bradley gets up and goes to the bathroom. He's gone for a long time. I sit with my hands at my sides, not eating. It seems disrespectful to shove my mouth full right now, no matter how much I want to. I lower my eyes to my pancakes. They've absorbed all the syrup and they're going to need another squirt. That's what I'm thinking about: a relationship I don't deserve and consequently will never have and dried out pancakes.

Finally, Bradley does return to the table. He just sits and stares at the floor, so I take my cue from him and do the same as my pancakes grow even colder. A taxi pulls up outside and the driver gets out, leaving the motor running. He opens the door to the restaurant and looks around. Bradley rises and meagerly waves an arm at him.

I open my mouth to say something, but no sound comes out. I look from the taxi driver to Bradley.

*How does he know a cab driver in Hilton Head?*

The taxi driver must be taking him back to his meeting. I'll put on a sweater and go down to the beach and make friends with the tourists. *It's gonna be okay. I'll resolve this issue soon, but not here and now. I'll set Bradley free. I'll grow old alone, hopefully with some family I've managed somehow to retain. Perhaps a distant cousin ...*

"Your ride is here, Amy."

My head swivels again.

"I think this is best."

I stay rooted to my seat. Bradley goes outside with the taxi driver, who seems to understand he's found himself in the middle of something very uncomfortable. I watch them get my suitcase out of Bradley's trunk and put it in the trunk of the taxi.

I throw my napkin into what's left of the syrup and walk out. *That's my suitcase! He can't just make this decision for me. I have a lawyer!*

I can't even afford a taxi across town, much less from Hilton Head to Flannery Cove. I try to grab Bradley by the shirt. "Can I just talk to you for a minute?"

"I've paid him upfront. We can talk later," he says, avoiding my eyes. "I just need some time away from you."

"Time?!" I turn my palms up, emphasizing my words. "Bradley, you can't just put me in a taxi. This is ridiculous."

"Yeah, well. Sorry," he says, not sounding at all sorry.

In the months I've known Bradley he has been arrogant at times, as well as boring, overbearing, possessive, and unpleasant. But today, he is justified in his proclamations. He and I both deserve better than this. Fine time to show some backbone.

The taxi driver looks from me to Bradley. I can see through the front window of the restaurant. Our waitress hovers close to it, keeping an eye on us.

I throw my purse into the back of the taxi like it's my decision to do this. Bradley walks toward me to say something or close my door for me, but I slam it before he can. "*Go!*" I hit the back of the driver's seat, and do everything I can to have some dignity and not look like a scolded child as we pull away.

I can't resist one look back. Bradley is standing in the parking lot looking smug, rocking back on his heels, his hands in his pockets. *How did I ever consider intimacy and a future with this man?* Twelve hours later and the notion is mind-boggling.

Ten minutes later I spot my taxi driver's name on his dashboard. "Rico?"

Rico turns slightly, then looks at me in his rearview mirror.

I have so many questions, but I can't put any of them into words. *When did he call you? What did he say?*

None of it matters anymore.

"Could you pull me through that McDonald's drive-through up ahead, so I can order some pancakes?"

# TWENTY-FOUR

I T'S COLD OUTSIDE the night I follow Andrew Bender from his office in downtown Flannery Cove to his house. I watch him through the blinds as he eats dinner with his family and throws his kids up in the air, planting kisses on their cheeks. From here I can see Mrs. Bender clearing the table and laughing while she seems to be telling him not to be too rough with the littlest one. Meanwhile, I scroll through my phone to check on Carly Brandt. No change. I listen to Deaton's fifth voice mail of the day and delete it.

I almost miss it. Andrew's standing outside on his front porch kissing his pregnant wife goodbye. They talk for a few more seconds, then he drives away slowly while she waves from the driveway and returns inside to the two children and the dog that is hanging over the back of the sofa.

He gets to the corner and turns right, and I start my car up and follow a few cars behind him. I watch Andrew Bender pull up outside apartment number sixty-seven at the Lighthouse apartment complex and leave his briefcase in the back of the minivan with the toddler seat, while he rings the doorbell.

THE FEW BOXES I'd packed were stacked nicely in the dining room, but now they're all spread out on the table, tape ripped open, contents spilling out. I haven't used a thermometer or a heating pad or a waffle iron in years, but once I packed these items I needed them back almost immediately. I've managed to get back to the hardware store to buy more paint rollers, but I've yet to find the energy to cover my walls.

"I just don't care about any of it anymore," I say to Deaton and Kristlyn. The bookstore is quiet this time of the afternoon. Kristlyn has just returned from an overnight trip and stopped by to spend some time with her boyfriend before going home to unpack. I'm a third wheel, but I don't care about that anymore either.

"So he just left you there?"

"A taxi? What was he thinking?"

I don't really care about this topic anymore either. It seemed important to tell them what happened initially, but now I'm sorry I didn't make myself the heroine of the break-up story. I could have been the one to stand on the curb and whistle Rico over, announcing that I'd had enough of Hilton Head, enough of pancakes, and enough of Bradley himself.

*"But that's not what happened,"* my therapist speaks in my mind. *"Own your truth, Amy. No matter how painful it may be."* Well, this is certainly a step in the right direction. A therapist giving advice is surely preferential to a hooker.

"And now this whole birthday thing," I say to no one in particular.

"When is that again?" Deaton asks.

I yawn. "Tuesday. Dad's birthday is Monday and mine is Thursday, so I dunno, Helena's got something arranged at the club Tuesday night." I make a pfft sound. "I don't even have a date for my own party."

Kristlyn claps her hands together. "I've got that thing," she says to Deaton. "You go with Amy." She nudges his shoulder like she expects him to protest.

I wave a hand. *No need to charity escort me.*

Deaton leans forward, considering. "I could," he says. "I could do that." It's like he's made peace with it.

Kristlyn jumps up. "Great. That's settled. Listen, I gotta run. I'll be back later," she says to Deaton. I turn away, trying to picture Kristlyn lying in bed later with a tightly wrapped robe and a towel turban, a mouth guard on her teeth. The picture is ridiculous. I'm embarrassed for myself.

Deaton and I are left alone in the silence of the store. It's time to close. "You don't have to," I say. "I'll be fine."

"No. No, really I want to. I'd be *honored* to," he emphasizes. "I just. I just want you to do something for me."

I snicker. "What's the catch?"

"Carly. I'll go with you to Kentucky, if you want. We don't have time to waste. We need to go see if—"

"Deaton." I let out a long sigh and pinch the bridge of my nose. "My kidney — it's probably not the healthiest one they could ask for. My mom's grandmother died from a blood clot when she was quite young. My paternal great-aunt had leukemia. We're not a stellar bunch."

"Your mom's mom may very well be Monique's mom." He raises his eyebrows and points at me. "You forget that. And anyway…"

"We don't know," I say loudly, backtracking on my original stance. My hands are tight fists. "We don't know anything about this Monique woman! Please leave me alone about this!"

He looks at me, his jaw open like he's stunned. We were holding hands on this project and moving toward the right door together and now I've dropped his hand and turned sharply in the opposite direction. "I thought," he says finally. "I thought that you thought — *that you felt.*" He holds a hand to his heart like I've shot him.

"I don't know what I think. Or feel."

"Tuesday," he finally says. "What time?"

TWO DAYS LATER Scott shows up, out of the blue. It's late afternoon. Hailey and I are the only ones working, and it's so dead I've got Hailey cleaning out the refrigerator while I tally up the day's totals. When the door chimes and I glance up, my heartbeat takes in what I'm seeing before my eyes do. Once my heart, my eyes, and my brain register and communicate with one another, something inside of me zings like that exhibit at the county fair where you take a sledgehammer to a scale and, if you're strong enough to reach the top, the bell sounds.

"Hi, Home Girl."

I shove the receipts I've been sorting into a drawer. Hailey comes out of the kitchen holding a gallon of milk. "Does this smell…" She stops in her tracks.

"Toss it," I say without taking my eyes off of him. "Then you can go. I'll lock up." Finally, I manage an acknowledgment. "Scott."

He steps closer to the counter and rubs at the light scruff across his chin as if he too is having a bit of trouble formulating a sentence. "I just… I stopped in to see what you had going on."

*"Whatever you'd like to have going on,"* I'd like to say, while pulling on his tie and leading him someplace private. *Silly, childish. Too many Sex and the City marathon*s. Instead, I shake my head to indicate there's nothing and slip out from behind the counter. Together we walk to the closest booth. The air between us is charged.

Scott studies me for a moment. I study him right back, unmoving, unblinking. I can tell he's measuring his words. "How have you been?" he says.

*"Where* have *you* been?"

He draws in a breath. "I've been working. I've been waiting."

We are engaged in a match of words. It's my turn, so I say, "Waiting for what?" I run my hand across the surface of the table and look down at it like I'm searching for crumbs. The table is smooth, as clean as an operating table.

"I've been waiting for you to break up with your boyfriend. Waiting for you to realize there have never been two more mismatched people. Waiting to collect the courage to tell you that."

My heartbeat is so strong, I'm certain it can be seen through my sweatshirt. I rub my lips together, stifling a smile that begins slowly and works its way out. I can feel it overtaking my features.

"Done."

Once I say that word, my smile turns into a laugh. "It's done. I don't have a boyfriend. I don't even have a date." I laugh like I'm announcing celebratory news. Indeed I am, judging from the look on Scott's face.

He leans back in the booth His shoulders are straighter. His chest more puffed out. "You broke up?" he asks incredulously.

"That's what done means."

He takes this news in, shaking his head, affirming it in his mind. "Thank God," he says. "That was so much easier than I thought it was going to be. Now obstacle number two. I hear you need a lawyer again?"

I get up and turn the lock in the front door. When I sit back down across from him I nod. "The appraisal was a problem."

Scott leans back in and folds his hands on the table. He looks to the side for a moment, then back to me. "Here's the thing, Amy."

I sit back deflated and very confused. *He doesn't want to represent me anymore. Doesn't want to...*

"I would like to date you."

The smile is immediate this time, no slow-spreading. An immediate high beam there's no way I can conceal. "Yes." I shake my head earnestly. "I want that. To date. Yes."

"But you're still my client until your house sells or the foreclosure process is completed. Which, as I've told you can be a lengthy process."

"Oh."

I can see that Scott has given this a lot of thought. "I can't see any getting around it," he says.

I blow air out, and my bangs dance on my forehead. "We were going to have dinner that one night."

"To sign papers. It wasn't a date. It was a meeting."

"I never signed them." I hold up my index finger as if I found our much-needed loophole.

"Yeah. I've tossed that argument around in my head a few times, but it's a loose one. You've left messages of intent to hire me. We've had meetings pertaining to the business at hand. You've stated to my secretary that I am your lawyer, and you are my client. The state of Georgia frowns on lawyers having relationships with clients. At the very least it's misconduct. At most, it's malpractice."

"I could get another lawyer."

"You could," Scott shakes his head in agreement, "If you have a very large deposit to hand over before they'll even talk to you. There's Henry Overton in Savannah. If he hasn't retired. He's had dementia for five years or so now. Some days he's lucid. Some days he's not. There's Russell Croswell in Shannings Bay. But he is running for public office, and I don't think he's taking new cases. If he is, you'll get his clerk, not him, and you'll pay top fees for his name. And there's Simon Dunlovey here in Flannery Cove. You won't call him. He will make it clear you can pay your bill off in various other ways."

"Let's just call the bank and tell them to come take the house." I fold my arms on the table and put my face down on them.

I feel his hands on my hair, stroking. "I can wait," he says. "I've *been* waiting."

I pop my head up. "What if we just meet again? No picking me up and driving me. Bring papers. I'll sign them all. I *really* don't have a date. I have my very own birthday party next week at the country club with my family, and I don't have a date. Well, I'm going with Deaton, but that's not a date. He can drive me, and I'll meet you there. Like we were going to do at Barristers." The words pour out of me. The idea takes shape in my mind. It seems doable. "That could work, right? It's not even technically *my* birthday party. It's a joint one with my father."

I can see him strongly considering it.

"It's no different." I shake my head convincingly, driving home my point. "If I'm your client, you should meet my family. I think it will help you represent me better, actually."

"You should be the lawyer," He smiles and concedes, "I want to meet your family. I want to know everything about you. *To represent you better.*"

"Tuesday night. The Flannery Cove Country Club. Seven o'clock."

"I'll bring papers."

"I'll bring a pen."

"There's one more thing," he says.

"Great. What next?"

"This one you're going to like. But I'm saving it for your birthday."

ON THE DRIVE to the club that evening, I'm reminded of all I've missed out on lately. "Aunt Patty's expecting a ring from Tommy Mobley for Christmas. An *engagement* ring," Deaton says.

"What? Tommy Mobley, the contractor? When did that happen?"

"I never told you this?" He says. "Oh gosh. They fell in love ages ago. So Tommy ended up finishing the house — did a great job on it, by the way, you wouldn't even know the place. Well, you never did know the place, but anyway, it's gorgeous. Then he took to 'repairing the broken relationship between Patty and L.J.' as my mother puts it."

I sit in rapt attention. I'm happy for his Aunt Patty, but sad too. "I had no idea. You never said," I say to Deaton, and he smiles like it's no biggie. I'd still thought of Aunt Patty living in demolition and brooding over the rubble. I've missed almost an entire year of my life while I was with Bradley.

*"Noooo."* My hooker friend apparently has a sensible side to her as well. She shows back up in my head and shakes a finger at me reminding me this is not *my* life I'm sitting here discussing — it's other people's. "You need to go claim your own," she says. *She's been talking to my therapist.*

Hailey has come home for the special occasion. She's made cake — such a spectacle, that cake — a big spectacle of pure sugar and love, just like her! It sits in the middle of the long table, all bright colors, and smooth, creamy decadence.

The big, brass clock in the entryway reads 6:45. Deaton and I are the last to arrive, before Scott. Dad rises and holds out his arms. "There's my sparkle."

I quicken my steps and hug him tightly and kiss him on the cheek. There's something about being done with Bradley. It's somehow made me miss my dad even more in the last few days, like I have a slot for personalities and that one already belonged to my dad. No one else can squeeze in there with him. People are who they are, good, bad, or indifferent. And sometimes they're all three rolled into one. But when they belong to you — well, you embrace all of it. And so I do.

Helena half-rises and holds up a hand, beaming. Jarod shakes Deaton's hand across dad's head. Hailey pats the two seats next to her that are empty. Deaton holds one out for me and I sit and look right into the scrunched up condescending face of Buffy Barrington and the always somewhat bewildered face of her husband, Hal. I smile tightly at them and look around the club.

I haven't been here in years. My last good memory is of a Shirley Temple by the pool, trying to pretend I was a teenager so I could attract the attention of the cute lifeguard. The inside of the dining room is in the middle of a remodel, but the section we're seated in still has the same regal red carpet, brass chandeliers, and the cloying aroma of old money. "Told ya it smelled like mildewed dollar bills in here," I whisper to Deaton while passing him the drink menu.

At 6:55 I begin to feel antsy, nervous, and exhilarated. At 7:02, Scott is standing in the doorway to the dining room, and a waiter is pointing him in our direction. He's holding a bouquet of lavender roses.

I have already told Deaton that my lawyer would be joining us for dinner, which led to raised eyebrows, a tilted head, and a blank stare. And that led to an explanation and an admission. "He's the best lawyer I've ever had."

"How many have you had?" he'd said.

"Two including him. My other one was an eighty-five-year-old business lawyer. When I bought the café."

"Well, sounds like he's had some tough competition. He *must* be good," Deaton said.

I rise and meet Scott halfway across the dining room. It's hard to say which one of us is grinning more. Everything seems funny. The fact that he is here with me is funny. The renovations, the people around us, the charge in the air: all funny. I stand straight and tall before him, attempt to compose my face into a serious expression and hold out my hand for a very business-like handshake.

"I'm not shaking your hand," he says. "I settled for that once. It was one time too many." He reaches for me, and I walk right into his open arms. His arms tighten around my waist. "Happy birthday, Amethyst." He whispers into my hair.

I arch my neck and look at him. *Amethyst*. "The deed to your house says Amethyst Chadwick-Hollander." He hands me the purple flowers.

"Dad. Everyone. I want you to meet Scott Warner." I begin to point everyone out while I hold on to Scott's arm. "Scott, this is my father, Raleigh, my um, my future step-mother, Helena, their friends Hal and Buffy, my daughter, Hailey, and her boyfriend Jarod, and my best friend in the whole world," I smile fondly at Deaton and present him with a flourish, "Deaton Dunklin."

Scott makes his way around the table shaking everyone's hand and making a bit of small talk: "Happy birthday, Raleigh. Great daughter you have. Nice to meet you, Helena. Hailey, you look just like your mom. Deaton, I've heard a lot about you."

Once he's settled comfortably by my side he leans over, "Stepmother? I had one of those once, straight out of a Disney movie. Do we like Helena?"

*We!*

I lean over and try to catch Helena's eye. She's wearing her bifocals and laughing at a card someone gave to Dad. "Oh that's priceless," she says.

"We do," I whisper back. "I guess I got lucky. She's more Hallmark movie than Disney vixen."

A waitress approaches holding a board of specials. "We're out of salmon and mahi even though they're still written on the board. I suggest the prime rib with asparagus."

"Oh we like the prime rib," Dad lets everyone know. "We don't care for the alfredo. Too sharp and pungent." Helena nods letting him know he got it right.

Dad catches my eye, and I smile and pick up my menu. But instead of looking at it, I reflect for a moment on the tingle I felt when Scott said, "We." A team. *I like what you like. I shun what you shun.*

"So you're just teasing us with the salmon and mahi?" Dad chuckles The waitress grins and smudges her finger across the board to try to erase them. Helena smiles a tiny bright-eyed smile, unsure what she missed. Buffy purses her lips, unsure anyone should be fraternizing with the help.

"So Deaton, how's literary life?" Dad asks.

"Can't complain," he answers, adjusting his glasses.

"Oh, do you write?" Buffy suddenly notices Deaton is with us.

"Oh no. I own a bookstore," he says, just noticing her as well. "But Amy—"

I step on his foot. This is not a conversation I want to have with Buffy Barrington. "So, the country club," I say looking around in awe like we're sitting in Buckingham Palace.

Dad and Hal start talking between themselves about "the board" and "the budget."

"I hear Earl Proctor tried to veto that," Hal says.

Dad shakes his head. "I'd like to see him try."

I'm not used to seeing my dad in a social setting with his cronies. It's strangely amusing. I'm hanging on every word, seeing a new dimension to him, as Hailey and Jarod and Deaton talk about Christmas break and Helena and Buffy talk about Shirley and Mac McDougall and the new house they just bought in the mountains, and Scott chimes in on everyone's conversations and reaches for my hand under the table.

"I thought I was here to sign papers."

"I'm stroking your fingers. Getting them ready," he murmurs. "It's a lawyer tactic."

The waitress brings our food to the table, and conversation lulls a bit. Everyone clinks and smacks and compares dishes. Hal finds fault with his prime rib, but I point out that mine was cooked to perfection.

Between chews, I lean over and take them all in — *my people*. I really need to warn Hailey to start now on the anti-aging creams — maybe a good stocking stuffer for Christmas, nip those beginning crow's feet in the bud. And for God's sake can Deaton ever learn to just pull a fork straight out of his mouth instead of that upwards thing he does? And what's up with Hal and Buffy Barrington? How are these people even still alive? They've been old forever.

"Who's ready for some of that delicious-looking cake?" Dad's voice booms down the table. Hailey smiles at the acknowledgment. The waitress asks if we would like her to take it in the back and cut it for us. "That sounds like a fine idea." Dad pulls his readers from his pocket and peers at her nametag. "Thank you, Katie."

Katie carries the cake through the swinging doors. "I think I'll just use the restroom real quick," I say to Scott, loud enough so that everyone around me hears. I tell Deaton, "I want to see if they still have those little soaps shaped like golf balls. I'll steal one for ya if they do."

I'm halfway across the room when I hear the recognizable ding of my phone. I start to turn around and go get it. It's lying there on the starched, white tablecloth where I left it. Jarod and Hailey both lean their heads down and peer at it. Hailey's hair is hiding their faces, so I can't see. They both look up when Buffy says something.

I pivot and begin to head back that way, but the small pockets of conversation seem to have stopped and everyone is now staring at my phone. Jarod has picked it up and is showing something on it to Buffy. He pinches his fingers together and places them on the screen then pulls them apart. My dad leans in, and I realize I've stopped in my tracks and I'm still standing in the middle of the floor watching this unfold. Around me dishes clatter, women laugh, men clear their throats and argue their points of view.

"*Aunt Mary?*" Buffy is shaking her head incredulously. "Blow that up again."

Jarod is smiling like she's crazy and he's about to prove it.

"Right there," Buffy says, pointing. "Her freckle, like Hailey's."

Hailey, who has said nothing in the last few seconds, holds a hand up to her ear and rubs at the small, dark freckle on her right lobe. The freckle she's so sentimental about that she's never allowed anyone to pierce through — the one she's always been told matches the freckle on her deceased grandmother's ear. Dark, round, centered.

"I don't see anything." Hailey's voice is high, shrieking. "That's just an earring.!"

Deaton looks up to find me, and his eyes bore into mine as Buffy announces to the table, "That's Carolyn Chadwick if I've ever seen her."

My legs feel like freshly boiled spaghetti noodles sliding off the fork, but I manage to walk slowly back to the table, in control, not alarmed — there's an explanation for this.

*Think of it now!*

There in the middle of the table is a blown-up picture of my mother, specifically her out-of-focus ear lobe, which she pierced after she became Mary Guthrie, and now bears a small stud, not a dark freckle. The picture is blown up so big it's pixelated beyond recognition, but the questions Buffy's words put in place have already started to form in everyone's minds. I meet the eyes of everyone there, but no one says a word except Hailey.

"This text came in, and it said something about an accident, and I could see an image was attached so I looked real quick and then..." She looks helplessly at me, confusion in her features. Her hand is waving toward Buffy, as if the doom and destruction she senses coming at us is all her fault.

In response, I pick my phone up and decrease the size of the picture. My mother is sitting up in a hospital bed, smiling with one hand held up, warding off the photographer. The text message is from Rhoda:

"We were in a fender bender. She's fine! Just

getting checked out."

"Mom?" Hailey again breaks the silence that hangs in the air like a thick fog. I've swallowed something huge — like my tonsils. They're stuck in my windpipe like an ice cube. I glance at Deaton. It takes him just a second. He adjusts his glasses and surveys the unfolding scene with roving, suspicious eyes, as if the whole thing may be a hoax, a birthday joke of some sort. He connects enough dots to make some sense of what's transpiring. I can see it in the way he's looking back at me, enraged, his face beet red. He inhales as if fire may erupt from his nostrils.

I look to Scott. He is startled, a deer in the headlights. *Wrong road? Wrong direction? What's happening?* It's all right there in his eyes that bore into mine. He starts to rise like he wants to help me, but then he sits back down. He can tell this is bigger than he is. There's a sense of it in the air surrounding us. No one can help me out of this.

Our waitress reappears and senses something. She leaves the sliced cake and dessert plates on the table next to us where I've placed my bouquet and whispers something to Helena. Helena nods without taking her eyes off of me.

I look at Hailey. She's still waiting for my reply. She wants it to come quickly and ward off this storm. She wants to defend me, believe me, align with me. "Hailey." It's the only word I whisper.

Someone has passed my cell phone down to my dad and he is staring at it in disbelief. He looks from it to me.

My dad: the pain and confusion on his face is a look I've never seen. There are feelings in there — real, raw emotion.

My eyes float back to Deaton. He looks away. "I don't belong here," he says to no one in particular, in an eerily calm voice.

I clear my throat, but I have no words for anyone. No explanations, no pretense of offering anything. "Jarod. Could you please take me home?" The tears are burning my eyes now. My heart is twitchy, like a butterfly that can't take off. I might be having a heart attack. Now would be a good time.

Jarod scoots his chair back, anxious to leave. Hailey places a hand on his arm to hold him in place, while still looking at me, but then she too scoots her chair back. She goes to her grandfather and leans down to hug him. She whispers something to him, and he nods and pats her back. The Barringtons continue to whip their heads back and forth, not missing a thing, as if they'd been given front row tickets to the match. Deaton carefully places his folded napkin on the table and walks away without saying anything more.

"Dad." I choke the word out, but my dad looks down at his lap. I can't tell anything by his face, but then he holds up a hand to ward me off, basically constructing an instant wall. *I do not want to hear you or see you.* "I." I drop my hands to my sides. "I."

I can't form words. It could be a stroke, not a heart attack.

271

Scott seems to have found his way to the other side of the road. He's had a few moments to take this all in and form some thoughts. "*I'm* taking you home," he says, rising from his chair.

My father won't look up. Helena won't look away. Her eyes are beady and piercing into my very soul. Hailey stands near her grandfather, patting his shoulder, an expectant look in her eyes. *Fix this now! Fix it or you're dead to me, and I'm counting.* I can almost see the mental roster keeping tune to the tapping of her hand. *One, two, three, four... still waiting!*

Scott takes me by the arm. My knees buckle slightly, and he gently pulls me back to a standing position. I hesitate, giving everyone a chance to stop me. I'll answer everything now. I'll tell everyone the truth, then I'll go in the bathroom and fill the basin with water and plunge my head under. But no one stops him. No one wants me to stay.

Scott holds me by the elbow like I'm an invalid. He opens the passenger door of his truck and helps me into the seat, closes the door, and goes around to the driver's side.

I stare at the floorboard. "Is this okay? I thought we couldn't be together on a date." I'm hoping to get out of there and catch Jarod. I'd rather be driven home by Jarod. I can hardly look at Scott.

He starts up his truck without a word or a glance in my direction then pulls out of the parking lot and straightens the truck into a lane, driving faster than the speed limit, I'm certain. His concentration is fully on his driving. The only sound in the quiet night is the *tsk tsk tsk* of the turn signal. "This is not a date," he finally says with defiance.

I stare at the lights of downtown Flannery Cove, as we travel through. It's decorated for Christmas, and green and red strobes stretch in my flooded vision.

Scott says nothing else to me until he pulls into my driveway, as if he's driven the route a hundred times before. He puts the truck in park, turns off the ignition, and stares straight ahead while I focus on the mailbox outside my passenger window.

When I finally turn and look at him, he's studying me, analyzing like I'm a math problem that won't add up. He opens his mouth to speak, then shuts it and looks out the front windshield like he's working things out in his head. Then he whips his head back and begins the tirade.

"Aunt Mary in Atlanta? You knew how much honesty and trust meant to me. How guarded I was against going through anything like I'd already been through. You said you understood completely. You did not. *You understood nothing about me!*" He emphasizes those last words, pointedly, delivering closing arguments.

I let him go at it. I face it head-on. And I wait for the verdict.

He doesn't deliver one, so I do. "I just lost everything back there. My father, my daughter, my best friend, and—"

"Still have your mom, though. That's what's important, right?"

I take a deep breath. I've stuck to a particular mental narrative for so long I'm not sure how to finally let it go, but the time has come because it's just not true anymore.

"I've never had my mother. I have a woman who claims to love me when it fits in her plans to do so. I am an heirloom she takes out and dusts off, admires a bit, and puts back to collect dust again."

Scott says nothing in return, and I'm sorry I uttered the words. These are private thoughts for me to come to terms with, and I certainly don't need, expect, or want his pity. I reach for the door handle and let myself out of his truck. I have the sense that I've just tossed something priceless off of a bridge. I even seem to hear the splash. All that remains are a few ripples that are fading fast.

I step out and start to close the door behind me. I pause when he says, "Did you ever think you could have trusted me? That I could have helped you?"

A wave of emotion so strong passes over me I feel faint. "No," I say. "I've never had anyone I felt I could trust with this. When I was fifteen, this was way too big. As I grew, it didn't diminish. It seemed to grow with me." I softly click the door shut.

Within seconds of watching me get inside my house, he drives away.

Hours later, I have no idea how I made it into the house. I scarcely remember walking up the walkway. I can't remember opening my door. I only know that I'm sitting on my sofa staring straight ahead when the front door shuts again, and a lamp gets turned on. The light is a shock. The actual flesh and bones Hailey is standing in front of me.

"What in the world have you done?" she says. Her voice rises once she gets past that. *"And how could you have done it?"*

# TWENTY-FIVE

IT'S BEEN DAYS since my life imploded, but it feels like I've been digging through rubble forever. When I look in the mirror I see ashy, tangled hair branching out in all directions, stained clothes, smudged skin. Yes, it's the result of a much-needed trip to a salon, being too preoccupied to do laundry — or even change — and of newsprint from packing. But it's my version of Armageddon.

"Please tell me you can handle the café, you and Jenna. I don't care," I say to Cory. "Work it out between yourselves. It doesn't matter anymore." Nothing matters anymore. I grab the few wrapped gifts I have in my office. "One for you, and one for Jenna. And can you deliver these things to Margo and Paulus? Please, Core. I just... I just can't right now."

"Scuse me." Two men maneuver behind me carrying furniture that's wrapped in moving blankets. Madame Bienve prances behind them. "Be careful with the pieces, please." Even the Madame is leaving me.

Cory squints, trying to figure out what I'm talking about. "I can deliver those." He points to the packages. "I *can't* run the café from now till Christmas. I have things. Plans."

"Whatever. Close it. Don't care."

"What about Hailey?" He calls after me before I reach the door.

"Hailey's at her grandmother's. No idea when she'll be back."

The door slams behind me. I look over at the bookstore. No activity. He hasn't called, hasn't even looked my way. Every afternoon before dark he runs with his head held firm, his gaze determinedly straight ahead.

I look at Otis sitting in the passenger seat next to me as we're leaving. He wants to go home. He's not the least bit interested in pursuing Deaton. I tug at his leash. *C'mon. Can't you muster up just a bit of stamina? I can't do this alone.* Otis smacks his tongue across his snout and puts his head back down where he doesn't have to see me either.

"I should get a new dog," I say to him. "One that can run. See how you'd like that."

*Meet my new pup, Paya. My dog, Matic.*

I dated Bradley for months, but it's Scott I think about when I'm alone, doing nothing but thinking. Not that I don't think about Bradley at all. He's the comfortable, old purse I finally sold at the yard sale. It had so many great compartments, but gosh it was so heavy — I never realized. But now I do. He was a tiresome man with a constant adding machine in his head and an unimaginative greeting. A numbers guy. He most likely would have been a puppet that stuck by me and sympathized with me, if he had been there that evening. The thought of such a man makes my stomach roil. But Scott and his gumption, I suppose I've gotten what I bargained for there.

I shut the door on my thoughts and pretend my mind is a road that has been blocked. The guard gate is up. *Detour. Turn around, Scott Warner. No entry.*

Over the next few days, I try to return my attention to my one other case. I still don't have a peg on Andrew Bender. I've sat by him at the park, and I've strolled adjoining aisles in the store, peering through the canned corn. I've followed him to work, to his house, and to apartment number sixty-seven many times. Finally, weary and dispassionate, I just ring the doorbell myself.

"Hello." The door is answered by a woman. She's fiftyish. She's plain, nothing spectacular. She's wearing a housecoat and slippers.

"Um, hi." I step back and look at the door number. "I was looking for someone." I keep a perplexed look on my face.

"There's no one here but me." She keeps a kind smile on hers.

"I must have the wrong place. I was looking for a business." It's all I can think of to say.

"Oh. I run a business. Well, kind of." She opens the door wider. I can see in the apartment. *Wheel of Fortune* is playing on her television. There's a TV dinner waiting for her at the little table next to a glass of milk. *Milk!* There's nothing sinister that I can find on this woman. "Were you needing a tutor?" She says.

I nod my head. "A tutor, yes. My daughter. She needs tutoring. I'm in the right place?"

"Yes." She smiles bigger, welcoming. "How old is your daughter?"

"Eight?" I say uncertainly like I'm asking her.

She cocks her head. "Eight? Oh, you must be in the wrong place."

"But the tutoring."

"I don't tutor children. I'm a G.E.D. prep tutor. I think I saw a flyer about a math tutor outside the gym. You might check over there." She shrugs apologetically and turns back to glance at her television and her meager meal.

I peer over her shoulder.

"You can't have…" She mumbles.

"You can't have your cake and eat it too," I say, just as Vanna turns the rest of the *E*'s.

My twelve-year-old self has been saying this to me ever since I left the country club and Hailey's vanilla frosted homemade masterpiece behind.

**From: Unveiled@officeweb.com**
**To: Benderfam@yahoo.com**
**Subject: Investigation**

**Mrs. Bender, can you verify whether your husband has a high school diploma or not? Is it possible that his "affair" could be GED prep tutoring?**

T HE NIGHTS ARE the hardest. They stretch so unbelievably. They're quiet. They're isolating. They taunt with the dawn of a new day that's no different from the one before. My heart has been broken, but it will mend. I won't cry. Spilling a full gallon of milk inside my refrigerator made me cry. Dropping a marble cutting board on my toe made me cry. But I will not cry over this. Until I do, and then the tears won't stop.

I feel like a late November pumpkin. Hollow. Unwanted. Expired. A daughter without a mother. A woman without a lover. I feel myself becoming bitter, broken, weighed down, and alone. I feel myself becoming my mother.

Most nights I stay up packing and waiting for the sunrise because one day soon this will be gone. The bank will come to handcuff me and drag me from the premises, and I have to be ready. And for now, I have to be busy.

I can't believe how much this house once meant. Now it means nothing. Less than nothing.

I wrap up all of my antique whisks and sifters for storage, then find the bride and groom champagne glasses wrapped in craft paper in the little cabinet above the refrigerator and pour glass after glass of the cheap stuff that was on sale at the grocery. I drink and wrap and tape and ignore any spouts of wisdom my head tries to shout at me. And when I knock over the entire bottle and grab the kitchen towel to mop it up, I try wringing the liquid out of it before tossing it into the laundry.

I wonder what my mom and Hailey are doing over their school break. Mom calls, but they don't invite me to join them — no family meetings that include me. Not that I want to be there. But Hailey... I don't know what to say about Hailey, my dad.

All Hailey will say is that she just needs to process this right now. "I can't look at you, can't speak to you, can't even begin to understand you, and frankly don't even know you," she had delivered on her way out the door, en route to Atlanta and the arms of her grandmother. Funny how Mary gets to be the savior in the chaos she created.

"You need to call your father," my mother says to me in occasional conversations.

"I need my father to call *me*," I reply. "Although I doubt he ever wants to speak to me again." Is it fair to wait for his timing? I don't see where I have a choice.

"Don't lose the only home you've ever had over this, Amy. That man is your home."

One week before Christmas, Fiona Bienve calls. I almost don't answer, but it's the curiosity that gets me — an unrecognizable number.

"Hello." My voice is weak, atrophied.

*When did that happen?* It's like my body has informed my larynx that we're about to go under.

"Amy? It's Fiona," she says. She doesn't seem to have noticed my frailty. I'm embarrassed by my weakness and try my hardest to muster some strength, clearing my throat.

"Fiona. How lovely." *Lovely?* It's what popped into my head. I hardly ever say lovely. I like it though — it sounds like I'm royalty. I'm going to try to use it more.

*Lovely seeing you again, Scott. That's a lovely tie you're wearing. Lovely to hear from you, Margo. Lovely that you've forgiven me, Deaton — Hailey — Daddy.*

*Turn around. Scott Warner. No entry.*

"We've finally got the last of mom's things moved out of the upstairs," she says. "I kept thinking I'd see you before, but you've been closed the last few days."

*I have?* The café will surely go under now. *Whatever.* I can't imagine serving up dill and salmon croquettes with any amount of pride ever again anyway.

"I have." I clear my throat once more and confirm this bit of news. "Yes. Um, I just had to take care of some things. Sorry."

"No problem." "I was just hoping I could stop by. I have a package for you."

I look around at the mess I've been living in for the last week. Boxes are piled on top of each other. Empty tape rolls are tossed onto the floor. I've been wearing the same clothes every day. Otis needs a bath. I need a bath. Garbage needs to go out. It looks like Charlie Sheen, Ozzy Osbourne, Oscar The Grouch, and a hard-core motorcycle gang have all moved in with me. They've taken over my home and my life.

"I'm not sure," I begin. "I think maybe after the holidays I'll be open."

"After the... Amy, are you all right?"

"I think so. I mean... I'm fine."

"Well, I'd like to come by. I'm flying back to New York and won't be back for a week or so."

I say nothing, I just look at the stairs that lead up to Hailey's room. Such a desolate, quiet space.

"I have the address. I'll be there in ten minutes." Fiona hangs up.

I figured out a few days ago that if I put a little toothpaste inside my mouth guard that it holds it on my teeth. Works great, but in the mornings my lips are scaly and filmy with remnants that seeped out. And I haven't even taken the time to scrub it off of them yet today. I've become such a slob.

I run into my room and rip my shirt over my head, throw it on the bed — which is made since the only sleeping I've done in the past week is cat naps on the sofa between packing — and rummage through drawers for something without holes. Facing into my underarm I sniff, then recoil. It's like I rolled in chili beans and taco sauce.

I wet the soap, glide it over the pits, shave, pat water, rub dry, and apply deodorant. I dress and run a brush through my snaggly, tangled hair and secure it with a band. Afterward, I scrutinize my face, pulling tightly at my eyelids. I've accumulated more lines and wrinkles since the last time I looked in a mirror. I wipe a baby wipe over my face and brush my teeth and my lips. My lips are brushed so hard they begin to bleed. The mission is completed and the result in the mirror is cleaned up crack addict.

I think I have a few minutes to put the crusty dishes in the dishwasher, but when I turn around Fiona is at my door ready to ring the doorbell.

"Come in." I fling it open like I'm just a bundle of energy, the picture of health and normalcy. I smile wide breaking more skin, then hold a hand to my burning lips. "Gosh, it's so good to see you."

Her smile is her usual high beam one. She's carrying a decorative bag with tissue paper arranged perfectly, sticking out the top. "Just a little something." She hands it over to me.

I take it from her and glance under the tissue: bath salts, scents, a loofah. "Oh, you know me well!"

*God, that sounds stupid! What's it even mean — you know I bathe?* Well, actually she's probably doubting that now.

She's not even listening to me. Instead, she's still standing in my entryway, her head pivoting one hundred eighty degrees back and forth, like one of those little figures on a dashboard.

"Your home is darling," she says brightly. "May I?" I turn around and she's slipping off her heels. She reaches into her bag and pulls out a pair of ballet slippers before moving off of the tile onto the carpeted area. I retreat to my sofa, motion for her to join me, and fold my legs while running my hand over the soft velvet on the cushion beside me. Fiona stands in the middle of the room doing the pivoting head thing again before coming to sit beside me. Only she doesn't sit back, she stays perched on the edge of the cushion.

"May I look around? Have the tour?"

"Oh. Of course." I mentally review the rooms. What kind of chaos have I left in my wake over the last few days?

"Well, this is the living room, obviously," I begin.

Fiona runs a hand over the velvet cushion as well, reluctant to avert her eyes. She seems fascinated by the way the material responds, lightening, and darkening. She is behaving quite strangely.

"I love this sofa," she says. "And this carpeting." She grazes her fingers over the lush pile. "Oh, look at the indentations," she says as she walks back toward the entryway and bends down to see the tile better. "Authentic."

I have never seen this kind of reaction before. Now I'm the one standing in the middle of the room with my mouth agape, being a bobblehead.

Fiona bypasses me and walks toward the kitchen. "Oh, thank God." She holds a hand to her heart. "Sensible black appliances. I abhor those cold metal ones. And look how those compliment that backsplash."

I look at my sensible black refrigerator as if I've never seen it before. There it is, standing proudly in all its sensibleness, a little line of black magnets with white letters on them that Hailey had left behind spelling out *Merry Kissmas* on the front — written before, well, everything. My sensible stove sits down the counter from it and on the other side of the island is my sensible dishwasher.

"I thought your last name was Hollander," Fiona says. We've moved on to the master bedroom. She's standing by the wall gazing up at the crown molding. She turns to where I'm standing in the doorway.

"It is."

"What's with the *W*?" She nods toward the wall where my lines from the ten minutes I spent attempting to paint over the mossy green are still there. It does look like a big *W*, now that she mentions it. She doesn't wait for my answer. "Do you still have that paint?"

"Oh yes. I bought enough to do the whole room. I just... I haven't had the time. I was just trying it out to make sure I liked it."

"I'm talking about the green."

"The green? Oh, yes, I still have the green, but..."

"What's upstairs?" She's already bounced from the master bedroom to the stairway.

*Is she on something?*

"Another master suite — Hailey's bed and bath. A small sitting area."

"May I?" She asks as she bounds up the steps.

She's gone all of one minute, then comes zipping back down the steps. "It's perfect."

"Well." I try to gather my thoughts. "Thank you?"

Fiona bites her lip.

"It was my..." I change courses. *Never mind.*

"Would you care for a cup of coffee?"

"Amy."

"Hmmm?" I turn, handing her a mug.

"I know your sign out front says you're renting. But, would you consider *selling* me your house?"

It was my new mug. The one with the dog that had just woken up on the front of it. I'd gotten it at that boutique by the pier. And now it's on the floor at my feet in too many pieces to glue back together.

"Why would you want to buy my house?" I ask. "Why wouldn't you want some nice condo over on the beach?"

"I abhor the beach," she says. Like silver appliances. I narrow my eyes at her. Is Fiona playing opposite day with me or something? This is quite suspicious. "That sticky sand. Those hurricanes." She shudders. "That broiling sun."

I look at her delicate, translucent skin that's still stretched tight across the topography of her face, and I can believe she hates the sun.

"But what about your mom's place?"

She wrinkles her nose. "No." she shakes her head slightly, very politely. "That won't do. Mother's neighborhood isn't so nice. We're selling while we still can."

*Well, be still my heart. Who would have thought?*

"He was right. This would be perfect."

I stop in my tracks. "I'm sorry? Who?" I'm more alert than I've been in days. "Deaton?"

She walks from room to room again, running her hand over the walls, opening and closing the doors. "Heavy. Solid wood," she mumbles to herself.

"Who told you my home was even available? Who told you it would be perfect? Was it Deaton? What did he say about me?"

Fiona finally stops her murmuring and admiring and acknowledges my questions. "Scott Walker, no Warner, I believe he said. He stopped in the café one day when we were finishing up with the movers, but of course, you weren't there. Where have you *been*, Amy?"

I shake my head. "Scott Warner came in? Looking for me?"

Fiona shrugs. "I'm not sure what he was doing. I mean... I guess? I assumed he was a friend of yours. Jenna was asking me about the move, and he overheard. Said I needed to come see if you and I could strike a deal. I think he said he was personally invested in seeing your house sell soon." She walks to the back sliding door and looks at the backyard. "Is he your realtor?"

"Fiona." I follow her to the door. "This is important. Did he say why he was invested in my house selling soon?"

"My gosh, that oak tree is beautiful. Is the swing staying?"

"Did he?"

Fiona hears my urgency and turns to me. She rolls her lips together and narrows her eyes. "I don't think so. I can't remember." Then she is back in house mode. "Perfect. I can keep an eye on Mother, but have my own space. She can be downstairs, and I can be up."

"Right." Despite my distraction, I try to get back to the business at hand. Could Fiona really be serious? "But the paint. The tile. The..."

"I know." She sweeps a hand, encompassing it all. "I won't need to change a thing."

From: Benderfam@yahoo.com
To: Unveiled@officeweb.com

**Subject: G.E.D.**

**Thank you! Thank you! Thank you! That diploma, or lack thereof, has been a point of contention in our marriage for too long. Andrew has been passed up for two promotions in the last five years. He'd wanted to surprise me before the baby was born, but after much prodding and questioning, he finally told me what he's been up to. He does not know I ever contacted you. I have deposited my final payment to your account. Please forget you ever met me.**

I TAKE ONE LOOK at it and think the deal is over. Fiona has left the sales price blank. I've told her the truth, what I needed to get out of it, and also what it had appraised for. "I need to at least split the difference or come close to be able to sell," I'd said. "I don't know where I'm going to get it. No idea how to make this work."

When she comes back with the contract, she has a plan. "That sectional," she says. "I'll give you two thousand dollars for it. And that dining room table and hutch, another one thousand."

I'm not crazy about the idea. A huge glob of something forms in my throat and sticks there. I finally shrug, relenting. "Seeing as how I have no idea where I'm even going, how much space I'll even have."

"Oh. I just assumed." Fiona wrinkles her brow. "Didn't your friend Scott…" She cocks her head to the side. "Do you even talk to your friend Scott?"

I blink.

"Amy, have you been upstairs to Mother's old studio? Your friend thought you and I should switch. I buy your house, and you rent mom's studio. Did I forget to tell you that part?"

As soon as she says it, I know. I look around at all of my furniture, minus the sofa, the hutch, and the table, and begin placing them. I mentally polish the wood floors and squeegee the glass windows in the upstairs loft. The place is spotless and furnished before she has finished her sentence.

"I'm leaving for New York tomorrow. You can take your time moving your stuff out. I know Mr. Deavers hasn't rented the space out yet." She begins to get very animated, talking with her hands. "I was just there dropping off the keys to him."

I grab a pen and fill in the sales amount on her contract. "Deal."

**I**T'S TWO DAYS before Christmas. Hailey says she'll be home tomorrow. She never mentioned talking things out. In fact, she'd said, "To get my stuff." I've no idea if it'll be a smash and grab and *Adios, Mamacita, it's been real...* or what to expect.

It has taken me multiple trips, but I've managed to move the necessities. I have two sleeping bags, toiletries, and food. I'm camping upstairs, on top of my café. It's fun! I've left behind those memories in my house that confuse me. "I'm onward and upward," I say to myself every time I hoist and heave another loaded box up the stairs.

And I keep an eye out for Scott Warner who apparently set this plan in motion. But he's nowhere to be found. I suppose he was being a good lawyer, nothing more.

If Deaton's seen me pull up twenty or more times over the last few days, unpack boxes and leave again, he never asks. He never surfaces, never offers to help, *nothing*. It's Kristlyn who shows up and knocks on the door between my trips.

"It's open," I yell. My heart thumps faster. I turn, expecting to see my friend back.

"Amy. What's going on?" She comes bearing gifts.

*He's not ready, but he's sent her with a peace treaty.*

"I've moved in." I twirl in the middle of the floor with my arms outstretched like it's just the grandest idea.

"But what about your house?" She puts the bag she's carrying on the top of a box and catches my elbow as I stumble mid-twirl.

"I sold it." I feel drunk twirling all around and talking nonsense, but nope this is the real me, with my real life. Even if I tried — even if I sat down with my back straight, my legs crossed and my hands folded as I related everything that's happened in the last few days — it would still sound like drunken banter.

*I rode away in the back of a taxi. My dead mom's BFF sent me a picture of her and the party was over. I sold it all and moved on up here.*

"I don't understand," she says.

"If I had a nickel for every time…"

I can't stop acting like an imbecile. Who cares anymore? All I've got left in life is my amusement.

She bursts out laughing. Kristlyn throws her head back, revealing her long, graceful neck, and breaks out into a deep, throaty cackle.

And I do too, only mine is more red cheeks, tears, and snorts.

"I brought tea," she says and goes to my new kitchen. She rifles through the open box on the counter and finds spoons and mugs. The small space is permeated with the scent of whatever she's put in the boiling kettle. It smells more like expensive perfume than food.

"What happened at that birthday party?" she asks once we're sitting.

I take the mug and sip. My eyes find hers over the rim of the cup. They're concerned eyes.

She stops me many times during the story to repeat what I've said. "So you were told she died on the train but then you saw that newspaper? So it was your dad's girlfriend that hired you and didn't know it was you? And you say it was Deaton's idea to help you investigate it?" She nods when she has it straight and I plunge ahead, letting it pour out.

When I'm done, she gets up, makes two more cups of tea, sits back down, and says, "Amy, you have to fix this."

"How in the world can I fix this? What does Deaton say about it?" I pick at the lint on my leggings and gaze out those two large front windows toward the bookstore across the street.

"What Deaton says right now cannot possibly be what he honestly means." She pulls her hand down across her mouth, over her chin, as if she's trying to come up with something.

"That bad, huh?"

I can see in her face I don't know the half of it.

HAILEY RELUCTANTLY JOINS me in the new apartment because there's nothing but furniture that's either too heavy or too big left wrapped up in blankets in the house. The movers won't be picking any of it up until after the New Year, and I have a few things I need to do here to get ready for it.

But before anything can be done, I have to take over nine thousand dollars to the closing table. It's hidden in a moving box under the sink. The cash advance limit on my credit card was thirteen thousand dollars. I withdrew it a while ago before my bad credit caught up with me and they cut me off.

Hailey hasn't said over two words to me but still, I'm happy that she came home for Christmas Eve and can even lay eyes on me until I realize she plans to stick firm to our annual ritual of Christmas Eve Mass.

"You want me to go like this?" I look down at my jeans, my Ugg boots, my oversized Old Navy sweatshirt.

"I would prefer you clean up a bit, but if that's the best you can do," she says, shrugging. I look at her for signs of sarcasm, our usual banter. There is none.

I kneel beside her. We are shoved in tight in a row with a grandmother and grandfather who have brought all their grandkids to mass. "Beloved, the grace of God has appeared," the priest begins.

"Okay, I get why you couldn't ever say. But I just, I don't get why you let it go on for so long. I mean, I'm eighteen now. You could have trusted me," Hailey whispers. *Okay, we're doing this now.*

"The appearance of the glory of a savior..."

"It wasn't a matter of trust." I answer her, "It was... I don't know. How could I, Hailey? It was her choice. If I wanted either of us to have anything with her, this was the way it was."

The child on my left is being quieted with a piece of candy. He takes it out to examine it before popping it back in his mouth. "Suck," his grandmother hisses, as he chews loudly.

"But Chappy. What about Chappy?"

"Who gave himself for us, to deliver us from our sins."

"I don't know." My eyes flood once again. I can't stand the thought of my father's face the last time I saw him, at that table. "I just don't know," I whisper, reaching for a tissue.

The grandmother nudges the grandfather. They both look at me and frown.

*We've got a devout one here, Harry. This isn't going to work.*

The grandfather reaches for the kid with the candy that's now stuck in his bangs, plucks him out of the line-up, and takes him and one other one out. The older kids all turn their heads and watch them walk out.

"Where are they going?" Their voices whine.

"Is it almost over?"

"Grandma, Tommy farted."

"Did not!"

"Let us pray," the priest says. And Hailey takes my hand and we do.


S INCE I HAVE no furniture aside from boxes and a sleeping bag, I've taken to sitting on the built-in shelves Madame had custom made to fit beneath the window. Now I can perch here and view all of Sandpiper Street, specifically the bookstore. Yesterday I noticed a smudge on the outside of the glass that's been driving me crazy ever since. I wanted to pop the screen, lean out and swipe it, but I knew people across the street would stop and look up, their hands shielding their eyes, their breath held in fear, and Deaton would just roll his eyes and assure everyone, "*Oh, get back to what you were doing. That's just Amy being theatrical, trying to get attention. You can't believe anything she says or does.*"

Deaton's not home. He left at six A.M. through the front door without looking up at me. I'm certain he is aware of my address change, but he's not caring about it one way or another. "Merry Christmas," I say to the empty street and my empty apartment.

Hailey left for Jarod's hours ago. "I'll be fine," I assured her, not that she'd asked. "No, I don't want to go sit at Jarod's parent's house next to his crazy Aunt Delores and hear about her flea infestation while she mixes up our cups and drinks from mine. One time was enough for that, thank you."

I've made myself a cup of the tea Kristlyn left with me. I'm looking at a book and wondering what Scott Warner is doing for Christmas. He probably went overseas to take those shoe-box things people fill up with treats for the poor children. Or maybe he's serving our troops on the front lines a big, hearty Christmas feast.

I hear a car door slam, but the car itself is out of my range of sight so I return to my book. Maybe Scott Warner is putting up decorations in all the Habitat houses he helped build last year so the new families feel the true Christmas spirit come alive inside.

*Oh!* There's a woman on the street below. She's dressed in cream-colored pants and a red sweater. She has a knit scarf wrapped around her neck and looped perfectly, hanging not too high and not too low, not too knotted and jumbly like so many of them do, strangling the person wearing them — just perfectly.

My mother!

You would think, with everything that has happened, she would look like chewed gum that's been left on the pavement. But of course, she doesn't. She's cool as ice.

She stands back and looks up at the sign above my door, just as I'm looking down assessing myself. I wonder if Hailey spent the entire week just studying her and wondering how in the world this piece of art gave birth to me. Maybe that's why she was there so long, unable to figure it out.

She looks up again and sees me there in the window. She waves and beckons me to come down and let her in.

"What are you doing up there?" She bustles in, running a sweeping hand over her outfit like snowflakes have fallen on it.

"Trying to think of my penance. A proper punishment."

"Mmm. And what have you come up with?" She follows me up the stairs. "This is charming," she mumbles. "The café. So sweet."

I open the door to my new apartment. "Nothing solid yet. Maybe traveling the country barefoot, walking town to town lecturing school children on the downfalls of dishonesty."

"Oh good grief, Amy. Always so dramatic." She puts her purse down on my window seat shelf. I glance at it. *Did she bring her pills? I could use some of those pills.*

"How's the arm?" I hadn't even realized she had a cast from the car accident. Hailey never said.

"Nothing serious," she says, waving her good hand. "Could've been a lot worse. My ribs hurt a bit. Don't make me laugh."

"Doubt there's much chance of that. If you want anything…" I wave a hand toward the kitchenette.

"I come bearing a gift for you. A long overdue gift." She tests the sturdiness of a packing crate then settles herself down on it.

Meanwhile, I stretch out a leg and rest my back against the wall in my window cubby. The afternoon sun is stretching its rays. I yawn. *Not really interested.*

"I've come to set you free."

I shake my head and roll my eyes and turn my gaze out the window. My thoughts are like a blender in my head. Round and round they go... and then the top flies off. "Talk about being dramatic," I say. "Thought you did that a long time ago."

But before I can let loose she interrupts. "Nooo," she says, drawing out the word as if teaching a slow to comprehend person. "The opposite. I chained you up a long time ago."

I glance at her then return my gaze to the street below.

"I loved Ian. Always had, always will." She smirks at her stupidity but continues trying to explain, to justify. "He left me and married someone else. Cassandra DeVanderal. Lots of money, but a size 12, mousy, thick-ankled. My friend Sandy sent me a picture — the newspaper clipping," she says, to prove she knows what she's talking about. "I took one look and knew that would never last, but I'd already agreed to marry your father. Such a nice, gentle soul." She pauses to give my father's grace and dignity its due respect, even though she was willing to take his only child to another country, away from him. "I can do this, I thought. I can learn to love this man." She stops and gets up to walk to the kitchen. She finds the paper towel on the counter and rips off a few pieces, then returns to the crate she was sitting on and hands one to me. I'm still wondering how someone can tell so much about ankles from a newspaper photo.

"But it turns out I couldn't. Ian stayed in touch with me. He said he still wanted me. And then came you."

I turn to look at her. She's dabbing at her eyes. "And then came me," I say, shaking my head.

"I despised my life. I despised Flannery Cove. I despised everyone around me," she says, ignoring my interruption. "Until you. I stuck you with that name you hate so much because you were going to be the beautiful jewel that would add some value and shine to my dull life."

"I don't *hate* Amethyst. It's just," I roll my eyes, "So over the top. Such a big name."

"A big responsibility," she says, sniffing. "An unrealistic expectation from a little baby. Unrealistic period. From anyone."

"I would have tried to live up to it if you'd given me the chance."
I turn and look into her face.

"Darling. You have."

We're both silent for a few minutes. I turn back to the street.
Mom finds the bathroom and stays in there for five minutes or
so then she finds a cup in the kitchen, washes it, and fills it with
tap water.

"So when you left…" I finally say once she's seated again.

"When I left," She sighs heavily as if she's shedding a lot of
weight at one time, "Ian kept saying he had a plan. I kept resisting.
Every time I thought about you."

"Pfft." I make a sound with my lips.

*We all know how long that deterred you.*

"That week. Ian was leaving, with or without me. I was so conflicted. I couldn't divorce your dad. I couldn't. The scandal… your
grandmother… that club… this town." She waves a hand around
the room — my little corner of this town. "There would have been
an enormous scandal. A custody battle. I would have lost."

I turn and start to say something, but she holds up a hand.
"You don't believe me, Amy, but it's true. Every judge in this town
belonged to the country club and was a friend to the Chadwicks.
Your grandmother used her charities for control, and she had it.
Ian was a questionable character." She flaps the hand she's holding up, indicating that's just the tip of the iceberg. "I didn't know
what to do. We were walking along the river that day thinking
about it all when we saw the train accident and my way out of this
God-forsaken town."

"Hmph. How'd that work out for ya?"

I'm not sure she's heard me. She doesn't answer for a few
seconds. Finally, "Not good, obviously."

There's one thing I've been turning in my head. One thing I've
wondered about. I look her in the eye. "Why did your documents
all say Mary Guthry? You said you hoped Ian would marry you, but
how could Ian marry someone who was already named Guthry?"

She flicks her hand over her sweater and reaches to untie her
scarf. She busies herself with that while she answers. "You must
have misunderstood."

"Which part?"

"Ian and I had a marriage certificate made as well. We were
as good as married."

After all this time, she's still so nonchalant. *As good as married?*
"You were not married, in any way, shape, or form, Mother. You
were someone else's wife. What do you do now? Consider yourself
as good as divorced?"

She flattens her lips. "It's certainly a lot less paperwork."

"Mary Guthry." I turn the name over, tasting its bitterness.

My mother shrugs. "Yes. Mary Guthry. Turns out I didn't like
my fake self any more than my real self."

"Turns out there wasn't much more to like," I say.

She does not acknowledge the cruel statement. We sit in silence
for a while, then I detect sniffing, crying. But I will not be moved
by it. I have lost the most precious thing. I never even had a chance
to hold it. All because of her.

"I am the descendant of two very selfish, manipulative women,"
I finally say into the quiet. "That's why you two didn't get along.
Your magnetism was identical."

My mother tries to speak. I can see her argument starting,
and I ward it off with an upheld hand. "You do not get to interrupt me. This legacy stops with me. I will spend the rest of my life
trying to convince my daughter that this is not normal." I take a
breath and continue. "I love you, and I want a relationship with
you, but it will be on my terms or it won't be at all. You will admit
everything. You will change your name back to what it really is.
You will be the woman who left her family, Caroline Chadwick.
And you will not control me. Ever again."

My mother is silent. Her sniffles have died down. She wipes
at her eyes and nods.

I return my gaze to the window. There's Deaton back. Kristlyn's
with him. Their arms are loaded down with bags and boxes as they
get out of the car and walk toward the door of the store. Neither
one looks up at me. I'm the forgotten girl in the window.

"I'm sorry, Amy. That day I left, I set your story in motion."

I turn my face halfway. My jaw is raised, my teeth are clenched
inside my closed mouth wearing away my enamel.

"I chained you to that story," she says. "With my departure,
you had no other paths, no other choices but that of an abandoned child. Always looking for a rescue. The gift I mentioned,
I've come to set you free from all this. The time has come. Go
forge new paths. Go finish your story with a world of alternate
endings, Amy."

# TWENTY-SIX

E VEN MR. KENT has a new significant other, but the closest
thing I have to love lately is Kristlyn. It turns out Kristlyn is
my friendship soul-mate. We share the same warped sense
of humor. She's a good listener, a sympathetic ear. When she doesn't
know the answer to my problems — *and who does* — she just nods
and looks off into space like she's thinking hard about them. And
though she hasn't said, I suspect she is defying Deaton's wishes by
visiting me every day.

I don't even need a man. I still have my business and a chic loft
apartment by the beach, and that's more than most people. What
I need more than anything is a way to convey to my loved ones
how deeply I regret not only the entire last year of my life but the
twenty or so preceding it as well. In the meantime, I couldn't care
less about everyone else coupled up, hustling and bustling around
outside, all wrapped up with each other against the cold. They
come through the café doors and stand as one, their faces turned
toward my menu. *"Whatever you want is fine with me. Hot chocolate?
Yes, hot chocolate. With whipped cream! Just one. We'll share it."*

I'm standing at the register waiting for two separate couples to
make up their stupid minds and *just freaking order something!* I smile
patiently. *How cute when you go back and forth like that twenty times.*

I don't even see my dad there until one of the couples parts a bit and there he is behind them, between them, like their shared little man. He's in his long wool coat, freshly shaven, his cheeks ruddy from the temperature. My dad is a good-looking man. My dad is my one rock that never rolled. God, I've missed him.

"Can you take care of this?" I grab Cory on his way to the kitchen.

He follows my wide eyes to my dad. "Uh, sure."

I walk toward him. We don't hug right away, but I do grab onto his coat and hold tightly to both sides of it for a second. I lay my cheek on his shoulder then I brush at a few stray hairs and compose myself. He stares at my face, trying to discern my mood, my well-being. He's been worried about me. I can see it there in his gaze.

"Follow me," I say. I lead him up the stairs. The supply closet on the landing that I've been filling with all the boxes and paraphernalia from my office stands open. I pause to close it and keep walking toward my apartment door.

"Well, this is it," I say, opening the door. "It's not exactly the way I want it, but it'll get there." I'm rambling, I know, but what else can I do with myself?

Most of the boxes are unpacked. Items that still need to be dusted and arranged sit here and there on the floor, but it's coming together. I sold a few more pieces of furniture, but what I kept and had delivered has taken on new life.

Dad looks around, smiling. "It suits you."

I stand in the middle of it and sigh. "Ah, Dad."

He rubs the top of his head like he's trying to rub some thoughts into it. What can be said after this? Where can we go from where we've ended up?

"Tea? Coffee?" I wipe at my eyes and stride to my kitchen and pull down two mugs. I know what he'll pick.

"Coffee. Black. Two sugars." He coughs and wipes at his nose with a tissue then reaches into his pocket and pulls out a throat lozenge.

We sit at the bistro table together. "Nice view," Dad says.

I nod and watch him. The memories take on a warm patina — the dad I've had my entire life, the dad that came to every volleyball game I had in school. Dad never said much about them. He cheered every time either team scored a point. I doubt he knew my jersey number or that I won the most improved player in tenth grade and the most valuable player in eleventh. *But he was there.*

We talk about the house sale. "I'm glad. I'm really glad," he muses. That snarky me that drips saliva from her fangs starts to remind me that my dad would say that even if I'd just announced I was cohabiting with Mr. Kent. But the better version of me shows up and kicks her like a football. She lands on the other end of the field.

"Yeah well, I guess it'll all work out somehow." I tell him about the appraisal. "I managed to get the difference from my credit card cash advance. I'll pay it back in bite-sized pieces." I shrug and tear at my napkin.

I don't know what else to say. I'm afraid once there's a rip this big the best seamstress in the world can't possibly mend it and manage to hide it. It's always going to be there, a fragile, vulnerable place waiting to be ripped again.

"Dad."

He holds up a hand. "No. no," he says. "This is on me." He sips at his coffee and moves his lozenge from one side of his mouth to the other. I grimace imagining the robust richness of my Jazz Blend coffee mixing with mentholated medicine. "What choice did you have, Amy? I get that. Your mom and I, we both…"

I reach across the table and hold his hand. We sit in silence for a while.

"Did you think?" I say. "Did you really?"

His grip on my hand tightens. "I never knew. I had my suspicions." He takes off his coat and lays it across the window seat. He looks down at Sandpiper Street for a bit before he turns back around and returns to his chair. "I knew she wasn't happy. The police didn't do much investigating. They said she was a grown woman, and if she left of her own free will that was her right. I got the impression that was their analysis of the situation." He drains his cup and puts it back on the table. "I took the peaceful way out and let the train accident stand as what happened. I never asked for the life insurance because they would have done an in-depth investigation, and that clearly wasn't what she wanted. It wasn't what I wanted either. Not for you."

I ponder this. The silence stretches.

"Let me rephrase that," he says, breaking the quiet. "It makes me sound saintly. What I should say is that I took matters into my own hands as well, from this side of things. I steered us down a path and allowed us to stay there. I just didn't want..."

His sentence breaks off, and I anticipate the rest of it. "Didn't want me to see her?"

"Didn't want you to be her," he says.

*Aah.* I nod sadly. Unfortunately, that plan may have backfired. "She used to call."

My eyes widen. "She... what?"

Dad shakes his head. He looks defeated, and quite old. "For years we would get calls, and there'd be no one on the line. So I suppose I knew. Deep down. I wasn't sure if I was on the wrong side of something right or the right side of something wrong, but I am complicit in this. Technically, I told no lies. But I evaded truths. Until Helena came along and questioned, and the more I evaded that, the more she questioned."

A memory of my lying in my canopied bed under a pink blanket comes out of nowhere. My dad's hand hesitantly stroking my back in a circular pattern while I cried over some fiasco in my life, and he tried his best to comfort me.

I shake my head. "Don't do that. I won't let you. I am the one that reeks of complicity, but we have to take our control back. It's the only way to survive this." I find a spot in the middle of the living area and stare until my eyes burn while my dad sips at his coffee and ponders what I've said. "I know everyone says I was young and didn't know better, but I did, Dad. I knew all along this was wrong. Even at fifteen. It's just I missed having a mom, and I had no real siblings to speak of, and I was struggling. I felt like I had no one.

"This might be stating the obvious," he says, "but you've always had me. I know bra shopping and various other things were a bit tricky, but I think we managed."

This brings a laugh. Then I get serious again. "That goes without saying. I love her because at the end of the day she's my mom, but it's nothing like what I feel for you. It's *in* me, but it's not *of* me."

He nods and wipes his eyes. "I kept any suspicions to myself. I think I do that a lot," he says. For the first time in my life that I can remember, I watch my dad's face crumble. Tears glide down his cheeks, between his lips.

"How did you find her?" he says.

I tell him all about the field trip to Atlanta, the P.O. Box, everything. He sits in wonder, his eyes going wide at times and narrowing at others. His mouth opening in shock then closing in confusion.

"I'm glad you've had that," he says, as he always does. But it's sincere, as if with my confessions I've absolved some sort of unwarranted guilt he's been carrying. "And *you*. All this time. *You're* Unveiled Investigations?!" He can't conceal the pride. He can't conceal the shock either. "How in the world did you ever manage that? When did all this happen? Unveiled has quite a reputation you know. Even at the country club."

"I know quite a few things about that country club."

He nods and shakes his head, incredulous. "Hal Barrington?"

"I don't sleuth and tell. But, I'll tell you something I learned during my marriage. If you suspect something then you probably already know it."

He lifts his mug in a mock toast. *Amen to that!*

I pause, then "Dad?"

"Hmm?"

"Where's Susan?"

This catches him off guard for a moment. His eyes flood again. "I don't know," he says. "I was thinking of asking Helena's investigator to try to find her after all this was over."

I roll my eyes and chortle.

"I bet she will too."

"I don't know about that," I say shrugging. "Some things are just left for us to wonder. And that's okay. In my search for whatever became of her, I've uncovered other things. Memories that needed to be brought to life and examined."

We both sit in silence. I make him a second cup of coffee and he sips it slowly, taking his time. Finally, he reaches for his coat. "You and me." He holds a hand to cover his mouth then forms a fist and thumps his heart. "We'll get through this."

I nod and watch him leave. I go to my window seat and watch my dad down below shuffling to his car. He stands at the car door before getting in and looking up to see me there, my palm flat on the pane. Dad thumps his heart again and waves.

It's only when his blinker flashes and he takes a right at the stop sign that it dawns on me. Every sentiment he uttered to me was his alone. In fact, he barely mentioned Helena's name.

From: Unveiled@officeweb.com
To: Benderfam@yahoo.com
Subject: **Another Case Solved** *delete*
Subject: **I've Still Got it** *delete*
Subject: **Thank God you took a chance on us and restored my confidence** *delete*
Subject: **G.E.D!**

This bit of news is the best we have received in a while. Much needed! I beg you not to make us forget it! However, it will never leave our lips, and we hope as well to never hear from you again.

Happy New Year.

# TWENTY-SEVEN

THERE ARE OVER fifteen Susan Blakely profiles on various social media sites, and there are five more revealed by searching the internet. "I should be unpacking," I say to Kristlyn. She keeps reading and ignores me.

"This Susan won a medal for women's pole vaulting in Rio." Her eyes rove back and forth on her screen.

"Hula hoop, I'd believe. Not so sure about pole vaulting." I glance at the image on her screen of a woman soaring through the air, her eyes closed as if she can't bear to look at where she might land. Her hair is back and her face is in a grimace. I'm not able to tell anything about her features. "Put it on the list." I close my laptop and lay my head down on it. "You sure you want to keep helping me with this?"

Kristlyn keeps reading. Her eyes move across the screen and then down and back to the next line.

"You should probably talk to the last person who helped me with an investigation."

She doesn't look up. "Do you know where Susan is? Did you secretly vacation with her last summer in Tahiti? If not, keep searching."

I smile, but I'm not searching, not really. I'm distracting. Keeping my mind in that closed gate mode, so Scott Warner can't gain entry. A girl I knew from childhood that I loved. A girl to

298

whom my family owes more than just a passing thought. That girl is allowed in. But that girl is also allowed to live the rest of her life in peace.

**Melissa and Andrew Bender of Flannery Cove announce the birth of their daughter, Sadie Olivia Bender, 7 lbs. 14 ounces, on January 6, 2016, at 6 P.M. at Mercy General Hospital. Sadie Olivia joins her two brothers, Matson and James.**

"Anyone you know?" Dad says, glancing at the paper on my kitchen counter with the black marker heart around the announcement and the smiley face I'd drawn off to the side.

"Huh? Nah. Just you know… doodling."

"So anyway," he says, reaching into his pocket. He pulls out a thick bank envelope. "This um. This might help with the money you need at the closing table."

"Oh! Oh no." I push it back toward him. "I closed last week." I smile big like it's a major accomplishment I single-handedly pulled together. "I had the cash advance, remember."

He nods. "I remember. But this," he pushes it back toward me, "will help with that too. Pay it off earlier. Too much interest."

I hesitate before opening the envelope and beginning to count. "Dad! There's five thousand dollars in here."

"I'm aware of that." He stirs his coffee.

"But how? Where?"

"Helena's engagement ring."

My eyes dart up from the bills I've just finished counting.

"Well, you know I proposed last Christmas. Christmas before last, actually."

"Yes, but —"

He cuts me off. "I didn't tell you then because she didn't accept. You know why. You know more than I do, probably." There is a hint of a scowl in his features, and a hint of a smile too.

"Aww, Dad. I'm so sorry."

"About?"

"Helena. Everything."

"Don't be, Sparkle. This is what she wanted."

"I don't. I don't understand."

"She said a simple gold band would be just fine." He shrugs his shoulders, no explaining women. "We want you to have this, the money from the other ring."

*We.*

"So you're still getting married?"

"Of course! April 12<sup>th</sup>. A small affair. At the condo. Mark your calendar. Tell Hailey we'll need a cake."

"Oh and Amy?" He says on his way out. "She also said to tell you to be expecting a call from a Morlinda Rowler. Something about an interview for the Courier. Said you'd know what she was talking about."

I KNEW THIS DAY would come, eventually. He couldn't avoid me forever. But I imagined we'd at least spar off in different corners. I even hoped for that. The calm and resolved manner Deaton left the country club in was not one I ever wanted to relive. It wasn't just angry, it was beyond. And at the time, I had felt certain that our relationship was beyond salvaging.

On a drizzly afternoon, Deaton finally strolls through the door of the café with the bell ringing behind him like he's come to borrow a cup of sugar. He walks right up to me, taps me on the shoulder, and, with a very stoic face, introduces me to a publisher who's visiting his bookstore that day.

The earth shifts a bit, but I'm the only one who seems to notice.

And then he pats Candy Walters on the shoulder, tells her he enjoyed their visit, and that he'll speak to her soon. Then he turns around and leaves me there with this woman who's looking expectantly at me, as though she's waiting for me to say something profound because most likely all of her clients spew brilliance in their every sentence. But all I manage is, "Well, this is a surprise. A secret agent, er publisher, um *friend* I never knew about," which I say with some weird, nervous giggle like an imbecile.

AFTER MY MOM first set up our post office box communication and I received my first letter from her, I immediately wrote back. My nana had raised me to be diligent with thank-you notes. I wasn't even allowed to play with a toy until I'd thanked the giver, and I couldn't use a gift certificate at the store until the card had been written.

I can't remember exactly what I wrote. Something along the lines of:

**Dear Mary,**

**Thank you for setting up this post office box. I have made friends with the lady that works behind the window here. She has a pet turtle at home named Linus. Linus likes broccoli, which I hate, so now I know who to save it for. Ha-ha! If you write to me next week it might take me a few days to get it. I am going on a trip to Stone Mountain. I will buy a postcard from there to send you. Please tell Ian that I said hello.**

**Love,**
**Amy**

**P.S. I'm trying out for volleyball.**

**P.S.S. I forgot — thank you for not being on that train too!!!!!!!!!!!!**

I wonder if I could send a thank-you card now to Deaton. Something along the lines of:

**Dear Deaton,**

**Thank you for sending over the publisher. I'm sorry I've been lying to you for the last year, but thank you for trying to find my mom with me. It was fun meeting all those people. Maybe we could do a reunion tour sometime and let them all know how things turned out. Let's make it a happy ending, shall we?**

**Love,**
**Your new neighbor, Amy Hollander.**

It's a piece of mail that does eventually provide me with an opportunity. It arrives with the café mail, but it's addressed to Stories by the Sea. It's junk mail, I can tell by the envelope, but technically it is his junk mail.

"Thank you so much," he says, his lips flattened and his arms folded across his chest when I take it over. "I'll be sure to call them if I ever decide to have the weeds in the sidewalk out front fertilized and maintained on a monthly basis."

I shrug.

We stare.

"You lied to me about what was right in front of my face," he finally says, scorn in his eyes. "You had me jumping through hoops and doing the most unthinkable, asinine..." He stops and composes himself a bit. "I thought I was trying to help you understand your mother's death, and then I thought I was going to be the hero and..." He shakes his head. "Stupid. I was so stupid."

"Deat." I can't look him in the eyes. "I couldn't. I didn't..." I have no defense. I stop trying. Because the truth is that I could... and I did... and he's right about everything. He's also right in his anger, his hatred, whatever he feels.

"There was like a millisecond," he pinches his thumb and index finger together, "where I thought you were just the greatest thing ever." He shakes his head. "Thank God it was short-lived."

I suck in a deep breath and wipe my eyes. I won't let him see me cry. Not because of pride, but because it's not fair. Deaton is not a mean person. I know this. He should be able to verbally punch at me without intermissions of compassion I don't deserve.

"God, I'm sorry. I'm just... so frustrated with you." His fists are clenched at his sides. "I didn't mean that the way it came out."

I nod meagerly. *I understand. I get it. Slap me on the other side, please.*

"What I meant is that Kristlyn is the greatest thing ever for me. And I think there's someone who feels that way about you. Someone who's not me. Someone suited for you." He moves behind the counter. "Someone who stopped by wanting to speak to me and try to understand things. Things I had no explanation for other than a girl caught up in a fantasy she saw no way out of. A quirky girl with a big heart that got detoured."

"Scott?" I say with more enthusiasm than I should have right now. I try to go back to solemn, but I can't. I'm too eager.

"Yes. Scott. That's one heck of a lawyer you've found yourself there."

"Deaton, I'm so sorry. All I can tell you is that I hope one day you'll forgive me. I was so wrong. I was…"

"So what'd the publisher say?" He goes to the register and begins to flip through the day's receipts, giving me very little of his attention.

I perch on the stool by the register. "She said you should forgive me?" My voice is squeaky with questioning.

"Mmm. What else?"

I give up. *Business only, got it.* "She was intrigued. She gave me her email. Said to please send a copy."

He pauses in his counting and starts over.

"So did you?"

"No."

He stops counting, puts down the stack, and looks at me. "Why not?"

I hesitate before answering. "I dunno. I just. I'm not sure anymore."

He squints and runs a hand through his hair. "What the… what aren't you sure of?"

"That I have any talent. That I have any imagination." My eyes are downcast, but as these words leave my lips I have to look up and see his expression. Even to my own ears, these words are ridiculous. Take a young girl, give her a mother whose demise leaves more questions than answers, give her a dad that doesn't question anything, or fill in any gaps. It's a bona fide recipe for imagination.

He squints harder and shakes his head like he's done wondering. Done questioning. Done with me altogether.

My colorful cast of characters line up on a stage in my mind and take a bow, offended that I've denied their existence.

*No imagination indeed!*

There's Samuel and Eleanor, Ghost Hailey, the hooker that gives me dating advice (haven't seen her in a while and she looks very disappointed in me.) Twelve-year-old me stumbles onto the stage a split second later, tripping over her big feet. Her hair is flipped out like Farrah Fawcett and she's wearing a tight AC/DC shirt and short — *really short, get some clothes on, girl* — shorts with baseball socks pulled up over her rapidly developing knees.

"So, let me get this straight." Deaton folds his arms across his chest again. "What about this Samuel and Eleanor you're so enamored with? They're like your family," he says, like he's not buying this one bit. "Like your parents or something."

"Yes, well." *My parents! Wow! How'd my therapist miss that one?* "Whatever."

"You're just going to forget all about them?"

I look off to the side, contemplating. Samuel and Eleanor exit stage left and appear in another setting. There's a bed, and they go to different sides of the bed and slip between the sheets. Eleanor lays still as a corpse, and Samuel tugs at the hand-stitched quilt. He pulls it up, just to their necks, and then he lays it down nicely, just below their chins.

*Not — I repeat not — completely over their faces. Whew!*

"Mental images tend to take on a life of their own," the website had said. It looks like mine have and know when to face facts just like genuine people — just like Margo! All my diversions are leaving me to do the same. No one needs my attention anymore except me, and I've learned new techniques on focusing, blocking everything else, getting down to business, learning to heal. I'm not crazy, not in need of medications and machines that zap my cortex, and not suffering from an extreme case of PTSD. I am just the product of a lonely, screwed-up childhood and a heap of troubles with a tendency to avoid them — and make them ten times worse. Step one: Owning it!

Getting back to Deaton I say, "No, I'm not forgetting about them or letting them die or anything, I'm just kind of busy right now. I have some things I need to figure out, and I need to make sure my café ledgers are in black, not red, and I don't know if you've heard but I've got this little investigation business too." I flatten my lips in a tired smile. I *am* tired!

Deaton nods for me to continue and drops his folded arms.

"I'm gonna let them rest awhile, figure out what I really want to do, and do it well." I look to the side and gather my thoughts on what I want to say.

I pause and swallow, then plunge forward. "I'm going to focus on my *own* story and see how it plays out."

# TWENTY-EIGHT

MORLINDA ROWLER IS a nervous sort of woman and kind of ditzy. I like her immediately. She hustles all over my little apartment, plugging in cords, doing lighting checks in various corners of my main living area, and studying her notes. She's all of a hundred pounds, bones, and hard edges, this Morlinda, even though her name sounds plump and round. I reach into the bowl on my end table and place a wrapped candy in her hand. "Have one. They're good."

She seems to be writing everything I say. When I assure my mom that her hair looks just fine, Morlinda grabs her notebook and scribbles fervently.

"I don't know what you're laughing about. You're no better, checking your phone every five minutes," Mom says, exasperated with both of us and our endless energy and estrogen.

"I have an um, a friend, in surgery today. Big surgery — kidney transplant. I'm waiting for updates."

"Oh. I didn't know. Well, I'm sure you can visit her when we're done here."

"Doubtful. She's in Kentucky."

"We're ready," Morlinda finally announces, after she's straightened things in the room and asked if I have a light bulb for the lamp on the end table. I've already told her I don't want to be

305

photographed, that I at least have to keep being able to sit anonymously on park benches beside my subjects and initiate random conversation.

"You can name me. You can't show me," I say again. "Anonymity has served me well. I'm giving it up somewhat in exchange for the publicity, but hopefully not completely."

She nods but continues to set some kind of scene around us. "Now," she says, adjusting herself into the chair and straightening her skirt. "Oh. Chewy." She tries to hurry past the caramel and swallow, then finally she's empty-mouthed again. "Amy," she begins.

"My name is Amethyst."

**Amethyst Hollander has been searching for someone since she was eight years old: her mother.**

**Watching them together, you would never believe they spent so many years apart. There is a closeness that exists between them as if no time at all has passed.**

**Amethyst was raised by her father, Raulerson Chadwick, here in Flannery Cove. She describes her childhood as loving and secure, and her dear father as her "rock." Growing up, Amethyst was told that her mother had died in the Flannery Cove train derailment of 1988. That is what everyone believed had happened to Caroline Chadwick.**

**In 2006 Amy began a new venture, the well-known Flannery Cove Investigation Agency, Unveiled Investigations. She has enjoyed much success in this endeavor and recently began a new investigation, initiated by her soon-to-be stepmother, into the truth of what happened to Caroline. To everyone's shock, Amy already knew her mother was alive and living in Atlanta under an assumed name.**

**"I was there that day the train derailed," Caroline says. "I saw the whole thing happen. I've had survivor's guilt ever since."**

**Caroline fled to Scotland but eventually relocated to Atlanta. That is where Amy tracked her mother to and where this story begins.**

**Continued-See Investigation Pg. B5**

I interjected a lot during the interview. I fought with my mother in front of Morlinda Rowler and her crew. I corrected her and reminded her continuously of her promise to tell the truth. And in the article, I apologized again to my family, as well as my community, as I told them all my truth.

I allowed the line, "I've had survivor's guilt ever since" to stay. Maybe that is her truth. I know firsthand that remorse can manifest itself in a myriad of emotions. The key to well-being is identifying them, but I'm not sure my mother will ever get there.

Unfortunately, that's the undeniable truth.

# TWENTY-NINE

I T'LL BE THREE weeks this Sunday since the article I spent
so much time and effort wording ran in the newspaper. It
appeared in the Flannery Cove Courier and a weekly publica-
tion in Savannah, and within days the Letters to the Editor started
rolling in. *"That's the girl that runs that café."* *"That's the place with
that prosciutto and Gruyere quiche."* *"Unveiled Investigations revealed the
truth about my husband and saved my marriage in the process."* And my
favorite, the one taped to my bathroom mirror: *"Wow! A woman who
can create the best lobster and linguine bisque I've ever tasted and runs
the town's five-star investigation agency? Is she single?"* That particular
comment was posted on the Courier's social media page, and at
last count had 101 comments and 162 likes. That bisque is going
to single-handedly bring my café back into the black.

I've brought two of the chairs from the old house that didn't
fit into the apartment down to my office. With the acquisition of
the coveted supply closet being part of my apartment agreement
I now have plenty of space. I'm trying to arrange them into a
nice sitting area in front of my desk, so I can get double duty
out of this room.

As I tug at the chair on the left and position it in a way that
will make whoever is sitting in it be attentive to both me and the
person on their right, I imagine my future clients: *I want to find*

*my birth parent. We believe Mr. So-and-So is working while filing for disability. I want to find the con artist who stole all my Granny's money.*

I feel just the slightest brush against my leg and then, "Amethyst." He is dressed in a school uniform: Khaki pants, a green polo shirt, and loafers. His features remain impassive, but there is a peacefulness to them. One can almost see or imagine a slight curve to the lips, a brightness to the eyes.

"Oh. Paulus. You scared me. Where's your mom? I wanted to tell her something."

He tries so hard to focus pupil to pupil, only occasionally reverting to the wall behind me. "My Uncle Jeremy brought me. He's a counselor. He wanted me to go to my new school a long time ago but my mom kept saying I needed to blend. He told her nuts like me and him and the rest of my family don't blend they just get chopped up and he knows it. Mom did not appreciate that but she let me attend my new school. Uncle Jeremy gets to come to visit more now because my mom is happy with him again, and he said she should know by now he's always right."

"Oh. Well. Good for Uncle Jeremy." I follow Paulus out of my office. The café is slow this time of day, after school. The dance moms come in the early hours now before school lets out then they spend their afternoons on the other side of town with Fiona at the new studio. God bless their loyalty to me! I send them with cookies and muffins to fatten her up and notes about the house.

*The heater thermostat is about two to three degrees off. I forgot to tell you to only use liquid soap in the dishwasher. Please drop this soup off for Mr. and Mrs. Westfield and tell them I'll be by soon.*

"So school is going well?" I ruffle the sandy brown hair that reaches my hip. Paulus doesn't shrink away.

"And here he is," he says with a flourish. "My Uncle Jeremy. He's alone, and God said it is not good for man to be alone. Mom says it's 'cause he's too picky and he's been waiting for the right one and he just hasn't met…"

I stop walking and look up, straight into the face of a young Chuck Woolery.

"Scott?" My eyes are big and round. My voice is so soft, I'm not entirely sure it made it out of my thoughts into the air.

He looks at me with a knowing gaze and a wry smile. "Jeremy Scott Warner the third, actually," he says. "Very pleased to meet you, *Amethyst*."

My heart thumps wildly, and the heat that starts at my heels quickly runs through my body up to my scalp and begins to fan out. I can't quite form proper words.

"I've been hearing about you for quite a while," he says. "Paulus' friend Amethyst, the one who needs a partner. Or was it a helper? A mate! That's what it was! I hear you need a mate."

My fingers find the chain around my neck and begin twisting, and I squint as I try to decipher this. "Did you? Did you know it was me all this time?" I look around almost as if I'm expecting people to suddenly jump out from under tables, appear from behind the doors and corners. *Surprise!*

"No! No." His head shakes assuredly. "I was going to tell you on your birthday. I'd only recently figured it out. I barely paid any attention to Paulus going on about Amethyst this and Amethyst that. It took me a while to go back to your paperwork and make the connection, and I thought, 'There can't possibly be two Amethysts.'"

"There can be," Paulus says. "But one might be synthetic. The chemical and physical properties of synthetic amethyst are so similar to real amethyst that it can't be distinguished without advanced tests."

I feel like I've run a mile and can't quite catch my breath. "You never said."

Scott nods solemnly. "I knew it was big. By then I was feeling things I wasn't even sure I wanted to acknowledge. I'm guarded, you know." He looks at me with raised brows and a wry expression. "Not just for myself. I guard this little boy as well. I can't…. I *won't* let him think something so promising and then take it away."

I glance down at the little boy standing at his uncle's waist. He's tugging at his eyelashes, pulling his eyelids over his eyeballs as if he's just discovered this neat trick.

"But Paulus said… I don't understand." There's something I'm not putting together, most likely a lot of things. My mind is a landfill. "Paulus said you were a counselor. I remembered that, and I specifically chose a female therapist to avoid ending up with Margo's brother. It's a small town, you know."

"I do know. A town with very few real estate attorneys. Thankfully."

"Counselor is a title often used interchangeably with the title of lawyer," Paulus says. "A counselor at law is a person who takes care of legal matters."

Scott smiles softly at me. "Everyone knows that."

"Uncle Jeremy passed by a bar to be able to dispense legal advice." Paulus sits down in a booth and begins to fold a napkin into little squares. The front door chimes with a couple exiting after paying at the register. Cory retreats to the kitchen, and only one other person remains in the café, a lone man hidden behind a newspaper.

I look back at Scott. "Why does Paulus call you—" I realize the answer before I finish the question.

"He's particular that way," Scott says.

I'm remembering more, recovering from the shock. "*But, you said* — you said I understood nothing about you." His words come back, just as painful as they were the first time and my pride, my stubborn pride, comes raging through.

I recall a movie I watched once where a very troubled, possessed girl burned down her mansion. I'd yelled, "No. Not the house. Drop the matches, you crazy." I have the sense I'm doing the same thing, but I hold my chin high, ready to blow this whole fate thing to bits and destroy everything.

"Yes. Yes, I did." His forehead wrinkles and his lips flatten — a touch of regret, perhaps, although I can't blame him for his words. "I've replayed that a thousand times. I needed time to process what I witnessed. I couldn't wrap my head around..." he stops and thinks what to say. "Well, I'm still not sure I've wrapped my head around it, but I'd like to try," he offers with a raise of his hands like he hopes it's not too little too late.

My chin lowers a notch. I can't figure out where to step in all of this. I'm floating in an ocean and I'm not sure I know how to swim, feeling emotions I have never felt. His coat is laying in the booth, and he reaches over and pulls something from the pocket and hands it to me.

I turn the little black plush toy in my hands. "A seal? I don't..." I look at him in confusion and then I see it. The little name tag made from letters strung and tied around its neck. O-f-a-p-p-r-o-v-a-l.

"It's yours. Our seal, Ofapproval." His eyes are crinkled in the corners with the faintest of smiles, his face full of anticipation. "Paulus made it. My hands were too big." He whispers, "Say you love it. His heart will break if you don't."

I make a noise in my throat. Cute, but I don't feel like playing stupid word games, and this isn't some movie starring Meg Ryan.

This is my life and my feelings. "I still just..." I stammer. None of this is making any sense.

*Scott and Paulus—all this time?*

Scott lays his big, warm working-man hand over mine. "I love you, Amy. I've loved you since the first time I saw you with your serious chef's apron and your sea-glass eyes, and the way you inhaled that sandwich like you hadn't eaten in a week. I loved my phone conversations with you. I loved everything, and that was before I even knew my family already loved you. Everyone loves you. I saw it in your family that night even when they were so hurt. I saw it in Deaton. I saw it in Fiona.

My former hooker friend shows up and takes a little pickax to the block of ice I'm encased in. With just one tap the whole thing breaks away.

"Fiona is buying my house."

Scott folds his hands and nods. "So I am officially resigning as your foreclosure attorney. No more obstacles. Amy, I'd like to date you now."

We stare at each other and start to draw close, magnetically pulled, but I place my hands in front of me and resist — awkward and uncertain — and still so confused. "I'm... I'm not good at this sort of stuff," I say. I want to make it clear who I am before we take another step. My past, my faults, my failings.

"Maybe you need some practice."

"Yes," I mumble, more to myself as I consider this, and gravitate back toward him. I drop the matches and step away from the gasoline. "Yes, I think I do."

And right there in front of Paulus and the man behind the newspaper and the window that looks out on Sandpiper Street and all of downtown Flannery Cove, Scott Warner takes me in his arms and we share our first soft, sweet, long, and passionate kiss.

# *THIRTY*

THE TWO OF them stand outside my closed office door. "You can't just hang it in the drywall. It'll fall. Right on her head when she's walking through."

Deaton shrugs. "Knock some sense into 'er."

Scott holds a nail between his lips and knocks on the wall. "Here's a stud. Hand me that hammer, would ya?"

I look up from the papers and bills spread out before me on the booth. There are twenty-seven dollars left in my account this week that I can pay toward my slowly declining credit card balance if I could only log on to the internet. Instead, I attempt to gather everything I need for tax time and add it all up. My handyman crew moves on to the landing, hanging the last of the new signs, and my eyes wander over to my favorite one hanging by the coffee grinding station:

**Grounds for Divorce?**
**Visit: www.UnveiledInvestigations.com**

It's been amazing the way I've been able to tie the café and the investigation agency together. I lost my anonymity but gained such a following. I even created a new salad with boiled eggs and

313

olives for eyes and named it the "Spy Salad." It's a huge hit just because people like to say the name.

Deaton reaches behind him for the hammer that's hooked on the ladder. Otis nudges the hand hanging at Deaton's side, but he wipes it on his jeans and places it back in his pocket, out of the way. Undeterred, Otis moves over to Scott's hand. Scott absentmindedly scratches him behind the ears and under the neck while standing back, checking his work.

Paulus marches behind them. "The first detective agency was in Paris, but the first unit in America was formed in 1846 in Boston, Massachusetts."

I glance over at little puppy Patere, splayed out on a blanket in the corner, all four paws barely reaching beyond the smooth, pink belly he displays to the world, before returning to my paperwork, but it's hard to concentrate. I wrap the blanket on my lap tighter around my legs. So cold! Even this late in the afternoon, ice from the freeze the night before remains on trees, awnings, even the few cars parked on the street.

"Hope they get the electricity up and going soon," I hear Deaton say. "Gonna be another cold one tonight. Kris' plane was delayed at O'Hare."

Paulus' murmured reply drifts down from above soft as snow-fall. "But then we'll have school tomorrow and Uncle Jeremy will have to do counseling, I mean lawyering, again."

I'm supposed to be on the adult's side. I'm supposed to think this whole camping thing — shutting down the shops and schools, lighting candles and fires and trying to come up with various ways to stay entertained without electricity — is a bother. "I'm with you, Paulus," I holler up to him, even as I see a flash of orange vest through the frosty windows. Electric company workers down the way trying to get Sandpiper Street back on the grid.

It's been a treacherous winter. "One for the books," all the newscasters say. My little upstairs apartment is drafty and every night, just when I've managed to finally get warm enough to fall asleep, the useless furnace roars to life like a lion going after a bloody piece of meat. My shower water runs cold after two minutes, and I miss soft carpeting under my feet when I rise in the mornings and walk ten steps to my kitchen area.

But I've never been so content. My skin has cleared up, and so have my thoughts. I sing in the shower and dance my way to the kitchen, despite the less than stellar accommodations and the frigid air.

I'm still navigating this new place I find myself in. Nothing is more important to me now than my small circle of loved ones. Some relationships will never be the same, but that's not necessarily a bad thing. They're better, stronger, healthy. My daughter, fortunately, inherited my staying power. She's committed to our bond.

This is the third time in two months that we've had a day with no power. The third time in two months almost the entire city has had to shut down. Someone told me last week that Sam Armstrong down at the auto parts store told them they've sold at least ten new batteries a week consistently since early January. Adjectives like brutal, miserable, and treacherous have become a part of the normal town folk chatter. Even the dance moms talk of nothing more pressing lately than whether it's okay to wear real fur when it's this bone-chillingly cold.

And yet, when I swipe my napkin across the frosty café window and peer out of the clear circle, when the only thumping I hear coming from up above is from Otis' tail, when I smell the lingering manly mingle of pine, leather, and mint on my collar left behind from an earlier tryst near the supply closet (I'm not frigid, after all!) and when I hear Paulus giggle — *actually giggle!*—at the sound of Mr. Kent's amplified antique car horn ringtone wafting through our neighboring interior wall, I'm reminded of something someone told me once.

Spring's a-comin'.

Best phrase ever.

### THE END

Tracy Bayle

# BOOK TWO IN THE SEA ISLAND SERIES

## Welcome to Shannings Bay

# *THE ROAD TO REMORSE*

JOE- WAYNE WATTS is a young, exhausted, and stressed-out new father with an equally young and exhausted wife. He and Carrie have just brought home a precious new baby and been dealt two unexpected and devastating blows.

But life has a way of working out, and the Watts family moves on and copes with their lot in life. Joe-Wayne is a dedicated husband and father, a tireless pillar of the community, a generous friend to all. Carrie manages a public persona as perfect and tidy as her home life. Alyson is growing up thriving, nurtured, and cherished.

But all that is only possible because of the night Joe-Wayne said he was running to the store for a package of diapers. Where he went and what he returned with changed the course of everything, but no one except Joe-Wayne knows the course didn't change on its own. If anyone knew it would shatter this perfect portrait, and not just for the Watts family. There are others whose lives would be destroyed if they knew what the result had been of Joe-Wayne's late night errand.

## About the Author

Tracy Bayle is a native of South Florida and currently resides in Central Florida with her family. She enjoys biking, beach days, cooking, interior design & home rehab, family time and consistently escaping into one novel after another. She has won many awards for essays and contributes to various blogs. A Convenient Catastrophe is her debut novel.

Follow Tracy Bayle at www.tracybayle.com
https://www.facebook.com/TracyBayleAuthor/
https://www.instagram.com/tracybayleauthor/

# A note from Tracy:

THANK YOU SO much for following Amy's journey. I hope you grew to love her as much as I did. She is a flawed individual that found herself in a desperate situation and unfortunately kept making it worse. – as lying and deception tend to do.

When an author spends months writing a book, editing it, polishing it and finally releasing it to the world it's a bit like giving birth. I have grown to love my characters. I have given them my all, and they are now ready for your enjoyment. Therefore, if you did enjoy them I would greatly appreciate your review. A beginning author depends greatly on these reviews, as well as word of mouth and encouragement and camaraderie, I might add, as writing can be an isolating job. You can find me on Amazon and Goodreads, and follow me on social media. Be patient with my social media, I'm tip-toeing in and busy writing book number two in the Small Town Strangers Series. If you would like to find out what became of Amy's foster sister, Susan, sign up for her story on my website and I will send you the link to download it as my gift to you. I will also keep you informed when subsequent books in the series debut and other relevant information. And maybe I'll make you laugh or smile every once in a while.

TO FIND OUT WHAT HAPPENED TO SUSAN-
DOWNLOAD FOOTPRINTS IN THE TIDE FROM
MY AUTHOR WEBSITE AND SIGNING UP FOR MY
NEWSLETTER AT WWW.TRACYBAYLE.COM

# Questions for Discussion:

Did you feel Amy had no choice but to keep up her charade, or were you angry with her?

Why do you think Amy was drawn to Margo and Paulus?

Were you surprised to find who Uncle Jason was?

What was your opinion of Raleigh as a father at the end of the book?

What do you think Amy was looking for in life over everything else?

Why do you think Caroline felt so stifled?

Do you think Amy's overactive imagination was significant?

Did you want Amy to end up with Deaton?

In the end, Amy tells her mother their future relationship will be with her conditions in her place. Would you have walked away from Caroline?

How do you think coming to terms with the truth about her grandmother helped Amy move forward?

How will Amy's relationship with her mother affect the one she has with Hailey?

Have you ever opened a side business that flourished beyond your expectations?

Which character was your favorite? Who would you like to see explored more?

Have you ever found yourself in a situation that someone else brought on you that made you feel like you had to lie and/or betray someone else you loved or choose sides?

Are you satisfied that Susan's story was left hanging? (Susan's story is available for download at tracybayle.com)

Printed in Great Britain
by Amazon

17839942R00187